THE SINGI
CALENDAR

Erin Green

www.ariafiction.com

About *The Single Girl's Calendar*

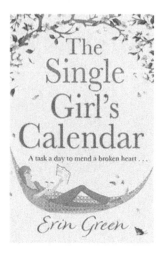

A task a day to cure a broken heart.

Esmé Peel is approaching thirty with some trepidation, but hope in her heart. If she can just get her long-term boyfriend Andrew to propose, she will have ticked everything off her 'things to do by the time you're 30' list. She didn't reckon on finding another woman's earring in her bed however, and soon she finds herself single, homeless and in need of a new plan. Her best friend Carys gives her the

perfect present – The Single Girl's Calendar – which
has a different cure for heartbreak every day:

Day 1: Look and feel fabulous with a new hair style.

Day 2: Step out of your comfort zone and try something new.

Day 3: Reconnect with friends and enjoy!

Despite thinking it's a bit of a gimmick, Esmé hasn't got any better ideas, so she puts the plan into action.
By the end of week one she has four new male housemates, and despite a broken heart she is determined to show Andrew she can do more than survive, she can thrive.

Dedicated: to all the single ladies

Chapter One

Thursday evening *had* started well.

'The air smells so different at the end of a working week,' said Esmé, stepping from Stylo Stationery onto a busy Birmingham street alongside her two work colleagues.

'That's your Friday night saying – surely it doesn't apply to Thursday night, too?' laughed Marianne, for whom a Friday night meant a take away and wine, snuggled on the couch alongside her Jimmy.

'Technically, this *is* her Friday night,' said Penny, whose Friday night goal was three loads on an economy washing cycle before watching the comedy hour.

'But it's true, smell how beautiful…' Esmé inhaled deeply, filling her lungs with the possibilities of a long weekend. When invoices for premium paper, double-sided sticky tape and multipacks of cheap biros would be forgotten until Monday morning.

A smattering of street litter flurried along the pavement as they stood contemplating Esmé's plans.

'I can't believe Old Steely Stylo granted you the day off,' added Marianne, checking her wrist watch.

'She's deducted it from my holiday entitlement, so no fear of favouritism,' corrected Esmé, determined to stick to the facts. She wasn't taking liberties. At Stylo Stationery the aged owner, Mrs Stylo, treated every employee in an equally harsh and abrasive manner.

'Even so, she must be softening in her old age!' said Penny, adjusting her scarf. 'Maybe we should all ask for long weekends come our anniversaries?'

'Like she cares about me and Andrew!' said Esmé, attempting to control her lengthy auburn locks in the spring breeze.

'She cares for no one,' said Penny.

'Seven years tomorrow, who'd have thought it?' laughed Esmé.

'Not me!' Marianne laughed as her dark fringe blew about.

'*Exactly*, so I need to make the most of it.' Esmé blushed in anticipation.

'You never know, he might not need your assistance, he might have pulled his finger out and organised a big surprise all by himself,' said Penny, having glanced at Marianne.

'I doubt it. He'd forget his own birthday if I didn't do a countdown. But tonight, could be the night...'

'Look at you, jumping the gun – you'll only be disappointed if he doesn't ask,' warned Marianne, buttoning her coat against the March chill. 'Most men need an arm up their back or an unexpected pregnancy to force them into marriage. Take my Jimmy... twelve years of dating and still *nothing*.'

All three women shook their heads, knowing the tale of woe which would follow, each was word perfect in their practised lines for the retelling of Marianne's one and only proposal story.

'You ruined your chances by pushing your luck,' began Penny.

'*Really?* said Esmé in a bewildered tone, feigning interest, much like a first-time listener.

'I made an appointment with the vicar, tea and sponge cake arranged...' explained Marianne.

'All proper and above board, then?' asked Penny, knowing her lines.

'I drove us to the local church and then bam... delivered the ultimatum – marry me or else!' announced Marianne, her cheeks flushed with embarrassment.

'Such a beautiful declaration of love,' said Esmé, her eye lashes fluttered at Marianne.

'Who'd have thought such a proposal could be perceived as a tad too pushy,' said Penny.

'Exactly,' giggled Esmé. 'Wasn't it your fairy-tale dream?'

Marianne nodded in a comedic fashion, her maturity enabled her to laugh at herself, unlike five years ago.

'I've lost count of the nights I'd dreamt of him springing such a gallant gesture, driving me to church and booking a wedding date.'

'Locking himself inside your car and performing a one man sit-in for eight hours, while you pleaded with the vicar, was a definite cry for help,' said Penny.

'A definite answer, though,' said Esmé, who hugged her friend.

'The vicar was none too chuffed given his wasted sponge cake and tea platter,' said Marianne, adding. 'Seriously, Esmé – joking aside, what have you planned?'

Esmé gave a cheeky grin, before she stared at each colleague in a bashful manner.

'Oh Lord, if that's not the face of a woman on a mission!' cried Penny, her wide eyes sparkling.

'I've got it all planned… candlelight, champagne on ice, bubble bath for two, a slinky silk number ordered from Agent Provocateur *and* a fresh set of Egyptian cotton sheets,' reeled off Esmé, trying to supress the shiver of anticipation that ran along her spine.

'A dirty night on clean sheets, hey?' said Marianne with a knowing smile. 'That should do it.'

'And not too much champagne… be giggly but not drunk,' warned Penny, her blonde curls bobbing from side to side. 'And above all… let him think it was his idea!'

'If *that* fails, hail a cab, drive to your local church, present him with the ultimatum and see if he does a sit-in,' laughed Marianne.

'Andrew wouldn't do a sit-in… not with a taxi meter running,' said Esmé, tying the belt of her new coat. Esmé doesn't like to criticise his habits, not even to her friends, but Andrew could accommodate both ends of the generosity spectrum. Self-indulgent with his own perceived needs such as designer suits, high-tech gadgets or boys' nights out whilst a smidgen stingy where others are concerned. Esmé could laugh it off, *everyone* had their faults. Being 'financially savvy' as Andrew called it wasn't Esmé's style, she liked to be generous with those she loved.

'Yet he'll waste good money on a snazzy rental apartment,' muttered Marianne. 'The man needs sorting out, and quick.'

'I'm trying,' said Esmé, trying to keep her tone light hearted.

'Enjoy,' Marianne gave Esmé a quick squeeze and an air kiss, 'but don't hold your breath, lovey.'

'Enjoy your weekend… whatever happens, OK?' added Penny, hugging Esmé tightly before she and Marianne hastily departed for the bus station.

Since starting at Stylo Stationery some nine years ago, the trio had shared so many of life's moments during office hours and coffee time: Esmé's first date dress dilemma, post-date dissections – of which there had been far too many for Esmé's liking, and numerous post-coital mishaps during her pre-Andrew existence, *obviously*. Since meeting Andrew, Esmé's daily chatter had been the detail of their seven year love story: the occasions, the memories and the day to day routines. Events slowly evolved, reaching today's pivotal moment – the evening of her happy-ever-after.

Come Monday, if tonight goes well, the three colleagues would be sharing celebratory drinks after work in a local bar. How exciting? But first, *tonight*.

St Martin's church clock shows six o'clock.

Esmé watched the pair disappear amidst the bustling crowd. Her heart pounding faster, with anticipation, that the very next time she'd see either of them, she could be, might be, correction, *would be* starting a new chapter of her life.

Chapter Two

Esmé did her usual quickstep routine through the city's pedestrian area towards the far side of the city *and* home. Or as Marianne called it 'the snazzy' rental apartment. A sophisticated rental for up and coming professionals in the trendy renovated canal side area for which Birmingham was now notorious.

'The area has more waterways than Venice' was Andrew's favourite quote, boasted a little too often to friends during nights out.

If only Birmingham could guarantee Esmé a love inducing moonlight cruise, which would secure her happy-ever-after, which Venice surely could.

The apartment hadn't been her ideal choice but Andrew had set his heart on the area, making it their *only* choice. She hadn't been too fussed about the location, just desperate to move their relationship onto a more permanent footing. Within weeks, Esmé had converted the bare magnolia two bedroom apartment into a fully fledged love nest thanks to an intuitive flare for interior design. A talent that had surprised even her. That, and her savings spent on investment pieces to add focus and colour contrast.

Esmé had memorised the estate agent's blurb too, and could recite it when family failed to understand Andrew's steadfast attitude.

'You're throwing good money down the drain by renting,' her mother frequently muttered.

'How can an open window and a wall mounted wrought iron railing constitute a balcony?' queried her father, having viewed the neighbourhood on more than one occasion. Esmé would smile, yet cringe, at the criticism, hoping Andrew couldn't hear.

They had her best interests at heart but everyone had to start somewhere. Andrew had decided that Symphony Court would be *their* somewhere. It wasn't Esmé's fault that her parents had started married life on the twelfth floor of a tower block in Chelmsley Wood. Attitudes and house prices had moved on since their time.

Wasn't she three years old before they had a garden with a lawn and a creosoted fence? But hey, if it made Andrew happy and meant they could start living their life together – what did she care?

Esmé walked towards home.

Could she put a price on coming home to Andrew? When you wake up each morning beside the one you love, money counted for nothing. Compromise. Wasn't that the foundation of a solid relationship?

Esmé could do a little give and take in order to please others. Anyhow, she'd waited five years for them to move in together, now, after another two years, she was more than ready for the next step.

Her mind was crowded much like the busy Birmingham streets. Esmé swiftly dodged the sauntering shoppers, nimbly jumped aside as rattling pushchair wheels nipped at her heels and gallantly ignored the early weekend revellers, who like her, were pretending tonight was Friday night.

Within thirty minutes, Esmé had walked the length of Birmingham city centre, from the bronze Bull statue, through Victoria Square and onwards past The Symphony Hall. Her feet had begun to ache but her plan was mentally choreographed, minute by minute, task by task and she was eager to begin. Finally, turning off Broad Street, she saw the welcome sight of the interconnecting bridges arched over the canal network. Home.

*

Taking the flight of stairs as fast as her stilettoed boots would allow, Esmé quickly entered apartment nine.

'Andrew?' she shouted, purely to be on the safe side.

No answer.

Esmé's plan required a ninety minute window of home alone time until his shift finished at the local airport.

Heaving her boots off in the narrow hallway, she peeled off her coat and threw it across the arm of their plush sofa. Esmé headed straight for their bedroom.

The room was immaculate. Esmé had made a conscious effort before leaving for work this morning to tidy her dressing table. A large room of minimalist décor, dominated by their king size bed, no clutter, no scattered clothes, no fuss – a show home standard of neatness, just as Andrew liked. All Esmé had to do was change the sheets before diving into a steaming shower to spend as long as she wished pampering herself knowing that fresh sheets were awaiting them.

There's only so much I can do to encourage him.

Relationship-wise, they'd been in a happy place for months. No bickering, nor arguments, no upset or issues. The last six months had been harmonious, so why wait any longer? She'd be alluring, irresistible and subtle – as Marianne had said 'let him think it was all his idea!'

Nerves trembled within her stomach, the magnitude of her precision planning and the possible outcome both excited and scared her. The constant replay, revisit, rearrange of the routine had consumed every waking hour for weeks and was about to become a reality. *This. Was. It.* If she could orchestrate tonight's plan, she would have achieved the one single thing she'd wanted for so long and before her thirtieth birthday. *Bonus.*

If there was one domestic job Esmé hated more than most it was wrestling with an oversized duvet cover trying to locate and align corners and seams. It usually took three rounds of pummelling, a frayed temper and a break-out of sweat before their bed was transformed into a billowing heaven of duck down and expensive cotton, complete with numerous scatter cushions. She'd arrange scented candles upon each bedside cabinet as a final touch.

Grabbing a bundle of freshly ironed Egyptian cotton sheets from her neatly piled airing cupboard, Esmé returned to the bedroom, unfurled the clean cotton sheet, ensured that the matching pillowcases were present and draped them over the wicker chair while she removed the spent bedding.

She'd even planned, paid and arranged for a gourmet meal to be delivered between their champagne bubble bath and the boudoir finale. If she played her cards right, this time tomorrow she would be wearing a brilliant-cut solitaire diamond on the fourth finger of her left hand.

It still baffled her why he hadn't proposed that night in Paris. The Temple Romantique was *the* dream setting, the sunset was picture perfect – it would have been the ultimate end to a perfect weekend. But no, not a hint of a proposal. Just a delayed flight back to Birmingham, a crummy cab ride in the rain and a disappointing discussion during coffee break come Monday morning.

And now, she was forced to mastermind and precision plan the situation which steered their relationship in the right direction towards them becoming Mr and Mrs Nixon.

'Mrs Esmé Nixon,' she said aloud to the room, slightly embarrassed and yet thrilled by the prospect.

Esmé drew the heavy curtains against the twilight, after momentarily pausing to stare at the neighbouring skyline of the Jewellery Quarter. Tomorrow they would spend all day in Vyse Street consumed by the four Cs of diamond standards. Esmé recited them like a well trained jewellery assistant: cut, colour, clarity and carat.

A swoosh of the curtain rail accompanied images of sparkling diamond solitaires nestled upon velvet cushioned trays in her thoughts. Delights previously ignored, with steely determination, whilst she browsed for gold cufflinks and tie pins each Christmas.

Esmé hastily moved around the bedroom illuminating and dimming bed-side lights. She knew what her future looked like – tonight was simply a means of ending one chapter and starting the next.

She wasn't the first, and feared she wouldn't be the last, woman to take matters into their own hands.

Esmé began tugging the spent duvet from the bed.

'Bloody hell, Andrew,' she muttered, repeatedly pulling to wrench the tucked in section of duvet from beneath the heavy mattress. One of Andrew's pet hates was his feet being uncovered during the night. It was one of hers that the bottom edge of the duvet was always firmly wedged under the mattress.

Finally, the mattress released. Esmé wrenched the billowing duck down duvet to the floor revealing a slightly bobbled white cotton base that had seen better days. Esmé's fingers nimbly located and worked at the buttoned edge.

Seven years with Andrew had prepared her for anything. They'd grown up together, enjoyed good times and endured a few rough patches, such as when holidaying with his pals in Ibiza was more important to him than her. Other couples might have split but they'd seen it through together. It was a phase, like any other. She'd supported his career choice and now his position at the airport was assured. He was working long, stressful hours but that was the nature of the beast as an air traffic controller. In return he'd gained a solid foundation, financial stability and the opportunity for future promotion.

Esmé was proud of him. Proud of herself too. She wasn't ambitious, unlike her cousins who frequently called hers 'a lowly office job'. She was happy selling stationery. Happy supporting her man. *Her* Andrew. Behind every successful man was a strong, supportive woman – Esmé knew she was a fine example. Supporting *his* career equated to supporting their future, their lifestyle and their future family.

With the cover gaping open, Esmé pulled frantically to retrieve the duck down duvet from its clothing.

Marianne was right. Some men need a little push in life. They knew what they wanted, *had* what they knew they wanted and yet, trundled along until someone pointed them towards the altar. Once on track there would be no stopping Andrew, much like a wind up clockwork toy on parquet flooring.

It wasn't as if she hadn't been planting tiny seeds for a while. It wasn't an issue she could force as boldly as Marianne had but the hinting, the constant references to other engaged couples and the barrage of wedding invites from friends – all helped to pave the way.

Andrew was comfortable in their relationship. Too comfortable, if truth be told. So tonight was the night. And tomorrow, their seven year anniversary, would be their engagement day.

'I'll get the worst part over with,' she sighed, collecting the fresh duvet cover from the wicker chair. 'Three rounds of wrestling, then my relaxing shower.'

Esmé's hands began gathering and rippling up the inside of the duvet cover fabric to locate the top corners.

A March engagement could easily become a June wedding; she'd plan like crazy between now and Easter – though seriously what was there she didn't already know? She knew which dress, knew which cousins would be bridesmaids. Money wouldn't be an issue thanks to Andrew's astute saving habit and her parents' additional gifts – she was their only daughter after all. The horse and carriage, the fresh flowers, matching rings, the once in a lifetime honeymoon in the Maldives and not forgetting the sumptuous reception at The MacDonald Burlington Hotel – perfect for a city centre wedding. How romantic would it be to have the reception where they'd first met? Or more precisely, *above* where they'd met in The Bacchus wine bar situated in the vaults beneath the hotel.

How had seven years passed so quickly?

A girls' night out with Carys, her life-long school friend, was not supposed to be a 'pick-up' night. Simply two ladies sharing a bottle of merlot, a good chat and a few girly giggles. Yet, every time Esmé had looked up to speak to Carys, his dark smouldering gaze interrupted her focus. Could he have been more obvious? His constant staring had been verging on improper. And finally, after thirty minutes, he'd braved the distance between his group and their table to introduce himself.

She'd played gooseberry to Carys's beaus on more than one occasion, so fair was fair.

Esmé smiled at the irony as her hands busily worked the duvet cover. Seven years of dating had led from one dimly lit room to another, though tonight would guarantee more than a scribbled phone number and a promise to call. Like then, she'd be ready and waiting. He'd made her wait three days. Carys had been certain he'd call in two given his reluctance to leave their table as his friends drank up and moved bars.

Esmé began flinging the medley of pillows and satin cushions to the far side of the room. The decorative headboard looked ugly and bare without the satin pillows. Another purchase chosen by Andrew, and which frequently embarrassed her in the throes of passion when it vibrated against the wall.

From the foot of the bed, Esmé grabbed the neatly folded hospital-bed corner of the spent cotton sheet, she gave one hefty pull in order to strip the mattress in one fluid movement and that's when it appeared.

An earring.

Esmé paused and stared at the offending item lying, as proud as punch, just off centre by their large headboard.

A gold dangling earring complete with a turquoise crystal. An earring that she had never seen before.

The handful of spent cotton dropped from her clutches and she slowly sidestepped towards the head end of their bed. She needed a closer look but any sudden movement might cause the item to disappear. It didn't. It stared boldly at her.

Had he cheated? And, in our bed! Had she slept all week with another woman's earring inches from her own gold studs?

Esmé wasn't sure how long she remained statue like, staring in silence, but when Andrew arrived home from his shift at the airport the silence was broken for several hours.

Chapter Three

The MacDonald Burlington hotel looked nothing like Esmé imagined. Esmé envisaged that her arrival at the grand establishment would be on a warm summer's day in June. Where she'd step from a glistening horse drawn carriage, in a beautiful bridal gown and glide through the entrance hall upon the arm of her new husband. They'd smile inanely and be met by the sweet smell of honeysuckle and delicate white roses amidst a cloud of gypsophila.

Instead, she stood alone, at ten minutes to ten, on a dark chilly March night staring up at the intricate masonry of the hotel façade, where sculptured ladies with pert breasts and scanty togas frowned at her from a great height. Esmé grimaced. She'd heard enough excuses from Andrew regarding pert breasts and cheap decoration.

Behind her, New Street railway station hummed with the busy footfall of travellers despite the late hour.

'When did an impromptu hotel stay become part of my Thursday night plan?' she muttered, as she dragged her overnight case towards the marbled lobby.

According to her schedule, she and Andrew should have consumed the champagne, dined on cordon bleu food and now be making the most of clean sheets and mood lighting. Instead, she was standing before the impressive reception desk booking a two night stay which felt awkward but necessary. Esmé watched the kindly features of the pretty receptionist prepare her plastic room key.

How many young women with red raw eyes and a hurriedly packed case had the uniformed blonde checked in this evening?

Having refused a morning paper, an early morning call and a continental breakfast in bed, Esmé handed over a suitable credit card and haphazardly scrawled her signature.

She stood in silence, appreciative of the receptionist's swift and precise booking routine, plus the speed with which she relayed the serving times for breakfast and ironically, bade her a cheerful 'good night'.

Room 325 was unlike the room Esmé had planned to sleep in tonight. Kicking off her shoes, she flopped onto the double bed, ruining the arrangement of decorative satin pillows.

A large abstract painting hung above the bed. An image of orange and blue swirls forming huge arcs of colour upon a square canvas.

'That's what my brain feels like,' muttered Esmé, twisting her head from left to right to make sense of the image.

Her argument with Andrew replayed in her head, word for word.

'How could you, after all we've gone through together?'

Silence. His dark eyes had darted around the room avoiding her direct gaze.

'I trusted you. I gave you everything and you repay me like this!' Esmé had flung her arms around emphasising the 'everything' element, making sure he was following her rant.

Silence. He'd loosened his tie, then stood dishevelled after a long day at work. Esmé could make out the tiny shaving nick on his chin that must have occurred after she'd left for work this morning. In her mind's eye, she could see him grabbing toilet tissue and applying a torn corner. He'd have been agitated, sworn and eaten his breakfast whilst bare chested, hoping the tiny cut would dry and scab before chancing his white shirt collar near it. She knew him *that* well. Or did she?

'Who is she?'

He'd answered immediately. Sadie. Esmé instantly hated the name, adding it to the shit list of her life. Sadie-from-work. Esmé's mind ran a photo-fit of each female she'd met at the airport's annual

Christmas bash or recent retirement parties. Sadie didn't appear in the attractive line-up.

Esmé imagined her as leggy, svelte and naked. Andrew had reluctantly confirmed naked sometime last week upon their cotton sheets while Esmé and Co. completed their annual inventory at Stylo Stationery.

Esmé hadn't waited for an apology as he pocketed the earring for safe keeping. Instead she'd verbally launched at him with accusations and hurtful name calling. Her questions had come thick and fast. Where? Why? When? How? She'd hardly given him a chance to answer before the next question was launched like a warped version of *Mastermind*. He hadn't 'passed' on any question.

'Are you leaving? Or am I?' On reaching question number two hundred and nineteen Esmé had fallen silent. There was nothing more to ask. She waited for his reply, a simple shrug was all he could muster.

What should she do? Demand that Andrew leave the apartment immediately? But did she want to be here alone? It wouldn't feel right, it wouldn't feel like home, not now.

She'd never walked out on a relationship before, let alone her home. Should she call her parents to collect her a.s.a.p. and bring a transit van to haul her belongings back to their house in Sheldon? Finally, amidst her rising panic, and before Andrew's staring gaze she thought of a new question.

What would Carys do in this situation? Esmé knew instantly. At twenty-nine years of age, having shared half her life alongside Carys, Esmé knew what she would do. Cool, calm Carys would take charge, she'd stand no nonsense. And, neither would Esmé, not this time.

Exhausted, tear-stained and hungry Esmé had grabbed handfuls of her underwear and a fresh set of clothes and stuffed them into her overnight wheelie-case before hastily leaving apartment nine.

She scurried back over the interconnecting canal bridges, closely followed by the distinct rattle of tiny plastic wheels, and made her way into the city centre seeking a bed for the night. She dashed past the early evening drinkers, the winos and other arguing couples silhouetted by lamplight.

She needed space to think. Apartment number nine offered no such luxury whilst Andrew breathed in and out. And her parents' semi-detached would instantly become a melting pot of parental smothering should she land there at this late hour.

I've done the right thing. I've taken control and removed myself from the upset. Andrew.

It's what the A-list celebs do in times of trouble according to Penny's trashy magazines. Frequently, amidst a relationship crisis, the rich and famous jet off to Dubai or some other far flung corner of the globe to find solace on a sun kissed beach. How many times during coffee breaks had they pored over a grainy image, shot with a long-distance lens, showing a model in oversized sunglasses in paradise. Now, Esmé was the damsel in distress. Thankfully, the paparazzi would never be interested in a gal from Brum with red eyes and dashed hopes.

Esmé imagined her parents' spare room and its trendy wooden futon with creaky slats and scratchy orange padding. What a joy that would be to snuggle up on each night. Maybe she should stay schtum rather than tell her parents?

Calling anyone right now would only complicate matters. They wouldn't be able to resist adding their point of view which would swirl around in her mashed head – much like the abstract painting in orange and blue.

Tears rolled down her cheeks as her heart grew heavy.

Was there any chance that *this* would pass? Any chance that she could look at Andrew's hands and not imagine them caressing another woman? Was there any possibility that she could ignore the basic facts? Andrew had admitted he had kissed, held and…

Esmé couldn't bring herself to name the act.

A fresh bout of tears erupted.

This wouldn't pass.

Tomorrow, their seventh anniversary, instead of smooching along Vyse Street she'd be holed up here where she'd relive tonight's discovery a million times before lunch. The shock would begin to lift and by morning the hurt of his lies, the loss of seven years and her new found hatred of a stranger called Sadie would surely descend at break neck speed.

Clambering to her feet, she plodded to the large window, pulling aside the cream voile and staring at the busy street below dressed in its finery of neon lights and looming shadows. A miniature world of busy lives dashed back and forth along New Street, wrapped up in their own existence and unaware of her pain and tear-stained scrutiny.

Had the caterers delivered their evening meal? Esmé recited the gourmet menu: lime infused chicken satay skewers, sumptuous steak Diane (basic but Andrew's favourite) followed by huge rum babas smothered in thick double cream.

Esmé shook her head to erase the image as if it were the *Etch-a-sketch* from her childhood.

She picked up her mobile and speed dialled 'Gourmet Delights Ltd'.

'Hi, can you confirm if a delivery has been made to apartment nine, Symphony Court?'

'Lady, we're closed. No more orders until the morning,' came the distant voice.

'Please, I need to know... was the Nixon order delivered?'

'Hold the line, please.'

Please say no, please say no, please say...

'Lady, yes. Delivered at 9:15 p.m. as instructed... the lady signed for it. Goodnight.'

'Lady... what lady?' asked Esmé. The phone line went dead. 'I left the apartment ten minutes before...'

The bastards! Those two had hooked up and hunkered down on her tailored menu, enjoyed her chilled bubbles – he deserved everything that would be coming to him. Would Sadie move in straight away or would he show some decorum and wait long enough for Esmé to remove her tampons and razors from the bathroom cabinet?

'There's no going back... not after tonight,' she muttered to the busy lives below. She watched a young couple holding hands and laughing as they walked along the street. How happy, how cute and yet, potentially destructive. How much time and happiness did they have remaining? Esmé craned her neck as they disappeared from view and her breath misted upon the window as her weekend plan emerged.

Tonight, she'd be brave. She wouldn't land on a girlfriend's sofa with a huge sob story – no, she'd bide her time. No rash decisions. No knee jerk reactions. The very thought of calling either Marianne or Penny crucified all her engagement dreams – Monday morning's coffee break announcement and drinkies in Bacchus bar were officially cancelled.

Chapter Four

Esmé slept with her mobile phone clutched in her hand. A scattering of spent tissues lay scrunched up on her duvet, alongside discarded screw caps and five empty liquor bottles from the hotel's mini bar. Esmé hadn't had a good night.

A film reel of last night's events played on a continuous loop every time she closed her eyes. Esmé was hoping that a vital scene would change and a different ending would magically occur. Sadly, it didn't. The sequence was simple: left work, made the bed, found the earring and then all hell broke out. Repeat unchanged.

Esmé lifted her shoulders, flipped the plump pillow onto the cold side and lay back.

Had Andrew slept well? Had he slept alone? Or had Sadie reunited her lost earring with its rightful twin?

'Enough. He isn't worth it,' she muttered, as she pummelled the pillow into shape.

It's not as if they'd *never* discussed infidelity. When his best mate, Steve, forgave his fiancée, they'd agreed reconciliation would never work in the Nixon/Peel relationship. How could they trust each other again? When his sister, Sarah, became pregnant by her old flame, Terry, they couldn't fathom how Simon, her husband, could entertain the idea of raising the boy as his own. And as for Bridie at work, when Nick walked out after just three weeks of marriage – did the woman have no self-respect as she begged him to come home? Esmé and Andrew had agreed. They couldn't face the social humiliation, the niggling doubts, the constant questioning or secret checking of pockets and purses for early signs of another torrid affair. They'd agreed calmly and maturely – you cheat, it's over.

And yet, he'd cheated. And, in *their* bed.

Esmé gathered her collection of empties and screw caps, ignoring the wave of guilt associated with the price of them. She could have bought a decent bottle of champagne for the price of those miniatures.

Her stomach growled.

Had she eaten anything last night?

Esmé pinched herself, hard. Ouch! Yep, she wasn't asleep. The nightmare had actually happened.

In her head, Esmé could see their kitchen calendar hanging beside their fridge. Today was the date she'd circled with gusto the moment the cellophane was removed. Her hands had eagerly flipped each page and finally, on reaching March, she'd grabbed a pen from the junk drawer. A red loopy circle had signified all her hopes and dreams. Who'd have thought she'd been counting down to a disaster!

By seven o'clock, Esmé could hear from New Street that the city was beginning to wake: the litter pickers with their yellow dustcarts and commercial waste collection crews were bantering between themselves.

Work? Urgh! Would it be entirely wrong for Esmé to attend the office and delete today from her holiday allocation? But the thought of disappointing the smiles that would instantly adorn Marianne and Penny's faces was enough to make her cry again. They would be so excited for her today, it would be all they'd talk about come coffee break.

Please don't text asking if we're strolling along Vyse Street, thought Esmé, as she grabbed her mobile and checked for text messages: nothing. Not even from Andrew.

Esmé flung back the duvet, she threw the empties in the bin and rummaged in her overnight case for her jeans and a sweater. She dressed as quickly as possible in an attempt to beat the mass of Andrew related thoughts that sloshed around in her mind. The quicker she buttoned her jeans, zipped her boots and pulled a sweater on, the more chance there was that her brain could be fooled into normality. Like forcing a delete and reboot on her computer at work?

Having dressed, washed and applied a small amount of make-up, she took the hotel key from the dresser and headed out in search of breakfast.

*

Esmé walked along New Street, where many of the shops' metal shutters remained closed and locked, as the staff commuted towards the city centre. Esmé had the empty streets to herself, fresh and clean, like a blank page on which to wander until the rest of the world caught up and awoke to Friday morning.

The early sun was shining, the sky was clear blue and yet the world was very different compared to yesterday morning. Yesterday, Esmé was a woman in love. Today, she was in limbo. Neither committed to a relationship nor single.

Beyoncé's 'Single ladies' song ran about her head. It was now so obvious; Andrew hadn't liked her enough to put a ring on it. A lump grew in her throat.

Esmé checked her mobile again – still no text, no apology, no call.

What was she supposed to do now? Start again? Reinvent herself at twenty-nine? Or return to the life she had before Andrew? A singleton, wining and dining with friends, with yoga and boxercise classes on alternate nights. Esmé couldn't remember her last day as a singleton. What had happened to the life she'd once loved? When had the group of girlfriends disappeared? The visits to the cinema for popcorn and late night chats? When had they stopped phoning? How long had it been since she had painted the town red on a girls' night out with old school friends such as Charlotte, Fiona and Deb? They were probably living the lives they'd all dreamt of living filled with weddings and babies.

I bet I don't even have their mobile numbers anymore, thought Esmé, sadly. Who'd have thought seven years on I'd be walking the streets purely to fill my time.

Esmé strolled the length of the pedestrian area, crossed the new tram line and went partway up the sloping gangway that leads to the Grand Central shopping area. And stopped.

I can't hold this together for a minute longer. I need to speak to Carys.

Taking her mobile, she stood against the metal railings and called her best friend.

'It's me.'

'*And?*' came the bubbly yet drowsy voice of Carys.

'We're finished – he cheated on me. What am I going to do?' Esmé's voice broke and tears flowed.

*

'I feel like my two year guarantee has expired and he's exchanged me for a newer model – much like the first sofa we purchased together from PlushSofasAtDiscountLand.com,' said Esmé, spooning froth from her skinny latte. 'He loved it at first sight but soon used the returns voucher in preference for the four-seater model.'

'Esmé, are you serious?' asked Carys, her dark eyes staring intensely over the rim of her tea cup. Her ebony complexion shone after having dashed into the city for lunch after Esmé's earlier crisis call.

'Yeah, the new sofa was being delivered as the store's removal guys were collecting the one they dropped off three days earlier. And now, he's exercised his consumer rights with lovers, too.'

'No, I mean about it being over between you two?' asked Carys.

Esmé balked at the question.

'How can it not be? We've just done seven years of promising each other a future and he wrecks it with a…'

'Mindless shag?'

Esmé paused.

'That's the worst of it. I don't think it was… he didn't make a single excuse, he simply stood and took everything that I threw at him. Carys, I don't think it was a mindless anything… from what he said… he was totally aware of what he was doing and how it would affect us. I've gone from soon to be fiancée to ex-lover in less than twenty-four hours!'

'I am sorry.'

'Maybe he's wanted out for a while. Played his hand and chanced his luck that I'd do as we'd always promised… threatened… without a fuss or a fight if either of us strayed.'

'Is there no way back from this?'

Esmé shook her head, her bottom lip protruded.

Carys reached for Esmé's hand and gently squeezed it.

'So, what have you done all morning?'

'Apart from visit cafes, I've walked around the city, stared in shop windows and had a meltdown when I found myself in the crime section at Waterstones…' Esmé coughed as a wave of nausea lifted to her throat. 'I felt fine until then. How many times has that store saved my skin with his birthday presents or stocking fillers? Not anymore. Those days are gone.'

'In that case, I have *just* the thing,' announced Carys, releasing Esmé's hand before rummaging in the plastic bag beneath her chair. 'Don't laugh, but this actually helped me through the break-up with Myles.'

'I thought I helped you get through that.'

Carys raised her head mid-rummage, her corkscrew curls bouncing as she disagreed.

'Nope! You know nothing about break-ups, Esmé. Seriously, your relationship has been so long-term you haven't a clue. But this...' Carys lifted a pink boxed object onto the table top. 'This might help.'

'What the hell?' said Esmé, staring at the advent calendar styled object with its tiny perforated doors.

'It's 100 per cent tack and it only cost a fiver but—'

'Carys?'

'Hear me out, Esmé... it's worth a laugh if nothing else.'

'Yeah, sure,' said Esmé, lifting the calendar to read the blurb on the reverse.

Want a sassy new way to overcome a break-up? Or simply an opportunity to focus on your life? The Single Girl's Calendar is made for you! Behind every door is a task that will help you focus on you, and you only! A whole month of pampering, mindfulness activities, caring and sharing ideas which in just four short weeks will have you feeling on top of the world! An insightful way to put a spring back into your step as a strong, independent woman!

'Are you serious?'

Carys nodded.

'It felt like a guilty secret when I did it.'

'You didn't tell me.'

'Believe me, I didn't tell *anyone*. *This* was my daily fix – a daily dose of chocolate plus a focussed task which helped to take my mind off Myles and our break-up. Go on, open door one and see what today's task is.'

Chapter Five

Day 1: Look and feel fabulous with a new hair style.

It wasn't her usual hair salon, but the stylish window of 'Guyz 'n' Dollz' was inviting when an emergency appointment was called for. Taking a deep breath, she pushed the heavy door open to enter the hair emporium.

The catwalk model perched at the receptionist's desk pouted in her direction.

'Hi, is there anyone available for a wash and restyle?' Esmé gave an apologetic grimace, hoping to hide her desperation.

'Sure,' answered the receptionist, flicking through various screens on her tablet. 'Tristan's available, he's one of our top stylists. He recently won the Snip, Snip and Snippet national award – you'll be in good hands. If you take a seat, I'll go and find him.'

'Sounds great,' replied Esmé, removing her jacket. She took a seat on the low sofa made of bamboo and coconut husk – giving thanks to her curves for providing some padding against such uncomfortable furniture.

Only fifteen minutes ago she was happy with her current hair style.

'Now dry your eyes, Esmé. Go and get your hair done – you'll feel ten times better for it. It's your first task – so, go!' It was clear from Carys's face she was pleased with the suggested task for day one.

'But Carys…' Esmé hadn't meant to cry on opening the tiny calendar door but doing so confirmed her new status: single.

'And, I'll meet you tonight – we'll go somewhere fabulous.'

'Carys, I can't…'

'You can and you will… now go! I've got to dash otherwise I'll be late back from lunch and my team leader will moan at me all afternoon.'

Esmé viewed her reflection in the huge mirror hanging behind the receptionist's desk. How long had she had this hair style? Eight years? It was definitely longer than she'd been with Andrew. Seven years with the same guy *and* the same haircut. And faithful to both.

'Change brings about change,' muttered Esmé, turning her chin left and right to view her appearance.

The bustle of the salon was visible from her vantage point. Beautiful, svelte people who happened to be talented stylists side-stepped and danced around each chair, snipping, combing, tinting and pandering to the needs of individuals draped in burgundy satin robes. The mirrored walls gave the illusion of row upon row of identical twins as each hairdressing station was reflected multiple times in opposing mirrors.

Esmé shrank a little within her own skin. How dare she bring her split ends into such a high brow establishment. Surely any minute now, Tristan will appear and demand that she leaves the premises and never darkens their door again.

'Hi babe, how are we? What's it to be? A shampoo and spritz? Or a total transformation?' A bald-headed Tristan appeared dressed from head to toe in the blackest of black apart from bright red patent leather shoes. He asked her a multitude of quick fire questions and then paused, waiting for answers.

'I simply want a change,' said Esmé, her hands lifting towards her auburn bob.

'Oh darling, you've got good hair, good cheekbones and beautiful blue eyes – all hidden beneath that bob... now, let me see...' Tristan's fingers gently lift and fluff Esmé's shoulder length hair.

Within seconds, Esmé is ushered towards the far corner where two juniors in matching jumpsuits perform a talented rub-a-dub-dub in oversized basins with heavily scented potions before wrapping her wet hair in a towel turban.

'Esmé darling, this way!' beckoned Tristan, swivelling a large padded chair in her direction.

Tristan pumps the foot bar and she lifts like Venus from the waves to face herself in the large gilt-edged mirror.

What a bloody mess! Her mascara was smudged beneath each eye and she instantly regretted opting for a no foundation day as her natural complexion looked sallow and waxy under the neon lights.

'Now darling, do you trust me?'

'Infamous words,' giggled Esmé, unsure as to how she should answer. Say no and she'd pay the price. Say yes and Lord knows what he'd do.

'Sweetie, wake up and smell the hairspray… this,' he said, lifting the ends of Esmé's bob 'needs a restyle. Trust me, you'll look fabulous.'

Esmé gave a weak smile followed by an unconvincing nod.

'A woman who cuts her hair is about to change her life!' sang Tristan, at the top of his voice.

'Really?' Esmé sat a little taller, eager to know more.

'And so, let us begin.'

Like an over active version of Edward Scissorhands, his blades flicked and spliced her auburn mane and discarded locks tumbled down upon the satin robe.

*

'Tadah!'

Esmé stared at the reflection and didn't recognise the young woman who stared back. Gone was the shoulder length bob. It had been replaced by an ultra-short, platinum blonde, pixie-style crop with an asymmetrical fringe dramatically splicing her forehead from left to right, or would that be right to left given the reversal of mirrors?

'I... I... I... love it,' she lied, her gaze frantically searching the reflection for anything that resembled her previous self. Wasn't this the kind of cut you gave yourself, aged four, having found the kitchen scissors in a drawer? A stranger stared glumly from the reflection. Esmé stared while Tristan did the flicky thing with his product covered fingers to fluff her fringe and by the time the double mirror routine to view the back was over Esmé was near to tears.

'Lovely, thank you,' is all she could repeat as she was de-robed and ushered towards reception. Would it be too cheeky to ask the trainee broom handler for her hair clippings in a doggie bag? Instead, she watched as they are swept into the corner and lost for ever.

Esmé knew the payment transaction was a race against time. Any minute now, the tears would start. Esmé was no superstar but this version was far removed from who she was. They wouldn't recognise her at Stylo Stationery come Monday morning.

'Fabulous… glad you love it. Come back soon and we'll treat you to a colour tint which will enhance your skin and eye colour!' said Tristan.

'That'll be seventy-six pounds fifty, please,' smiled the model receptionist, pouting her plump lips as Esmé rummaged through her purse seeking a wrap of notes.

Great, that's twice in twenty-four hours I've been screwed over, thought Esmé. She handed the money over swiftly, trying to make it less painful like swiping off an *Elastoplast*. The eight crisp ten pound notes were fresh from the cash point. Esmé hadn't planned on spending them all at once, but hey, if Carys's calendar advice was anything to go by she'd feel like a new woman in no time, with new hair and no money.

'And another appointment?' prompted the receptionist, flicking the tablet's screen.

'I think I'll leave it for now, see how… what my…' Esmé wanted to say boyfriend, fiancé, husband, but the words snagged in her throat. She failed to finish the sentence and left it hanging in mid-air, then retrieved her offered coat before she scurried from the salon. She struggled to open the heavy door and squeezed through the tiny gap as it closed swiftly on her backside.

Esmé imagined that once the door was closed, every high-brow customer and stylist would look up and nod smugly to each other, knowing full well she'd never grace their wash basins again.

Would it be awful if I went straight round to 'Hair by Milly' and asked her to correct the fringe? thought Esmé, trying to gaze in each shop window without making it too obvious that she was eyeing herself up.

Esmé sighed.

If this ever grows out, I'll stick with my usual. Now, I'm mourning the loss of a relationship and my hair.

Esmé quickly texted Carys.

'Haircut. Don't feel fabulous. Feel robbed. Woolly hat needed!' Esmé speedily sent the text, hoping for an instant reply. Nothing.

Esmé perused the shops. Within minutes, she spotted a wire basket containing clearance items, a hand-written sign pegged above it announced, 'Everything £3.50!' Following a quick rummage through the mix of colours, Esmé selected a deep claret colour with a contrasting banding in pale blue.

'Bargain,' muttered Esmé, as she purchased it and instantly covered up her expensive hair-do.

Chapter Six

Esmé inserted the Yale key and twisted. Had it only been two years since this key was her actual door key? Willclare Road, a wide leafy residential street of red brick homes where the pavements are dominated by oak trees and lined with parked cars.

Given the events of last night, was this now home?

Her heart was racing. *This* wasn't the plan she'd made last night. The plan was to wait another day before telling her parents and yet here she was, thanks to that sassy calendar reminding her that today wasn't day one of singledom – that started last night – today was actually day two!

After her emergency hat purchase Esmé had browsed the busy stores of the Bullring, only to sidestep the flow of shoppers and lean against the railings by the top of the escalators to retrieve the calendar from her shopping bag.

Esmé's finger nail dug deep at the serrated edge of door two, and prised it open. She scoffed the tiny slab of chocolate before reading the task.

Day 2: Step out of your comfort zone and try something new

Wasn't walking out on a cheating boyfriend enough? What about her unscheduled stay in The MacDonald Burlington? Or could returning to her parents' home represent something new? The scratchy orange futon in her mother's spare room definitely couldn't be described as a comfort zone.

Esmé quickly re-read the back of the calendar packaging. There was no mention of backdating tasks. Did she have to apply Carys's stringent rules for the entire month?

Esmé quietly entered the hallway and closed the front door. She needed a moment to ready herself for this family announcement. She looked around at the familiar gold flock wallpaper, the dainty telephone table and the lopsided Yucca plant – nothing had changed.

The forever home of the Peel family. A national statistic of two parents and two children, living, breathing, fighting and laughing within these four walls for nearly thirty years.

From the kitchen drifted a rabble of voices offering familiar warmth as she took off her coat and dragged the woollen hat from her hair. On passing the hallway mirror she stared at herself open mouthed.

'A bad idea, I hate it. Step two of getting over a slime bag should be regrowing your hair, which explains why step one is getting it cut – it gives a girl focus,' muttered Esmé at her reflection. She quickly pulled a few blonde strands down to frame her face and jammed the woollen hat into her pocket.

Esmé kicked off her shoes in a teenage manner and plodded towards the commotion in the kitchen.

She hesitated, her hand on the kitchen door handle. She felt sick. Never had her left hand, fourth finger, felt so bare.

Despite the rental situation, her mother adored Andrew. At times, she sided with him rather than Esmé. It was one thing to take a boyfriend into the bosom of the family, it was quite another to adopt him in favour of your own daughter. Lord knows what would be said when she broke this news. Esmé needed to play this carefully.

She and Andrew were finished. She wanted it to be dignified, she wanted a clean break. As long as his testicles fell from his body after having caught a serious, yet incurable, STD which he had instantly shared with Sexy Sadie during their love tryst. What she didn't need was her mother berating her for losing the only decent man that had walked into her life, and how she'd obviously disappointed him to the point where he had to look for another woman.

What am I doing here?

'Sod off, you *never* said that!' came the muffled voice of Kane, her older brother, through the kitchen door.

Great! I don't need an audience for this.

Esmé conjured up a brave face and entered the kitchen. A large kitchen that had seen homework tantrums, late night cheese on toast making and the aftermath of many Sunday morning hangovers around the scrubbed wooden table that held pride of place.

'Get real, man... surely you can wait another week?' chuntered Kane, seated at said kitchen table in jeans and a faded Jack Daniels tee-shirt.

'My hands are tied, you know that... you knew that last week *and* the week before,' retorted Russ, his best and oldest friend, seated on the Formica worktop and slapping his hands on his spread knees.

'Bollocks! Do it for me, please.'

'Hi,' interrupted Esmé, staring between the two men but ending up face to face with Sue, her surprised mother, turning from the stove as she tended a grill pan of spitting bacon. 'Only me.'

'What a nice surprise! What the bloody hell have you done to your hair?' screeched her mother, her own auburn hair tied back in a knot.

'Scalped, more like,' snorted Kane.

'I fancied a change!' said Esmé. 'I'll have you know the stylist who did my hair has just won a national prize at...' Esmé had forgotten his credentials but it suddenly mattered that others knew he had some kudos. 'I may go back and have a colour tint applied in a few weeks…'

'Hello, Esmé,' said Russ, and his dark monobrow moved as he spoke, before proceeding. 'Kane, you knew the deal, man – I was honest and upfront and now… this.'

'Mr Gallagher… long time, no see,' said Esmé to Russ, before returning to Kane's remark. 'I fancied a change, if you must know.'

Esmé took in Russ's profile and a fleeting blush came to her cheeks, how had her brother's best mate grown from a gawky, spotty teenager into a sturdy man with a five o'clock shadow at just three in the afternoon.

'You look like a boy – is it finished?' asked her mother, pointing at her fringe. 'What's Andrew say about that?'

'It's the new me!' said Esmé in a bullish tone, though deep down she agreed with them.

Esmé looked around at the faces – did they all really need to hear her news first hand?

'He loved it,' muttered Esmé, annoyed with herself for bailing out and avoiding the truth.

'*Really?*' snorted her brother. 'It's hardly feminine.'

Russ stared at her as if he could see through her lie.

'How long's it been since you had a girlfriend, so don't give me the male talk about what's desirable and what's not!'

'Get over yourself, woman… I've got eyes in my head and that… doesn't do anything for the old libido.'

'I'm glad, given that I'm your sister!'

'Sod off,' scowled Kane.

'What's happening?' asked Esmé, as she slumped into the seat opposite Kane and looked between the two friends. Never in all their years of friendship had she heard a cross word between the two and yet, a definite undercurrent was brewing.

'Nothing,' snapped Kane.

'We were securing a deal but it looks like it has fallen through,' muttered Russ, his eyes flicking a glance towards Kane.

'Intriguing.'

'He hasn't got the deposit for his share of the rent,' explained Sue.

'Leaving me and the other guys in the shite.'

'Two more days, that's all I need,' muttered Kane.

'You said that two days ago *and* two days before that… and now look at us.'

'Bollocks, you could lend it me if you weren't so tight but nah, you'd prefer to cut me out.'

'Stuff you, Kane. We've had a month's notice. We all attended the viewing, we all agreed and still…' Russ held his hands up for effect.

'Moved out, have you?' asked Esmé. *Ironic, I'm about to reverse the process and beg to return like the prodigal daughter.*

Russ nodded before adding, 'Trying to.'

'About time, too,' added Sue, removing the grill pan from the heat and forking the cooked bacon onto white rolls.

'Cheers Sue, I bet my mother's thinking the same, though she's pretending to be heartbroken.'

'Don't kid yourself, Russell. I'm sure she's heartbroken at the thought of less washing, less ironing and an end to the stream of blondes sneaking down her staircase at the weekend,' laughed Sue, squirting brown sauce onto each cob.

'What's the set-up?' asked Esmé.

Kane shook his head.

'A house share across the city,' explained Russ.

'Where?' asked Esmé, eyeing the plates her mother handed to each bloke. *Had she eaten lunch?*

'Edgbaston,' added Kane.

'Montague Road, it's a renovation job on a Victorian property… the landlord has done it out pretty smart. Swish-like. There was supposed to be five of us but this waster can't get his act together,' explained Russ.

'Waster? Sod off… I've got a crisis,' growled Kane, between mouthfuls of bacon.

'You've always got a *bloody* crisis and it's usually financial – that's why I kept reminding you.'

Silence descended as the two men bit into their butties. Esmé watched as her mother pandered to them. If only she knew that while she fussed in her motherly way over these oversized boys Esmé's heart was lying shattered and broken on her freshly mopped tiled floor thanks to Andrew's cheating libido.

'Esmé, you want some putting under?' asked her mum, pointing to the grill pan.

Esmé shook her head; eating was not on the agenda while her stomach somersaulted at each imaginary flashback of Andrew and a blonde on her Egyptian cotton. Esmé gulped down the lump in her throat. This was too much to bear.

'Where's Andrew?' asked Kane. Her mother looked up from the sink.

'I have absolutely no idea. Probably in bed with a woman called Sadie!' Esmé said, as calmly as she could muster.

The silence was deafening. The trio stared, unable to fathom who should take charge of the conversation. Sue was dumbstruck, her bottom lip trembled.

'I thought that you and he…' said Russ.

'You said he liked your hair,' said Kane.

'Yes, so I did. And yeah, I lied, but so did he. Apparently, we're not and haven't been… what's the word?'

'Exclusive?' offered Russ, finishing his first cob.

'Exclusive… I was thinking faithful, but hey, apparently not. Anyway, forget him. How much?' asked Esmé hastily.

'Esmé!' exclaimed her mother, her wet hands dripping on the kitchen tiles. 'Where's Andrew?'

'A grand and a half, which was to cover the basic deposit, rent for the month and the electrical stuff we've had to buy for communal living… kitchen stuff, kettles, pans and a cheap plasma tv for the lounge… don't shake your head, Kane. I told you everything as it was agreed, so don't try blaming me.'

'Have you moved in then?' asked Esmé.

'Me and two others moved in last Friday, this weekend Kane and Dameer were supposed to pay up and move in, but it looks like the rest of us will have to cough up more cash if this one bails – the others aren't going to be happy.'

'But Russ, if you lend it to me,' whined Kane, between mouthfuls of bacon.

'I'll do it,' said Esmé, her voice eager and refreshed.

'Cheers, Sis.' Kane said through his stuffed mouth, adding. 'Nice to see someone would lend me *that* much.'

'Nah, I mean I'll move in, if you've bailed.'

'Get stuffed, Esmé!' snorted Kane.

'Would you?' asked Russ, choking on his bacon cob. 'It would save us having to pay more each month.'

'Esmé!' snapped her mother, slamming the fridge door as she tidied her kitchen.

'Another time, Mum... I'm getting myself sorted here.'

Amidst a chorus of 'you can't do that', 'your father will go mad' and 'that's great stuff,' Esmé gave a valiant nod.

This felt right. It was hasty, but it solved an immediate problem and meant she didn't have the undignified prospect of sleeping in the old box room on a creaking futon.

'Will this afternoon be OK for the money? I'll fetch it now if that's OK with you, Russ.' Esmé stood, eager to complete her mission.

'Hang on a minute!' shouted Kane.

'Perfect. I'll tell the guys we've got a woman joining us,' smiled Russ, as he polished off his second cob.

'They won't be happy,' interrupted Kane, licking his fingers and scowling. 'Dam's family will object.'

'They won't be happy having to fork out extra to cover your ass either, so what's the difference?'

'Call me when you've told Dam or better still… Asa, then we'll have a chat about you lending me the money, Russ.'

'Kane, mate.'

'On second thoughts, *they'll* probably offer me a loan rather than have a girl bunk up with them.'

'Right, I'll be off then, could I bring it round to you in an hour or so, what number was it?' asked Esmé, ignoring the protests.

'Number seven, Montague Road, just off Portland Road,' instructed Russ, jumping down from his Formica perch. 'I'll be in, I'm still unpacking boxes.'

'Esmé?' said Sue. 'What's happening with Andrew?'

'It's a long story, Mum, but we're through and this… *this* sounds perfect for me stepping out of my comfort zone and trying something new. See you all.' Esmé grabbed her woollen hat from her pocket and pulled it tight about her ears.

She turned to leave, eager to get to the bank before closing time.

'I never thought I'd see the day when my little sister did the dirty on me,' said Kane, standing up in annoyance. 'Twice in one day.'

'Kane, get over yourself… if you wanted it badly enough you'd have got the cash ready,' answered Esmé, over her shoulder.

Kane shrugged and pouted.

'Gazumped me with a deposit and then disrespects me in a Villa hat!' he scoffed, turning up his nose.

'A what?' Esmé stared in bewilderment from the half-open door.

'Since when have you been a Villa fan?'

'That's a travesty when your dad and him are true blue noses,' added Russ, pointing to Esmé's woollen hat.

Esmé dragged the hat from her head and viewed the large badge sewn on the rear side. *Shit.*

'Esmé, I *want* to talk about Andrew – where does he stand with all this?'

'Another time, Mum. I've *got* to go!' Esmé shoved the offending football hat into her handbag, pecked her emotional mum on the cheek and walked confidently from the family home to return to the city centre.

Chapter Seven

Esmé approached the corner of Montague Road warily. It was a popular area, one of many renowned roads boasting huge Victorian houses on each side of a leafy avenue – some tastefully renovated and modernised, others shabby looking and run down.

Was this the right move? So much had happened since yesterday.

On leaving her parents' house, she'd caught the bus into the city, reached her bank just before closing, withdrawn the cash and returned to meet Russ Gallagher, her new roomie.

Esmé's feet slowed as she counted the house numbers down from twenty-one.

Was common sense beginning to catch up with her? Or the fear of new adventures?

What if I pay my deposit and then hate living with four men? What if they chain me to the kitchen sink and demand roast dinners and non-stop house cleaning? Should I complain if I get lumbered with the box room that's too small to stash a Christmas tree in? What if they pinch my food from the fridge?

Esmé stopped dead in her tracks.

Of course, they're going to pinch my food, that's the whole advantage of sharing a house, other folks' food purchases were always far better than your own – so, why shouldn't they?

At number seven's wooden gate, she stopped and stared at the newly fixed brass digit. Seven *was* the luckiest number. Seven colours in a rainbow. Seven dwarves helped Snow White. Seven days in a week. Even, seven horcrux in Harry Potter.

Esmé smiled. This felt good. Yes, she'd be returning to the hotel room for one more night but tomorrow she'd start afresh here at number seven, Montague Road.

She unhooked the gate latch and paused. Ahhh, *but* seven deadly sins. Seven years bad luck. And cruelly, seven years of dating Andrew. Esmé gulped back the tears that sprang to her eyes. She had to be strong. What was the alternative? Phone Andrew up and ask what their chances were, before washing the stale smell of Sadie from her Egyptian cotton sheets? Or sleep on a creaky futon at her parents'?

What's Andrew doing right now? She glanced at her watch: half past five on a Friday afternoon.

A fresh wave of anger flared from her boots.

I didn't cause this, that hairy arsed git started *this* ball rolling and…

Esmé paused and viewed the property before her. Large bow windows and an ornate front door created a warm welcome. *Home.*

She flung the gate open and entered the neat garden.

At the front door, Esmé pressed the gold button and listened as a deep rhythmical chime sounded somewhere inside. The front step was laid with tiny black and white squares in freshly applied cream grouting. The thick wooden door proudly bore a large door knocker and a substantial looking letter box slot. Everything gave the appearance of being solid, expensive and brand new.

No expense spared here, she thought admiringly.

Through the frosted glass side panels Esmé could see the fast approaching fuzziness of a male outline, the slant of the shoulders suggested Russ, who flung the door wide open and offered a cheeky grin.

'Welcome to our humble abode.' Russ stepped aside, allowing her to enter.

'Wow, this is beautiful,' she stuttered, taking in the mosaic floor, the elaborately carved newel post on the staircase and the overhead plaster mouldings that scrolled down each wall.

'Amazing, isn't it? The landlord reckons it's taken him four years to renovate and us guys… and gal… are the first to rent it after completion,' explained Russ.

'I can see why you wore so keen to secure the place even without all the deposits up front… which reminds me.' Esmé plunged her hand into her oversized bag and retrieved the brown envelope bulging with cash.

'I'm surprised you weren't mugged walking through town with that lot,' said Russ, taking the offered bundle.

'It's all there, I made them count it twice.'

Russ hesitated for a moment, then grimaced.

'Please feel free to check, I'd hate for you to assume and then find part of it missing.'

'Are you sure, it's just that we're all on tight budgets... I've stretched myself to the limit and there's little room for manoeuvre financially for any of the other guys either. Mr Joshua's a decent sort but I can't see him slashing the monthly rent over a sob story.'

Russ crouched, emptied the bundle of cash onto the bottom stair and began to count the crisp twenties into piles.

Esmé waited as Russ counted.

'Perfect, best to be sure,' confirmed Russ, losing the sheepish look before stuffing the envelope into the back pocket of his jeans. 'I'll call him to collect it as soon as you've seen your room and settled in.'

Esmé's nerves had begun to dry her mouth.

'I'm sure the room will be fine, Russ,' she interrupted, eager to view what she'd just spent her hard-earned cash on. Even if the room was a dump in comparison to this hallway it'd be better than crawling back to the apartment shared with Andrew.

'This way…' Russ led the way up the galleried staircase, while she followed. The navy carpet sprang beneath her step and her hand drifted along the polished banister – it felt like a day trip to a stately home where you pretend that all you survey belongs to you and yours.

As they ascended, the view through the wooden spindles to her right was of a row of closed wooden doors running the length of the first landing. As they reached the final stair onto the vast expanse of landing the second door along sprang open and a dark skinned male rushed out. His face was framed by a thick wiry beard which reached down to a tee-shirt that proclaimed 'Time Lord'.

'Oh Dam, this is Esmé… I mentioned her earlier,' said Russ, waving an introductory hand between the two.

'Nice to meet you,' his hand shot forth and warmly shook Esmé's limp offering. 'I'm dashing out to collect more belongings. It's like a Tardis in there, every box I open gets swallowed up and it *still* looks barren.'

She recognised Dameer but couldn't recall much about him. He'd filled out from his willowy teenage form, though his thick black hair still lolled uncontrollably over his forehead. Pleasant enough as a teenager but he rarely spoke other than 'yes, Mrs Peel' or 'no, Mrs Peel' whenever he came around their house to play FIFA. It would be easy to be friends with Dam.

'Catch you later, Esmé.'

'Laters,' muttered Esmé as Russ pushed on ahead towards the furthest curve of the landing and a second flight of stairs.

She watched through the carved spindles as Dam's dark hair bobbed down the lower staircase.

'He's a decent sort, is Dam.'

'Did he move in today?'

'Yes, he works and studies at the university, so was too busy last week.'

'I see.' Esmé didn't know what else to say having never entertained the idea of university herself. 'What subject?'

'Physics related, I think…' Russ gave a shrug. 'He's too clever for the likes of me – I'm lost whenever he talks about his studies. His parents pushed him education wise and it's paid off.'

'So, he didn't complain about a female moving in?' she asked, as they climbed the second staircase, which was identical to the first in every manner.

'Oh no, he wasn't bothered, he'll be spending most of his time between here, his parents and university – I doubt you'll see much of him. Dam's fine about it, his parents might not be pleased, but hey.'

Ascending the second landing a sense of déjà vu consumed Esmé, she half expected to see Dam dash from the second door along as he'd done minutes before on the landing below.

'The bathroom for this landing is here,' said Russ, indicating the first closed door. 'Asa has claimed the room next to yours, so you're not alone up here.'

She didn't recognise that name, but clocked him as housemate number three.

'Less bodies to share the bathroom then.'

'Exactly, there's three of us on the landing below. And this…' said Russ, leading Esmé up the final few stairs to the second landing. '… is your room.' He swung the door open and snapped the light switch on to illuminate the most delightful room Esmé had ever seen.

A huge metal bedstead dominated the middle of the room, adorned with a bare mattress still wrapped in thick plastic. A white marble fire surround and hearth, deep sash windows and ornate ceiling roses portrayed a tasteful renovation.

'It is beautiful!' cried Esmé, dashing to the centre of the room. 'And all mine.'

'Sure is, now you can see why your brother got the hump.'

'Served him right, he shouldn't keep relying on others to sort his life out.'

'But that's Kane, through and through, deep down I knew he wouldn't produce the dough on time.'

'And he chose this room?'

'Oh yeah, dashed up the staircase ahead of everyone else and bagsied it three weeks ago when the estate agent brought us round for a viewing... a decent choice really.'

'Hmmm, I am surprised. Kane has more taste than I gave him credit for.'

'A decision based purely on the size of the room, I think. So, don't remove him from the Neanderthal category just yet,' laughed Russ.

Esmé began opening and closing the doors of the fitted wardrobes and shelving units which spread along an entire wall. She could see herself living here. See herself filling this room with her belongings, spending time creating an afterlife from Andrew, being alone when she chose and amongst housemates when she wished.

Four men. What the hell had she done? Come Monday, Marianne and Penny would never believe her story.

Her shoes sank into the thick carpet as she crossed to the rear window and peered outside onto a large garden of sweeping manicured lawn with a colourful rockery, a cascading pond and even a hammock swinging lazily between two aged trees.

'The landlord hasn't scrimped on the renovations, has he?'

'It's cost him a pretty penny, I'm sure. Mr Joshua reckons everything works perfectly, though to be fair none of us have lit a fire yet,' explained Russ, pointing to the fireplace and blackened grate.

'It's just beautiful, Russ – thank you for letting me take his place.'

'His misfortune is your lucky day.'

'And the other guys don't want to switch rooms?'

'If Jonah knew this room was going begging, believe me, he'd have had it last week,' said Russ, turning round to leave the room. 'But he's settled where he is.'

'Jonah? From St Joseph's?' Esmé tried to steady her voice as her eyes widened at hearing his name. Jonah Jones! Surely not.

Russ smiled.

'The very one… funny how the ladies never forget Jonah.'

'I haven't seen him in years… Mum barred him from our house for being a bad influence on Kane.' Her heart beat fluttered uncontrollably, taking her back to a school girl crush.

'She wasn't far off, he is *that* sort… he'd pinch and crash cigarettes from his mates but never got caught round the back of the bike sheds smoking them. Funny, because we always did!'

Esmé laughed.

'I haven't seen Jonah in years, has he changed much?' she said, suddenly aware that any comment may reveal her teenage secret.

'The same as he ever was, so don't hold your breath,' joked Russ.

Deliciously sexy then, thought Esmé, as the image of a nineteen year old Jonah filled her head after an absence of ten years. Boy, had she made a prat of herself swooning after him at every opportunity.

'He doesn't still wear a vintage army trench coat by any chance?' she asked optimistically, choosing not to enquire about Jonah's knee high laced boots. His style was like no other individual in their street, his long mane of blond straight hair was constantly flicked and thrown over his shoulder and as for his fashion sense – boy, he was on another level compared to the crowd who wore chinos and loafers.

'Not any more. Anyway, he's a model now... catalogue and poster stuff mainly but... ackkk, he'll bring you up to date with his career,' said Russ, leading the way to the landing. '*Happy?*

'Absolutely... but Jonah can have the room if it matters that much,' said Esmé quickly, hoping she sounded nonchalant.

Earlier on her return journey into the city centre, she had tried to predict from Kane's line up of friends who was likely to be sharing the house. Russ obviously. Dameer was now confirmed. She'd imagined their mate Matty but she'd heard he'd married a Swedish girl and moved abroad. Or Andy H, though hadn't he had a biking accident and needed a specially adapted home nowadays? Jonah Jones being part of the posse would prove interesting. Asa's identity as the fourth guy no longer mattered, Esmé was to be housemates with Jonah Jones.

Back in the day, he'd stand inside their hallway, leaning against her mum's flock wallpaper, waiting for Kane. Waiting for ages as it usually turned out, for Kane was always disorganised or late. Regardless of how much notice Esmé had before his arrival to apply blue eye shadow and plenty of cloggy mascara, she felt dumbstruck whenever he stepped inside the house. It's amazing how many times a teenage girl could dart back and forth up thirteen stairs for essential items from her bedroom while her dream date stood in the hallway. Seventy was the record. Hadn't it become a household joke? Hadn't Kane banned her from talking to him at one point? All she'd wanted at the time was a date with Jonah Jones.

Russ led the way downstairs. Esmé followed in his wake but her mind had regressed ten years to the giggly teenager.

Let's hope my hormones have settled, she thought. Otherwise my thighs will be toned to perfection with the workouts up and down these stairs.

'Are the others at home?'

'Nah, Jonah's probably out with a lady friend and Asa works most of the time.'

Esmé noted the fourth name again.

'Thank you, I can't wait to move in.'

'You don't have to thank me, you did us a favour. Who knows what Asa's face would have been like if I'd returned to say we needed to put up another three hundred and seventy-five each... Jonah would have probably gone ape-shit too.'

'Thank you.'

'The guys will give you a hand up the stairs with any heavy stuff.'

'So, who's the fourth guy?'

'Asa Henson... you won't have met him before.'

Esmé nodded as Russ hesitated.

Russ lowered his voice and continued, as they descended the staircases.

'I think he's the nicest guy in the world, honest, trustworthy, a top bloke – though don't tell your brother that,' added Russ.

'I won't.'

'Not everyone *gets* Asa. Dam's with me. Jonah thinks he's a total loser… but you'll need to figure him out for yourself.'

'A bit like marmite then?'

'Exactly! Anything else you'd like to know or do you want your deposit back?'

'No thanks, I'm as pleased as punch.'

'Even with the return of old Jonah Jones?'

'Yep, though don't tell my mother, he'd be banished from this house too.'

'Deal. Come on, let's show you the rest of the house.'

Esmé automatically followed Russ's eager gait.

'Actually no,' she stopped, pointing back up the stairs. 'I'll catch you up in a second, Russ.'

'OK. I'll be downstairs… organising your door keys.'

Esmé dashed back up both flights of stairs and entered her new room. Slightly breathless from the exercise and excitement, she pulled her single girl's calendar from her handbag.

'You had better sit somewhere special,' she whispered, placing the cardboard box on the mantelpiece, before stepping back to admire the tackiness of her first possession.

She picked up her handbag and chased after Russ.

On the way, she whispered to herself, 'one thing is certain, I'll be the first to volunteer to take responsibility for buying toilet roll,' she laughed. 'And if Russ hurries up and organises my key... I could move in tonight rather than return to the hotel.'

Who'd have thought stepping from her comfort zone would be so easy. Far easier than being the sensible and cautious Esmé of yesteryear or was that just yesterday?

She gave a beaming smile. Task one's haircut may have been a disaster but task two's comfort zone had worked out perfectly.

Chapter Eight

'Hi Esmé, it's Russ... we're in the Ivy Bush pub... if you care to join us for a drink.'

Esmé listened to her voice mail and didn't need asking twice. She was grateful that her first night at Montague Road wouldn't be spent home alone.

It wasn't a pub she frequented but, much like the area, it was one she knew well. Esmé deleted his message and immediately called Carys.

'Hey babe, you'll never guess what I've done?' It took five minutes to bring her friend up to date and arrange to meet at the Ivy Bush. 'You might as well meet the guys too.'

*

'Loving the hair, lady,' said Carys, as she and Esmé met outside the corner pub just before nine o'clock.

'I'm not so sure myself, I'm hoping it grows on me by Monday morning otherwise I'll be wearing head scarves to work.' Esmé tugged at her fringe as she spoke in a poor attempt to lengthen it.

'Please tell me that Andrew won't be joining us,' said Carys.

'Seriously, are you kidding? He hasn't called or contacted me. He hasn't a clue what I've done or even where I have been for the last twenty-four hours… so no, as painful as it is to admit, he's shown his true colours.' Esmé checked her phone for the time. 'It's an entire day since I left Symphony Court and I've heard nothing.'

'Good riddance, then.'

'Exactly. Come on, let's introduce you to my new housemates.'

Esmé led the way though the glazed double doors of the Ivy Bush, where a noisy yet pleasant atmosphere greeted them. The bar was heaving with bodies and voices were shouting over the jukebox despite the early hour. Esmé clutched Carys's hand as they wove their way through the crowd towards Russ and Dam seated by the window. A selection of empty and half-full glasses filled their table.

'Esmé!' shouted Russ, immediately standing to make room at the table. 'Dam, move your feet from the chair.' Dam, still wearing his 'Time Lord' tee-shirt, slid his feet to the floor.

'Hello, I thought I'd bring my friend, too.' Esmé did a quick introduction before she settled at the table. Russ dashed off to collect two glasses of white house wine from the bar.

'No Jonah tonight?' asked Carys, failing to restrain a wry smile.

'He's here, somewhere… don't worry, he's never far away where alcohol is concerned,' laughed Dam, searching the crowd for his friend. 'He pops up like a bad penny.'

'Carys remembers Jonah from your FIFA playing days at our house,' added Esmé, pretending not to scan the crowd for a familiar face.

'Great days, shame we outgrew the technology… gaming isn't something I focus on nowadays,' said Dam, emptying his coke glass.

'What is it you do?' asked Carys.

'I lecture at the university, and you?'

'I sell advertising space to local businesses – have you seen the billboards above the station?'

Dam nodded.

'That. Not the most interesting work.'

'It pays the bills, Carys,' added Esmé. 'I'll switch for a day – you can sell sticky back plastic and I'll phone round securing local advertising.'

'Is that your job?' asked Russ, returning with a tray of drinks, before squeezing himself back behind the table.

'Yep, stationery… I used to be obsessed by it but nine years at Stylos has successfully cured me,' joked Esmé, having thanked Russ for the drink.

'Just to businesses or the general public too?' asked Dam, sipping his fresh pint of coke.

'Both, the boss isn't fussy as long as stationery sales are being—'

'Well, look who it isn't?' called a voice, interrupting the conversation. 'Kane's little sis, Emma! How are you?'

The girls turn to view Jonah, his long blond hair cascading over the shoulders of his leather jacket, his ripped denims displaying tanned thighs. With his chiselled jawline, cleft chin and piercing blue eyes he could justify his role in the Davidoff advert.

'It's Esmé, actually,' said Esmé, shaking his extended hand. 'Nice to see you again, Jonah.'

'Once seen never forgotten, hey?' laughed Russ, sipping his pint of Guinness.

'Oy, less of your cheek, Russell. And who is this little lady?' Jonah points to Carys and winks.

'My friend Carys, Carys this is Jonah Jones,' said Esmé, adding 'We were just talking about her job in advertising and—'

'Blar, blar, blar… bloody advertising, it doesn't get you anywhere nowadays… networking with the big boys is the answer,' said Jonah, pulling up a spare seat beside Esmé and settling himself. 'I'm still modelling… your brother might have mentioned it, anyway I've found that…'

Esmé lost track of time listening to Jonah talk about his modelling career, his desire to be signed by a leading agency and his pursuit of high quality shots for his portfolio. Within no time, she's learnt that he's been all over the world: Milan, Paris and most recently New York City, on an all expenses paid photo shoot. She couldn't take in all the details as she couldn't drag her focus away from his fine features. It was so unfair when men had wonderfully thick eyelashes, along with flawless skin. Esmé felt quite plain in comparison.

The bustle of the pub continued around them, the jukebox churned out endless hits and Carys was busy talking to Dam and Russ. At one point a fresh glass of wine was nudged against Esmé's hand as Jonah kept her spellbound.

Good company, good surroundings and good conversation. *This* felt good for a Friday night.

'Emma, I think your mobile is ringing,' said Jonah, as he tapped Esmé's forearm.

'Oh sorry, sorry… I was quite… and it's Esmé, *not* Emma.' Esmé opened her mobile to see Andrew's number illuminating the screen. *Shit!*

On seeing Esmé's expression drop, Carys leant over to view the caller's details.

'What do I do?' whispered Esmé.

'Go outside and answer it,' said Carys.

'But it's taken him until ten o'clock to even contact me.'

'Yep, but now that he has, you need to speak to him, go on… I'll come out with you if you like.'

Esmé silently mouthed her apology to the three men before heading for the exit with Carys in tow.

'Hello?' The cold air and the noise of the traffic hit them hard as they exited the Ivy Bush.

'Esmé, is that you?'

'Yes, what do you want?' Carys stood close and Esmé tilted the phone so they could both hear.

'Esmé… please don't.'

'Me don't? What about you?'

'Look, we need to talk… I want to…'

'Andrew… it's not convenient right now.'

'But I've waited all day to speak to you and now…'

'Hey, you don't get to call all the shots, you know. I gave you plenty of chances last night to explain and you were hardly forthcoming. I had no choice but to leave.'

'We both needed time to cool off but now we need to talk, Esmé.'

'Andrew. No!'

'Tomorrow then. I'll come around to your mum's.'

'What makes you think I'm staying there?'

'*Esmé*, don't make this difficult.'

'Seriously, you think you know everything don't you, well, I've news for you, Andrew – you know nothing. Today was supposed to be our seventh anniversary and you ballsed it up the night before.'

'I can explain, just—'

'No. I heard everything I needed to last night… you cheated, not me. Goodbye!'

Esmé killed the connection and burst out crying. Carys wrapped her arms around her friend and they leant against the pub wall.

'Was it too much to ask? *This* is actually worse than Marianne's ultimatum, at least Jimmy's faithful and committed to her, by his own admission he just can't do the wedding bit,' cried Esmé. 'All I've ever wanted was to fall in love, get married, have a family and live happily ever after – instead, I'm twenty-nine and back where I started all those years ago!'

'Shhhh now, it'll be alright. You've found somewhere to live, a couple of decent guys to share with and you've got me.' Carys rubbed her friend's back as she spoke.

'I know, but just hearing his voice, hearing him say my name and knowing that we've got to unpick our lives from each other's after seven years… oh Carys, this isn't over by a long way, is it?'

'Nope, it'll take time but you've made huge steps today, giant steps in fact, and tomorrow you'll take some more,' she whispered, adding 'Unless you want to try again with him.'

Esmé's head lifted to stare at her friend.

'I can't forgive him, so I can't go back.'

Esmé buried her head in Carys's shoulder as a fresh wave of sobs erupted from her.

*

'Ah great!' muttered Kane to his mates, as Esmé and Carys returned to their table. 'She's now gate crashing our local too?'

'Hey, that's your sister,' said Dam, shocked by the remark.

'You don't live here so it's not your local, ha!' crowed Esmé, her red rimmed eyes looked around the table for the missing male.

'I invited her actually… thought it would be nice to re-acquaint ourselves now she's moved in. Do you know Carys?' said Russ, moving aside the empty glasses.

'He knows me, don't you Kaney-boy. Where's Jonah?' asked Carys. 'We only nipped out for a second.'

'He'll have gone – there are no flies on that boy,' said Dam.

'Oh.' Carys and Esmé took their seats and re-joined the group.

'So how are you liking your room?' asked Kane. 'Good choice?'

'Ten out of ten, big bro… you picked well… shame you couldn't stick to your word but hey, it's my lucky day,' said Esmé, her tone slightly sharp.

'Don't you just love siblings? Dam, would your sisters do you over like this?' asked Kane, as he sipped his pint. 'Did Russ tell you about the Villa hat?'

'Kane!' shouted Esmé, 'Really, is there any need?'

'Yes, you've disrespected me twice in one day.'

Esmé squirmed as Kane retold the woollen hat story to Dam and Carys, who smiled and nodded politely.

'I honestly thought she was offering to lend me the cash, seriously, Carys – I did. But no, she jumped in and snatched the opportunity from under my bloody nose. *Thanks,* little sister, thanks.'

'Kane, she didn't,' said Dam. 'You hadn't got the cash ready.'

'She bloody did and for all you lot know… she'll be running back to Andrew in a day or so – that'll serve you lot right.'

'No, I won't. Don't bring Andrew into this… you haven't the slightest idea what's happened,' said Esmé, as she glared at her brother.

'Wait and see, that's all I'll say, wait and see,' said Kane, nodding at Russ and Dam, who exchanged a glance. 'Then who will you want moving in? Me!'

Chapter Nine

Esmé couldn't sleep.

Having returned to Montague Road with Carys, who'd had a guided tour whilst waiting for her cab, and generously helped tear the protective cellophane from her friend's new mattress. Esmé was now alone. Lying on a bare mattress, dressed in her pyjamas and wrapped in a giant lilac fleece felt somewhat make-shift but it was only for a night – it was no worse than camping. At least she *had* a roof over her head. Having been so impulsive earlier, it felt right to finish the day in her new home.

She repositioned her head, without the support of a pillow her neck was beginning to ache, and Andrew came to mind.

Why had he waited all day and evening to contact her? How had he filled the hours? Had he spent the day explaining to his family? Explained to hers? Nope, Kane would have said if he'd ventured to Willclare Road, but still.

And now he wanted to talk. To tell her that her belongings were piled inside a large yellow skip? Or that he and Sadie had spent the day in Vyse Street choosing a solitaire ring?

How much of their seven years had he been faithful to her? When he'd slagged off Myles for cheating on Carys, was he at it too? The questions roamed round and round as Esmé tossed and turned, trying to fall asleep.

'Focus on the here and now. Here in this room is my new life. A brighter life. A calmer life. A sweeter life. A slightly empty and unplanned life but one I chose,' she whispered into the darkness.

A new improved version of Jonah filled her mind. He hadn't really changed, broadened across the chest and shoulders but his smile, his perfect skin and charisma were unchanged from his teenage years. Boy, after all these years he still had the charm that turned her stomach to mush.

Esmé sighed. How had she ended up moving into a house with Jonah Jones? Her teenage self would be in seventh heaven, if only she'd known what the future held.

There, that feels better.

'A life that I can unpack in the coming days. A life that won't cheat behind my back, nor disrespect my choices…' Her breathing calmed down and her eyelids began to flutter.

Crash! A noise outside in the garden caused her to start and sit bolt upright. Silence. Esmé sat motionless, listening, her ears strained to hear the unfamiliar sounds in the unfamiliar darkness. She flicked her mobile on to check the time: 1.27 a.m.

It could be one of the guys returning from his Friday night out, Jonah hadn't returned to the group after she'd taken Andrew's call. Had she heard Russ and Dam come in having left them in the Ivy Bush?

Esmé kicked off her lilac fleece and slid from the bare mattress. At the large window, she moved the heavy drapes aside and stared into the night and the garden below. Empty. Her nose touched the cold glass in an attempt to see directly below her window.

Was there a drain pipe? A rambling clematis which could put her at risk of climbing intruders? Why hadn't she thought to check during daylight hours?

There was a long scraping sound. The sound of a metal chair leg being dragged on slabs?

I'll wake Russ.

Esmé left her room and dashed down the stairs to the lower landing. A row of closed doors greeted her.

The second door is Dam… Esmé stared at the other four doors, but which is Russ's? The end one must be the bathroom for this floor, so two out of five are accounted for, but still, which one should she hammer on first?

She placed her ear to the first of the three choices. She couldn't hear anything, no snoring nor breathing. She repeated this at the second door. Nothing.

She nipped along the landing to listen at the third and final door. Instantly stepping back in surprise at the murmuring and groaning emanating from the other side.

Someone's definitely awake, and with a guest.

I can't disturb them and how embarrassing would it be if it proved to be a tom cat or a hungry fox sniffing around the bins.

Esmé quietly backed away from the bedroom door and tiptoed down the final staircase to the hallway, after which a quick dash across the cold tiles led her to the kitchen door.

The moonlight softly lit the kitchen-come-morning room through the glazed back door making the electric light unnecessary. She stood barefoot, ears pricked, listening to the sounds of the garden. Nothing. Had the fox gone? Had the tom cat found a mate? She neared the kitchen area's main window next to the sink unit but the large roller blind was pulled down and she wasn't tall enough to lean across to peer out behind it. Listen was all she could do. A whistling noise came from the open fireplace.

Esmé turned to listen.

And breathe. How pathetic am I? It was probably the wind as it rattled down the old chimney in my room.

Russ said everything was in working order so the chimney wouldn't be blocked up.

She could return to bed, no drama.

First she took one of the many coffee mugs from the draining board and boiled the kettle. Helped herself to the semi-skimmed milk in the fridge and sugar she found in a top cupboard, vowing to replace them once she'd been shopping in the morning.

She rinsed the coffee spoon beneath the scalding tap and settled herself in the adjoining morning room, sinking into the wide two-seater couch.

This was nice, a beautiful moonlit night and total silence. Esmé glanced at the clock: quarter to two. If she still couldn't sleep after this drink, she could doze here and watch the sun come up on a brand new day. What bliss?

An image of Andrew lying awake burst into her head. The rhythmical sound of the apartment's dripping bath tap quickly followed, along with the thumping of the radiator in their bedroom.

Esmé sipped her coffee.

If I hadn't found the earring, how long would Andrew have kept his secret? A week? A month? A year? And all the time I'd have been living my life hoping that each holiday would bring a proposal and a diamond ring when in reality we'd be a day nearer to…

Esmé listened as a scraping noise filled the morning room. Was this the equivalent of the apartment's dripping bath tap? The noise continued. Esmé looked around the room, leaning forward to view the section of kitchen through the archway – was there anything dripping? Had the fridge door sprung open? Nothing.

The noise became louder: footsteps on gravel. Having peered through her bedroom window she knew the layout of the garden, there was no denying someone *was* outside.

Now what?

A tall dark shadow swept past the morning room's window blinds.

What should she do? Where's the nearest police station? What's Mr Joshua's emergency number?

The back door handle rattled back and forth.

Esmé's heartbeat was as loud as a dinner gong.

She placed her cooling coffee mug on the tiled floor and stood, reaching for the ornamental poker from beside the fireplace. Her fingers tightened around the metal rod, it didn't feel snug in her grip but its sharp edges were reassuring.

One good swing.

Esmé froze as the scraping noise continued outside the kitchen window.

Oh, no, they're checking out the windows now.

She leant forward enough to see the roller blind on the main window by the sink. A large shadow loomed like a shadow puppet monster, and a hand lifted towards the top window latch before reaching through and unhooking the large side window catch. The roller blind buckled and bulged as the figure heaved itself up and climbed through with ease.

She was transfixed by the clambering shape of a pair of jeans and a sports jacket, as it descended backwards over the sink unit and onto the sleek marble effect work surface.

Keep calm and breathe. One good clout will do the job. Make it good, make it swift, make it hurt!

The figure stepped through the kitchen archway. Esmé launched, bringing the iron poker down repeatedly on the offender's head and shoulders.

'Woo! Woo! Woo!' shouted the figure, buckling to its knees to lie supine upon the tiled floor, elbows bent, hands raised to protect its head.

'Take that, and that!' screamed Esmé, as she belted the fallen figure with the iron poker. Her knees pinned the intruder to the floor and her free hand clutched his clothing.

The electric light suddenly snapped on revealing a startled Dam standing in the doorway wrapped in a navy dressing gown.

'Quick Dam, call the police, we're being burgled!' shouted Esmé, as she continued to rain blows upon the figure beneath her.

'Get this crazy wench off me, Dam! Before I retrieve that poker and shove it where the sun doesn't shine!'

Esmé paused, the poker halted in mid-air.

The intruder knows Dam. *Shit!*

She stared up at Dam's frozen stance and then at the curled up person clutching his head, anticipating a further onslaught. Dam's look of horror dissolved into laughter.

'Oh man, that's the funniest thing I have ever seen,' he laughed, stepping forward and removing the poker from Esmé's fist. 'Seriously, where's a video camera when you need one?'

'Fuck you, Dam!' came a voice from the floor.

She released her hold on his clothing and stood back. Her hands shook and her heart pounded.

'You're quite safe, I've disarmed the female,' said Dam, as he wrapped a protective arm around Esmé's shoulders and the intruder slowly unfurled and got to his knees.

'Esmé, *this* is Asa, and Asa, *this* is Esmé – Kane's little sister and replacement who moved in today and who…'

'You're a savage one, aren't you?'

'You scared me!'

She watched as the guy removed his beanie hat and his dark eyes stared at her. A sharp gasp escaped her on seeing the colourful tattoo in emerald and navy that crept from beneath his sweatshirt collar and spread across the left side of his features from jawline to temple and disappeared into a dark crew-cut.

'I'm so sorry... I thought,' stammered Esmé, embarrassed and unsure of where to look for fear of causing more offence than she already had.

Asa staggered to his feet and stood tall, blocking the artificial light supplied by the fluorescent tube.

'No problem. I'm used to being used and abused by women, though usually I've dated them first but hey doll, if you want to skip the introductions... be my guest.'

Dam roared with laughter.

'Shut it, Dameer. It might have been nice if my friends had briefed her a little but obviously not,' said Asa, who stepped nearer and turned his tattooed face towards her. 'Go on, you can look. It's not rude to stare if you have permission.'

Esmé instantly averted her eyes to stare at the tiles.

'Asa, don't,' interrupted Dam.

'It starts at my lower back and snakes up my neck and yes, across my face. You're not being rude, you're being curious – here, get a decent look.' Asa pushed the side of his face nearer to Esmé, who ducked beneath Dam's arm to swiftly remove herself from Asa's advancing tattoo.

'I don't need to see, thanks,' blurted Esmé, as she squirmed away from the coloured mass.

'Stop it, Asa. You'll scare her,' ordered Dam, holding a hand to Asa's chest. 'I take it you've just finished your shift and forgotten your key *again?*

'You know me, Dam – I always love to make an entrance. It must have dropped out of my pocket during the day. I'll get another tomorrow,' said Asa, adding. 'Lady, you've certainly learnt how to crack a poker over a guy's head. Did they teach you that at school while us lads were playing rugby?'

Esmé watched as he rubbed his scalp and then leant against the sink unit, arms outstretched supporting his weight, eyes closed and head bowed.

'Sorry, but can I get you anything? Pain killers?' she asked.

'Vodka?' he muttered.

She glanced at Dam.

'He's joking, don't let him fool you. I say, we all go to bed. We'll laugh about this in the morning,' said Dam.

'I need coffee first,' muttered Asa, raising a hand to wave. 'See you.'

'OK. Well, I'm leading this one back to her room and we'll see you in the morning so enjoy your coffee.' Dam gently led Esmé from the morning room.

'Is he always like that?' she asked as they walked through the hallway.

'Nah, but if you catch him on a bad day there's no telling what mood he'll be in. Honestly, he's one of the nicest guys you could wish to meet but that... that was pure comedy seeing you knock ten bells out of him while he scrambled around on the floor. Wait till I tell Russ.'

Having climbed two flights of stairs, Esmé stopped outside her room as Dam turned and began to descend back onto the first floor landing.

'What's with the tattoo on his face?' asked Esmé.

'Oh *that*. That's a long story... which is his to tell. Goodnight.'

She watched as Dam retreated partway down the staircase to his own landing.

'Dam.'

'Yeah?'

'Thank you.'

'No worries, sleep tight, Esmé.'

Chapter Ten

The morning sunlight crept through a chink in the curtains like a searchlight. Esmé propped herself up on her elbows, remembered where she was and listened: someone was playing a musical scale. Was it a clarinet or a flute? The repeating sequence continued up and then steadily down. She strained her ears to tune into the sound and decided on a flute.

But who? Russ *never*. Tattooed Asa? Dam perhaps? Or Jonah?

She scrambled from beneath her fleece which was curiously wrapped around her legs. This she must see, though if it was Dam she wouldn't be so surprised. She was still grateful to him for looking after her last night when that oaf played his face.

She grimaced.

She mustn't mention his face.

Living with Asa might prove more difficult than expected. Esmé's forte was mentioning the elephant in the room during difficult situations. Andrew's granddad had a prosthetic leg due to his diabetes – how many times had she unconsciously referred to pirates and wooden legs whilst visiting?

She spied her calendar perched on the mantelpiece.

'Day three, here I come,' she said as she searched for today's door with its tiny chocolate.

Day 3: Reconnect with friends

Interesting, given that I did that yesterday thanks to Russ, Dam and Jonah. Maybe I'm getting ahead of myself in this calendar malarkey.

Esmé rummaged through her wheelie case in search of something more suitable than pyjamas for this morning's first breakfast.

A fluffy housecoat would be nice if it looked cute, though given that hers still hung in the Symphony Court bathroom and doubled her waist measurement whilst looking dowdy, it wasn't an option.

Esmé hauled on her jeans and a tee-shirt – though, a quick look down at herself suggested she was recycling yesterday's clobber as it looked so similar. Russ and Dam had seen her – would they notice it wasn't the exact same tee-shirt? Were these guys that observant? She peeled off the outfit and grabbed her red leggings.

But they clung to her hips and made her feel self-conscious so she peeled those off too.

'If I waste much more time the flute playing will have stopped.'

A quick peek beyond her bedroom door ensured the landing was clear and two large strides later, wearing grey leggings and a fresh tee-shirt, Esmé was bolting the bathroom door.

Running the washbasin taps, she started on seeing her reflection.

Bloody hair, how long does it take?

After a wash, a quick brush of her teeth and a ruffle of *the* new hairstyle – she was ready to face the breakfast table.

She bound down the staircase onto the lower landing, where all the doors remained closed so she sped past them and descended the lower staircase. The flute scales were louder but not as much as she expected, maybe someone was playing in the lounge?

Esmé popped her head into the main lounge – empty and very tidy. She closed the door and tried the dining room – empty too.

The guys must be in the kitchen.

'Morning!' Esmé burst into the morning room like a ray of sunshine. She was met by the panda eyes of a blonde woman slumped at the central table, cradling a mug and staring aimlessly at the fireplace. She hadn't tidied her hair or washed, and her bare legs protruded from an oversized man's shirt haphazardly buttoned down the front.

'Eh, oh yeah, morning,' muttered the woman.

Dam's head appeared around the archway, a wooden spatula in hand.

'Morning Esmé, did you sleep alright?'

Esmé looked from Dam to the woman and back again.

Best not to ask.

'Yes thanks, and you?' Esmé darted through the archway to join him at the cooker only to find Asa seated on the marbled work top, bare chested and clad in jeans, cradling a coffee mug too.

'Morning, precious, am I in for another beating today?' he said, to her surprised face.

'Let's face it, you deserved it, frightening me like that,' she replied, diverting her eyes from his bare chest to the blobby eggs Dam was nudging around in a frying pan.

Oh shit, she'd mentioned face again.

'Hardly premeditated though, was it?' he muttered.

Esmé stared at him, noting the tattooed formation of peacock feathers clearly visible in daylight. His dark eyes stared straight back, before his brow quivered and she returned her gaze to Dam's eggs.

Dam lifted the pan, took his plate from the other work top unit and swiftly tipped his eggs onto the white crockery. Esmé watched intensely, purely to avoid looking up at Asa.

'You want this?' Dam asked, offering her the handle of the frying pan.

'Please.'

Dam returned the pan to the stove, vacated the hotspot and settled at the table opposite the blonde. Asa sipped his coffee and watched her.

Now what? I stupidly said yes, when I should have said no. This tattoo guy heard me say yes, he's now expecting me to cook. I could simply put the frying pan into the sink and make a drink, he'll probably never notice. But if he does, he'll think I'm weird. Which I am for saying yes when I don't want fried eggs, I'd have liked…

'Are you alright?' asked Asa, staring down from his perch, obviously witness to her hesitation.

'*Me?*'

'Yep, you with the frying pan.'

'Fine.'

'You haven't been shopping, have you?'

'What?' snapped Esmé, her brow furrowed in irritation.

'You moved in yesterday, you haven't had any boxes delivered by your parents and you didn't get around to going shopping, did you?' he repeated.

'No, but I don't see what that has to do with you.'

'Because… you'll need eggs if you're going to cook any… you can borrow two of mine if you want – they're over in the fridge, top shelf.'

'*What?*'

'Borrow, lending… you pay back later when you've been to the shop, get it?'

She looked up at Asa, who started to chuckle.

'Damn, you're hard work, babe.' At that Asa jumped down from the worktop, opened the fridge and grabbed a box of six eggs. 'Here, take two but make sure you replace them. I'll let you off for using my milk and coffee yesterday.'

'I… I… thank you.'

'You're welcome,' said Asa, and walked through into the morning room where Dam continued to chomp his eggs. '… if it saves me from getting a beating.'

Esmé's head whipped round on hearing the end of his comment, her eyes taking in the length of his retreating back – olive skin smattered with colourful tattoos. She could see his muscles ripple beneath his painted skin.

Dam laughed and nodded his head while his jaws continued to chomp. The blonde sipped her drink, picked at her finger nails and ignored Asa as he joined her side of the table.

Who was she anyway? Russ's girlfriend perhaps? Should I have introduced myself. How rude of me not too.

Esmé removed the frying pan from the stove, refilled the kettle and flicked the switch.

'I'm making a fresh brew, anyone want one? Dam? Asa? Ummm…' she approached the blonde. 'Would you like a top up? Sorry, I didn't catch your name earlier.'

'*Me?* It's Crystal. I'll be off in a minute, I'll just finish this,' she said, lifting the mug to show the dregs at the bottom.

Crystal. Who in their right mind called a kid Crystal?

Dam lowered his head.

'You can borrow my coffee again if you wish, but remember that once you've been shopping you're on your own,' laughed Asa, swigging his cooling drink. 'No free loading.'

She made her coffee before returning to the stove to cook the eggs.

'I heard someone playing the flute earlier,' she said, breaking the silence.

'Next door,' said Dam, putting his dirty plate into the dishwasher. 'You could hear it when we viewed the house, couldn't you, Asa?'

'Yeah,' was all Asa said.

Crystal suddenly stood up and placed her dirty mug in the sink.

'I'll be heading off then, see ya... thanks for the coffee.' Her shirt-come-dress barely covered her behind thanks to a shaped front and tails.

'Oh right, see you again,' said Esmé, looking up from plating her eggs, before she grabbed cutlery from the drawer.

Neither male spoke. The morning room door closed as she seated herself beside Dam at the table and began to tuck in.

Several minutes passed. Esmé was engrossed in her eggs when she heard a snort and from the corner of her eye saw Dam's shoulders shudder uncontrollably.

'What?' Looking up to see both blokes dying with laughter. 'Have I got something on my face?'

Asa stopped laughing, Dam roared even louder, throwing his head back so that his beard danced as his jaw moved up and down.

'What, have *you* got something on *your* face?' asked Asa, leaning across the table. 'Are you for real?'

Esmé sat, knife and fork suspended, and stared from one to the other as both men belly laughed.

What's the joke?

'You've no idea, have you?' spluttered Asa.

'Seriously, another comedy moment... woman, you kill me,' hissed Dam.

Esmé picked up her plate of half eaten eggs and stood up.

'I'll go and eat elsewhere if it's alright with you pair, maybe you'll grow up and learn some manners for the breakfast table.'

Breakfast with Andrew was always civilised: drink coffee, eat and chat about the day ahead. *This* would take some getting used to.

Esmé left the morning room, balancing her coffee mug on her plate, and headed for the dining room. As the door closed behind her she heard Asa mutter, 'see you again' before a new eruption of laughter bellowed out.

*

The heavens opened as Esmé walked back from the bus stop lugging three plastic carrier bags which cut ridges into her palms. Being thrifty seemed like a better idea than ordering a cab but being drenched to the skin wasn't part of her plan. The sight of their gate post quickened her pace along with the thought of hot chocolate topped with freshly whipped cream and the marshmallows currently at the bottom of one of the heavy bags.

As soon as her key turned in the lock, she could hear the commotion inside: male voices loud and deep coming from the lounge. She closed the door, dropped her handbag and removed her dripping coat. Quickly flicking off her shoes revealed her soaked feet as she tiptoed towards the kitchen with the carrier bags banging against her legs.

Once unpacked, with Asa's small stash neatly repaid on the work top, she headed for the lounge. A moment of hesitation saw her linger outside the door trying to count the number of voices she could hear within: Russ, Asa, possibly Kane and Jonah. It's now or never.

Esmé entered the lounge, the four men were in various positions, sitting and lying about on couches, armchairs and pouffes, all mesmerised by and shouting at a football game on the large plasma tv. An array of cans, coke bottles and crisp packets were either clutched in their hands or scattered around the shag pile carpet.

'Hi,' she said, as she stood between the couch and the single armchair.

No answer. Not a single grunt.

'Hello,' she called a little louder, above the rant of the four referees pointing and shouting at an on screen foul.

No answer.

How bloody rude! This is exactly how Andrew used to behave when a match was on, cheering, swearing and ranting at the screen as if the referee could hear his abuse and advice. He can't! Why does every man think he's the world's best football manager from the comfort of his armchair?

Without thinking she crossed the room and swiped the neon blue light at the bottom of the screen. The football match died. Silence instantly descended. Esmé turned, hands on hips, to face the rabble.

'Hi fellas, I'm home,' she sang sweetly, turning to each stunned bloke in turn. 'Asa, I've left a pile of goodies on the worktop to repay you for lending me coffee, milk and eggs.'

Asa simply nodded and looked around her body at the blank screen.

'Oh Kane, nice to see you again… have you come to check how I've settled in?' Esmé smiled sweetly at her brother.

Kane remained mute, eyes wide, biting the inside of his cheek.

'Jonah, where did you get to last night, not even a goodbye?'

Jonah emptied a bag of crisps into his open mouth, but choked on being addressed.

'I… left…' he spluttered, eyes watering.

'No Dam?' asked Esmé.

'Having dinner at his parents' house,' chorused Russ and Asa in unison.

'Russell, have a good night, did you?'

'Yes thanks... Esmé, would you mind?' Russ waved his hand in a passing motion towards the tv.

Kane got up and swiped at the screens 'on/off' area. Esmé remained standing, unsure of what to do.

'Now, can we please—' Russ pointed to the screen.

'Esmé... I mean can *someone* ask my sister to move!' shouted Kane, who pulled a face at the other guys.

'Seriously, drop the whole silent treatment,' snapped Asa. 'You spoke to her last night and she can hear you saying it.'

'Are you not speaking to me, Kane?'

'Someone tell my sister, what do you think?' asked Kane, addressing the males.

'Seriously, how old are you?' said Russ.

'Oh did-dums...' Esmé's bottom lip protruded towards her mute brother.

'Will *someone* tell my sister it's not a Villa game, so she won't be missing anything if she leaves the room!'

'Esmé, please!' snapped Russ, as he pointed to the blank screen.

'I hope your girlfriend wasn't offended at breakfast... Dam and Asa hardly said a word to her, did you?'

'*My girlfriend?* asked Russ, and his eyes widened.

Jonah choked for a second time.

'You alright over there, Jonah?' asked Asa, 'Anything you want to say?'

'Crystal. She only had a coffee but still, you were hardly pleasant to her, were you?' said Esmé to Asa.

'Jonah... seriously, anything to add?' asked Asa, with a bemused expression.

Jonah looked away, brushing crisps from his front.

Esmé looked from one to the other. She was slightly lost in the conversation or how to proceed given the sea of smirking faces, so moved from centre stage as the football commentary came back to life and the lounge breathed a sigh of relief on seeing an unchanged score.

Instantly, the volume of cheering, shouting and beer swigging resumed as though no interruption had occurred.

'See you again!' mimicked Kane, as Esmé left the room.

As the lounge door closed, Esmé heard Asa say, 'Shhhh, we told you that in confidence.'

'Don't shhhh me about my own sister, I told you about the Villa hat, didn't I?'

She returned to the kitchen, peeled off her wet socks and began making her hot chocolate.

What's so bloody funny about being polite and interacting with housemates? Obviously in this day and age, manners don't exist and everything is highly hilarious. Surely if they were going to share a house they needed to communicate with everyone, even girlfriends at the breakfast table.

She heaped the cocoa powder into a mug and boiled the kettle.

Neither of the blokes had kissed Crystal goodbye so obviously she was neither of theirs. Russ should be glad she was polite and made an effort. Her mobile rang in her pocket interrupting her thoughts.

Carys.

'Hi,' said Esmé, instantly brighter, putting her friend on loud speaker.

'Just checking you're still alive.'

'Certainly am… are you free to talk?'

Esmé continued with her drink as she explained last night's antics. Within minutes she was seated on the morning room couch, chatting away, with a pile of the pink and white marshmallows melting down the side of her mug.

'Hardly normal behaviour from a grown man. How were you to know?' came Carys's voice over loud speaker.

'I had no idea… did I?' said Esmé, lost in conversation.

Asa came into the morning room, walked to the kettle area and began making a drink.

'That's what I said, who in their right mind enters a house by…' Esmé stalled as her gaze met Asa's. She blushed, switching her call from loud speaker to her ear.

'Please continue… don't mind me,' he said, as he turned his back on her conversation and reached for a collection of mugs.

'Exactly,' said Esmé into her phone, avoiding looking in his direction in case she stared.

Pause.

'*Exactly.*'

Pause.

'Er, erm… not quite but yeah. Arse about face really.'

Asa whipped round from his coffee making. Esmé blushed, yet again she's mentioned the 'F' word.

'You haven't mentioned the poker yet, tell her about smashing me one with the poker – a pretty decent defence strategy for a young woman. She might want to buy one too.'

'Sorry,' said Esmé to Asa, her hand covering her mobile mouthpiece.

'The poker… don't forget all the details, she'll want to know it all.'

'Excuse me, Carys. I'm being interrupted, just a second,' said Esmé into her phone. 'Asa, do you mind? I'm on the phone.'

'I know but you're missing out the best bits just because I walked in, don't… I really don't mind.'

'Well, I do, thank *you* very much,' retorted Esmé. 'Hi Carys – I'm back. No, no. Yes.'

Silence.

'Rudeness really,' said Esmé.

Asa collected the multiple handles of the coffee mugs and made his way from the kitchen into the morning room.

'Bye Carys!' he shouted as he passed the couch.

Esmé frowned.

Asa smiled.

'Nobody, don't worry,' said Esmé, into her phone.

The door swung closed as Asa left the room.

'A bloke called Asa, don't worry,' she explained, adding, 'He's just an arse.'

'No, I'm not. I'm adorable,' shouted a voice through the closed door.

'You're an arse!' shouted Esmé in temper.

She sat stunned and open mouthed, her mobile clutched to her chest in disbelief at her own rudeness, before continuing her call.

*

Esmé lay on her bed reading a glossy magazine she'd picked up in the supermarket, when a sharp rap on her bedroom door disturbed the peace.

'Yes?' she called, hoping it wasn't her brother come to convince her to swap homes.

When there was no answer, she slid from the mattress to open the door.

'Oh, it's you!' she said, as Asa filled the open doorway.

'Yep, me, the arse… just come to see how you're settling in at Chez Montague.'

'Fine.' Her arm remained outstretched, her hand firmly on the door handle, visibly blocking his path.

Don't stare at the tattoo. Look him straight in the eyes. Don't look. Oh shit, I *looked*.

Asa looked over her head into her empty room.

'Need a hand moving any boxes?'

'Er no. I haven't collected my belongings yet.'

'I see, parents delivering them, are they?'

'Nope. I just haven't arranged collection yet.'

Asa leant against the door jamb.

'You leaving that calendar on the mantelpiece?'

'What?' Esmé turned to view her room. 'No, well, yes for now, but no.' She pulled the door a little further closed behind her body to block his view.

'Hardly an ornament to admire on the mantelpiece, that's all, but if it's all you've got?'

'What? No.' scowled Esmé, puffing out her cheeks. 'What do you want, Asa?'

'You nearly called me arse then,' smiled Asa.

'No I didn't, you don't know me well enough to predict what I was about to say. You know nothing about me, so please don't try...' Her eyes drifted across his face to the blue and green tattoo before snapping back to his dark eyes.

'To finish your sentences?'

'What? Urggh!'

'I'm only kidding with you,' he peeled himself from the wooden frame surround. 'Look, I've come to apologise, OK?'

'What for?'

'For earlier when you were chatting on the phone, and then this morning when we rudely laughed at you for not understanding our guest at breakfast, and for mimicking your goodbye to her and then for telling your brother the whole story which gave him a bloody good laugh too... so, sorry.'

'Well don't.'

'But I want to.'

'But I don't want you to.' What didn't I understand? What did I say that was so funny?

'You're thinking now, aren't you?' asked Asa. 'I can see the cogs whirring.'

'No, I'm not.'

'You are, I can see it. You're thinking what's he on about? What didn't I get? What didn't I understand? And that's OK because I think it's sweet that you didn't get the breakfast situation.'

'Yes, I did.' Esmé released the door handle and folded her arms.

'Did you? Oh sorry, in that case sorry for overestimating your naïvety but I felt certain that the actual situation had gone right over your head and that we'd been rude enough to laugh when we really shouldn't have, though it was mighty funny.'

What the hell was he on about?

'It was fine. I wasn't offended by your laughter, nor Dam's… there's no need to apologise.'

Asa nodded slowly, his eyes scrutinised her. Esmé averted her eyes from the tattoo by staring at his nose.

There's a spot forming under the surface by his nostril. Should a female housemate point out such a detail? Would she have pointed that out to Andrew? Not usually necessary, he always scrutinised his skin after a shower or a shave.

A wry smile began to dawn across his lips, it developed into a dimple within his left cheek.

'What?' snapped Esmé.

'Nothing, just admiring the view.'

'Well, don't!' Dear Lord, please remove this man from my doorway. I have no idea what his game is or what the hell he's apologising for and somehow, he bloody well knows all of that.

'Crystal.'

'Yes, that was her name, quite a nice name actually.'

'Do you think?'

'Yes, it conjures up lovely images.'

'Go to school with many Crystals, did you?'

'No, but if I had, I'd probably have been friends with her…'

'*Really?* What lovely images have sprung to mind then?'

'Oh loads, dancing lights, sparkly Christmas trees, glitzy earrings…'

'Hookers.'

What did he just say?

'Hookers?'

'Yeah, hookers, ladies of the night… you know?'

'No, I don't know *actually.*' Esmé's tone lifted to indignation.

'I initially thought that by your 'see you again' line as she left.'

Esmé's mouth performed the perfect goldfish impression for several seconds, as Asa watched from the doorway.

'But given that you knew… I feel really daft wanting to apologise for mine and Dam's rude behaviour of belly laughing *at* you when all the time you were fully aware of her occupation, the cash in hand situation and were simply playing it uber cool. Sorry, my mistake. In fact, you should probably give lessons on just how coolly you handled that, such a poker face, because we could have sworn that you had no idea, when actually you did!' Asa shoved his hands into his jeans pockets and sauntered off along the landing towards his room next door.

Esmé stood speechless as Asa's bedroom door closed softly. Hers followed suit, then she leant against the closed door before sliding down its entire length to her haunches, her hands raised to her mouth.

OMG! *This* would take some getting used to. A hooker? Russ *or* Jonah? How embarrassing if she'd barged in and interrupted them last night?

She remained in a crouched position for a lengthy time before stifling her giggles as she heard herself repeat, 'see you again' in a light fluffy tone.

Chapter Eleven

Day 4: Acknowledge your true values

The sound of childish wailing drifted from downstairs.

Esmé wrenched the warm duvet over her head on her Sunday morning lie-in. Obviously, someone's family were visiting for an early morning house call. She could image a young nephew or niece running amuck downstairs while flapping parents were begging them to be quiet in Uncle…

Which name filled the blank? Uncle Dam? Uncle Jonah? Uncle Asa? Uncle Russ?

She gave a snigger and plumped her pillow, snuggling down for an additional thirty minutes of sleep.

The wailing continued, louder than before.

She chastised herself for moaning, before flinging the duvet back and getting up and dressed. What did she expect in a shared house? With the comings and goings of five adults, surely peace, harmony and Sunday lie-ins couldn't be guaranteed.

'*Morning*,' sang Esmé, entering the kitchen to find a little boy aged about three devouring toast at the table, his dungareed legs and football slippers swinging gleefully. Asa was cooking sausages at the stove, while Kane swept up dried Coco pops scattered across the floor tiles.

'Morning,' said Kane, looking up from his housework.

'Hi,' shouted Asa, as he turned round from the grill pan.

'Who owns the little one?' she pointed to the dark haired boy and pulled a quizzical face.

'Russell's little lad,' said Kane.

'*Really?*

'A previous relationship. His mother dropped him off for his visiting day. Toby, meet Esmé, my sister,' said Kane, quite formally for a child to adult introduction.

'Hi, little fella,' said Esmé, heading for the kettle. 'You're early?'

'I dropped by to see how you were…' said Kane, adding. 'Mum's really concerned, that's all.'

Esmé began to make her morning tea. So, he's talking to me today.

'I know but I need some space to get my head straight before she starts with the questions.'

'Where's Russ?'

'In bed, I think,' answered Asa, without taking his eyes off the sausages.

Esmé screwed her face up, looked at Toby and then at Kane.

'Are you serious?'

'Yeah,' said Kane, emptying his Coco pop collection into the bin.

'His child is visiting and he's in bed?'

'Shhhh,' said Kane, and dragged her through the archway towards the sink area. 'Little piggies.'

'I know but still, that's taking the piss, Kane... a guy should look after his child, not leave it up to his housemates or even his best mate. That's not right. It's not fair on the little piggy as you just called him... The mother wouldn't be happy, would she?'

'No,' answered Kane, in a monotone.

'No,' added Asa.

'Sorry... but I'm *not* having this.'

'Esmé, please...' is all she heard of Kane's protest.

In two seconds she flew from the room, darted to the first landing and rapped sharply on Russ's door. She was determined to follow her plan, and the calendar had said to acknowledge her values, so she would.

'Russ!'

'What's wrong?' came his sleepy reply.

'*This*... and by that, I mean you still being in bed while little Toby is downstairs, it really isn't acceptable,' she began. 'And before you say it's none of my business, I beg to differ. I live in this house and I know that any mother would not be too happy thinking she'd dropped him off, as you obviously haven't collected him and now you aren't even up nor dressed and my brother has taken responsibility to feed him breakfast… which I presume he has naughtily thrown all over the kitchen floor and then demanded toast.'

'Uh!'

'Russ, are you listening to me?' she rapped on the bedroom door again, purely for good measure.

'Esmé, go away!' shouted Russ.

'How dare you!'

'Please?'

'No, I have every right to come up here and say my piece.'

'Esmé, *please* leave it.'

'I won't. You're expecting the rest of us to entertain your child in our house and then when his mother appears later you'll want to take all the glory for being such a great father… well, I don't think that's right!'

Silence. Today's task was far easier than she'd imagined.

'Russ, you had better get up and get dressed now, otherwise I'm phoning the mother – this isn't acceptable… you've got responsibilities and you need to start putting his needs before yours.'

She could hear shuffling behind the closed door.

She stepped back from the door as it was wrenched open.

'And later when she gets here I am going to…' her voice died, as a woman's face and body appeared, tousled hair, panda eye mascara, with a bed sheet draped around her body.

'Do you mind? We're trying to… you know?'

Looks like she would *need* to get used to such encounters, thought Esmé.

She pushed past the tousled siren and entered Russ's darkened bedroom.

'And *this* is absolutely shocking… you're up here… doing *this*…' she screamed, as Russ quickly grabbed the quilt making himself decent for his unexpected guest. 'Have you no shame? Your little boy is downstairs, eating toast made by *my* brother – who, may I add, doesn't even live here and… and…' Esmé stopped as the woman climbed back into bed and nuzzled up to Russ's body. 'Shame on you – that's all I can say!'

Esmé marched from the room, her arms flailing, a look of disgust etched on her features. She descended the staircase to find Kane standing open mouthed at the bottom.

'What did you say?' he gasped.

'I told him straight. He has definitely gone down in my estimation… this is shocking. How any man can be up there with some tart while his little boy is eager to start his visiting day is beyond me. What a lowlife?'

'You didn't say that though, did you?'

'Of course, I did. I told him.'

'And… then what?'

'Then nothing, she climbed back into bed without batting an eyelid about his paternal responsibilities… shocking.'

'There's no need to cause trouble – you've said your bit.'

'He needs to be a father and step up to the plate,' Esmé said, walking back to the lounge, where Dam was watching morning tv. 'Don't you think so, Dam?'

'Sorry, I heard the shouting but thought I'd keep out of it.'

She flung herself down in the armchair.

'Russ and Toby… it's not right, the little boy is playing football alone in the garden – I've a good mind to phone the mother and tell her.'

Kane stood at the door and stared at Dam.

'You haven't got her number, have you?' asked Dam, muting his programme.

'No, but that's not the point… if I had, I *would*.'

Kane sighed. Dam sighed.

'I could phone his mother,' she added.

'Whose?'

'Russ's mother… She'd go mad if she knew…'

'No!' cried Kane. 'I wouldn't.'

'Yeah, I agree with Kane,' added Dam. 'It might spoil the surprise.'

'What surprise?'

'Russ is taking Toby round for a surprise visit later today.'

'Oh,' said Esmé, as she hugged the sofa cushion to her chest. 'I suppose it's not her fault her son is some low-life father that can't respect his kid… oh, I see what you mean, why should she pay the price for his low morals.'

'Exactly!' chimed Kane.

'That's more like it,' said Dam, glancing at Kane.

Esmé played with the seam of the cushion.

The wind had been taken from her sails.

'But still, she should know that he's not doing his job as a father.'

'No!' chorused the men.

'Seriously?'

'We'll have a word with him… won't we, Dam?'

'Oh yeah, a strong word with him about his responsibilities,' added Dam.

'You can tell him what I said,' she added.

'Word for word,' said Kane eagerly.

'Absolutely,' muttered Dam, as he turned back to focus on his tv programme.

Chapter Twelve

Day 5: A financial make-over

'What the hell?' cried Marianne, as Esmé charged into the offices of Stylo Stationery at just gone nine o'clock on Monday morning.

'Sorry, I'm late… I promise it'll never happen again and… what's that?' she pointed at the helium balloon dancing on its ribbon beside Penny's computer. The balloon bobbed revealing the message 'Congratulations!' 'Oh yes, long weekend, long story.'

Marianne fell back into her seat, wide-eyed at Esmé's new hair.

'Do you like it?' Esmé theatrically framed her face with her hands.

'I think I'll like it more after an explanation… where have your auburn locks gone?'

'Same way as the—'

'*Congratulations!* Show me, show me!' cried Penny, entering with the tea tray and quickly depositing it on the first free desk before grabbing Esmé's left hand.

'Urgh! Problem.' Esmé grimaced. 'No ring.'

'No proposal?' asked Marianne, wincing.

'No, nothing. Over. Finished. Totally *finito!*'

'No!' exclaimed Penny, supporting herself on the nearest chair back. 'Are you serious?'

'Ladies, you won't believe what's happened since Thursday.'

The three women gather around Esmé's desk, cradling their coffee for a minute by minute update, totally ignoring the ringing phones, the Monday morning routine and the arrival of Ollie, the new IT intern.

'I swear on my life, you've shocked me. I wouldn't have brought that if I thought there was any doubt... I feel a prat now, hoicking that in on the bus,' said Penny, pointing to the metallic balloon.

'And a waste of a tenner,' added Marianne. 'And now, you've hooked up with four guys in a house off the Hagley Road – excellent move.'

'Marianne, don't... they might get through this... they might...'

'No way. I'm done. Of all the guys I've dated... I never thought Andrew would cheat on me.'

'And there was a fair few in your younger years,' adds Marianne.

'Well yes... of course, but I never saw this coming and so, it's right what they say... you never know someone, *ever.*'

'Oh, come now, I *know* my Jimmy,' said Marianne. 'I know he'll never marry me, but he'll never cheat and he'll probably sweet talk me into having a baby someday.'

'Yeah, same here. I know my Keith… as miserable as he is, moaning about everything the kids or I do in and around the house… he'd never cheat in our marriage,' adds Penny.

'Looks like I'm the lucky one then… unfortunate enough not to see this coming, not to be playing the field and to have put all my hopes and dreams into one basket!' said Esmé, her voice cracking. 'So, that's the news. Hence, the new hair and why I arrived late.'

'Seriously, he wasn't right for you… I don't care what Penny and your mother said about him… You're now free to spread your wings and have a bit of *fun*,' said Marianne.

'You wait seven years to tell me that?'

'Yep, long time actually. Where was the romance? The passion? Andrew was a dead squid.'

'Marianne!' cried Penny, a look of horror on her face.

'I'll be honest, I never liked him the first time I met him… too… what's the word? Arrogant! Up his own arse!' declared Marianne, opening her desk drawer and grabbing a packet of custard creams. 'Here… let's celebrate!'

Esmé leant across the desk and took two.

'Marianne, you really shouldn't comment,' whispered Penny, refusing a custard cream.

'No, seriously, I thought, oh no, a total mistake,' explained Marianne, stuffing biscuits into her mouth quicker than a Guinness book of records attempt.

'Hmmmm, cheers,' added Esmé, nibbling the layers of her first biscuit.

'This might be a rollercoaster break up… so don't comment so freely,' repeated Penny.

'A what?' muttered Marianne.

'Weekend break up but they're back together on a high by Wednesday… a rollercoaster break up.'

'No way,' mumbled Esmé.

'No one knows what the future has in store.'

'I do… he got caught doing the dirty in our bed. Her name's Sadie and I hate her guts.'

'Sadie… oh, one of those, is she?' asked Marianne, curling her lip.

'One of what?' asked Penny.

'The new generation of Sadie, Selina and Sapphire – all slinky and kinky and chasing your man.'

'Anyway, it's over… I can't forgive him and I certainly won't forget.'

'You don't deserve that,' said Marianne.

'You're right. I deserve better.'

'You'll be joining us at the bus station each evening?' said Penny, moving onto safer territory.

'Yep, new bus route, new bathroom routine with a guy called Asa and…' Esmé pointed to her throat. 'That awful knot that sits just here and won't allow you to swallow or eat properly, reminding you that your heart has been broken.' Esmé's eye filled with tears.

'Oh lovey, this will pass,' said Penny, jumping up to give her a hug.

'It'll probably pass as painfully as a kidney stone but yep, it'll pass,' adds Marianne, standing to join in the group bear hug.

'And in the meantime,' came Esmé's muffled voice from under the commiseration of her colleagues. 'I need to arrange to clear my belongings out of the... *his* apartment, visit the bank, change my address... urgh, the list is endless.'

'And your mother?' asked Marianne.

'Urgh! Don't remind me. As much as she hated the rental apartment... and pushed for a mortgage commitment...'

'The woman doted on Andrew.' Marianne completed the sentence as Esmé began to sob.

*

'In nine years... I have never been late for work, Mrs Stylo. I can only apologise on this occasion and promise it will never happen again,' panted Esmé, determined to convince her steely eyed boss sitting opposite.

'Mmmm,' growled the old lady, eyeballing her carefully. A back drop of metal filing cabinets and a withered spider plant failed to contradict the 'You don't have to be mad to work here... but it helps' sticker that had constituted office humour for the last three decades.

When did bosses become *this* difficult? Stavros Stylo, Esmé's original boss and the late husband of this witch, had been the warmest, kindest man she'd ever encountered. Since his untimely death from cancer a few years ago, not a working day had gone by that Esmé hadn't recalled with fondness the day he interviewed her. A simple four questioned interview, at that.

'You like stationery?'

'You can tap, tap, tap on the computer thingy?'

'You can make coffee without wasting time?'

'Yes, yes, and yes,' had been Esmé's eager reply as a naïve twenty year old, in desperate need of work and independence.

'You can start after lunch time then?'

Her first proper interview and her first proper job after walking out mid-afternoon from her original job in the box factory, where she was used and abused and asked to clean the toilets.

How she missed Stavros Stylo, with his fatherly mannerisms.

'I assure you there are reasons but it will *never* happen again,' pleaded Esmé.

'Your hair, there's something different?'

Esmé touched her once lustrous locks, feeling instead the crispy texture of styling product and was reminded, yet again, that her long hair had gone to the big dust pan in the sky.

'Oh yes, a slight trim.' An understatement, Tristan took ten inches off from all over transforming a glorious young woman into a pantomime page. 'But that is not the reason I was late…'

'The colour?' Stylo's hand flaps around her own head of fine grey hair.

'Yes, I was auburn last week and now…'

'White?'

'Platinum, actually… though if you wish to call it white, then yes, white.'

Esmé watched as the old lady's hand absentmindedly touched the nape of her wrinkled neck, and fingered the texture of her own greying locks imprisoned in a severe bun.

'You think such a colour would…?'

Kill me now. The devil of all bosses wishes to copy my haircut, my life is seriously in trouble.

'I'm not so sure…' she muttered, not wishing to sound rude but definitely not wishing to gain an aged twin.

Mrs Stylo frowned, her steel grey eyes bore into Esmé.

And now I've annoyed her twice in one morning.

'Are you having a crisis?' asked the elderly lady.

Possibly.

'To be honest Mrs Stylo, life has changed pretty rapidly in recent days to such an extent that—' Esmé began to explain.

'You want leave Stylo?'

'To be honest no, but…'

'You here with my husband, he called you his top girl and yet you come in here saying you want out, you having crisis – which leads to change, which ultimately means you will be going for the interviews, yeah?' said Mrs Stylo. She continued to tut long after her sentence. 'How much?'

Esmé's ears pricked up. What did she say?

'I ask you, how much? How much for you to stop having the crisis and stop looking elsewhere for more pennies?'

Esmé wondered fleetingly if it would be entirely bad manners to jump up and dash from her office for an emergency conflab with Marianne and Penny about the best way to negotiate something she hadn't even thought about. Instead, she sat tight. Her last pay rise was two years ago and that was only enough to cover the increase in her bus fare to and from work. If her new lifestyle was to be stress free she needed to ask for much more, more than she'd have dreamed of but hey, what had The Single Girl's Calendar, day five, said 'a financial make-over'.

'Three thousand,' whispered Esmé, watching the old lady's reaction. A figure plucked from the air but at roughly twenty quid a week per thousand before tax that would be a nice amount to cushion the blow should any unexpected bills come her way. Andrew had never been her safety net but he would never have seen her go short, not while they were living together, anyway. But Andrew was history and so was his safety net.

Mrs Stylo grabbed her calculator and punched buttons for a considerable amount of time.

'Three thousand, you say?'

Esmé nodded, speaking was not an option.

After a few more button presses, the old lady gave the tiniest of nods. If she'd blinked, Esmé would have missed it.

'OK, OK, but no more of this crisis and you stop looking for new job, right?'

You suggested a new job, not me, thought Esmé.

'Oh yes, definitely… right, from this point onwards no more crisis… no more… finished, gone, done and dusted,' said Esmé, as she scrambled up from her seat and edged towards the office door. Through which she shot, closed and then instantly returned in a fluster to say. 'Thank you!'

'And my Stavros, he thought you were the best, men, phah!' muttered the old lady, shaking her head and returning to her paperwork.

*

Esmé climbed the office stairs in a state of shock. How could this be happening? She thought she'd been called in for a dressing down but instead walked out with a pay rise. How? Why? When she'd opened door five of her single girl's calendar she'd imagined the task related to balancing her current account, denial about her overdraft and arranging to sell a whole load of her belongings on eBay purely to make ends meet. Instead, she was entering the shared office with a huge smile on her face.

'What's wrong with you?' asked Penny, viewing her stunned expression. Marianne stopped shuffling paper and stared too.

'If I told you, I'd have to kill ya,' laughed Esmé, slumping into her seat, eager to start work.

*

Esmé felt like a survivor for most of the morning but a mid-afternoon break found her weeping in the ladies' toilets. With damp red eyes, she peered into the wash basin mirror, in need of a pep talk.

'There's no going back. He's shown his true colours. He can beg as much as he wants but I'll put the phone down. I don't want to hear his sob story. If he calls, I'll say 'Andrew, you had your chance and you blew it.'

Argh! Esmé cringed, bringing herself back to the reality of talking to herself in the toilets.

She splashed cold water onto her face and vowed not to talk to herself – it only gave the game away.

'Quick, where have you been? Reception want you downstairs,' cried Marianne across the office as she returned from the ladies. 'Katrina is all of a flap.'

Esmé trotted down to the main reception desk to be greeted by a smiley, plump lady in a tabard, holding an arrangement of fresh flowers. Katrina, the receptionist, looked longingly at them over her high desk.

'Esmé Peel?' cooed the florist, offering her the colourful arrangement.

'*No.* I don't think so,' was all Esmé could muster, before the smiley lady bade her a good day and swiftly departed.

'I'll have them if you don't want them,' offered Katrina, her receptionist's head-set skewed around her lower jaw.

'I'll let you know.' Esmé climbed back up the stairs, her arms quivering with the weight of the delivery.

'Oh, how beautiful,' squealed Penny, as Esmé entered the office peering through foliage and ferns.

'Predictable,' muttered Marianne.

'Now what? Accept them and take them home or donate them?'

'I'll have them,' snapped Penny, blushing on receipt of a cold stare from Marianne.

'Your shout, but be careful... how many times has he ever bought you flowers, let alone sent you flowers?' asked Marianne, cautiously eyeing the arrangement as Esmé placed it on the centre desk.

'*Never.*'

'Exactly.' Marianne gently touched the delicate rose and lily petals.

'He's sorry... he's acknowledging that he messed up,' offered Penny, her eyes pleaded with Esmé to accept or donate to her. 'Are you going to read the card?'

'Nah, you can throw it in the bin.'

'Esmé,' said Penny, looking to Marianne for reinforcement. 'You really should read it.'

'I was only ever thinking about us and he was thinking about them! I don't feel bad, if you wish to read the card then go ahead, be my guest, but I refuse to be manipulated. However much this has cost it doesn't come near to what it has cost me!'

Esmé sat at her desk and stared at the bouquet. It was beautiful, it had probably cost him a small fortune and yet, the very sight of it turned her stomach. Had she asked for this? No, all she'd wanted was a faithful, committed Andrew. It was too little, too late.

'Penny, take them home.'

'Whoop.' Penny gushed at the prospect, before piping down and making certain Esmé was sure.

'No, seriously… I can't accept them, on principle, and I'm not carrying them on the bus only to ignore them for a fortnight. Please, you'll be doing me a favour.'

'Brave choice,' whispered Marianne.

'Though you might want to sneak past Katrina on the way out tonight,' laughed Esmé.

＊

Esmé knocked on the door of apartment nine, her key was in her hand but it didn't feel right to use it.

Andrew opened the door wearing scruffy jeans and a crumpled tee-shirt. His look of surprise was touching.

'What's with the bleached hair?'

'Hi… I fancied a change.'

'It's different from your usual style.'

'Good different or bad different?'

'Hmmm…'

'Never mind, it doesn't matter what your opinion is, to be honest. Anyway, sorry to disturb you but I've brought some boxes to…'

'I thought you'd send your parents to bag and box… I was dreading…' he stepped aside, embarrassed by his response. 'Anyway, come in.'

The door shut firmly behind her. The hallway felt smaller than ever with them both standing silently observing each other. How many times had they stood together here prior to going out, arriving home, waving off friends or welcoming family – so many times and yet, now, urgh!

'Go through.' Andrew pointed towards the lounge doorway.

She wasn't expecting this. Esmé was half expecting him to be the normal Andrew, bouncy, boisterous and a tad bolshie but this shell of a man with his crumpled tee-shirt, a five o'clock shadow and uncombed hair wasn't the Andrew she knew.

Esmé looked around the lounge, the curtains were drawn, the tv was on mute and an empty pizza box lay open on the floor by the couch.

'Is she here?' asked Esmé, standing in the centre of his lounge.

'Sadie?'

'Mmmm.'

'No. Esmé that was—'

'Don't. Please. I haven't come here to discuss things… I've come to collect a set of bed sheets, a change of clothes and a few personal belongings,' she said, adding 'but thank you for the flowers, they were beautiful.'

A flash of hope flickered in his eyes.

'I wanted you to know how sorry I am.' He took a step forward, his unshaven face puffy and tired.

'Sorry but no. You made a choice when you and her… now, I need to… and I've decided. I can't forgive.'

Andrew flopped backwards into the nearest arm chair, his crestfallen expression stared at her.

'We're through?'

'Sadly, yeah.'

He shook his head, his eyes glistened.

'You cheated. What do you expect me to do? Forgive and forget?'

'I *want* to make amends… Let me make amends. We'll get engaged, married – do whatever you want, just say it and we'll do it.'

She shook her head as a wave of emotion snagged in her throat.

Andrew launched himself from the arm chair, dropped to one knee and grabbed her left hand, his eyes were desperate, his lips trembling.

'Esmé.'

She snatched back her hand as if electrocuted by his touch.

And now, he asks. After all those years of hoping, he asks now!

Esmé wanted to cry. What wouldn't she have given for him to even suggest getting engaged prior to Thursday evening.

'I can't.'

Andrew rose from the carpet and stood before her, staring.

'It would be a mistake,' she muttered, not able to look at his face.

She didn't know where her calmness was coming from but if she could just hold it together for ten more minutes she'd be out of there and heading home to Montague Road.

'Look at me,' muttered Andrew.

Esmé lifted her gaze to see the man before her. His pain was clearly visible. Yet, it wasn't a face she loved, or knew any more. It was simply the face of another human being that was suffering and hurt and whose heart was probably breaking as they spoke. His large hands were not the hands that had once held her tight, caressed her skin and wiped her tears away for they were now tainted by the skin of another woman. Since Thursday, she'd imagined those very hands hastily unbuttoning a blouse, unzipping a skirt and then guiltily being washed and dried to dial up a takeaway ready for her return home after the late-night stock take.

'Do you mind if I help myself, or do you want to fetch the things I need?'

'You,' was all he could muster.

Esmé left the lounge and swiftly collected bits from the airing cupboard, her dressing table, wardrobe and the bathroom. She couldn't help but look to see if anything new had been added to the medicine cabinet as she removed her razors and tampons.

Chapter Thirteen

'You're late,' snapped Jonah, just after eight thirty, as Esmé dashed to join those around the kitchen table.

She pouted at his unexpected tone but settled opposite him in the only available chair, Crystal's yet-to-be-bleached seat.

A selection of snacks in cereal bowls were scattered along the table and a sea of hands were grabbing and snatching at various corn puffs and peanuts.

'Can we start this house meeting?' shouted Russ, above the chomping.

'Who made you chief?' snarled Jonah, stuffing a handful of peanuts into his mouth.

'You're in a fine mood, I can see this will go well,' offered Asa, directing his comment to Jonah.

'So?'

'Is Dam not joining us?' asked Esmé, conscious that her newly found ally always seemed to be absent.

'He's having dinner at his parents,' said Russ, before banging his fist on the table top. 'So, I've called this meeting, which probably gives me the right to be chief, Jonah. Anyway, we now have our five paying occupants so we need to organise how this is going to work.'

'I think Dam should be here, it should be a face to face discussion,' said Esmé to Russ, before she cringed. Why did she keep using that word? Asa, seated diagonally to her, didn't flinch.

'So do I, but as we said, he's at his parents' house enjoying a family dinner,' said Russ.

'Get on with it, I have people to see,' sniped Jonah, flicking a cheesy puff at him.

'Cleaning, rent collection, emergency details, security, visitors… how do we envisage it working when we're all coming and going?'

'I don't care,' said Jonah, tearing open another peanut packet before holding it to his open mouth and tipping the contents in. 'I left home to avoid such duties and constant moaning.'

'OK, first things first, emergency contact numbers – can you fill in your details and phone numbers,' said Russ, producing a piece of lined paper.

'Where is this going to be kept?' asked Asa.

'Back of the kitchen door, unless you want to make a note in your mobiles as well, just in case,' suggested Russ, scribbling down his info before sliding the piece of paper to Asa.

'Yeah, right.' Asa slid it straight past to Jonah.

'Is it optional?' asked Esmé, eyeing Asa.

'Not really,' said Russ, finding the contacts app on his mobile.

'So why's he allowed to pass—'

'No family. That's me,' said Asa, his tattooed features grinning at her.

'Who do we phone in the case of an emergency?' she asked.

'An ambulance... do you need me to write that number down for you?'

Surely everyone had somebody. Even if it was relatives you didn't like or didn't get on with... who had nobody?

Asa looked up and caught her staring.

'Seriously, no parents, siblings or grandparents remaining... so, whose details do you want me to put?'

Esmé's heart sank, as Jonah completed his details and pushed the paper and pen in her direction. Esmé filled in her parents' contact details and added Kane's as an afterthought.

'Dam can fill in his later,' said Russ, taking the paper back on completion.

'Dam will already be with his family in an emergency, because the likelihood of him being here long enough to have a bloody emergency is slim,' laughed Jonah, reaching for more snacks.

'Is he always at his parents' then?'

'The majority of the time... there was no point to him moving in,' said Jonah, looking at Russ and Asa for confirmation.

'His choice,' said Asa.

'He can do as he pleases as long as he coughs up the rent each month,' added Russ.

'The umbilical cord is yet to be cut,' whispered Jonah, leaning across the table.

'That's unfair and you know it… it's his choice to be family orientated, so cut it out,' said Asa, who leant along the table to deliver his retort to Jonah.

Esmé watched their interaction. What was it Dam had said? Somebody thinks someone else is a loser. Clearly feelings were mutual.

The discussion continued in the same manner covering toilet roll, using the washing machine, forgetting house keys and pinching food from the fridge. Occasional spats and an underlying tone of hostility lengthened every discussion point.

'Guys, please, back to business.' Russ looked irritated, his monobrow furrowed deeply as the other two men out-stared each other. 'Next discussion, please.'

'I was wondering…' Esmé looked around her housemates. 'Who'll vacuum the staircases and communal areas?'

'*What?* Asa pulled a quizzical face.

The other two simply stared

Esmé blushed.

What an idiotic thing to say.

'Good point,' said Asa. 'Such questions keep me awake at night because the list is endless – who'll empty the kitchen bin, clean the filter in the tumble dryer and replace the rim block in the bog... but hey, if you want to figure out the vacuuming, be my guest. Or you can lighten up and live a little.'

'I was thinking more along the line of guests,' interrupted Russ.

'Interesting point given Saturday morning's visitor,' laughed Asa, glancing at Esmé, who instantly blushed.

'We're all adults, so why have rules?' asked Jonah.

'That's what I'm asking, do we say guests don't get to use the shared areas so it's bedrooms and bathrooms only or...'

'That'll prove interesting when Kane drops by... because he's likely to become a permanent fixture now that he's failed to move out of his parents' house... no offence, Emma,' said Jonah.

'It's Esmé. And none taken.'

'OK, Kane's slightly different given he's a friend or brother to all of us,' said Russ, looking around the group. 'Guests of the opposite sex then?'

Asa shrugged.

'No thoughts?' asked Russ.

'Not an issue, as far as I'm concerned. I don't bring people back, friends or otherwise and I'm not offended by others having guests around the place when I am here, so no opinion from me,' explained Asa.

No friends, nor family. How odd?

Esmé continued to watch Asa from the corner of her eye.

'If I'm paying a fifth of the rent on this whole house then I'd like full use to be fair,' said Jonah.

'Agreed, but I wasn't up yesterday when a young lady stayed for coffee so I can't remark on how the others felt about it.'

'I was fine,' adds Asa. 'Dam was too.'

'Are you saying, I wasn't?' interrupted Esmé.

He shrugged, giving a wry smile.

'If you call *that* comfortable, then hey, you were comfortable, babe.'

'I *was* fine.'

'So, there's no need for a ruling,' said Jonah.

'Are you sure Dam was OK?' asked Russ.

'He was fine, the guy has different values but he's still OK with what the rest of us do,' said Asa, giving a deep sigh.

'Touchy tonight, aren't we?' said Jonah. 'Bad day?'

Asa flicked a dark stare in his direction before focusing on Russ.

'What is it you do?' asked Esmé.

'Me?' He seemed surprised that she asked, before replying. 'I work at the hospital.'

'Children's?'

'Queen Elizabeth.'

Esmé sat back, that wasn't what she was expecting. She'd have said labourer, driver, warehouse work, security... well, anything that would allow such defiant tattoos. Employment couldn't be easy to find given his choice of body art. But still, there were plenty of jobs within a hospital where contact with the public was minimal, cleaners, porters... the morgue.

Esmé visibly shivered as her thought hit home.

'Are you alright?' asked Russ.

'Yeah, someone just walked over my grave,' joked Esmé.

'And your job?' Asa's question was unexpected, Esmé thought that conversation had passed.

'I work in a stationer's in Digbeth.'

'Any chance of freebies?' asked Jonah.

'Hardly, the owner's widow is as stingy as they come.' She blushed.

'Zip then, if there's nothing to gain from having contacts with you as a housemate,' muttered Jonah, drawing his fingers across his lips.

Bloody cheek!

'This is taking much longer than I'd planned, so, to the final point. What if one of us doesn't cough up the rent for next month?' asked Russ, looking around the table.

'I'll hunt them down,' spat Jonah, his flawless brow crumpled into a valley of lines. 'Seriously, don't screw me around where money's concerned.'

'He's being realistic,' added Asa, looking around the table. 'One minute you have a job, the next... gone.'

'Yours maybe, mine never,' scoffed Jonah, picking peanuts from his teeth.

'I thought modelling was pretty risky, job wise,' said Esmé, as the table of males stared at her.

'Unemployed, mio?' he said, his hand touched his chest in a dramatic fashion. 'Dooh! I'm a model. I'll find work anywhere... the agency was honoured to have me sign.'

'Any chance of freebies?' asked Esmé.

'*You* wish!' snapped Jonah, before turning away.

Esmé glanced around the table to ascertain whether he was joking or serious. From Russ and Asa's expression, Jonah wasn't joking.

Asa grinned and shook his head.

'Back to business, please,' hissed Russ. 'We need to take this seriously... we've all opted to live here, based on our incomes and lifestyles – it would be a pity if someone needed out.'

'Wouldn't it be best to wait for Dam to be here?' asked Esmé again. 'We've only just moved in and you're discussing the possibility of one of us leaving already... surely we can move on to another subject?'

'If you want Dam to be present, call him, he can join in via his mobile,' snapped Asa, rolling his empty crisp packet into a ball and throwing it at the kitchen bin.

'For fuck's sake, I'll get Dam,' snorted Jonah, retrieving his mobile and speed dialling. 'Hey Dam, we need your input... what's going to happen if one of these losers gets kicked out or leaves this place?'

The group listened as a tinny version of Dam joined the house meeting. Jonah switched his mobile to loudspeaker and placed it on the table.

'It puts a whole new outlook on the finances for us all, so stop kidding about please... listen,' continued Russ, his irritation simmering.

'Did you hear that, Dam?' shouted Jonah, towards his mobile. 'Pathetic! I don't get the negativity, this is like living with my mother.'

Esmé smirked, having known the Jones family when they lived in their street.

'Look, if we fail to plan, we plan to fail...' said Russ.

'Did you really just say that?' laughed Jonah. 'I hate frigging corporate talk at the best of times but seriously man, at home during a house meeting?' Jonah shook his head. 'Dam, did you hear that?'

'But it's true.' Russ looked from Esmé to Asa for back up but neither one wished to back such robotic phrasing. 'So?'

'I say we split it between the remaining ones should anyone leave, it gives us control over who moves in,' said Jonah, reaching for more crisps.

'We were hardly in control this time thanks to Kaney-boy… no offence, new girl, but I didn't choose to include a female. Kane bailed out and Russ agreed Esmé could take his place without consulting the rest of us… where was the planning in that?' said Asa.

'I hardly had a choice. We'd already waited a week for Kane's deposit and then he bailed,' explained Russ. 'Was I supposed to say no, then?'

'But you didn't consult us, did you?' adds Asa.

'Hang on a minute, I am here, listening to this you know… let's face it, Russ may not have consulted you all *but* it's hardly difficult living with me.' *Face* again, second time in a matter of minutes.

'I wouldn't choose for the house to be mixed, would you?' Asa asked Jonah, and suddenly they were allies.

Jonah shrugged.

'Dam, back me up here?'

'I'm not too fussed to be honest, she seems OK, so far. Except the football match trick… that wasn't funny,' said Dam's tinny voice.

'You weren't even here!' Esmé retorted.

'Yeah, but Kane phoned and mentioned it,' said the tinny voice.

Great, another display of male solidarity.

'I wouldn't have chosen to move in with four guys but needs must, so like it or lump it. You'd think I was a leper the way you're all reacting.'

'She's got a point,' laughed Asa. 'And, she's definitely more entertaining with the house guests than Kane would ever be.' He snorted as a rapture of giggles bubbled from the mobile.

'Yeah, that's a point,' adds Russ, smirking.

'News travels quick around here,' said Esmé.

'It was too good to waste, let's put it like that,' said Asa, raising an eyebrow.

Esmé huffed and shook her head.

'We aren't getting anywhere, are we?' moaned Russ.

'How can we decide anything when Dam's not present and we can hardly hear what he's saying,' said Jonah.

'Give it a rest, will ya,' snapped Asa, sliding his chair backwards. 'I'm off before this one winds me up any more.' He pointed at Jonah before adding. 'Esmé, let me know how you get on with your vacuuming quandary.'

Ha, ha. Now, he thinks I'm an idiot too.

'*And* meeting adjourned,' sneered Jonah, banging the table top, before following suit and leaving.

'It wasn't actually, but given the lack of progress, it might as well be postponed until another night,' said Russ, as he watched them depart.

Esmé looked at Russ's doleful expression.

'Sorry, have I caused you a problem?'

'If anything, you saved the situation. It was your brother that created the issue. He promised us the money and then dragged his heels.'

'That's kind of you to say but they were expecting a houseful of lads and they got lumbered with me.'

'They'll get over it,' said Russ, as he pinned the emergency contact sheet on the rear of the kitchen door.

Chapter Fourteen

'Esmé? Are you awake?'

The rapping on the door woke Esmé with a start. Her mobile read twenty past midnight.

'What?'

'It's Dam.'

'Yeah, I know.'

'There's a bloke on the doorstep asking to speak to you... he's refusing to go away until he's spoken to you.'

So Andrew had found the address. She'd kill her brother.

'Esmé, are you coming down to see him?'

'Yeah, I'll be two minutes.'

'OK, I'll tell him.'

'Don't let him in though, leave him on the door step.'

Silence.

'Dam? Are you there?' Shit, he'd gone. Did he hear that final part?

Esmé pushed back the duvet and leapt from the warm confines of her bed. Having rummaged about for clothing, she pulled a hoodie over her pyjamas, and ruffled her hair. A wet finger wiped beneath each eye removed any sleep.

The landing light blinded her as she left her bedroom. Barefoot, she plodded down two flights of stairs to find the rear view of Andrew seated on the bottom step.

'What do you want, Andrew?'

He jumped at the sound of her voice and looked startled by the sight of her.

'Esmé! Hear me out, please. Earlier when I said that we could…'

'What are you doing here?'

'Please don't do this.'

Esmé pushed past him, walked to the front door and opened it wide, sweeping her free hand in the direction of the garden path. 'If you don't mind, I need to get my sleep, I have work in the morning.'

'Esmé,' said Andrew, as he leapt to her side trying to place his arms around her.

'Get off, you have no right to touch me.'

'But…' Andrew took a few steps back, giving her some space but not as much as Esmé wanted. Her desire was a large wooden door separating them.

'No! I mean it. We're finished. I'm not happy with the decision but I have no choice. I spent seven years with you… we weren't even engaged in that time, that's how serious you were about me.' She held up her bare left hand. 'See, no diamond ring.'

'If that's what you want…'

'Andrew, no! It was what I wanted until I walked in to find that earring and now I want nothing more than to return to my bed, alone. So, goodnight.'

'I think she's made it quite clear,' came a male voice from the direction of the kitchen. 'You need to act like a well-mannered gent and do as she asks.'

Esmé and Andrew turned to see Asa casually walking along the corridor, coffee mug in hand. His face was expressionless, and his body language non-threatening but his eyes were directly on Andrew.

'Sorry mate, but who are you?' Andrew stepped back on seeing the tattooed features.

'That doesn't matter. I heard her ask politely, so now's the time to leave.'

'Excuse me, who do you think you're talking to?' snapped Andrew, his chest inflating.

Asa calmly walked to the front door and stood beside Esmé.

'You. I'm speaking directly to you, Andrew,' said Asa, before he sipped his coffee and stared at him over the rim of the mug.

Andrew's jaw tightened, he was agitated by the interruption.

Esmé watched as Andrew's eyes travelled back and forth across the tattooed skin. Asa's casual manner was annoying the hell of him.

'*Esmé?*

She shrugged, trying to control the grin that was threatening to spring to her face.

'Seriously, she asked you to leave and so, you need to go.'

'Do you want to take this outside, mate?' asked Andrew, his bolshiness finally emerging.

'Sorry, but I'm not your mate and I don't remember suggesting anything of the sort. You've been asked to leave our premises. Esmé asked you politely and now, *I'm* telling you.'

'Or?' Andrew took a step towards Asa.

The lounge door opened, Russ and Dam appeared bang on cue.

'Is everything OK out here?' asked Dam, coming into the hallway.

'Fine mate, just fine. Thanks for fetching her,' said Andrew, as if Dam was his new-found buddy.

'See you,' said Esmé.

'*Esmé…*'

'Bye Andrew.' Esmé left the front door wide open and started for the staircase. 'Thanks fellas, I'll see you in the morning.' She climbed calmly to the first landing determined not to look back until she was around the corner. Then she leant over the banister and peered down into the hallway.

Andrew was staring at Asa, who in turn stared back.

'Now, me and the lads are fully aware that you've been parked over the road for the last few hours watching the house. We can see you're upset. I'm sure you've a million and one things to discuss. But *that* doesn't excuse your behaviour, OK?'

'Hey mate, she's my girlfriend... I can...'

'No, you can't. She made it clear she doesn't wish to speak to you. In future, I suggest that you call her and make suitable arrangements to sit down and discuss your business. Harassing her at this time in the morning and making demands isn't right. It's not fair on her, *or* us.'

'You can't tell me when I—'

'If I need to call the police, I will. She doesn't need you stalking her.' Were Asa's final words before the heavy door closed firmly on Andrew's heels.

Esmé watched as Asa calmly turned to the other two and shrugged.

'Don't ask because I haven't a clue. I was in the kitchen making a drink but that didn't look nice.'

'Is she alright?' asked Russ.

'Who knows?' replied Asa. 'He's been parked outside all night staring at the house.'

'I'm not sure she realised,' added Russ.

'Which one of us is going upstairs to check she's OK?' asked Dam.

Silence descended on the hallway. On the first landing Esmé silently eased herself away from the banister and hastily tiptoed up the second flight of stairs.

Rap a tap tap

'Yes?'

'It's me… Russ.'

Esmé climbed out of bed, wrapping her duvet around her pyjama clad body before she opened the door.

'Hi Russ, what's up,' she said as casually as she could.

'The guys were wondering if you were alright?'

'I'm good, thanks.'

'*Sure?*

Esmé nodded, but dropped her gaze

Russ tilted his head to catch the line of her eye.

'Need a cuppa?' he asked, on seeing the glisten of a tear and the redness of previous tears.

Esmé shook her head.

'Asa said you can beat him with the iron poker if it makes you feel better,' he added.

Esmé cracked a smile.

'No thanks, another time maybe.'

'OK. I'll leave you be, get some sleep and… shout if you want a drink bringing up.'

'Cheers, Russ.'

'Good night, Esmé.'

Esmé closed the door and returned to her tearstained pillow.

Chapter Fifteen

Day 6: Accept an invitation

It had been an emotional day.

Esmé's feet ached by the time she arrived home on Tuesday evening. She'd missed two buses on her homeward journey from work so had to jump on the next best route and was dropped off a fair distance from home.

She breathed a sigh of relief on entering number seven's gate, soon she'd be feet up, tea in hand and chilling.

She slid her hand into her pocket for the keys: empty. Instantly, she knew where they were – sitting on the hallway table inside number seven. A burning sting sprang from behind her eyes.

Could today get any worse?

'The Dolman order has fallen through,' complained Steely Stylo, as soon as she arrived in the office. 'I asked you to phone last week to confirm the order but, oh no, too busy to care. A two thousand pound order up the swanny.'

Esmé tried to protest but Mrs Stylo's retreating figure was hard to argue with. It wasn't her fault, she had phoned as she'd asked.

An hour later, the office door burst open and a young man in a crash helmet and biker leathers walked in carrying a large bouquet box.

'Esmé Peel,' he announced, without lifting his visor.

'Yes, that's me.'

'Delivery. Sign here please?'

The office stood still for a minute while Esmé got a grip of her senses. The delivery guy plonked the box on the nearest table and offered her his pen and clipboard.

'Since when did Katrina send the delivery guys up here?' asked Penny, peering over the top of her computer screen.

'Since she started having this many flower deliveries,' said Marianne, pointing at six different arrangements displayed around the office that had arrived earlier in a similar manner.

'What's the card say?' asked Esmé, making her way between desks.

'Dunno. I just deliver them, lady. Can you sign here?'

'Let's guess. It might read 'I'm sorry. Please forgive me', the same as the other six delivery cards, or he might be developing a flair for this flower sending business and start cracking a joke on each card.' Esmé stared at Marianne, it helped to divert her anger.

'Does he really think that sending me flowers will erase what's happened?'

'Fresh flowers cost a lot of money, it would be a waste not to accept them,' added Penny, as she peered up from her paperwork.

'Plus, it gives me a choice in selecting the arrangement that I'll be taking home on the bus, given that Penny had one yesterday!' said Marianne.

'You can have the lot, Marianne, enjoy!'

Esmé snatched the clipboard and signed the delivery slip.

The door slammed shut on the delivery biker. Esmé and the ladies gathered round as she broke the cellophane seal to open the cardboard box. The smell of lilies took them all by surprise.

Esmé lifted a tall glass vase in which an arrangement of orange tiger lilies was pre-positioned and set it down on the nearest desk.

'They are beautiful,' swooned Marianne.

'They are… but I don't want them!'

'Esmé!' cried Penny. 'Any girl would die to receive such beautiful flowers… you really should—'

'… send them on to Sadie because that's who he's been playing away with?'

Both woman hovered and stared enviously at the tiger lilies. This delivery was in a different league to the previous ones.

'Seriously, which arrangement do you want to take home, Marianne? This is past a joke!'

It was all too much, Esmé's emotions had got the better of her so she dashed from the office in tears.

'Do you want to go after her, or shall I?' asked Penny.

Marianne followed Esmé.

'Esmé, it's me, Marianne. Are you OK?'

The toilet door swung wide and Esmé crossed to the sink area.

'OK? Do I look OK to you?'

Marianne shook her head.

'Do you know what's the hardest thing?'

Marianne remained silent, which Esmé took as a sign to continue.

'I was busy dashing home last Thursday to ensure we had a great night because all I could think about was us getting engaged on our anniversary – how ridiculous am I?'

'You're not ridiculous. You loved him and only wanted what every girl wants.'

'Exactly, how pathetic!' Esmé had dissolved into tears as Marianne wrapped her in a tight hug.

'You are not ridiculous, you're hurting and you want to hurt him for causing this but Esmé please don't lose sight of what you could have by forgiving him… surely there's a way past this.'

Esmé had shrugged free of her embrace.

'You don't even like him…'

'Yeah, but you do,' whispered Marianne.

And finally, to complete her tear-stained afternoon.

'Esmé, phone call for you,' said Penny, sheepishly putting a call through and mouthing. '*Andrew.*'

They'd argued. In ear shot of her colleagues, they washed their dirty linen in public and hung it out to dry.

'Are you coming to Bacchus Bar for a cheeky vino?' asked Marianne, pulling on her coat come home time.

'I should but I'll give it a miss, thanks. I could do with getting home.'

Esmé wanted to kick herself as the two women headed off towards the city centre but it was no good pretending, Andrew's phone call had got the better of her.

Despite day six of The Single Girl's Calendar throwing her the perfect excuse for an after work drink at barely seven o'clock this morning, Esmé knew that her mood was low and heading home was best.

Instead she was now standing on the doorstep looking up at the guttering and trying to figure out whose bedroom was situated on the first floor at the front, and whether he would really mind if she managed to scale the drain pipe, and break in?

If the rear kitchen window was still open she could nip in via Asa's route.

Esmé dashed along the side entrance leading to the rear garden, to view a firmly closed kitchen window. She looked around the garden for anything to aid an entry into the house, a spade, a long-handled broom or a patio chair. Nothing, everything was locked securely in the shed, on the door of which she could see a firmly closed shiny padlock.

The block paving, gravel edged patio and expanse of lawn covered a far greater area than she had realised from the view from her bedroom window. Esmé tried the back door handle, purely on the off chance, as she returned to the front of the property.

Nothing. Everything was locked as tight as a nun's knicker elastic.

'Bloody typical.'

Esmé settled on the wall and prayed for it not to rain again. That's when she heard the flute being played. The gentle melody was coming from the house next door hidden by a huge laurel hedge.

How lovely to be so talented.

Within minutes, the heavens opened and horizontal rain bucketed down.

Esmé jumped up, nipping round to the front door of number five, her apology ready for whoever opened the stained-glass door. The flute playing ceased and a gentle shuffle could be heard from within.

'Hello?' came a feeble voice. 'Who is it?' The front door remained firmly closed.

'I'm Esmé – I live at number seven. Sorry to interrupt but I've locked myself out of the house. I was just wondering if I could borrow an umbrella.'

The front door opened as far as the door chain would allow. Two piercing blue eyes peered through the gap.

'From number seven, you say?'

'If I could borrow an umbrella, I'll return it tomorrow, I promise.'

In one swift action, the door chain was released revealing a tiny lady in her dotage, sporting a warm cardigan and a pair of M&S slippers.

'No need, dear… we'll go one step further. How about a cup of tea and a nice slice of walnut cake?'

'I couldn't possibly intrude.' *Day 6: Accept an invitation* floated around in her mind.

'It's no bother at all, come in, lovey.'

'You're so kind. They shouldn't be long,' explained Esmé, stepping across the threshold and removing her damp and dirty shoes. 'I only moved in on Friday and I've locked myself out already, ridiculous.' The carpet was a welcome relief to her throbbing feet.

'There's nothing worse, and without ladders you're stuck,' said the old lady, her eyes sparkling. 'Come through, come through.'

'I'm Esmé by the way.'

The old lady plodded towards the kitchen.

'Grace MacDonald. Mrs MacDonald… though I'm a widow now.'

'Nice to meet you, Grace, sorry to intrude.'

'Think nothing of it, I was only practising.'

'I heard a flute being played.'

Grace nodded vigorously. Her face lit up as they passed into a dark kitchen lined with aged oak cupboards.

'I've played since I was a wee girl,' she said, adding. 'Please take a seat.'

'It sounded beautiful. I think I heard you playing on Saturday morning too – I thought it was one of the men,' said Esmé, as she settled herself at the table.

'I've lost my touch now, what with my arthritis, but in my younger days I used to play the concert halls back home in Glasgow and I taught the flute at the local school,' explained Grace, lifting the kettle to the cold water tap.

'Here, let me do it, you sit down… just tell me where everything is.'

'Would you?'

'Sure.' Esmé jumped up and buzzed around the kitchen; Grace watched from the table.

'How long have you lived here?' asked Esmé, mashing the tea.

'Getting on for forty years. Me and my Jack moved in as newlyweds... the area was very different then.'

'How?'

'The Number 76 used to come straight by the corner of this street, which would be a godsend now.'

The two chuckled, as Esmé delivered the china cups and saucers to the table.

'And you?'

'Me? As I said, literally a few days and already I've forgotten my key.'

'Does the man with the tattoo live there too?'

'Eh, oh yeah... Asa.'

'Not a friend of yours?' asked Grace.

'We haven't exactly hit it off, to be fair.' Esmé chuckled. 'In the early hours of Saturday morning I hit him with a poker...' Esmé spent the next ten minutes retelling the story much to Grace's delight.

'A tortured soul, I fear,' muttered Grace, sipping her tea.

'Really? You wouldn't say that if you lived with him.'

Grace laughed heartily.

'Honestly, he's one of a kind...'

'The kind that gets my back up,' laughed Esmé.

Grace spent a further ten minutes laughing as Esmé role played her phone conversation with Carys and then the misunderstanding about 'Crystal'.

'There used to be a load of those types around here a few years ago, the area went through a bad time, lots of drugs, prossies—'

'*What?*'

'Prossies... prostitutes.'

'I know *what* you meant, I just can't believe that *you* said it.'

'I'm old but not naïve, you know.'

'I can see.'

'Though honestly, it makes you wonder what awful experiences those people must have endured to resort to that, you know... it's a real shame.'

Esmé smiled politely, unsure what to say.

'And you, living with four handsome men. It would have been frowned upon in my youth. Woo, you girls of today, you don't know you're born!'

Esmé pulled a face.

'None of them take your fancy?'

'I've just broken up from a long-term relationship. Last Thursday in fact.'

'Busy weekend, my dear?'

'You could say that.'

'Our tortured soul, what's the thing with his face?'

'I daren't look. He tried to make me the other night but I was too scared to. I'm dying to know why… it's peacock feathers in blue and emerald swirls. Quite frightening to look at really.'

'He has such a lovely smile, yet he's not said why?'

Esmé shook her head and sipped her cooling tea.

'He's quite defiant in his mannerisms, I reckon it's to break with social norms – he seems a bit of a free spirit.'

'What's his job?'

'At the hospital but he wasn't specific.'

'And the long haired one?'

'Jonah's a male model posing for adverts and catalogues.'

'The Asian lad?'

'Lectures in physics at the uni.'

'Clever boy! And the plain one?'

'An engineer, I think… well, he was when he was younger. He's my brother's best friend… my brother was supposed to be the fifth housemate but he ran out of cash, so I stepped in instead.'

'Lucky you,' chuckled Grace.

Esmé watched the vibrant blue eyes twinkle throughout their conversation.

When would life become easy enough to laugh at?

'Do you work?'

'I couldn't afford to live here otherwise, I do admin for a stationery company.'

'Enjoy it?'

'Nope.'

Grace's brow creased.

'So why are you there?'

'Hmmm, good question. I've been there nine years and never had the urge to leave.'

The light in the kitchen had faded without either of them noticing. Their tea cups had cooled and the dregs in them scummed over.

'I guess there's a chance one of the men has arrived home by now,' said Esmé, getting to her feet. 'Thanks for the tea.'

'Thank you for the chat, it's been lovely. Oh, we forgot the walnut cake!'

'Never mind. Another time.' Esmé collected the dirty cups and took them to the sink.

'Leave them, it'll give me something to do when you've gone,' said Grace.

Esmé gulped.

Her own nan had said words to that effect whenever they visited as children.

'Have you any family?'

'Yes, my David, he pops by when he can.'

Esmé watched as her bright eyes dimmed just a fraction.

'You'll have to come round to ours one night for a meet and greet. I'm sure the fellas would like to get to know our new neighbour.'

'In time, in time,' muttered Grace, as she saw Esmé to the front door.

'Take care, and shout if you need anything.'

'I will, dear. Thank you.'

Esmé hesitated on the doorstep.

'Do you like fresh flowers?'

Grace's face lit up.

'Doesn't everyone?'

'At the moment, I don't.'

The rain was still lashing down as Esmé trotted down Grace's drive and over to her own pathway. Grace stood on the step and waved heartily.

I hope I'm as bubbly as that at her age, thought Esmé, hammering on the door of number seven.

She dashed through the door as soon as Dam released the latch.

'Thank you, not at your mum's tonight?'

Dam pulled a face, closing the door.

'I'm not there every night, you know.'

'Aren't you? I thought you were,' said Esmé, as she dropped her handbag down by the coat rack and darted up the stairs two at a time.

Dam returned to the lounge and the blare of the tv.

Esmé continued to climb, and a waft of aftershave greeted her as she reached the top.

'Hmmm, someone smells nice,' she muttered, reaching her bedroom door.

'Why, thank you, so nice of you to say,' answered Asa, coming out of the bathroom, dressed head to toe in black, his wet hair glistened.

'Oh, I didn't mean…'

'Don't look so surprised – I scrub up quite well, if I say so myself,' he added, strutting past her down the flight of stairs.

Esmé watched the painted face flicker through the banister railings – the blue and emerald tattoo in full view along his left side.

Why would anyone in their right mind have that done? He wasn't a bad looking bloke but then to ruin it all was a ridiculous idea. If both sides of his face looked like the right side he could give Jonah a run for his money in the looks department. Which is probably why they didn't get—

'You standing there catching flies?'

Esmé started as Asa ran back up the staircase, catching her in a day dream.

She didn't answer and turned to enter her own room.

Rap a tap tap.

The sudden knocking made Esmé jump. She wrenched the door open, half expecting another one liner from Asa, only to find Kane glaring at her – with Russ at his side.

'Russ, please tell my sister the information,' said Kane, turning away childishly having spoken.

'Kane here,' Russ deftly pointed to her sulking brother, 'would like to inform you that your mother's house is filled with fresh flowers sent from Andrew and that she and your father would like you to go round and collect what you will, as soon as possible.'

Esmé leant against the wooden door frame, folding her arms.

'Tell my stupid ass brother the answer is no. Andrew can do his fancy deliveries as much as he wishes but I am not changing my mind based on him flashing his cash. Tell Kane, to tell my mother, she can give the flower arrangements to anyone in her neighbourhood for all I care. Thank you, Russ.'

'No problem. Kane, your sister said…'

'I heard her. Now, tell her that…'

'Kane, sod off – either talk to me or don't… you spoke perfectly well only the other day, now you return to this. I've had a long hard day with similar flower arrangements being sent to the office – just deal with it.'

'Russ, tell her that I'm still mad at her for ruining my plans. And Mum said—'

'Bugger what Mum said, she knows enough people to give them away to, the W.I., the doctors surgery, the dental practice – I don't care who, OK?'

'Russ, tell my sister that…'

Esmé didn't hear the remainder of the sentence, she shut the door on the crazy world of men and flowers, switched her iPhone volume to high and enjoyed drowning out her brother's whinging.

'Now *that* feels like home,' she laughed, stripping off her work clothes and donning her comfies. As she removed her make-up and freed herself of the stress of the day, she wondered what Grace was doing?

Esmé hoped she wasn't too lonely, that simply wouldn't do.

*

'What are you doing there?' asked Esmé, jumping back in fright having found Kane sitting outside her bedroom door.

'Waiting.'

'If you think I care about your sorry ass messages from Mum or your money worries then you're wrong. Now please, can you move aside so I can step out of my room without tripping?'

Kane reluctantly moved his long legs but continued to stare at the navy carpet.

Esmé walked to the top of the staircase and looked back.

'Kind of childish, don't you think?'

'You are, jumping into my place… you can go home now you've had your fun.'

She peered through the banister's wooden spindles at her brother.

'Nah, the fun is only just starting for me, big bro,' and with a devious chuckle Esmé flew down the staircase, heading for the kitchen.

Her mood had definitely lifted since her chat with Grace. She burst through the kitchen door to find Jonah standing in his underwear making a drink. He was decent but none-the-less, tight, white boxer shorts left little to the imagination.

'Oh sorry, I didn't think… I didn't mean to intrude…' her eyes finally settled on his face, having sneaked a peek at the rippled torso, broad shoulders and footballer thighs.

Esmé blushed as her heartbeat accelerated.

'No worries, Dam and Russ are watching the box… your Kane was here a while back,' he said, unabashed by his lack of clothing.

'I saw him, he's upstairs sulking.'

Jonah continued to make his drink. Esmé tried to hide her flustered face in the fridge as she opened the door and attempted to look interested in the cheese, yogurt and egg box laden shelving.

Andrew had never looked so desirable in his boxers. Though he always wore the loosely fitting cotton grandad style ones. But even if he had purchased skin tight shorts, would his thighs have ever looked so plump, firm, soooo…?

'Are you cooking?' asked Jonah, stirring his coffee.

'Yes.'

'Something nice?'

'*Possibly*,' came her muffled reply, not wishing to remove her face from the fridge in case her eye level was inappropriate with him standing so close.

'Any chance of making a bit extra and bringing it through to the lounge – I could cook for you in return one night?'

Hmmmm, now there's an offer. It made sense to double up and share, once in a while.

Esmé reversed carefully from the fridge, beaming with delight and happy to oblige.

'Deal! Are you allergic to anything?' she asked as he retreated towards the kitchen door.

'Do I look like the sensitive sort?' he said, turning to face her and waving his free hand up and down his body.

Esmé cheeks burned intensely.

'No *but…*'

I'd hate to ruin that beautiful physique and bring him out in a rash.

Eagerly taking ingredients from her shelf, she began creating a culinary delight worthy of impressing him. Though the prospect of him suffering from a rash and asking her to smother or dab such a perfect body with calamine lotion three times a day would be her idea of heaven.

Esmé checked herself. Less than a week after leaving Andrew and her thoughts were drifting elsewhere already. *Really?* In reality she wouldn't know what to do with such a physique if Jonah did give her the come on. Andrew had a decent body but he wouldn't fall into the Adonis category.

Within half an hour she had a culinary delight of pesto and pasta dished up into two deep bowls, with a sprig of parsley to garnish. Chunks of garlic bread graced the side salad.

'Here you go,' announced Esmé, carrying his laden tray into the lounge. 'I hope you're hungry, Jonah.' Esmé looked around the occupants of the lounge: Dam, Russ and Kane all agog from their seated positions.

'Jonah's gone,' said Dam casually from the sofa.

'What?' screeched Esmé, scouring the room.

'Smells good,' said Kane, lifting himself out of the armchair. 'I think he said he was hooking up with some woman.'

'Are you joking?'

Russ gave an apologetic smile.

Great! What a waste of my time. And my food. Esmé stood grasping the tray handles, wishing the earth would open up and swallow her whole.

'So, who's hungry?'

'I ate at my mum's,' said Dam apologetically, turning his attention back to the football match.

Russ shook his head.

'Sorry, I ate before I came home.'

'Can I have next dibs before it gets chucked?'

Esmé was too angry to argue or force feed either of them, so she handed the tray to her brother.

'Cheers,' said Kane, greedily tucking into the pasta. His latest silent phase was obviously over, *again*.

Chapter Sixteen

Day 7: Create, make or bake

The working week continued much as it had begun with a stream of florists and their arrangements parading through the office as if a royal wedding was imminent.

'When is this going to stop?' asked Marianne, peering through the flower arrangements adorning her paperwork piles.

Esmé shook her head.

'When he finally gets the message that I am not coming back – flowers or no flowers.'

'I think it's cute,' said Penny, absentmindedly, while doodling a ladybird on her notepad.

'*Cute?* Are you serious?'

'Yes, he's trying, which is more than some men do,' she added.

'I'd have much preferred it if he tried harder to stay clothed and with his body parts away from his work colleague, but hey, this….' Esmé waved her arms around at the numerous flower arrangements that her colleagues had refused to take home, 'is just *so* cute!'

Marianne hid behind her computer; a storm was brewing.

'Kissing me by moonlight was cute. Sharing a bag of chips on a blustery beach on Bank Holiday Monday was cute and my dream of him proposing would have been cute whether it had been beneath the Eiffel tower or in the foyer of Birmingham library, but nah! I got the discovery of a lost earring and an office that looks like an *Interflora* convention!' The tears had been threatening to erupt all day and finally they came.

'Oh dear, sit yourself down and we'll get you a coffee,' ushered Penny, aiming for damage limitation to Esmé's mascara.

'I can't look around this office without having a flashback… the two of them naked in our bedroom!' wailed Esmé, snatching the box of tissues offered by Penny before frantically dabbing her eyes. 'And you think… you think *this* is cute, I think this is… harassment!'

Penny swallowed the guilty lump in her throat.

'You've got a point.' Penny looked around, it was a little overwhelming. 'I've got a plan, let's call a taxi and send this lot to the City hospital?'

Esmé cried a little more.

'I've already phoned. They won't accept flowers… an issue with health and safety,' sniffed Esmé, blowing her nose.

'How ridiculous, some old bugger could well be cheered up by looking at these blooms.'

'I took Grace, our neighbour, two arrangements yesterday. They swamped her lounge, even she was surprised by the combined size of them. "Who'd have thought that flower arrangements could take up more space than my Christmas tree?" Seriously ladies, that's what she said.'

'I bet it smelt lovely in her lounge though,' said Penny soothingly.

'It did but there's a chance she'll develop hay fever before the vase water needs changing.'

'Oh Esmé, dry your eyes... you need to stay positive, lovey,' came Marianne's voice from amongst the foliage.

*

'Have I told you about my calendar?' said Esmé, dabbing her eyes. Penny and Marianne stared back with blank expressions. 'Well Carys, you know Carys, don't you?'

'The one whose boyfriend cheated?' asked Penny, offering round her packet of bourbons.

'Dooh, that could be a multitude of us,' jibed Esmé.

'Afro ringlets? Beautiful skin?' said Marianne, as she dunked her biscuit in her coffee.

'Yep, the one. Well, she bought me a single girl's calendar – total tat of course, a five pound job from the book shop but…' Esmé continued to explain that every day she had woken, dressed and then opened the tiny door for her task of the day. 'There's chocolate, too.'

Marianne laughed.

'Are you serious?'

'Honestly Marianne… I think it has helped me. I know yesterday was a tearful day but I've been more together than I thought I would be. I thought about phoning in sick on Monday and self-certifying myself for the entire week. I didn't think I could face coming in each day and yet…'

'And yet you're here,' said Penny, her face beaming. 'Positive mental attitude, that's what it's down to.'

'And that's down to the calendar?' asked Marianne, turning to Penny.

'I think so,' said Esmé, nibbling her biscuit.

'Me too. I remember when I broke up with a long-term boyfriend years ago I didn't get out of bed for a week… now, if I'd just had a small incentive such as a daily task, who knows.'

'The daily task is to survive the break up – end of,' said Marianne, adding. 'You don't need a calendar to do that.'

'You're being too harsh,' said Penny, shaking her head. 'Have you never had your heart broken?'

'Yes, plenty of times but I've never needed a cheap fix…'

'I do.' Esmé jumped in to defend her calendar. 'Strange things have occurred on certain days. relating to my set task.'

'Really?' said Penny, who shuffled her seat nearer to listen.

'Falling in line with that day's task… how weird is that?'

'*Really?* said Marianne, her tone dripping in sarcasm. 'Or have you looked for it?'

'Day five was Monday… right?'

Both her colleagues nodded.

'A financial make-over was my task of the day. During my bus ride to work, I listed my expenditure, plus changes I needed to make with standing orders and direct debits when I visited the bank,' said Esmé, knowing she was about to go against company ethics with what she was about to say. 'Stylo gave me a pay rise.'

Penny and Marianne exchanged a glance.

'No way!'

'Never!'

'See, told you… now, how did that happen on the day it needed to happen?'

'I thought you had a telling off about being late,' said Marianne.

'I did… but then the conversation led onto my new haircut, she mentioned a crisis and I explained that a lot had happened over the weekend and… one thing led to another and bingo, I walked out with a pay rise,' explained Esmé to the open mouthed pair. 'So, explain that?'

'I can't,' said Marianne.

'What else?' asked Penny.

'Yesterday, day six, accept an invitation.'

'You refused ours for a drink after work,' laughed Penny. 'So, you failed that day.'

'I did, but my next door neighbour invited me in for coffee and cake and I accepted her offer as I was locked out,' said Esmé, her face beaming with triumph at proving her wrong.

'What's today then?' asked Marianne, draining her coffee mug.

'Day seven: create, make or bake… which I feel I did yesterday as I cooked Jonah an evening meal last night.'

'Ohhhhh la la!' sang Marianne, waving her empty coffee mug. 'Tell us more.'

'Yeah, sadly he didn't eat it, but still… I made it.'

'Technically, you're a day ahead of yourself,' said Penny, collecting the coffee mugs. 'I say anything that helps you in the first few weeks is a bonus – don't listen to what she said.'

'I just don't buy the positive attitude, mumbo jumbo stuff, calendar or no calendar,' said Marianne, as she wheeled her office chair back to her desk. 'In life, you have no choice but to face the tough stuff.'

*

Esmé's desk phone rang.

'Hello, Esmé speaking.'

'Katrina here, could you come downstairs please?' came the receptionist's tinny voice.

'Not *more* flowers?' Esmé hung up. 'This arrangement must be too big to carry up the bloody stairs.'

'Where are we going to put it?' cried Penny, looking around at the flower arrangements crowding the office.

'I might leave it in reception, Katrina can enjoy it,' said Esmé.

This was beyond a joke now, Andrew needed to stop, respect her decision and move on.

Maybe Carys could buy him a single guy's calendar?

Esmé smiled at her own joke as she approached the glass doors leading to the main reception. There was no flower delivery guy. No humungous flower arrangement. Just Katrina seated behind her pristine desk, an expanse of tiled floor and a young woman seated on one of the hard back chairs.

Esmé presented herself at reception as requested.

'Yep, what's up?'

Katrina's eyes widened and her lips pursed.

'What?'

'There's a young lady to see you…' Katrina nodded in the direction of the seated woman.

Esmé froze. There was only one woman that she wouldn't recognise but who might wish to speak to her.

'Sadie!' Esmé turned to face the pale, slim young woman.

She stood up, albeit rather nervously, before speaking.

'Could I have a word?' she stepped forward, dressed in a pretty printed frock, pleated and preened, accompanied by pale ballet pumps and a blonde ponytail. Esmé took in the peaches and cream image in one glance. Where was Sexy Sadie?

Really, who'd have thought it? Andrew had fallen for the angelic, sweetheart look. Not what she'd expected.

'Not really. I think you and him have caused enough damage, but thank you for dropping by. Please show yourself out.' Esmé turned to leave the reception area but the woman's outstretched hand brushed her forearm. 'Please don't touch me.'

'I just wanted to say…'

'That you're so sorry for shagging my boyfriend while I was busy earning a crust… is that it?'

Sadie shrugged.

'No, not that? Or do you simply want to have a good look at me, see how we compare in appearance – was that it? Well, now you've had a good gawp you can leave.' Esmé suddenly regretted wearing her favourite top to work, it was slightly faded and had seen better days.

'I just thought we could talk… woman to woman.'

Esmé turned to Katrina, who was now open mouthed, her heavily painted face frozen in horror.

'Is this a wind up?'

'Totally legit, she walked in and asked for you, by name,' said Katrina, her head-set suspended before her gaping mouth.

'Does Andrew know you're here?'

Sadie shook her head.

'Did he ask you to come here?'

Another head shake.

'So, what the hell have we to discuss?'

'Look, I wanted to explain… so you know that it wasn't your fault…'

'Too bloody right, it wasn't my fault... I've been faithful to my partner, unlike him and... you! Do you have a boyfriend?'

'No.'

'So, you were free and single to chase whoever you wanted and yet, you chose *my* man?'

'It just happened,' said Sadie, fiddling with her handbag.

Was this really happening?

'Affairs don't just happen. One of you, both of you, needed to want it, chase it, flirt after it before something actually occurred. Simply working alongside people doesn't mean that something will automatically happen and you fall into bed.' Esmé stopped as Sadie's pretty brow creased.

'I don't understand?'

'You, him, you work together.'

'No,' said Sadie, her voice a bare whisper. 'I live in the same block, apartment two on the ground floor.'

Esmé stepped backwards, shocked by the discovery of another lie.

'You don't work at the airport?'

'*No.*'

'He said that you and him... oh, never mind, it makes no difference... He can lie his ass off for all I care.' Esmé recalled the gourmet food boss confirming '*Delivered at 9 15 p.m. as instructed... the lady signed for it*'. So, it was Sadie! Andrew had called her up from downstairs – how bloody convenient.

'We met…'

'I don't care, do you hear me. I don't want to know about the lying, cheating scumbag and you, all prim and proper in your cotton dress looking as if butter wouldn't melt in your mouth… you are welcome to him! You deserve each other. And, I hope in seven years' time when you're nearing the point of commitment, that he does exactly the same on you!'

Sadie's mouth opened and closed without a word being said.

'And finally, thanks for bringing my private life into the office… I really do appreciate it but I think Katrina would rather work in peace. And I would prefer to get on with my job rather than creating a scene down here!'

'I came to say I was sorry… last time we spoke, he wanted you back.'

'He can go to hell!' shouted Esmé, as she stormed through the glass double doors and made her way up the stairs to her office.

Day seven create, make or bake – surely, creating a scene at work wasn't meant to be the task of the day?

Chapter Seventeen

Day 8: Take yourself to dinner

Esmé had phoned the restaurant first thing that morning.

'Just to confirm, madam – that's a table for one at eight o'clock in the name of Peel, is that correct?'

'Yes, please. Could I request a quiet table, please?'

'Madam is very welcome.'

Esmé looked around the candle lit restaurant and wondered which of the staff she had spoken to. She had the warmest of welcomes from the maitre'd who escorted her through the busy restaurant and made sure she was happy with her quiet table, table ten, before fetching her a large vodka and orange, plus a jug of chilled water. Her waiter was equally as attentive and approachable when she ordered from their large leather menu. And as for the nimble waiter who briskly worked the tables alongside hers, he had to be doubling as an actor or a model with such dark smouldering looks.

'Is there anything I can get for madam?' asked the nimble waiter, stopping at table ten as he whizzed by.

'No, thank you… the mussels are perfect,' smiled Esmé, unsure how to receive such solicitous attention.

'Excellent news.' His smile reached his eyes before he headed back to the kitchen.

Esmé felt a contented glow ignite deep within, she was proud of herself for being open minded and taking herself to dinner. Technically, she'd taken herself on a date, and so far, so good! Why should she be denied fine dining simply because she was not accompanied by a male?

It felt good to sit alone, amongst a scattering of strangers at nearby tables busy discussing their own lives and issues, and eat her dish of piled mussels without interruption.

She couldn't say what she'd been frightened of. In the taxi, her stomach had flipped with nerves from the house into the city. When seated, cradling her large vodka and orange, she had to consciously slow down each breath for fear of hyper-ventilating.

It felt good to take her time, do as she pleased, linger over her starter rather than eating at the pace of her companion. For once, she felt very grown up.

In no time, she was surrounded by the happy chatter of numerous diners – none of whom even noticed her.

Esmé savoured the final mussel.

Why did seafood always leave her wanting more? But the thought of her carbonara with a green salad was enough to make her mouth water.

'Has madam finished?' asked the nimble waiter before her own could scurry to collect her empty dish.

'Yes, thank you, could I order another vodka and orange please?'

'Certainly.'

Esmé sat back drying her fingertips. She could get used to this life, folk fetching and carrying, scurrying back and forth in the name of excellent service. She'd leave a generous tip, she believed in rewarding good service but... she stopped and stared across the restaurant.

The maitre'd was walking a couple through the tables in her direction. The woman was stunningly beautiful, her mane of teased blonde ringlets swept her shoulders, she had an hour-glass figure and a cleavage to die for, and behind her walked Jonah, his smug expression announcing how delighted he was to be walking behind, checking out her assets.

Esmé lowered her head as they swept past.

Their arrival had ruined her night.

He was the last person she wanted to see, well other than Andrew.

The maître'd seated them at a nearby table. Thankfully, Jonah's back was positioned towards Esmé, and she silently gave thanks for small mercies.

As their waiter handed them the menus, Esmé saw that the woman's foot had escaped her shoe and was easing along the inside of Jonah's leg.

Esmé peered through her asymmetrical fringe, fascinated. Jonah pulled his chair a little closer to the table and repositioned the linen cloth that covered his lap.

Had they no respect?

Esmé's main course was delivered, but it couldn't compete with the entertainment provided by Jonah and his date. All the neighbouring tables were transfixed. A pair of high heels lay abandoned beneath their table, visible to all, as the frantic movement of the white table cloth on Jonah's lap left little to the imagination. Jonah's face must be cataclysmic with pleasure.

Their waiter focussed upon his service and delivered their ice bucket and champagne order.

Esmé absorbed every detail to recall once home, she would savour the giggles that would arise from sharing this gem.

Their champagne cork interrupted all conversations, her delight clear to everyone. As apparent as her wedding ring.

Jonah might be a perfect man with his model looks, perfect complexion and dress sense but was clearly a dog when it came to morals: lying, cheating and skulduggery. Though the woman was equally to blame.

Why would any man choose to dally with a married woman when he could have a wealth of single women without the threat of being cited in a divorce or a good thumping?

Esmé cringed.

Had Andrew behaved like this with Sadie? Out and about around the city before falling into their bed?

Esmé pushed her empty plate aside.

Was it too much to ask that a single guy meet a single girl? Add a splash of romance, lots of kissing and a good dollop of lustful passion – wasn't that a recipe to be content with?

How would she ever know which men were genuine and who were players?

Esmé watched as Jonah's laughter grew louder with each glass of champagne, his hand beginning to rove around the woman's left thigh as his manners were sent packing.

She was contemplating her coffee choice when a commotion at the front desk interrupted the restaurant's ambience. A young man in a leather jacket dashed past her table.

'Melissa, would you care to introduce us?' He stood before Jonah and his wife, and stared between the pair. Esmé watched the woman's feet rapidly re-appear beneath the table to be thrust into her expensive shoes.

'Gareth, what are you doing here?'

'I was just about to ask you exactly the same thing... and this is?'

The young man thrust his hand into Jonah's personal space demanding it be shook.

'Gareth Thompson, and this is my wife, Melissa, though it appears you two have already met. So, what's on the menu?' He grabbed the nearest chair and plonked himself down alongside the startled lovers. 'Champagne! Excellent. Bring me a fresh glass,' he called to the waiter. 'So, what is it we're celebrating?'

Jonah looked around the restaurant as Gareth helped himself to his bottle of bubbly. Melissa sat open mouthed and squirming, unlike the other diners and some of the staff, who were all enjoying the show.

Esmé ordered a liqueur coffee with accompanying mints – the entertainment was worth staying for.

The nimble waiter delivered a leather-bound wallet to her table with a generous smile and a fresh rose.

Esmé smiled politely.

The wallet revealed an itemised bill alongside a piece of paper torn from a small note pad.

You have a beautiful smile. Don't dine alone, dine with me. Roberto. Tel number 0770 6442

Esmé looked up to find Roberto watching her from across the room. She blushed and re-read his note.

Her fingers trembled with excitement as she fumbled through her purse.

Should she leave a tip? Would it look condescending after his act of chivalry?

She placed a handful of money inside the wallet and indicated that she wished to pay. Roberto darted across the restaurant to retrieve it.

'And madam's answer?' he whispered.

'Madam is unsure what her answer should be…' replied Esmé, a fleeting glance at his bare left hand suggested he might not be married.

'Madam *simply* needs to phone, when Madam has a free evening,' he said, his steady gaze holding her attention.

Esmé blushed. She was taking a chance but maybe single girls needed to take chances in order to live a little. She pocketed his telephone number, she could decide if and when she was free.

Chapter Eighteen

Day 9: Dare yourself – face your fear

Friday night arrived before Esmé could catch her breath. What a week it had been? A list of self-promises floated around in her head during the lengthy bus journey home: a combination of a bubble bath, a face pack and a magazine would help sooth her tired bones.

On arrival, the noise emitting from number seven Montague Road suggested her housemates' activities would not be conducive to a tranquil evening.

As her key slid into the lock a barrage of Toby's screams filled the air. In the hallway, the little boy was running around waving a toy aeroplane above his head.

'Nawwwwwwwww!' he screamed, running at Esmé, his aeroplane heading towards her face.

'Hi. Steady on, you'll have my eye out, Toby.' Esmé said, as the boy swung around the tiled floor.

'Hiiiiii,' said Toby, in a sing song voice, as he circled his plane for another attack.

'Toby, come here,' called Kane, entering the hallway from the lounge. 'Oh, hello, you're early.'

'Nice aeroplane,' said Esmé, turning to Kane. 'Are you here again?'

'Love you too, Sis.'

'Toby, go and find Russ,' said Kane, as he ushered the boy towards the lounge.

'Kane, you should call Russ daddy or dad when Toby's about.'

'Why should I call him daddy if he doesn't choose to himself, he's Russ?'

'Because it's modern father bullshit – that's why. Parents should be called dad, papa or pops, he's supposed to be a parent not a best buddy.'

'OK, lecture over. I'll tell Daddy Russ.'

Esmé headed straight for the staircase. 'I'll be upstairs, should any one call.'

'With more flowers,' laughed Kane.

Esmé stopped mid-stair.

'*What?*

'You might want to take a look in the morning room before you—'

'You had better be joking?' Esmé raced to the morning room, flung the door open and was greeted by a sight befitting another annual *Interflora* convention. 'For fuck's sake!'

'Oy, mind your language, there's a kid about!' snapped Kane from the hallway.

'Says you, Mr Potty-mouth,' chimed Esmé, allowing the door to close behind her.

On every flat surface was a pastel coloured flower box from which a rainbow of fresh flowers sprang. Tall artistic designs sat alongside traditional posies, alongside single stemmed roses, dramatic arching orchids and delicate unknowns with their strange shapes and colours.

Esmé was speechless, moving slowly around the arrangements.

This must have cost him a fortune. It's wrong, it's almost cruel to allow him to continue wasting money.

She grabbed her mobile from her back pocket and dialled his number.

'Andrew, you need to stop with the flowers.'

'Why?'

'Face facts,' there was that word again. '… I'm not coming back. I'm happy here.'

'Without me?'

Esmé gulped.

Was she truly happy without him? It wasn't her original plan but she'd coped for the majority of the week.

'Esmé, don't answer but think about it, maybe we needed this space in our relationship. There's no need for us to be over, we could still date – you living there, me here. I could get a lodger to share the expense of the apartment and then we'd find a way to make this work for us.'

'I'm happy as I am.' The words spilt from her lips and surprised even her. 'Sorry, but yes, I'm hurting. Yes, I'm sad and tearful when I think about us, and then angry when I remember you and… her. But in the gaps in between when I am not thinking about us, I have enjoyed doing my own thing every day without having to consider another person.'

'Cheers Esmé, you know how to kick a guy when he's down!'

'Andrew, I was your girlfriend for seven years and arranged everything around you, my work life, my home life and this week… after what you and she did – not me, you and her! I have had a week of just being me. And yeah, I've coped. Sorry if that wasn't what you wanted to hear but you should have thought about that when you were rolling about with Sadie.'

There was a lengthy pause.

'The flowers need to stop, Andrew… and purely so you know, Sadie paid me a visit at work yesterday.'

'Don't bluff me.'

'Very girly-girly with long blonde hair, which was tied in a ponytail, she wore a cotton summer dress even though it's spring, ballet pumps and she carried a…'

'Esmé stop… I believe you… I never asked her to visit.'

'But Andrew, you lied. She lives on the ground floor, she's not a work colleague.'

'I want you to know—'

'Andrew, you called her the minute I was gone. She signed for the gourmet food… did you enjoy the steaks? Cooked medium rare – just how you like them?'

'Esmé, listen!'

'Bye Andrew, I'll be in touch about the apartment.' Esmé hung up the call, killing his final sentence.

*

'Any idea when the morning room will return to normal,' asked Jonah, swanning in as Esmé leant against the kitchen sideboard.

'In about a week when they start to die, I should think.'

'We can't have that – you need to move this shit out of here.'

Esmé pulled a face at him, and peeled her body from the furniture.

'Do I look like a magician that can make things disappear – so please, give me a break.'

'Seriously, the whole house can't move for flowers. A break-up, wasn't it?'

'No, I died. People are sad.'

'Boy, you're arsey tonight!'

'Maybe you need to put your brain in gear before speaking and secondly, I may have good reason to be arsey with you?' Esmé contemplated mentioning the restaurant visit, or could that wait for another day?

'*Moi?*

'I made you dinner the other night and you didn't even hang around to eat it, remember?'

'Oh yeah. Apparently Kane said it was delicious.'

'Hmmm. So, are you cooking for us both tonight?'

Jonah screwed his face up.

'Nah, nah, nah, It's Friday. I've got plans.'

Esmé left the morning room, she'd been had but never mind, it wouldn't happen again.

*

Esmé lay on her bed listening to the sounds of the house around her. Everyone seemed to have plans. She heard Asa plod up the staircase and enter his room next door. Sounds of him opening and closing wardrobe doors and cupboards followed. Jonah had begged the use of their bathroom as Dam was getting ready in theirs below. From their bathroom, she heard the shower running, Jonah's muted singing and the hot water pipes gurgling deep inside the walls.

Was singing in the shower a male thing? Andrew never sang in the shower, or had he? She couldn't remember. Was this her new game in life? Continually comparing every new male to Andrew?

Esmé stared at her new ceiling, the shadows and abstract light danced upon the white pimpled plaster.

She viewed the bedside clock: eight thirty. Another hour and surely the house would fall silent as they each left to embrace their respective Friday nights out.

What a difference a week and a day had made?

Esmé replayed the sequence leading her from Symphony Court to the hotel, The Single Girl's Calendar, the new haircut, her mother's warm kitchen with bacon butties and banter and then the offer she couldn't, and hadn't, refused. So much had happened in such a short space of time.

Her gaze came to rest upon her single girl's calendar still propped on top of the mantelpiece. Day two had told her to 'step out of your comfort zone' while today's door had demanded she 'face your fear' – she'd definitely done both throughout *this* week.

A series of banged doors and jovial shouts confirmed that the males had left the building, in her mind's eye Esmé could see each of them striding along Montague Road.

'I'd better empty the morning room,' said Esmé, leaving her room and plodding downstairs.

Within minutes, she'd selected and re-positioned appropriately sized arrangements around the house. A large display for the lounge's bay window, a dramatic centre piece for the dining room and an abstract floor standing display for the hallway. Still, the morning room remained full of flowers.

'This is hopeless,' she whinged.

'You off out?' came a voice from behind her.

Esmé whipped round to see Asa, dressed in jeans and a tee-shirt, obviously not going out, stride into the morning room.

'Sorry, you made me jump – I thought everyone had gone out.'

Asa shook his head.

'Has Toby gone?' A flush of guilt consumed her, she hadn't given him another thought after initially arriving home.

'What?'

'I thought I heard everyone go out but Toby was here earlier… has he gone too?'

'I believe he's gone visiting.'

'Makes sense. I didn't know he had a little one before I moved in.'

'Hmmm, I keep out of it. From what I hear there's been loads of issues with the mum… and her family… anyway, what's your plan, Stan?'

'For my evening?'

'No, the flowers?'

'You noticed as well? Jonah complained earlier.'

Asa raised an eyebrow, and walked around the morning room staring at the remaining arrangements.

Esmé watched him, prepared for a verbal sting or a smart alec answer.

'Seriously, what's the plan?' His eyes stared at her, patiently waiting.

Was he enjoying her struggle? He's going to mock anything that I suggest, so why bother?

'Aren't you heading out too?'

'Later, probably,' he said. 'So, the flowers?'

She had to come clean.

'I. Don't. Know. I gave some to work colleagues, the receptionists... I nearly offered Sexy Sadie an arrangement the other day but held back as she truly doesn't deserve one.'

'*Who?*

'The woman Andrew cheated on me with... never mind, it's a long story.'

'All this...' he waves his hand at the flowers. 'is linked to your break up?'

Esmé nodded.

'Now, I get it... poor sucker he's got it bad.'

'Work, my parents' house and now, here... I just want him to stop, it's not in his nature to be generous or spend money on stuff like this.' Esmé's voice cracked, as huge tears spilled over her lashes. 'I can't bear to look at them.'

'Hey, don't cry, it's not that big a deal. Order three taxis to arrive as soon as possible – I know where we can take these.'

*

'Hamstead Road, Handsworth, please?' said Asa to the taxi driver.

'Where?' asked Esmé, steadying numerous arrangements with her feet, whilst her arms were wrapped around another balancing on her lap.

'You'll see.' Asa sat back, staring at the darkening sky as the taxi pulled away from the kerb. Two more taxis filled with flowers followed in convoy.

Within no time the three taxis pulled up in a neat line alongside a set of green railings on a busy road.

'Unload, quickly now,' said Asa, standing each arrangement on the pavement beside the taxis. 'I can't believe you've talked me into this, on a Friday night, too.'

'I didn't, you offered, remember? Now please hurry up, the meter is ticking,' huffed Esmé. 'There's nothing like freely volunteering to help and then complaining and withdrawing your offer at the first available opportunity, is there?'

'Me, volunteer? Never,' He muttered, diving for another wobbly arrangement from the floor of the first taxi.

'You did and you know it!' said Esmé. Once all three taxis were emptied Esmé stood staring at the display of flowers arranged haphazardly upon the pavement.

'We'll keep this taxi, go and pay the other two and let them go,' instructed Asa. Esmé darted along the pavement to taxis two and three to pay them.

She soon returned.

'We'll be a few minutes, so please don't leave,' said Esmé through the open window to the driver.

'I'm not staying without cash in my hand to stay put, love. I've had too many youngsters like you rip me off. The clock says eight pounds sixty already…'

'You said…' said Esmé.

'It's Friday night, love, I can't afford to wait for a crazy girl with flowers, OK?'

'Here,' Asa thrust a twenty pound note at him. 'Now, sit quiet, we'll be back in five or ten, then I'll have my change back depending what's on the clock. Sorted?'

The taxi driver snatched the money and sat holding the purple note.

'Thank you.' Esmé began to move the flowers to the bottom of the railings, as Asa followed suit.

'You're paying me back, right?'

'You thought I *wouldn't* pay you back?' she snapped, lugging another arrangement across the pavement.

Asa raised an eyebrow.

'Thanks for the vote of confidence but I. *Always*. Pay. Back.'

'OK, don't lose the plot over a loan,' sniped Asa, clearly wishing he'd stayed at home.

'Where are we? And what's the plan?'

'To deliver these to the empty graves,' said Asa proudly, pointing at the green railings.

'A graveyard!'

'Yep, a very old graveyard where, if you look carefully, you'll notice there are no flowers.'

Esmé peered through the railings at the rows of lichen covered headstones, the stone angels, crosses and scribed open books, the twisted trees and even the smattering of litter blown amongst the graves. This was easily her worst nightmare. Esmé didn't watch horror films as the ghosts, ghouls and cobwebs spooked the hell out of her for weeks afterwards.

But Asa was right, from where they stood, there wasn't a single flower in sight, just wisps of overgrown grass between the monuments.

'I thought graveyards closed.'

'They do.' Asa pointed further along to the elaborate gates and their swatch of chains and bulky locks.

'So how are we getting inside?'

'We're going over,' said Asa, looking up and down the street.

Esmé stood staring between the carpet of flowers and the locked gates, her mouth open wide.

'Can I remind you the meter is still running,' said Asa, noticing her indecision.

'I really don't know about—'

'Well, I do… live a little, babe,' Asa approached the railings and launched himself athletically over them in one bound, landing lightly on the other side. 'Quick now, pass me some flowers.'

Esmé quickly handed him the arrangements. Asa plonked them down on the other side until they were all behind the railings.

'Give me a hand getting over?'

'No, stay there. I'll be quicker on my own.'

'No. These are my flowers, not yours, Asa!'

His name sounded foreign in her mouth.

Asa paused.

'Bloody women, here, give me your hand,' muttered Asa, offering his.

Esmé grasped his hand and lifted her leg as high as her tight jeans would allow. The denim cut into the top of her thigh. Her slip-ons slipped on the metal railings.

'Hurry up.'

'Oy! I'm trying, don't mock,' said Esmé, trying to hoist herself over the railings without causing herself physical damage.

Asa took hold of her under the arms, like a child, and dragged her over in an ungainly fashion that she wasn't expecting. Esmé landed safely on the ground beside him.

'Thank you, I *think*.'

Esmé could see the taxi driver shaking his head.

'Now where?' she asked.

'Anywhere… the graveyard is so old nobody has flowers, which makes it seem forgotten and unloved,' said Asa, pointing to the nearest selection of tilted graves.

Both chose an arrangement and headed off, then went to and fro with the rest of the displays. The moon was bold in the night sky, offering just enough light to see by.

Esmé looked around at the aged graves, the lingering shadows and low hanging branches, all that was missing was a dense mist. Her heart beat remained fairly rapid but the scene was beautiful and the atmosphere restful. How peaceful to lie here for eternity, asleep amongst the ivy and yew trees.

This wasn't as scary as she'd imagined.

In a matter of minutes, Esmé and Asa had run around the graves in a very haphazard manner, tripping over branches and grave edgings, and distributed all the flowers.

'This feels like some freaky Halloween style horror stunt,' said Esmé, standing back to admire their handiwork.

The gravestones were still tilted and toppled but now a breath of colour was dotted here and there.

'Are we done?' asked Asa, as he wiped his soil stained hands down his trousers.

'Done. Give me a leg up and we're on our way home.'

They jogged to the green railings over which they had jumped, and viewed the black outline of their waiting cab. Behind it stood a police car.

'Shit!' hissed Esmé. 'We're in for it now.'

One officer was out of the car, waving his torch light over the graveyard railings, awaiting their return to the cab. The other officer was sitting in the patrol car's driving seat.

'And can I ask what you are doing in the graveyard at this time of night?' his voice was deep and loaded.

Asa helped Esmé over the railings before climbing over himself.

'Officer, you won't believe us, but I'll give it a go,' said Asa.

'Oy, why do you always butt in?' snapped Esmé at Asa. 'I'll explain.'

'Be my guest.' Asa waved a hand towards the officer and stepped aside.

Esmé stuttered and stammered her way through a detailed explanation, the police officer stood listening intently, while the taxi driver became agitated.

'My meter's still running here, seventeen pounds thirty,' he called.

On completion, the officer simply stared at her.

Esmé held her breath. Asa dug both hands into his pockets.

'So, you're telling me you've scattered flowers around the graveyard in an attempt to be kind and generous at this time of night?'

'Yep. It was his idea but my flowers,' said Esmé, beaming with pride.

'Stay here, I need to see this.' The officer walked along the railings and peered over to view the graves by torchlight. Esmé watched him with bated breath.

'Can you cut out all the detail next time,' said Asa to Esmé, as they watched PC Plod do his thing. The officer put his radio to his mouth and spoke numerous times before returning.

'A nice gesture but I need your details, we've had numerous reports of vandalism over recent weeks and we'd like a little more information.'

'Surely not,' moaned Esmé.

'Oy, my meter's at twenty pounds and ten pence,' shouted the taxi driver.

Asa poked his head inside the open rear door.

'Sorted then, because it looks like we've got a new ride.' Asa slammed the taxi door and the cab swiftly pulled away.

'If you wouldn't mind?' said the officer, indicating the rear of his vehicle.

'Now look what you've caused?' moaned Esmé.

'Me? You've got a nerve, blaming me. You wanted to explain, you shut me down when I tried.'

Esmé began to cry as they settled in the rear of the patrol car.

'Great, because *that's* going to help immensely,' muttered Asa as the patrol car pulled away from the graveyard.

Chapter Nineteen

'A caution, how embarrassing?' stuttered Esmé, as they returned home, walking the dark streets of the city. 'I could die with embarrassment.'

'You don't say? I'd never have guessed given that you've only mentioned it a million times between the cop shop and here,' said Asa, stopping in the middle of the pavement. 'This is one mighty fine Friday, I can tell you.'

'Sorry, you shouldn't have volunteered then,' sniped Esmé, stopping and turning to look at him.

'I thought I was doing a good deed,' said Asa, 'Next time, I won't bother.'

'Who for? Me?'

'For the dead, actually?'

'The dead!'

'*Women.*'

'Oy, your mother wouldn't be proud of hearing you say that.'

'My mother's proud of *everything* I do.'

'*Really?*'

'Yes, really.'

'I doubt it very much… given the state of your…' the final word disappeared and crawled towards the gutter.

'Given what…?'

'Nothing,' muttered Esmé, a growing sense of shame bubbling within.

Silence enveloped them.

Esmé wondered why he grated on her nerves so much. Was it that he knew everything? Or that he bragged and boasted about himself? Who had that much confidence or ego?

'She's dead by the way,' said Asa, breaking the silence.

'Who is?'

'My mother.'

Esmé stopped walking and stared.

'Asa!'

'What?'

'You can't say it like that.'

'I can. She's dead.'

Esmé regained her stride and jogged to catch him up.

'Asa?'

'Stop bugging me, she was *my* mother, I can say it how I like.'

'But…'

'But nothing, you're being overly sensitive about something that has no connection to you, so why the sad face?'

Esmé swallowed the lump in her throat. They continued in silence, while Esmé tried to figure out what to say and how to say it. Asa simply studied the stars.

Minutes passed by.

'Sorry.'

'What for?'

'Your mum.'

'Are you still on that one?' he laughed. 'Move on, I have.'

'How?'

'It takes time but…'

'No, how did she die?'

'In a fire.'

His voice changed partway through his sentence. His tone recovered in less than a heartbeat, it was a miniscule change but Esmé heard it.

'That's awful, how old was she?'

'Thirty-four…'

'That's no age,' said Esmé, adding. 'That's shocking… like me dying in five years' time.'

'You need to start living a little then, don't you, because it could be over before you know it?'

'I *do* believe, I've had a pretty busy week…' Esmé stopped, before adding. 'You've got a cheek, you know that.'

Asa smiled.

'Fancy popping for a drink, given that it's Friday night?'

'Around here?' Esmé looked at the back street area which they nipped down a few minutes ago and doubted there was anything near.

'There's a decent boozer round the corner,' Asa pointed ahead. 'You can say no.'

'Why would I say no?'

'Because...' he pointed towards his tattooed face. 'Some people are offended by such things.'

'I haven't a problem, it's your face,' she lied.

'Some think that I must be a lout and a night out with me will end up in a police station...'

'Aw well, done that.'

'Excellent, come on then. The Shakespeare's just along here.' Asa walked towards the end of the road, heading for the corner. 'That's interesting, because I'm a decent judge of character and I seriously had you marked as one that would be *sooooo* bothered by tattoos.'

'No,' lied Esmé. He can read me like a book.

*

Asa led the way, pushing open the double doors into a traditional bar, decorated with coloured tiles and engraved glass. The happy atmosphere enveloped you on entering. The customers lined the length of the wooden bar, chatting to an elderly landlord who stood cleaning glasses. The bar staff dashed to and fro between the beer pumps and optics and the jukebox kept a trio of men busy scanning the tunes.

'Evening, Sid,' called Asa, as he settled on a bar stool. 'What's your poison?'

Esmé eased herself onto the high bar stool with the usual elegance of those with short legs.

'A JD and coke, please.'

'Two JD and cokes, please Sid – doubles.'

'This your regular haunt then?' asked Esmé, looking around at the wooden alcoves where a mixture of singles and trios seated at the various tables cradled drinks.

'Not really, yours?'

'No. I've never been here before…' retorted Esmé. On seeing Asa's grin, she added 'Oh, you're pulling my leg again, I get it.'

'Yeah, but that's the thing, seriously, you don't, do you? You pretend you get it all but… nothing really makes sense, does it?'

The two drinks arrived and Asa handed a tenner in Sid's direction.

'Cheers, me dear.' Asa snatched his drink and took a swig, before giving a huge sigh.

Esmé gently sipped hers, the ice clinking in the glass.

'What don't I get?'

'Life.'

'Yes, I do.'

'Nah. You've hardly lived. Your head is full of daydreams and you're afraid of everything, even your own shadow.'

Esmé ignored him.

He doesn't know me. I moved in one week ago. I could have been out with Roberto, the waiter, tonight being wined, dined and romanced, had I chosen to phone him.

Esmé had kept his number safe, but it was only day nine since the break-up. She hadn't cleared the apartment and her head was still muddled, why rush in and muddy the waters?

'Now you're ignoring me because I touched a nerve,' he said.

'I'm not. You think you know everything… you don't.'

'I know that despite just nine days away from the boyfriend you've got your hopes set on Jonah.'

'Sod you,' snapped Esmé. 'He's just a friend.'

'You're single, you can take your pick.'

'You think you know people, well you can't pigeonhole human nature, not everyone reacts as you assume.'

'Really? Prove me wrong.'

Esmé held her hands wide. 'How?'

'Go and put on a tune that people in here would react to, the choice is yours. Let's see how well you read folk.'

Esmé looked around the crowd, people of different ages and backgrounds filled the pub.

'Go on, don't dawdle…'

Esmé jumped down from her stool and headed for the jukebox.

Asa watched as she leaned against the plastic hub and flicked the selection pages, searching. She pumped her cash into the slot and walked back as frantic piano music filled the air. She evaded his gaze, climbed awkwardly back onto her stool and nonchalantly swigged her drink before acknowledging his company.

'Meat Loaf?'

Esmé shrugged.

'Decent choice but nah! You think these punters listen to this?' asked Asa, nodding towards the customers. 'As I said, you're not a very good judge of character. Watch!'

Esmé watched a few individuals mime the odd line, tap a finger or two on the table. She had to admit there wasn't a great reaction, not as she'd expected.

'A nice chick like you… you should have gone with your first choice.'

'I did.'

'You didn't. You wanted to impress so you went with what you thought was the right choice, so you've crashed and burned.'

'You know nothing about me and yet… what's the point?' Esmé fell silent.

Asa smiled.

'Please carry on, you were verging on interesting then. I'll tell you… you, Esmé Peel, are a nothing person.'

'I am not!'

'You are. You have no plans, no true dreams, nothing to look forward to… you wait around until something happens and then tag along until the next thing happens, filling your life with other people's dreams and hopes.'

Esmé was speechless, her mouth fell open. Asa smiled.

'Prove me wrong. Did you have plans for tonight?'

'No, but I could have had a date, if I'd called him. Anyway, neither did you by the looks of it.'

'I had plans. I always have plans. I had a sleep this afternoon because I was meeting friends from work at around eleven and heading for a club. My plans changed once I realised *you* needed a hand.'

'You can still go,' said Esmé, injured by his accusation.

'Given that it is half eleven now… they'll know to go ahead without me.'

'Yeah right, *friends* from work… who really has friends at work they go clubbing with?'

'I do.'

'You're lucky then, apart from two, mine are simply colleagues that just happen to work where I do. Where do you work then?'

Asa paused.

'The hospital. I told you that at the house meeting.'

'Sorry. You did.'

'You looked surprised then, and now.'

'It's that with that…' she pointed to her cheek. 'I didn't think they'd employ you… doesn't it scare the patients?'

'No, just *you*, by the sounds of it. See, I knew you were uncool with the whole thing,' he said, adding. 'I'm not a porter, kitchen or laundry staff either if you're trying to suss out which department – all feasible roles for someone with a facial tattoo.'

'Let's face it, it just isn't normal, is it?'

'You mention face every time I am around.'

'I can't help it, it's like that 'don't mention the elephant in the room…' you're OK till it's mentioned then it's all you can think about.'

'*Really?*

'Not like that!' Esmé's annoyance was growing. Was he playing with her or was this his usual style?

'I'm kidding you.'

A lengthy silence occurred.

'Was that lover boy that turned up the other night?'

'Ex-lover boy. Actually, thank you for the other night, I did mean to say the next morning but…'

'You slipped out really early – I figured you avoided us all on purpose.' Asa sipped his drink. Esmé stared at his side profile. Her eyes followed the contours of the blue and green, wispy lines, shading, colour and shadows.

'Why the tattoo?' she asked, openly looking at his face.

'Why not?'

'But it's your face… surely it could have gone somewhere else?'

'Not really. I wanted it there. I like peacock feathers.'

'But there's no face or a beak.'

'That's lower down my back. Peacock feathers symbolise immortality and resurrection.'

'I thought the eyes warded off evil spirits.'

'It would make my life a whole lot simpler, if that were true,' said Asa, giving a deep laugh.

'How come you always have something smart to say?'

Asa shrugged.

'It's what comes of being an arse.'

'I shouldn't have called you that, it was rude of me. Sorry.'

'You could be right, I might be an arse. I call it being honest... but being an arse works as well.'

Esmé laughed.

'I'm honest, if nothing else.'

'Even so, I'm sorry for calling you that during my phone call – though it did make us both laugh when you answered.'

Meat Loaf finished wailing. Asa looked towards the jukebox, then around at the other customers.

'Is it my turn?' he asked, jumping down from his stool. Esmé watched as he walked to the jukebox, studied the plastic cards and then pumped his money into the slot.

Esmé's ears strained to hear the intro of the track.

The piano bursts from the beginning of... it couldn't be, Asa wouldn't choose Abba?

Asa walked casually back to the bar, his eyes holding her gaze. Coolly ordering another round with a wave of his hand while climbing back onto his stool just as 'Dancing Queen' burst forth from the jukebox. Numerous customers stared across at the pair as the distinctive tones played loud and proud.

'They are staring,' laughed Esmé.

'Yeah, but watch them,' whispered Asa. Esmé loved this tune, she'd have jumped up and run to the dance floor had she been with anyone other than Asa.

'Are you watching?'

'Yes.'

From every inch of the busy bar Esmé could make out the tiny bopping actions made by every customer, be it a lively foot tap, a finger dance on the table top or the twitch of a shoulder. Every customer was moving, tapping, jigging or mouthing the words, unconsciously or otherwise, along with Abba.

'The one song everyone loves to hate and yet, they know every word. They can't resist joining in as if it gets inside each and every one of us.'

'And you?'

'*Me?* I love this song!'

Esmé burst out laughing.

'Now, I know you're kidding me.'

Asa's face stayed deadpan.

The refilled glasses appeared on the bar.

'You're not joking, are you?' laughed Esmé.

'What's not to like about 'Dancing Queen'? It reminds me of my childhood and happy times, dancing around the lounge with my mother... why would I dislike a song that instantly brings her back to life?'

He was right. Be it a wedding, an eighteenth birthday party or a retirement do, the dance floor is always full when 'Dancing Queen' is played. A crowd pleaser, if nothing else.

The seated jives continued until the track finished and a fresh set of memories were revived by the next track.

'Where did you grow up then, after your mum…?'

'Aunty Judy and Uncle Jim… took me in, I can't complain, they gave me everything I needed, apart from my mum.'

Asa collected his drink and knocked it back in one.

'Steady on,' said Esmé. 'I can't do that.'

Asa held his arms wide.

'See what I mean… come on, live a little, Esmé.'

Esmé knocked back her drink in one before spluttering and almost toppling from her high perch.

Asa summoned the barman again.

'Two more, please?'

'I'll pay for these – I owe you a twenty anyway.'

'OK, pay your way, Esmé.'

The final hour of the day passed in a blur at the bar, knocking back a range of spirits recommended by a wayward Asa.

'Now, the real test… can you still walk home or is it a taxi job?'

'I can walk,' said Esmé, as she tested her legs by climbing cautiously from her high stool.

'Great, we can spend the money on a final round. Climb back up.'

'I can't. I'll stand,' she laughed.

'So now that we're housemates and drinking buddies – what's the story with ex-lover boy?'

'History.'

'Boy, he must have mucked it up big time?'

'Yep, his cheating was the quickest exit of my life.'

'Did he know that it would be?'

'Of course, I couldn't stomach a cheating partner.'

'So, where are you pitching your cap?'

Esmé pulled a face.

'What's your type?'

'Hmmm, now that depends.'

'On what?'

'My tastes may have changed. Andrew was a nice guy but I'm now wiser, maybe it's time for me to widen the range a little by taking an interest in people I'd never looked at.'

'Sounds promising,' said Asa leaning on the bar and closing the gap between his and Esmé's shoulders.

'I like blonde, athletic bodies and maybe... I'll step out of my comfort zone with something a little different next time.'

Asa watched her face enter into a dream like trance. He'd got as close to her as he dared but now, on hearing her wish list, he gently eased his frame backwards, distancing himself as she spoke. One thing was certain, housemate or drinking buddy, it was clear who she'd set her cap at.

'Shame to ruin the fun, lady, but it's time to stagger home.' Asa jumped down from his stool and made slowly for the door, and Esmé tottered and swayed in his footsteps.

Chapter Twenty

Day 10: List three future dreams

Esmé staggered into the lounge, dressed in her pyjamas and a towelling housecoat, carrying a glass of water and a packet of paracetamol.

'Morning, nice of you to join the land of the living,' laughed Russ from the sofa with little Toby tucked under his arm, watching cartoons. 'A little hung-over, are we?'

'Please don't be cheery on my account, I want to die.'

'Serves you right. Was it 'Dancing Queen' you were singing as you staggered up the path?'

Esmé flopped into the armchair and swallowed two tablets.

'Really?'

'Seriously, as loud as you could.'

'I didn't.'

'You did. Ask Asa.'

'He'll be just as bad as this,' said Esmé, taking some comfort.

'He's not. He's up and out… it's eleven thirty.'

Is this some sort of joke? Had she been downing shots and he just had water?

'We drank enough to kill a buffalo, he can't be OK.'

'You don't know Asa, he can take his booze.'

Esmé watched the two on the sofa, snuggled together and chuckling over the cartoon. As the excitement grew, Toby's tiny slippered feet jiggled to and fro.

'How old is he?'

'Three.'

'They're funny at that age, aren't they?'

'This little fella is, though he was running around at six this morning so I came down here.'

'We watched cartoons,' gabbled the child, his bright face looking up into Russ's.

How cute.

'I'm off then but…' said Kane, bursting into the lounge. He halted on seeing Esmé. 'You look dead rough.'

'Talking to me now, are we?' she smarted.

Kane ignored her, and spoke to Russ.

'I'm off then. You all sorted, know what to do?'

'Yes, I know what to do, thanks.'

'Toby, I'm off.'

Toby scrambled from his seat and ran like a puppy to give Kane a cuddle.

'Catch you later, bye,' said Kane, before disappearing. Toby returned to his spot beneath Russ's arm.

The front door slammed. Esmé watched as Russ's brow furrowed and his mouth twitched as if talking to himself.

'Don't let him put on you,' said Esmé, after a moment of heavy silence.

'Sorry?'

'Kane, don't let him put on you, he's a sod for making others do his dirty work... just tell him no.'

'Ah that, no, he's fine.' Russ jumped up with sudden exuberance. 'Come on, Toby, let's go to the park and play football.'

'Yay!' cried the child, following him.

Esmé watched the two disappear, so cute, and yet, so sad.

Esmé stared at the plasma screen as a mouse chased a cat with a frying pan.

How different life would be if she had a child to consider last weekend. Could she just have upped and offed? Would Andrew have made a decent father? Possibly, though given his latest actions and irresponsibilities, no.

'Morning, how are we?' asked Dam, charging into the room, trainers in hand.

'Dying.'

'Thought you would be, good night though?'

'I think so.'

Dam sat on the edge of the sofa and pulled on his trainers.

'Sorry if I woke you.'

'No worries, it was funny. Asa said you got cautioned for being in the graveyard. That's hilarious.'

Esmé cringed.

'Off out?'

'Yeah, to a family meal, it's a must on Saturdays… though I've plenty of studying I could be doing.'

'What, you're studying as well as lecturing?

He nodded.

'Studying what?'

'Physics.'

'Oh right. *More* physics,' Esmé said, as if she understood the subject.

'You don't have to pretend to be interested, no one ever is.' Dam stood and straightened his trouser legs.

'Even so, I'd like to take an interest in my housemates,' said Esmé.

Dam smiled.

'And your plans for today?' he asked.

Esmé realised she had no plans.

'To get showered and dressed once I feel slightly better.'

'Bye, Esmé,' said Dam, shaking his head.

'Bye.'

In an instant he'd gone and the front door slammed.

Asa was right. She had no plans, not for today, or tomorrow or… well, ever.

Esmé felt an irritation deep in her stomach.

Did he actually tell me, *'You've hardly lived, your head is full of daydreams and you're afraid of everything, even your own shadow'?* Cheeky git, well she'd show him!

*

By mid-afternoon, her head had ceased to bang like a drum. Having consumed a plate of pasta to line her stomach, Esmé sat reading in the lounge when there was a hammering on the front door.

Who the hell was that?

She hadn't heard any of the guys return home but waited to see if one of them answered but they didn't and the hammering continued.

Esmé peeled herself from the armchair to peer through the lounge window and see the noisy visitor. A young woman in a green coat, her black hair swept into a messy bun and her face bare apart from a smudge of pink lipstick. She turned round as Esmé peered. Her frown didn't ease to a smile on seeing she was being watched, and she hammered on the door again.

I'll be polite and calm, she'll be fine.

Esmé dashed to open the door. As the latch left the cradle the woman pushed it hard and stormed inside.

'Excuse me…'

'Where is he?' she demanded, striding back and forth at the bottom of the stairs. 'Toby!'

'Toby's at the park with Russ.'

'Are you joking me?' she snapped, her delicate features twisted into a knot.

'Yes, they went a couple of hours ago.'

'What a frigging joke this is!'

'Sorry, but I'm not sure what time they're coming back… do you want to walk up to the park? I believe it's only in the next street.'

'Do you live here?' She began to pace.

'Yes and…'

'Has he been upset?'

'Not when I've seen him. He's watched cartoons while snuggling on the sofa, played football in the back garden and, from the dishes in the sink, ate a bowl of scrambled eggs – I haven't seen him crying.'

The woman relaxed and stood still, suddenly extending her hand.

'I'm Rita… you are?'

'Esmé.'

'I see.' The pause seemed to last for an eternity before she continued. 'I'll take myself off up the park then, sorry to disturb your Saturday afternoon.'

'No worries, see you.' Esmé closed the door. This could well be the downside to living with others, their dramas entered your world, and with so many individuals under one roof maybe there'd be one every day.

*

An hour later Russ returned, swinging a bag of shopping and no Toby.

'Rita called by... did she find you?'

Russ stared.

'Yes, thanks.'

'I told her that you'd gone to the park and that Toby hadn't been upset – sorry if I've said the wrong thing but she seemed to calm down once she knew.'

'Yeah, she's like that is Rita. Thanks. He was late going back, she panicked,' said Russ, as he disappeared into the morning room.

Another of life's complications that he had obviously learnt to live with. How difficult it must be having a lifelong connection to an ex-partner?

Esmé spent the remainder of the day around the house, cleaning her room, doing laundry ready for work on Monday and steadying her delicate stomach.

She heard the front door unlock, footsteps and then the morning room door open and close.

'*So?*'

That sounded like Kane.

'I told you,' answered Russ.

Are they arguing? Never had Esmé heard a cross word between the two and yet, like in her mum's kitchen last weekend, this sounded like another disagreement.

'What's the harm?'

'Kane!'

She heard the morning room door open and then the lounge door opened revealing Kane.

'Hi, Esmé, you OK?'

'Me? Yeah.'

'Good good, at home all day, are we?'

'Yeah. Why?'

'Nothing, just asking… aren't I allowed to ask?'

'You weren't speaking to me earlier and now this… what's up, Kane?'

'Nothing, just being polite.'

Esmé stared.

This wasn't like Kane. Why did he keep flitting in and out of the house? What was going on?

'Right, I'll be seeing you then.' Kane disappeared and re-entered the morning room.

'Fine.'

'Kane, it's not fair.'

'It's fine, I tell you.'

Esmé put down her magazine and listened.

Kane's footsteps traipsed through the hallway and the front door slammed. She jumped up to peer through the lounge window at his retreating figure.

How come he'd got a key if he wasn't paying any rent money?

She jumped as Russ joined her in the lounge.

'Are you OK?' he asked, as she blushed having been caught at the window.

'Kane has a key?' she asked, ignoring his question.

'For emergencies, yeah, we all thought it best given you were living here.'

Esmé returned to the couch as Russ settled into the armchair with his coffee mug.

'Have Dam's family got a key?'

'No.'

'Your family?'

'No.'

Esmé pulled a face.

'*Just* my family... do you think I need looking after?'

Russ slurped his drink.

'Being female, we thought it best, that's all.'

She returned to her magazine. Her gaze flickering between the page and the frowning male in the armchair. The silence lingered for near on thirty minutes until the front door slammed.

'Hello, anyone home?' called Jonah, in a jubilant tone.

'In here,' called Russ, emerging from his trance. Esmé sat up and fluffed her hair. Russ looked away when their glances met.

Jonah burst into the lounge with an energy unseen in number seven today, carrying a small cardboard box.

He was wearing a beige army coat and a pair of expensive leather boots, which made quite an outfit.

Esmé's stomach flipped.

Seriously, when would this teenage obsession go away?

'You'll never guess what I've bought?'

'I'm not in the mood for games,' moaned Russ, staring at the box.

'A pet.'

'Seriously?' said Esmé, who jumped up to take a look.

'A Chilean Rose!'

'A what?' asked Esmé, peering closely as Jonah lifted the lid to reveal a tarantula. 'Oh my life!' Esmé darted backwards to stand on the couch cushions pointing at the box.

'Not your thing then?' asked Jonah, laughing.

Esmé wanted to cry. She was in a room with a spider. A living breathing spider. And Jonah was laughing.

'Russ, please make him close the lid!' wailed Esmé.

*

'Then what did he do?' asked Grace, handing Esmé a fresh cuppa in her cosy kitchen.

'He just laughed. The very thought gives me goose bumps.'

'He'll get rid of it – the others will make him.'

'Do you think so?'

Grace brought an old biscuit tin with her to the table and settled opposite.

'I'm certain, the tattoo guy will see to that… he's more…' Esmé waited for Grace's character reference but it had faded, unlike her fear of the hairy tarantula.

Esmé sipped her sweet tea, dunking her ginger nut biscuits as Grace looked on.

'Don't fret…'

'What if it gets out of the tank?'

'Tank?'

'He's taken delivery of a huge glass tank for his room. Apparently, they live in there amongst a load of green foliage and some kind of humidity making machine to make it tropical.'

'Seems like hard work to me, he'll get bored with it soon, believe me. I've seen it so many times.'

Esmé shook her head.

'I don't think so, he said he'd wanted one since childhood and now, moving into his first proper adult home… tadah! He bought one.'

'Surely someone else will protest.'

'Jonah moaned that he's expected to put up with our interests and belongings so why shouldn't he be allowed to buy what he wants?'

'And he wants a pet?'

'Yep.'

'I've never really had pets.'

'I had loads as a child, gerbils, guinea pigs, rabbits… but nothing exotic.'

'I can imagine cats and dogs being good company.'

'We always wanted a dog but my dad said no.'

'A far nicer pet than a spider. Argh, I wouldn't be best pleased either, but have faith, the lads won't ignore your reaction.'

'Well it's hard to ignore, I jumped up and down on the new couch, screaming,' laughed Esmé. 'He was trying to tell me how he'd called her Rose, I simply screamed at him.'

The terror that had risen within had been monumental, every nerve of her body wanted that spider dead. How was she to live under the same roof?

'My idea of a Chilean rose is chilled in the fridge before drinking,' said Esmé, finally raising a smile.

Feeling calm and safer, Esmé switched topics and relayed the details of last night's graveyard delivery.

'This morning they all knew about it, so Asa must have filled them in before I woke up.'

'A lesson learnt there, nothing is kept quiet between the men then,' laughed Grace.

'If you tell one, you might as well tell them all! The police issued us with a caution but nothing else… boy, what next?'

'Nothing, life will settle down for you and then you can breathe,' suggested Grace, as she collected the empty tea cups. 'Time for another?'

'I will, if I'm not holding you up from doing anything.'

'The dusting can wait, believe me… there's no rush left in me to do anything else these days.'

As Grace pottered around her kitchen making fresh tea, Esmé told her about little Toby, his cute slippers and an irate Rita.

'Such a pity, but at least young families aren't hidden nowadays – they were in *my* time. Girls were sent away to their aunts in the country and then came home without their babies. We all knew about it but nothing was ever said… taboo, if you get my drift? But still such a struggle to raise a little one outside a relationship.'

The afternoon slipped slowly past, by the time Esmé had drunk all her offered tea, the kitchen was losing the light and the dark night was drawing in.

'We'll have to nip out for a walk next time, visit the local park on a fine day,' suggested Esmé, knowing her own grandmother had enjoyed such visits when she'd been alive. Nanny Peel had enjoyed the spring colours and the blue sky on a fresh day.

'That sounds lovely, now take care and don't you worry your head about that spider.'

'I'll try not to,' said Esmé, knowing all too well she wouldn't be sleeping tonight if the new lodger remained in the house.

Chapter Twenty-one

The thunder of feet on the staircase woke Esmé early on Sunday morning. She heaved her bedding over her head and tried to return to her slumber. The image of an eight legged fiend filled her mind.

'Errr,' she jumped, as she felt something touch her left foot. Whipping back the duvet just to be sure, a dash of cold air ensured she was fully awake. 'So much for a Sunday lie-in.'

She plodded to the mantelpiece to collect her single girl's calendar.

I never completed yesterday's task! Fancy failing on day ten having been so good every other day?

Only last night, she had thanked Carys for such an intriguing present. Carys had phoned to say she and her younger sister, Jenny, were going to the cinema, did Esmé wish to join them? Esmé had jumped at the invite, having made no plans of her own.

'You can't spend a Saturday night home alone…' said Carys. 'I predict you'll end up watching *Casualty* while downing a bottle of vino and bed before half ten.'

'What's wrong with *Casualty?* asked Esmé, when they met in the cinema's foyer.

'Single woman's cheesy tv,' explained Carys. 'The actors are super fit but the storyline's total mush.'

'That covers half the tv I watch anyway... *so?*

'*Change*, my dear girl... it'll be good for you,' giggled Jenny, her dark eyes sparkling like her older sister's.

'The last ten days have been nothing but change... one step at a time, yeah?' Esmé had joked before giving Carys a quick update on the week's events, especially the flower deliveries and their subsequent disposal of them.

'Pretty busy then... yet another way of getting over a break-up,' soothed Carys, after Esmé's detailed summary. 'And now, time for a bit of Firth and Bridget.'

'Always a good shout. Come on!' Jenny had ushered them briskly towards screen five, laden with popcorn and candyfloss.

Esmé returned to her bed clutching her calendar. She re-opened day ten, not such fun without the tiny slab of chocolate, to re-read yesterday's task: list three future dreams.

What were her dreams? Nothing came to mind. She used to know – Esmé held up three fingers and counted.

'To get engaged, to get married and to have my own family in a few years,' she said aloud to the empty bedroom.

Simple *but* ruined. She needed Andrew to succeed at each one. Esmé folded her arms in disgust. How can one person mess it up for someone else on such a grand scale?

The three things she'd wanted most in the world he'd now wiped from her reach. What new dreams had she to replace them? None.

Esmé didn't wish to be richer, thinner, fitter, more fashionable, more intelligent, more out-going, less frightened of spiders, more charitable, less reflective… she smiled at the irony.

She still wanted to be engaged, married and planning a family – had she specified Andrew's family? No. She wanted a guy who a, wouldn't cheat b, would commit to her and c, commit to their future family. Simple. Though not so simple when you're starting all over *again.*

She could feel the hollowness growing deep inside.

Leave well alone before the memories make you cry. This isn't the way to start a Sunday morning. Sunday morning is supposed to be a joyful, bright part of the week.

Esmé jumped from her bed, pulled the covers straight and headed to the wardrobe and grabbed a colourful tee-shirt and her favourite jeans.

Within ten minutes, she felt a whole load better, vowing to leave yesterday's task until later but instead to focus on today. She took the calendar from the bed clothes and searched for day eleven, a mouthful of chocolate was guaranteed to brighten her mood, she read the task.

Day 11: Spring clean your wardrobe

Esmé looked down at her outfit.

Did she need to spring clean her wardrobe? She'd never followed fashion trends but was comfy and ticked the boxes of clean, tidy and presentable. Did anyone she know, apart from Jonah, consciously choose a particular fashion style? Penny shared her clean and tidy category, Marianne was older, yet stylish in a classy way. Carys and Jenny had definite styles or was it simply cultural expectations which determined their colourful appearance and choices?

Esmé opened the wardrobe doors wide. Despite still needing to collect most of her clothes from the apartment she stared at the foundation of her possessions: tee-shirts in a rainbow of colours that had complimented her old auburn hair, jeans and a variety of boots: some heeled, some flat, with round or square toes.

She knew she had a selection of other clothes in the apartment but honestly, for the majority of the time, Esmé was happy as she was.

She could wear a pink tutu, Doctor Martin's and a wet suit – but would it make her a more interesting person? She doubted it.

Wow, she'd struggled with these tasks. The first week was easy but yesterday's lowered her mood and today's had made her feel like a dowdy frump. What's wrong with clean, tidy and presentable? Wasn't changing her hair style enough?

Esmé was having none of it, this wasn't the way she'd hoped her Sunday would start, so she left her room and began the day afresh.

'What are you doing here?' asked Esmé, as she entered the morning room to find her brother eating cereal. 'You don't pay rent, you don't have a room and yet you're here all the time.'

'No, I'm not,' said Kane, with his mouth full.

Esmé snapped the switch on the kettle.

'It feels like it,' she muttered, taking a mug from the draining board. 'Seriously, you had the chance to live here, and you blew it.'

'You jumped in my grave by waving your cash around, isn't that right, Dam?'

'Sibling argument – please leave me out of it,' chuntered Dam into his toast and pâté. 'I have enough when I visit my parents.'

'And another thing… you can start paying towards the food you keep scoffing when you do come around… you ate all the biscuits last time and my last piece of bread!'

Kane pulled a face at his sister, mimicking her mood.

'Woo, little Miss Arsey today, are we?'

'No, Little Miss Not-Putting-Up-With-Brothers any more, that's who!'

'Pity, I had planned to put in a good word with Jonah for you!'

'You arse!'

'I thought you'd given Asa that pet name, not me?'

'Seriously, you are a total waste of space, waste of a heartbeat, waste of standing space, an oxygen thief and waste of a skin!' Esmé stirred her coffee and swiftly left the room.

'Woo, what's up with her?' asked Kane.

Dam simply shrugged.

Esmé stood in the hallway, coffee mug in hand. She wanted to cry.

What had just happened? Why did it bug her so much that Kane was here?

'Are you OK?'

Esmé turned to see Kane slip through the kitchen doorway. 'You seem a bit…' He pulled a grotesque face.

'I'm sorry. I didn't mean any of that… It's me, I suppose, I'm all over the place.'

'Come here.'

Esmé put her coffee on the bottom step as Kane wrapped his arms around her shoulders and bear hugged her mighty tight.

'I get it. You're allowed to feel this way... just don't let it get the better of you, that's all.'

Esmé cradled her head under his chin and wobbled it from side to side, a trick she'd done since his teenage growth spurts.

'I know. I've had a good week considering. I've coped well but *this* morning I feel like... Blar!'

'Maybe it's catching up with you... you've kept yourself busy and now, Sunday morning, the blues kick in.'

'Maybe.' Esmé thought about The Single Girl's Calendar, had yesterday's task been too much to deal with so soon after the break-up? Or was the idea of spring cleaning her clothes that hard to take? 'Do you think my clothes need updating?'

'You're asking me?' scoffed Kane, releasing his hold.

'I'd say yes,' said Jonah coming down the stairs. 'And your platinum hair needs toning down, too.'

'I wasn't asking you! And what's wrong with my hair?'

Jonah pulled a face.

'I only had it done a week ago... Tristan said...' Her words fade, Tristan had mentioned a return visit, hadn't he?

'Bleach blonde just isn't now, whereas vibrant reds, mmmmm irresistible!' Jonah smoothed his long blond hair over his shoulder. 'What I wouldn't give to spend some time with a red haired lover...'

'You think everyone's image needs updating,' laughed Kane.

'I'll ignore that remark, Kane. Esmé, you're a woman, I think you need to start dressing like one.'

'Excuse me! I think you'll find us women can please ourselves with what we wear and when.'

'You can, but seriously,' he waved a hand up and down indicating her clothing. 'You've worn something similar every day you've been here... where's your panache? Your finesse? Your vavavoom?'

'Jonah!' cried Esmé, laughing.

'Only saying, you asked for *his* opinion so why not take mine? Treat yourself to a personal shopper for the afternoon – they'll work wonders for your wardrobe,' said Jonah, heading towards the kitchen.

'Has that tarantula gone?' asked Esmé, calling after his retreating frame.

'Yep, I returned it yesterday actually... thanks to you and your hysterics!'

'Thank you! It's not my fault I have a phobia.'

The kitchen door swung shut.

'A personal shopper's not a bad suggestion…'

'Well, it's your bank balance,' muttered Kane, and kissed the top of her head. 'Call me, if you need me.'

'I will.' Esmé collected her coffee mug from the stairs and watched him pull on his trainers by the front door. 'Kane, thank you.'

He looked up from tying his laces.

'I get it, seven years is a long time… you must have thought *these* days were over.'

'I did.'

*

'Aren't you taking the rest of your clothes?' asked Andrew, as Esmé slid closed the doors of their fitted wardrobes.

'Not at the moment,' she said, as Jonah's suggestion churned over in her mind. She could turf the remainder of her jeans, sweater tops, hoodies and faded tee-shirts into several black bin liners but what if she failed to be impressed when out shopping. How many times had she returned empty handed from her favourite store? She'd kick herself for throwing out decent quality clothing. If nothing else she could leave these clothes here, replace the items and then donate these things to charity.

'Good, I don't mind,' said Andrew, seated on the edge of their double bed watching proceedings.

'Sorry, I know… that wasn't easy.'

'So, don't do it.'

Esmé paused.

'I have no choice. We aren't the same people as we once were. I can't pretend it hasn't happened.'

She turned away and busied herself emptying the top drawer of her dressing table into a cardboard box. She could feel his eyes on her back, drinking in her every move, but she couldn't bear to see the sadness in his eyes.

'Have you told your parents?' she asked, casually.

'Yep, and my brother and both sisters – they all know I messed up. They all know you've moved out, I even explained how and why.'

Esmé folded the flaps on the box and set about filling another with her cosmetics.

'You didn't have to go that far but thank you for being honest… I didn't relish the thought of bumping into them in the city and having to defend myself.'

'My mother was gutted, if you want to know. Said she couldn't believe I'd acted so foolishly and that I deserved everything that I had coming to me. My father didn't say much, but he never does, does he?'

'Not usually.' Esmé carried on packing in silence, working her way through the drawers.

Who'd have thought that Diana Nixon would have sided with her? They'd got along well but still, Andrew was the apple of her eye. That *was* a turn up for the books.

'Are you heading straight back?' asked Andrew, breaking into her thoughts.

'Yep, my dad's outside waiting with his friend's van.

'Oh.'

'I said he could come inside but he didn't want to intrude, you know how it is?'

'OK.'

Within fifteen minutes, Esmé had packed the majority of her possessions from their bedroom and the few that remained in the bathroom. Andrew helped her to carry the bulging bin liners and boxes down the stairs towards the entrance where the white transit was parked.

'I'll leave these here, if your dad's not too keen on speaking,' muttered Andrew.

'Thanks. Well, bye, sorry for interrupting your Sunday afternoon but... I needed...' her throat closed up with a wave of sadness.

Why had this happened to them? Why wasn't today about Sunday roasts and choosing a design for wedding invitations. Instead, Esmé was frozen to the spot amidst a sea of bin liners, desperately trying to say a cheery goodbye to an ex-boyfriend whose pain was etched on his face.

Andrew gave her a clunky hug that was roughly and hastily delivered, before he traipsed back up the stairs to apartment nine.

Opening the entrance doorway, Esmé beckoned to her dad as she dropped the first of her bags outside on the block paving.

Chapter Twenty-two

Day 12: Smile at ten strangers

Monday morning, Esmé anxiously walked into the office.

Would Andrew repeat last week's flower deliveries and refurbish the office with round two from *Interflora?* Esmé opened the door and cautiously peered inside. Empty surfaces.

'Morning Esmé,' called Penny, as jovial as ever. 'It's safe to enter. We gave the flower arrangements to the cleaning staff on Friday night. How was your weekend?'

'You'll never believe me, so we'll start with yours first.' Esmé settled at her desk as Marianne delivered a tray of coffees and the weekend analysis. Penny explained how her new winter boots had cost the earth and hubby hadn't been impressed so the guilt trip forced her to take them back on Sunday for a full refund.

'Do you know how hard it is convincing one of the sales assistants that you haven't worn them outside the house when you've clocked up an hour inside on carpet to break them in but forgot to take them off when you fetched the washing in off the line. Polishing that scuffed sole took some doing, phew!'

'Did you get your full refund?' asked Marianne.

Penny and Esmé exchanged a glance and laughed.

'Of course, I'm the Queen of refunds.'

'I'll remember that come Christmas time – you can stand in the queue and collect my refunds in place of me,' said Marianne.

'I'll do it. I'm yet to buy a party frock for the Christmas party without returning it two days afterwards.'

'Are you serious? Even that shimmery blue one you wore last year?' asked Marianne, shocked by the confession.

'Absolutely, *even* that shimmery blue one. Actually, I nearly kept it but no, I took it back in the end. Never cut your labels out, a stitched tack here and there to keep it from falling out on the night, then return. I'd never wear them again anyway.'

'Penny, I'm shocked! You're always so honest,' said Marianne, trying to change her expression.

'I was given a caution by the police on Friday night.'

Both ladies turned and focused on Esmé, both open mouthed.

'Why?'

Esmé relayed her Friday night adventures.

'And afterwards? Go straight home, did you?' asked Marianne, a sparkle twinkled in her eye.

'Not quite…'

Work in the office failed to begin until the ladies had received a full account of Friday night.

'I've got a feeling about this one,' said Marianne, draining her coffee mug.

'Ergh! No way. Not Asa. He would take the micky out of everything a date would ever do, he knows everything about everything and doesn't mind reminding you at every opportunity. Worse still, you can't relax when you're talking to him because of his tattoo.'

'That sounded very shallow,' said Penny, shaking her head.

'I thought I wasn't judgemental about how people look, but hands up.' Esmé lifted her hands above her head. 'I'm Esmé, and I am totally judgemental when it comes to accompanying a tattooed man into a bar and talking to him face to face. I also can't stop using that bloody word in his presence. Now, go ahead, judge me.'

'He might have his reasons,' said Marianne, having settled at her computer and pressed the 'on' button.

'For sure, and you're bound to feel bad when you find out why?' added Penny, copying Marianne.

'He's defiant in the face of social norms, that'll be why,' announced Esmé, adding '*see* I can't stop myself, can I?'

'How's Jonah?' asked Marianne.

'Ah Jonah, Jonah is a different kettle of fish.'

⋆

During her lunch break, Esmé smiled at an elderly gent, a sulking toddler and the assistant as she queued at the local bakery. None of them returned her gesture, instead they simply stared back at her before turning away.

Armed with paper bags containing warm sausage rolls she hot footed it back to the office. She smiled at the biker carrying his tinted-visor helmet at the cash point. She gave a warm smile to the security guard patrolling the delivery entrance to the warehouse next door to Stylo's. She even smiled at the young man, suited and booted, seated in reception as she walked through.

Nobody smiled back.

'Nobody smiles any more, do you know that?' she announced, arriving back at her desk to unpack her food.

'Sure, they do,' said Penny, as she scoffed salad from a Tupperware box.

'They don't. Today's calendar task is to smile at ten strangers. I've smiled at six and not one has returned the gesture.'

'It's Monday, maybe you'd have better luck if it were a Tuesday?' said Marianne, spreading her *Ryvita* with soft cheese.

'Friday would be a dead cert, everybody smiles on a Friday.'

'I didn't smile much the other Friday, I cried for most of the day,' muttered Esmé, biting into her lunch, and scattering pastry over her lap.

'Show us your smile, then?' asked Marianne. 'I can be number seven.'

'Yeah, maybe it's you.'

Esmé quickly swallowed her mouthful and ran her tongue over her teeth before giving the pair her best smile.

'You're grimacing rather than smiling,' said Marianne. 'You need to include the eyes for a proper smile.'

'I agree. I think those six people think you gurned at them, rather than smiled.'

'Thanks for the confidence boost, ladies,' said Esmé. 'You're supposed to be supportive.'

'We are, now try again but be more natural…'

'Try to portray a warm glow, as if you're delighted to see them,' added Penny, her salad fork suspended and watching.

'Like this?' Esmé leant forward, widened her smile in an ear to ear move and crinkled her eyes.

'Not quite so much, but better… you need practise,' laughed Marianne.

'Practise smiling? No way,' snorted Esmé, eyeing her colleagues suspiciously.

*

The Personal Shopper suite situated on the top floor of the department store was classy beyond belief. Scarlet velvet curtains hung in front of each changing room cubicle which was big enough to house a party of ten plus the shiny silver mobile hanging clothes rails.

Esmé was early for her six o'clock appointment so sat nervously waiting, watching the service and attention devoted to a middle aged man. His male shopper, Gregory, was dressed to impress in a three piece suit, his designer beard clipped to perfection and his startling blue eyes never wandered from his client. Other Personal Shoppers whizzed back and forth collecting, carrying, fetching and returning garments.

It reminded Esmé of the *Pretty Woman* shopping scene.

Esmé smiled as a whirlwind of energy, dressed in a stylish two piece in pale lilac, leapt forward with her hand extended to introduce herself. Her name badge read 'Minnie'.

'Nice to meet you, I'm Minnie and I'll be your Personal Shopper for today's visit.' Her vibe was infectious and her hand shake firm, Esmé instantly felt at ease. 'And can I say, what a lovely smile you have.'

'Thank you, I'll remember to mention it at work tomorrow,' said Esmé.

'Your booking form said "looking for a spring clean" for your wardrobe – all tee-shirts, jeans and boots. Is that correct?' asked Minnie.

'That's me, the comfy but clean look,' said Esmé, shrugging with a continuous smile.

'Am I correct in saying a size twelve?'

Esmé nodded.

'Anything in particular or an occasion that we could focus upon?'

'I'm recently single, so hoped that in the next few weeks I might be enjoying a few days and nights out.'

'Perfect. Describe an outfit that you'd hate to be seen wearing?'

Esmé took a long time to think.

'Struggling, clothes not your thing, hey?'

'Not really. As long as I'm presentable and it doesn't break the bank – I'm happy.'

'Let me get you a coffee, and then I'll nip downstairs and select the first outfit... and there won't be any tee-shirts, jeans or boots. OK?'

Esmé sat back enjoying a large latte with extra sprinkles as Minnie exited the plush suite, and she listened to the dominating voice behind the next curtained section repeatedly saying 'No, not suitable. No, not my style. No, I'm not interested in stripes, or checks, or dots.' Gregory came from behind his client's changing room curtain at record speed, his brow furrowed, dragging behind him a large hanging rail laden with men's clothing.

'Here we are!' called Minnie, speed walking into the suite. 'If you'll come this way please.' Esmé discarded her empty mug and went behind the billowing curtain held open by Minnie.

'Now, trust me, these are going to look stunning on, hangers never do the garment justice,' said Minnie, snapping each hanger from the clothing rail. 'First a straight leg black trouser, with a classy white blouse and a beautiful scarf – just to add a little something special. While I was on the shop floor, I also selected a second outfit, which I hope you'll love... just as much.'

*

'How much did all that cost?' asked Kane, as Esmé proudly strutted her imaginary cat-walk in the morning room.

'Cost is irrelevant, Kane,' she said, striking a pose in the window reflection.

She hardly recognised herself, as she turned and re-traced her steps, hand on hip, chin lifted and pelvis sashaying. Esmé was delighted with her 'new image'.

'You'd better have next month's rent, that's all I can say.'

'Fear not, Bro… all sorted.'

Four outfits, one for going out and three for casual wear, was more clothes than she had intended to purchase but still, she deserved a bit of pampering. Esmé felt good in her new attire. And confident. And feminine.

That wasn't the first time today she'd had that thought. Walking into the city straight from work, she'd tried to smile at everyone. Specific smiles were saved for the young man waiting outside the sports shop. He'd smiled in return which had made her blush. A young woman struggling through a shop doorway with a double buggy pushchair had also returned her smile albeit tinged with motherly frustration. Number nine had received Minnie's welcome compliment. And finally, smile number ten had caused the man who worked the flower stall on

New Street to do a double take and shout good evening to her. It had taken some effort but afterwards she'd felt good, positive and yes, confident.

'Where's Jonah?' asked Esmé, reaching a standstill, hand on hip, holding her model pose.

'Out on a photo shot… missing him, are we?'

'Do you really have to talk like that?'

'What? You asked.'

'When I see him, I'll thank him for suggesting a Personal Shopper – she was worth every penny.'

'Lucky Jonah, he's got all the girls flocking to thank him, whereas me… well, I'm plain Kane.'

Esmé stopped posing.

'Don't say that, you've got your faults Kane, but don't put yourself down.'

'Look who's talking. You're a fine one to talk, you criticise yourself all the time.'

'I know. But not anymore, I'm trying to stay positive, and do you know what, if I thought there was a male version of my single girl's calendar which Carys bought for me, I'd buy you one too.'

'Don't make me laugh.'

'Honestly, I laughed too, but there's a difference about me, a positivity that I haven't felt before.'

'Flashing the cash more like, nothing else, my dear,' laughed Kane, getting up to leave. 'Anyhow,

I'm glad you're pleased, I'll tell Mum you're doing fine.'

'How is Mum?'

'Mmmmh.'

'That bad? I know I need to explain to her but I can't bear to see her upset over my decision.'

'I told her that he cheated, she knows that.'

'Thank you, I promised Dad I wouldn't avoid her but…'

'Esmé, focus on you – Mum's upset but she'll be fine. Don't you worry. She just had high hopes for you both, that was all.'

*

Esmé hung each new item of clothing in her wardrobe. It felt right that a new start in life should have a new selection of attire. She wondered what adventures and memories were in store for her wearing these items.

She looked at the pile of jeans stacked neatly on the wardrobe shelf above her head. Hopefully a lot more fun than I had wearing those.

Esmé quickly undressed and climbed into bed. She looked at the mantelpiece and her single girl's calendar and instantly felt guilty.

Today's smiling task was completed. Yesterday's wardrobe task had been started, though possibly not completed. But *still* Saturday's day ten remained outstanding.

She climbed from her bed to retrieve the calendar. She must complete it, she'd promised Carys. She re-read day ten: List three future dreams.

She found paper and a pencil in her bedside cabinet and wrote down her three dreams for the future without thinking.

To fall in love *again*

To get married

To plan a family

Esmé scribbled the date in the bottom corner 'March 2018' as a memento. She knew she could still have all three dreams, they just wouldn't include Andrew.

A knot of emotion swelled in her throat.

That was the hardest part to accept, for so long his name was attached to every dream but now, he had been erased.

Esmé let the tears fall. She didn't jump up for tissues, or wipe her eyes on her sleeve. She felt guilty for causing her parents upset, she felt unkind for taking Kane's place in the house, she even felt unsure why she was crying when today had been a good day. Esmé simply let the hurt roll down her cheeks and drop from her jawline onto the duvet. She hadn't cried properly in days. Alone in her room, it just felt right.

*

Esmé peered from behind her bedroom curtains into the rear garden. There was definitely someone out there standing to the left of the bench by the rear fence. As her eyes grew accustomed to the light and dark the outline became apparent.

She darted towards the bedroom door and switched off the main light so she could peer without being seen. Kneeling before the drawn curtains she made a peep hole and took another look.

It felt wrong to be spying but surely, it's wrong to stand out back and stare.

She could hear the goings on downstairs. Three adult men gathered their nibbles and beers to watch their Monday night football. Recorded earlier in the evening to be watched in a male huddle, if they could avoid hearing the final score on social media. Their muted banter filtered through the house, the fridge was opened and closed, the cutlery drawer searched for the bottle opener, even the slam of the crockery cupboard door. Russ's excited chatter predicting scores, penalties and sending offs and the stunted reply, possibly from Dam, who'd stayed home.

Esmé knew that Jonah was down there too.

Why did she always feel like the child?

She balked.

Possibly because she was crouched on her bedroom floor peering through a spy hole at an unknown shape in the garden just as she had at the Boogieman aged just five.

The outline moved. Esmé imagined a side step or even a shuffle but what appeared to be shoulders definitely moved. No tree in the garden was that symmetrical. And none of them would tiptoe across the lawn towards the shed.

Burglars after Dam's bike!

Esmé hastily scrambled to her feet, stumbled on the empty boxes scattered around her room and dashed downstairs.

'Dam! Someone's nicking your bike! Quick!'

She burst into the kitchen disrupting the male bonding session of opening Pringles, Monster Munch and popcorn.

Three males, two dressed in Aston Villa away kits, stared in surprise at Esmé's pyjama clad appearance.

Why do men watch football wearing team shirts – surely, they know they haven't been selected for the squad, right?

'Quick, they're breaking in right now?' Esmé flung back the bolts on the rear door and stood aside so the men could charge out.

Nobody moved.

Huh? Cheesy puffs had won the day over superhero status or Dam's precious bike.

'Come on.' Barefoot, Esmé took the lead, the men slowly followed.

Charging along the side of the house and around the corner, she reached the patio area. A crunching of gravel behind her boosted her courage, the men *had* followed. She tiptoed up the steps, her eyes scouring the shed area for the intruder but nothing was visible.

'Great shout, Esmé,' muttered Jonah, standing close behind her. 'I was ready for some pre-match action!'

'I swear, I saw them from my window…'

'You need your eyes testing, love,' called Dam, from the corner of the house. 'And my bike?'

'Relax Dam, the padlock is intact. I can see it from here – the girl's gone crazy. She's seeing things,' called Jonah, returning to the house.

I wasn't. I hadn't.

The three men returned inside. Esmé stayed where she was, poised on the stone garden steps.

Sod them, they can all think what they want but she knew what she saw.

She peered into the darkness, the large trees loomed ahead, the giant conifers and pampas grass waved rhythmically as though taunting her for her error. She'd seen the cut of their shoulders, the dark outline of limbs against the dark background.

'If I wait long enough they'll have to come out of hiding. And when I scream, Jonah and Dam can apologise for not believing me.'

'Talking to yourself again, are you?'

A voice from behind made her jump. Her hands flew to her heart as it lifted to her open mouth.

'Asa! You scared the life out of me!' She turned to face him, a few feet away on the patio.

'Sorry, but you do that a lot, you know.'

'So?'

'Just saying.'

'I'm not going crazy and I don't need my eyes testing. I saw them standing over there,' she pointed towards the back fence. 'I watched them move across the lawn to the shed and that's when I came down for the guys but…'

'They didn't believe you?'

Esmé shrugged and turned away.

In the distance, a child in a neighbouring house began shouting for their mum.

'I believe you.'

He said it so quietly that she nearly missed it.

'I believe I saw someone the other night.' He took a few steps towards her and pointed towards the far corner of the garden. 'A bloke standing over there. He'd gone by the time I got outside, but I was certain.'

'You didn't say?'

'I took it to be your fella.'

'Andrew?'

Asa nodded.

'No.'

'Us men act in funny ways when we don't get what we want… I think he's been loitering outside the front some nights and has now ventured to the back of the house.'

Andrew wouldn't do that.

'He's got my number. He could phone any time he wishes…'

'Us blokes, we're not logical. Easiest thing would be to call, say you're sorry, ask to meet up for a chat… try to impress and talk you round but nah… we don't save face that way, do we?'

'We want to know everything, without having to ask basic questions. I reckon he wanted to know if you're shacking up with one of us four?'

'Be bloody serious.'

'I am being.'

She turned away.

'He's checking out the competition before he makes his move… then he'll know how to play it to win you back, see?'

'I thought us women were supposed to be complicated creatures.'

'Not compared to us men.'

'Do you reckon he's gone?'

'Probably… but he'll be back like a tom cat scenting his patch.'

'Err, that sounds horrible…'

'Depends if you want his attention or not, doesn't it?'

'We're finished… so he can go spray elsewhere for all I care.'

'Hmmm, I believe he already did that!'

'Yes, and I found her earring in our bed!'

'Are you coming in?'

'Nah… I'll stay out here for a moment.'

Asa returned to the house.

Esmé watched as he disappeared from view, then re-appear through the kitchen window on his way to the lounge.

'Esmé!' a whisper came from the direction of the shed.

She jumped.

'Esmé… here!'

'*Andrew?* Esmé peered into the darkness to witness a dark figure emerge from behind the shed. 'What the hell?'

'Shhh… he'll come back otherwise.'

'*Good.* It'll prove how accurate he was.'

'He knows *nothing…* come here?' Andrew beckoned her to join him.

Esmé shook her head.

'I'm busy… if you want to speak to me do it in the correct manner.' Esmé turned on her heels and darted inside.

Esmé stood in the kitchen window staring out, knowing perfectly well that Andrew could see her – just as she had Asa. She grabbed the roller blind chord and gently lowered it, blocking out the garden view.

Chapter Twenty-three

The throbbing at her left temple was intense when she opened her eyes.

Please no, not a migraine.

Esmé scrunched her eyelids closed and pulled the duvet over her head. Her right hand fumbled around on the bedside cabinet feeling for her mobile and within minutes she'd sent a groggy text to Stylo Stationery and the office girls excusing herself from work.

A series of electronic bleeps 'wishing her a swift recovery', pierced the duvet darkness and tweaked at her migraine.

Esmé lay on her back to see if the head pain eased. No. Her right side. Her left side. Nothing helped.

She needed tablets before she was sick.

She visualised the route she needed to take. Down two staircases, through the hallway, morning room, kitchen and into her cupboard above the fridge. The very thought of the effort made her feel sick. Her mouth filled with watery saliva, her stomach rolled and jumped. Throwing the duvet back, she slowly moved, her eyes firmly closed, from the bed towards the bathroom. With every step her head pulsed with pain.

She cried when the bathroom on her landing was locked.

She banged on the door, the noise ricocheting around inside her head.

'What?' came Jonah's voice from within.

'I need…'

'What?' the door was wrenched open and Jonah stood finishing his facial routine by side slapping his face. 'What?'

'Shhhhh please, I've got a migraine… I need…' Her stomach lurched, and she ran past him to kneel before the toilet.

'You going to be long?' he asked, watching the curled figure in fleece pyjamas retch.

Esmé didn't answer but continued to vomit.

'*Great!*'

Esmé heard him bounce down the staircase to his own landing.

'She's chucking up and I'm going to be late now.'

Uncaring bastard. This wasn't his bathroom anyway.

Esmé wiped her mouth with toilet roll, flushed the pan and eased herself onto the hard floor, awaiting the next bout of sickness.

'Are you alright?' asked Dam, his face appearing around the door frame. 'Need anything?'

'My tablets are in my kitchen cupboard… if you wouldn't mind fetching them.'

'Sure.'

Esmé felt a weight lift from her, all she needed was two tablets with a little water and then sleep... if she could rest she'd feel fine, delicate but fine, when she woke for the second time migraine free.

Sitting on the cold bathroom floor, eyes squeezed tight, it felt like hours before Dam returned.

'Here... I brought some water,' he said, nudging her gently.

Esmé opened her eyes a fraction solely to view the offered box, before closing them against the dim light. She popped two tablets from the blister packet and swallowed them with water, her eyes firmly closed the whole time. Dam remained by her side and watched.

'Thank you, Dam.'

'Do you need a hand?' he asked.

'No... I want to stay here for a while and wait for the tablets to kick in, but thank you. I'll be fine.'

'You sure?'

'Honest, I'll be fine now I've had those... but thank you.'

'See you later,' he said, before Esmé sensed he had disappeared.

She dragged the hand towel from the hoop beside the sink and pushed it beneath her head.

Don't think about the germs, the dried saliva or toothpaste resting beneath my head.

Esmé lay down gently and the coolness of the wooden floor was welcome after her bout of sickness sweats.

She lay completely still, reciting nursery rhymes in her head as a means to distract herself from the thumping pain.

*

'Esmé!'

The alarmed shout woke her with a start, and a second later she cringed with the pain.

'What are you doing down there?' asked Asa, crouching beside her.

'What time is it?'

'Just gone four o'clock… what are you doing?'

'I woke up with a migraine, then I was sick. Dam fetched my tablets and then I was sick again and then I just lay here because I couldn't be away from the toilet because the sickness just carried on and—'

'OK, shhhhh,' soothed Asa, feeling her forehead. 'Does your head still hurt?'

Esmé squeezed her eyes tight and nodded.

'Have you taken the tablets?'

'I took two with Dam earlier but I was sick almost immediately so I must have brought them back up but then I didn't know whether to take any more or not, I don't want to overdose by taking more but my head still…'

'OK, I hear you. Have you been here all day?'

Esmé gave a sorry nod, and tears rolled down her cheeks.

'Don't cry, it'll be fine.'

'But I haven't eaten, or drunk anything and now look, I'm shaking and my mobile phone is in my room and…' Esmé dissolved into sobbing gulps.

Asa gently rubbed her back until she calmed down.

'When were you last sick?'

'Ages ago, I think.'

'So, let's get you back into your bed,' he said, raising himself from her side. 'Here, take hold.' He held out his hands for her to clasp.

Esmé gave a feeble pull but remained on the floor.

'As weak as a kitten, hey?'

Esmé felt his arms wrap around and beneath her, then she was lifted from the wooden floor.

'I don't usually do this… so don't start any rumours, right?'

Esmé gave a snort.

'Like that, is it?'

Esmé felt the warmth of his torso through her pyjamas as he carried her. A gentle sway and he navigated them back to her bedroom. He gently placed her onto the bed before throwing the duvet across her.

'I'll be back in a minute.'

'I'm not going anywhere,' muttered Esmé, relieved to be back on a comfy mattress.

Asa dashed out, returning seconds later.

'Here, lift your head.'

Through squinting eyes, she could see he was holding two tablets and a glass of water to her mouth.

'Just sip then swallow the water.'

Esmé followed his instructions before lying back on her pillow.

'Sorry.'

'For what?' asked Asa, standing clear of the bed.

'*This.*'

'This is nothing.'

'Really?'

'Believe me. Hopefully the tablets will start to work. I'll be back in a minute.'

Esmé nodded and began to count in her head, one, two, three, four…

She heard the bedroom door open and close.

Five, six, and seven…

*

'Esmé?' whispered Asa.

Esmé squinted to see him holding a wooden tray.

'Here, try to sit up, even if you keep your eyes closed.'

Esmé blindly shuffled to raise herself into a slumped position as he placed the tray across her lap.

'Some toast and sugared tea.'

'I don't think I can.'

'You need to, just a few mouthfuls will help,' he said, seating himself on the edge of her bed.

Esmé took the offered toast and bit into the doughy delight, the salty butter dancing on her tongue. Eyes shut tight, she focussed on each chew.

Asa sat in silence watching.

'I bet I look a right mess, don't I?'

'Beautiful.'

'In my pyjamas... I haven't even brushed my hair.'

'As I said, beautiful.'

'You're taking the rip. You're *such* an arse, you know that?'

'Yeah, I know.'

Silence descended.

'How long has this lasted?' he asked, breaking the silence.

Esmé explained about getting Jonah out of their bathroom this morning by being sick, how Dam had collected her tablets for her.

'You've been there all day?'

'I slept for some of the day.'

'But even so, that's not on. Did the guys just go out to work?'

'Yes, but it wasn't their fault.'

'Have they checked on you? Phoned you during the day?'

Esmé shook her head, as she finished the first triangle of toast.

The change in his mood was immediate, even with her eyes closed Esmé could imagine his furrowed brow, his glaring eyes and stern expression.

Within fifteen minutes, Esmé couldn't eat any more toast.

'You've done well, at least your body now has carbs and fluids so the shakes should stop soon. I'll be downstairs, call me on my mobile if you need anything, OK?'

Esmé shuffled down to lie flat beneath the duvet.

She felt his seated body lift from the mattress and heard him approach the doorway.

'Asa.'

'Yeah?'

'Thank you.'

'My pleasure, phone if you want any more toast.'

'Maybe you're not *such* an arse after all,' she muttered into the darkness.

'Cheers, thanks for that.'

'My pleasure.'

Esmé listened as he chuckled to himself going down the staircase.

*

After another lengthy sleep, Esmé woke to find her migraine had eased. A quick look confirmed it was gone ten o'clock.

She gently prised herself to a sitting position, then gently again to standing, for fear that any sudden movement would re-ignite the migraine, and made her way towards her single girl's calendar.

She leant against the mantelpiece searching for day thirteen. Once open, she hesitated before opening the foiled chocolate.

What if it triggers another migraine?

But still, she unwrapped the tiny slab and ate it quickly as if speed were of the essence.

Day 13: Re-read your favourite children's book

That was an easy task. She knew exactly where her favourite book was.

Esmé grabbed her mobile and called her brother.

'Kane, are you at home?'

'Yes.'

'Great, will you do me a favour?' she asked, continuing before he could refuse. 'Go into my old bedroom, on the small bookcase you'll find a Ladybird book, a hardback cover. Bring it around here a.s.a.p., would you?'

Esmé crawled into bed and awaited her book delivery. She knew Kane wouldn't argue or fuss, or have trouble finding the treasured possession from her childhood.

*

'Seriously, I'm running book errands?' said Kane, arriving in her bedroom some twenty minutes after her call.

'Thank you, love you, bye!' called Esmé, snatching the hardback book from his hands.

'*That's* it? Well, bye!'

The door closed as Esmé snuggled down with *The Princess and the Pea*. She stared at the illustrated cover, distinct in design and soothingly old fashioned. A large Ladybird bug sat proudly in the corner.

Did all olden day queens wear such magnificent ruffles as day wear or were they purely for special occasions or when helping a young woman to bed? I bet they never found an earring between their sheets.

Esmé disappeared into a world full of colour images, silvery greyhounds and dashingly handsome prince charmings, complete with sheer tights and pageboy haircuts.

She loved reading as a child but it had faded from her life much like the long neglected friends and exercise classes.

Esmé couldn't remember the last book she had read.

As she turned the pages the years rolled back – all she needed was a glass of cold milk and a couple of gingersnap biscuits and she'd be seven years old again.

Chapter Twenty-four

Day 14: Make a gesture of friendship

'Esmé, hello my sweet... your hair looks lovely,' cooed Grace, opening the front door.

'Thank you, I fancied a change from platinum blonde... I've never been a true red head before,' she giggled, stepping inside. 'I've made you a sponge cake, too.' Esmé placed the cake tin in her hands.

'Come in, perfect timing for a cuppa.'

Esmé quickly removed her boots and followed Grace into her warm cosy kitchen.

'Day off work?'

'Sickness really... I had a migraine yesterday so was ill all day, today I feel washed out and delicate so didn't feel ready to return.

Grace busied herself with the kettle and china cups as Esmé settled at the kitchen table.

'You should have called. I'd have nipped round to make sure you were OK.'

'Thank you, the blokes were useless... apart from Asa, who found me lying on the bathroom floor when he returned from work so made me tea and toast and fetched more tablets.'

Grace turned from the sideboard and grinned.

'What?'

'I've got a soft spot for him, that's all,' smiled Grace, adding '… big piece or small?' moving the cake knife back and forth in an arc above the Victoria sponge.

'A decent piece,' laughed Esmé.

The two sipped their tea, ate cake and tried to refrain from succumbing to a second helping.

'I shouldn't really, as I've made another one for us next door… so you should enjoy this one,' explained Esmé.

'Thank you… so tell me, what's with the hair colour?'

Esmé touched it nervously.

'I felt washed out after yesterday's migraine, I'd bought the hair dye a few days ago so with the whole day to myself, I thought why not.'

'Why not indeed, it accentuates your blue eyes,' said Grace.

'Do you think so?'

Grace nodded, adding. 'What do you think Jonah will say?'

'He probably won't *even* notice.'

'He'll notice – believe me.'

Esmé sipped her tea and smiled.

*

'Tadah!' sang Esmé, presenting her Victoria sponge to the men after everyone's evening meal was cleared away.

'I love cake,' said Dam, taking a plate and holding it towards Esmé. 'The one thing my mum never makes is cake.'

'Seriously, I thought your mum was the best cook ever,' said Russ.

'She is but it's more savoury food than baking.'

Esmé divided the sponge into five equal parts as best she could, then dug deep to separate each piece, lifting Dam's onto his plate.

'Look at that!' he exclaimed in excitement.

'Calm down man, it's only bloody cake,' muttered Jonah. 'A Victoria sponge shouldn't have cream, just jam.'

'Are you a bloody expert?' said Esmé, sparkling with energy.

'There's a baker on Paris Road that will sell you one for just a quid,' added Jonah, eyeing her up and down.

'Not one like this they won't,' argued Dam, tucking in as fresh cream squirted at the side of his mouth.

'Such a pig,' muttered Jonah.

'Oy, cut it out!' snapped Russ.

Jonah shrugged. Dam's tongue poked out licking at the escaped cream.

'Jonah?' Esmé indicated to the cake.

'Nope.'

'You don't want a piece?'

'I don't do cake… all that fat and cream sticks to your guts… and your ass.' His eyes travelled downwards over Esmé's figure, before faltering to a smile.

Esmé's smile faded.

Russ looked at her and turned away. Dam focussed on his cake.

'One piece won't hurt,' she said.

'Not for me. You lot can load up on calories but I've got a body to think about and if this bad boy gets fat… I'll be out of a job, so no, thank you,' he said, adding. 'Dam won't say no to another piece, will you Dam-my-man?'

'I'll have his share, if he doesn't want it,' shouted Dam, as Russ began to protest.

'This is exactly what I can't stand – vultures around food… grabbing and snaffling cake which turns you from a mean machine like me into Mr Blobby… like these pair. Enjoy!'

Dam gleefully grabbed his second piece.

'You git, you could have shared,' moaned Russ, staring as Dam tucked into Jonah's share.

'You can have my piece,' offered Esmé, plating up seconds for Russ.

'You sure, don't you want it?'

Not now, after hearing Jonah's opinion.

'Nope, I ate a piece earlier with Grace – I made her one too, you see.'

'Thankee thankee,' said Russ, who gleefully grabbed seconds.

Jonah watched, shaking his head.

'Blobby, blobby, blobby,' he sang, before leaving the table and heading to the lounge.

Esmé looked at the solitary piece of sponge cake.

Would Asa want his piece? Or could she sneak it to her room and eat it away from the table?

'That was gorgeous, Esmé,' said Dam, patting her on the shoulder. 'Ignore Jonah, you bake as much as you want – I'll eat it every time.'

'Thanks Dam.' Esmé mustered a smile, while deciding on the final piece.

'What's with the hair?' asked Dam, pointing to her red locks.

'I just fancied a change, that's all.'

'Kind of suits you, though I prefer…' Russ stalled, licking his fingers.

Esmé looked up and saw the two men exchange a glance.

'What?' she asked swiftly.

Dam shrugged, collected the empty plates and headed for the sink.

'Dam, I'll have a coffee if you're on drinks duty,' said Russ, leaving the table.

Esmé cling filmed the cake plate and placed it in the fridge for Asa.

Jonah was right, another piece would stick straight to her thighs so what was the point. He'd probably notice that straight away yet, he hadn't mentioned her hair.

*

'Hi,' said Esmé looking up from her new book, as Asa entered the lounge.

'What's happened to your hair?'

Esmé smiled and gently teased her fringe.

'I fancied a change.'

'Does it wash out?'

'No, it grows out.'

Asa nodded and left the lounge.

'There's a piece of cake in the fridge for you,' she shouted after him.

'*Thanks.*'

Esmé watched as the door closed gently and returned to her reading.

What was wrong with him? Grumpy ass. One minute he was sweetness and light looking after folk, the next he was all grouchy and moody.

The wall clock said twenty minutes past midnight. She should really go to bed, but the just-one-more-chapter gremlin had kept her up way past her bedtime. She returned to her book and continued to read.

A tiny voice in her head kept interrupting.

'He frowned at my hair', 'what's happened to your hair?', 'does it wash out?'.

Esmé put the book aside, jumped up and took a look in the mirrored glass of the wall unit. She pulled and tweaked at her fringe, turned her head this way and that inspecting what Asa had just viewed.

Looks great to me.

The lounge door opened making her jump.

'Thanks for the cake,' said Asa, dolefully.

'My pleasure.'

He stared at her, glanced at her hair and turned to leave.

'Doesn't it suit me?' she asked.

He shrugged.

'Grace, Russ and even Dam said it suited me and yet you... you frowned when you saw it... and then the does-it-wash-out comment?'

Asa turned back, tilted his head and stared.

'Does it really matter what everyone else said?' he asked, adding. 'But hey, if everyone else said it's *great* – then yay!'

Esmé stared at him.

'That isn't it though, is it?'

Asa sighed, rubbed a hand over his face before looking back at her.

'You don't want to hear it.'

'I do, you can be honest,' she said.

'We both know why you've dyed your hair red... so, I hardly need explain.'

Esmé frowned.

'Don't pretend. I heard him talking to you and Kane in the hallway.'

'Who?'

'Jonah.'

'Jonah?' Esmé's face lit up.

'Are you for real? A mention of his name and the heart flutters, doesn't it?'

Esmé pulled her chin in and she could feel the flush creep up her neck.

'Jonah told you how much he adored red hair, '*irresistible*' and '*What I wouldn't give to spend some time with a red haired lover*' I believe was his exact phrase. Surprise, surprise, you now have red hair.'

'Asa!'

'Forgive me, but I thought you had more sense than that,' he turned to leave the room. 'Thanks for the cake, by the way – it was nice but...'

'What?'

'Did Jonah say he loved Victoria sponge sometime last week?'

'You're such an arse, do you know that?' she spat.

'Sorry to mess up your illusions of love but the guy doesn't even notice you... so go dye your hair any colour of the rainbow.'

Asa left the room, Esmé heard him cross the hallway and start up the staircase.

'Touchy git...' Esmé went back to the armchair, furious. 'You're only jealous because he's better looking than you. You've ruined your looks with your tattooed face.'

Chapter Twenty-five

Day 15: Take up a new interest or hobby

'So, how's tricks?' asked Carys, settling herself opposite Esmé for a cheeky merlot straight after work. 'And, I'm loving the new hair colour.'

'Do you like it? Couldn't be better, though I had two days off due to a migraine, but other than that… I'm coping.'

'Understandable, given the recent upheaval. And Andrew, he's not bugging you too much?'

'Did I text you about him stalking me from our back garden?'

Carys sipped her wine and shook her head.

'*Well…*' Esmé launched into a detailed account, talking Carys through the evening as if she were watching it unfold on a screen. After fifteen minutes, she finally drew breath.

'What a bloody cheek!'

'I know…' agreed Esmé. 'He didn't mind admitting it either, quite happy for me to know what he's up to.'

Carys winced.

'He'll be sucking up to your parents next – so watch out.'

'Kane said he hasn't been anywhere near them. Dad helped me clear the apartment of the majority of my belongings last weekend.'

'And your mum?'

'Well, there's a question. Two weeks on and I can't face her. Kane said she'd been low about the whole thing but I don't want her to try to talk me into going back. Hopefully I'll clear the rest in a week or so, then be able to visit Mum. Her knowing that the apartment is cleared should underline that I'm not going back.'

'It'll confirm there's no going back.'

'The guys are packing for two days away this weekend so I have the place to myself... I was wondering if you fancied going out on Saturday night?'

Carys pulled a face.

'No can do, babe – Jenny's boyfriend's sister's hen do, *sorry.*'

Esmé quickly deciphered the relationship connection like a tongue twister in her head.

'I've got to go, they're lacking in numbers and the bride-to-be has had a hissy fit because the surprise hen do that she requested from the maid of honour has gone tits up, despite the bride-to-be keeping a close eye on proceedings, and now she's had to wade in, trying to rescue her own surprise party from being a shambles.'

'How does that work then?'

'Don't ask. I don't like hen dos at the best of times but even more so when the pressure is on to have the time of my life with my sister's prospective in-laws knowing that I'm being judged by some giggle-o-meter measuring device. The bride-to-be might cattle prod me if I don't consume three times my own weight in Prosecco.'

'Rather you than me. Anyway, I've got loads to do… I could even pamper myself by being home alone.'

'*Sorry.*'

'No, seriously, don't fret. I'll be fine. I'll view it as a mini retreat in my new home.'

'Sounds great, wish I could join you,' said Carys, adding. 'Are they all going?'

'Oh yeah! It'll end in a brawl though, with Jonah and Asa in the same camper van.'

'Dam's going?'

'I know, that was my reaction… I know he's a grown adult but his family sometimes hold him a little too close, if you get what I mean.'

'*Really?*'

Esmé gave a cheeky smile.

'Interested, are we?'

'You know… maybe. He seemed pleasant enough at the pub the other Friday.'

'He's such a sweetheart at home, mmmmm, nice choice.'

'Don't breathe a word, OK?'

'I won't, not unless you want me to…'

'No, I just thought… he was nice, that's all.'

Esmé sipped her wine, trying desperately to control her smile.

Carys simply shook her head.

'Now, I wish I hadn't said anything.'

*

Esmé walked to the bus stop in Moor Street.

Did matchmaking count as an official hobby or not? Was it true matchmaking as Carys had asked about him? It wasn't as if she'd spotted a connection last Friday and then attempted to bring them together. Fail. She'd been far too busy talking to Jonah. Definite fail. But still they might be a good match, if he was interested.

She stood at the bus stop, iPhone in hand browsing the internet for books. She didn't recognise half the names in the current book charts – had it been that long since she'd purchased books for herself?

Rankin, McDermid, Billingham and Patterson – all Andrew's favourites but hey, she'd never be buying those again.

Her heart sank.

When would that feeling disappear?

Some days seemed easy compared to others. Carys was right, the migraine probably was connected to it and her weepy Sunday evening was definitely a delayed reaction to the break-up. Maybe love died little by little, fading each day…

Today was a good day. Work was good, the ladies were on top form with their banter, she had a quick drink with Carys and considered the possibility of matchmaking.

What more could I ask for?

The number 126 bus pulled in and the queue shuffled forward.

Esmé settled herself before continuing her on-line book search.

'Hello?' came a voice from the seat behind.

Esmé turned to view a young man with a beard and dazzling blue eyes gazing at her.

She hesitated a fraction too long in placing him.

'The Personal Shopper suite… I had a particularly awkward guy who was refusing any advice…'

Yes, Gregory.

'Hi… yes, I remember "No checks, no stripes and no dots", wasn't it?'

'Greg. Esmé, isn't it? Though your hair colour has changed…'

She gave a brief nod.

He'd remembered.

'Exactly his phrase. He left long after you did and with only one outfit.'

'I left with four… though it wasn't difficult given the lovely clothes Minnie had selected for me.'

'You were pleased?'

'Oh yeah, delighted. I'd have never selected those for myself, I'm more a tee-shirt and jeans girl.'

'Good to hear…' the pause lengthened, as Greg shifted in his seat. 'Would you mind if I?' He pointed to the vacant seat bedside her.

'Not at all.'

I must be dreaming. The good looking guy usually asks to sit next to the girl in front of me, *but* never me.

Greg swiftly resettled himself, his brown leather man bag riding on his knees.

'OK?'

'Oh yes, sorry, I was in a world of my own… anyway…'

'I've only got two stops, so you'll be free of me in a second.'

'*Really?*

More's the pity. Since when had decent young men started taking an interest in her?

The bus drew to a halt and several passengers left before they continued.

'I was just searching for books… I've just got back into the habit, it's been so long since I read anything. I was just browsing really but… anyway, less of that.' Esmé tucked her phone into her pocket.

Stop waffling, and smile.

'I tried to speak to you as you were leaving but my client wasn't the easiest so… I'm glad I bumped into you.'

Esmé blushed.

'Would you be interested in going for a drink sometime, if you're not busy?'

'I'd love that,' said Esmé, a little too eagerly and loudly for her own liking.

'Excellent, if you could scribble your number on there,' he said, 'I'll give you a call tomorrow night, we could work something out for this weekend perhaps.' He passed her a slip of torn paper from his pocket. Esmé rummaged in her hand bag for a pen and quickly wrote her mobile number on it.

The bus drew to a halt.

'My stop. I'll call you, tomorrow,' he said, before standing and leaving.

That'll fit perfectly with my free weekend.

Esmé watched him make his way off the bus, and gave him a lingering look as the bus pulled away from the kerb and passed him walking. He smiled back.

Could Greg count as a new interest for my daily task?

*

Esmé jumped off the bus one stop earlier than usual. It wasn't her plan to introduce exercise into her daily routine, instead she wanted to nose in a particular shop window: Second Chances.

She pressed her face eagerly to their grimy window to view two objects: a sewing machine and a knitting machine – both old but the sign clearly read: good working order.

Esmé entered, the tiny wind chime danced and immediately an elderly lady appeared through the beaded curtain at the far end of the cramped shop.

'Hi, I wanted a price for the sewing and knitting machines in the window,' called Esmé, as the old lady approached.

Her walking stick made a rhythmical thud and her feet shuffled.

'Back in fashion, they tell me,' she said, threading her way between the collection of vacuum cleaners, battered suitcases and old tea chests.

'In a way, yes, but the modern machines do a lot of the work for you… these older ones are the kind my mother had when I was a girl – I know how to use them.'

The old woman drew the window backdrop aside so Esmé could examine the machines for herself.

They had a few scratches and knocks but looked in fair condition. No worse than her mother's Singer machine that she'd used on Saturday afternoons.

'Could I buy them as a pair for cash?'

'I see, what price had you in mind?'

Esmé smiled.

Cute and very shrewd.

'What's your best price for the two?'

The old lady smiled, her crepe paper skin wrinkled excessively.

'You young ones know it all, hey?' she said. 'I blame those damned tv shows for teaching you how to haggle.'

'I'm a fair person – I'm sure we can come to a fair price.'

'One twenty-five,' said the old dear, as she peered through tiny specs.

'One hundred and fifteen and I'll pay now,' answered Esmé.

'Deal!' The old woman spat on her hand and shook Esmé's firmly.

Deal? That was easy but urgh!

'Excellent.'

'Boy, that was swift bargaining…' muttered the old lady, writing out her receipt.

'I know a fair deal when I see it,' said Esmé, adding, 'now... what time do you close?'

*

'Are you serious?' moaned Russ. 'I've got to carry that to our house?'

'Yep, Dam is going to carry that one,' said Esmé, delighted that both men were at home when she'd phoned. 'Do you hear him complaining?'

'Not yet,' muttered Dam, loading the sewing machine onto his thigh before he heaved it up into his arms. 'This'll be down by my knees by the time we get it to the end of Montague Road.'

Russ hoisted the knitting machine high on his shoulder.

'It'll be like the Strongest Man competition with the stones... remember those, Dam?'

'I'll have had a heart attack before then,' said Dam.

'Are you ready, the lady wants to close for the night?' asked Esmé, eager to get going with her new toys.

'The things we do...' said Dam, as he managed a few steps carrying the machine close to his body and high against his torso.

'Sorry Dam... her offer was just too good to refuse... we should have waited for Kane to get his cash together and we wouldn't be doing tasks like this,' moaned Russ, looking around at Esmé.

'Oy, I made you lot a cake the other night, I've got my uses too,' shouted Esmé, walking steadily behind the pair of waddling men.

Please don't drop them, please don't drop them.

By the time they'd reached the end of the street Dam was asking for a rest, so he placed the sewing machine on top of a nearby wall and stretched his arms.

'Fancy switching for a while?' he asked Russ.

'No chance, I can balance this one perfectly on my shoulder.'

'How about I have a go at balancing it perfectly, and you take this one...? It'll give you a biceps workout as you're carrying it.'

'Jog on, lad, just two streets to go' laughed Russ, walking off and leaving Dam to hoist the sewing machine back into his arms without help.

'And two flights of stairs,' muttered Esmé, walking slowly behind them. 'Unless I'm allowed to use the dining room for sewing.'

Chapter Twenty-six

Day 16: Break an annoying habit

'I haven't got any annoying habits, have I?' asked Esmé, making her morning tea.

Dam gave her a sideways glance as he collected his cereal bowl from the cupboard.

'What's that supposed to mean?'

'Nothing… apart from you have!' he laughed, emptying half a box of cornflakes into his bowl and adding milk.

'Excuse me, what about you?'

'I've got loads… I annoy myself half the time.'

'You spray that poison hairspray every morning so the house is filled with that nausea gas… it sticks to your throat,' offered Asa, drinking his coffee at the table. 'And, you act like a sheep following what others do rather than thinking for yourself.'

'I don't!' Esmé swung round, knocking her mug over and sloshing the contents over the sideboard.

'Plus, you never wipe up after yourself in the kitchen,' continued Asa, smirking.

Esmé grabbed a cloth from the sink and began to wipe.

'And you snore!'

Esmé and Dam stopped what they were doing and stared at Asa.

'No. I. Do. Not!' shrieked Esmé, wide eyed as she choked on her first sip of tea.

'How would you know, mate?' asked Dam, his spoon suspended mid-mouthful.

'She does. You can hear her through the wall, Dam. Every night since she arrived she's snored,' said Asa, giving her a grin.

'That's not true.'

'Morning,' chimed Jonah, entering the room and looking around at the three intense faces. 'Boy, what's happening here?'

'I've just informed Esmé that she snores,' said Asa. 'She's calling me a liar.'

'I didn't.'

'I believe you just did.'

'You kind of did, Esmé.'

'Seriously, *you* snore?' Jonah pulled a face. 'Wow!'

Esmé's face turned scarlet with embarrassment.

'I do not snore, Jonah.'

'How would you know, really?' said Jonah, helping himself to breakfast.

'Precisely!' said Asa, getting up from the table to put his dirty crockery into the dishwasher.

'Jonah, he's pulling my leg, saying it purely to rattle me.'

'Seriously, I'm not.'

'I once slept with a girl who snored, never again…
what an awful night that was,' muttered Jonah,
searching for a teaspoon. 'I kept having to ask her to
turn over onto her side…'

Asa pulled a face at Esmé.

'What's that supposed to mean?' she snapped.

'*Nothing.*'

'What does what mean?' asked Jonah, turning
round to look at the other three.

'Him pulling faces,' said Esmé.

'Boy, have you gone red,' said Jonah.

'Jonah, I nearly got out of bed the other night to
knock on her door purely to ask her to roll over,'
laughed Asa, enjoying her embarrassment.

'You can't sleep on your back if you snore,'
explained Jonah to Esmé.

'I don't sleep on my back! I can do any position.'

A moment of silence occurred. Esmé looked at
each male, their faces flickered with wry smiles.

'See you all, have a nice day!' called Asa, heading
for the door.

'Asa!' Esmé followed him.

'What?' he turned in the doorway.

'I don't snore, so I'd appreciate it if you didn't say
I do, OK?'

'OK. But ya do!'

The kitchen door closed.

'He's doing it to wind me up.'

'It worked then,' said Dam, as he finished his cereal and cleared his dirty bowl away.

'He can probably hear it through the wall,' offered Jonah, slurping his coffee.

Esmé took a deep sigh, brightened her face and turned to Jonah.

'For the last time, I do not snore… that arse is saying it purely to tease me.'

'Oh right, I get it,' muttered Jonah.

'Get what?'

'You and him… you know?' Jonah waved a hand casually between Esmé and the closed kitchen door.

'No! That wasn't it! Heaven forbid!'

Jonah looked up from his breakfast and smirked.

'It's not difficult – you're easy to wind up.'

'On that note, I'm out of here. Seriously, I came down to enjoy a peaceful breakfast and this is what I get…' said Esmé, throwing half of her tea in the sink. She put the dirty mug in the washing up bowl and headed for the door. 'Bye.'

'That's another…' said Dam.

'What?'

'Another annoying habit… never washing your mug up or putting it in the dish washer.'

'Oh, shoot me down!' called Esmé, leaving the morning room.

*

Esmé spent her lunchbreak surfing the internet for sewing patterns for a flared skirt.

'It's all a bit boho, isn't it?' asked Marianne, joining her at the computer screen.

'Maybe, but I was thinking the other night, I loved crafting and making things as a child. Just like reading, I don't know when that actually stopped.'

'Probably when you discovered boys,' added Penny from the other side of the office, chomping her salad.

'Hmmm not really, I made my own prom dress. I think it was when I came here to work.'

'Earning a wage and having spare cash?' said Marianne. 'I remember you used to wear a little burgundy skirt with stitch detail on the waistband – I remember asking you where you bought it?'

'I made that. Wow, where did that go? I *loved* that skirt.'

'I loved it too,' said Marianne.

'I don't remember it, but even so, why go back to making your own clothes. It's so easy to buy.'

'My calendar task was to start a new hobby so I bought myself a sewing machine last night on the way home from work.'

'Are you serious?' asked Penny.

'Two of the guys helped me to get that and a knitting machine back to our house before half six. Second hand, but both in good nick.'

'I bet Stella McCartney's quaking in her boots,' laughed Penny.

'Oy, don't knock it, at least she's trying to do something with her life. What are me and you doing, hey?' said Marianne, over the top of Esmé's head to Penny. 'Seriously, I work here, go home, clean, cook and scrub before I do the same again the next day.'

'Just joking,' muttered Penny into her plastic food box.

'My life has evened out to a whole load of routines... That's it as you get older, life becomes routine...'

'So, change it,' said Penny.

'Aren't you sick of it?' asked Marianne.

'I haven't got a minute to myself to think about it, between Keith, the two kids and the house I don't get time to myself, let alone time to worry about routines. I do what I do in the time available to me so I can do the next job. That's it. My life. Wife and mother.'

Esmé looked up at her colleagues.

'Ladies, really... is this necessary?'

'We're not arguing, lovey. We're just saying how it is once you get to our age, so mind you try and make the most of the things you want to before you turn into us!'

'Or you, Marianne. I'm quite happy with my lot.'

'Mmmm.'

'What's that supposed to mean?' asked Penny.

'Maybe you are, you've got the children to look after but me and our Jimmy – we're comfortable but…' Marianne's voice faded.

Penny and Esmé watched as she returned to her desk.

'I don't know, maybe it's my age… I've been here fifteen years and what am I *actually* doing?'

'You need telling now? I suspected you never understood the training,' laughed Penny, pulling a face.

'No. I know what I'm *doing* but in the grand scheme of things spending eight hours a day organising orders for the warehouse is hardly riveting, is it? I could be doing so much more.'

'Do it then, Marianne. Sounds like you need a calendar like hers,' said Penny, pointing to Esmé. 'A stuck-in-a-rut calendar – which you knocked the other day as pure mumbo jumbo.'

'It's been great so far, if I think back just two weeks – how much has changed because of that calendar.'

'Phuh!' snorted Marianne. 'Things have changed because *you* have been open minded, that's why.'

'Do you think? Yes, Carys's gift has made me face each day and make changes. The house move, my hair, my new wardrobe… all those things came via the calendar.'

'No disrespect, but she'd probably still have been snivelling into her breakfast whilst living at her parent's,' added Penny. 'Which is what we all did after a break-up.'

'Maybe Carys can buy me a married woman's calendar?' laughed Marianne. 'I'll just pretend to be married.'

'Or the mid-life crisis calendar, more like,' said Penny.

'Either way, fingers crossed, Esmé won't be here to clock up fifteen years like we have.'

Esmé peered from behind her computer screen at her colleagues.

This was going to be a *long* afternoon.

*

Esmé offered to make the tea on the hour every hour purely to escape the unusual 'vibe' in the office. She knew they hadn't fallen out but the tension might not clear until a fresh work day began. On her fourth trip with the tea tray, her mobile rang.

An unknown number illuminated the screen.

Leaning against the canteen's sink unit, with a dripping tap as a background irritation, Esmé took the call.

'Hi, is that Esmé?'

'Yes.'

'It's Greg… you gave me your number last night.'

He had rung. He'd actually done what he'd promised.

'How are you?'

'Fine thanks, we're having a busy day here so it'll probably be a late finish… so, I was wondering if you were free tonight for dinner. I'll totally understand if you're busy, it is short notice but I thought I'd ask.'

Esmé stopped herself from answering straight away.

What were the dating rules? Wasn't he supposed to wait? Wasn't she supposed to make out she was ultra-busy and make a date for the weekend?

'That would be fine,' she said, quickly adding. 'I can switch plans, no problem. Busy weekend and all that.'

Should I have said that? If tonight goes well he may want to see me again over the weekend.

'Great stuff. Shall we say eight o'clock? I'll pick you up and we'll catch a bite to eat… Chinese, Italian – what's your favourite?'

'Italian.'

'OK. So, your address is?'

Esmé quickly gave him the details and after a swift goodbye, Greg was gone.

Chapter Twenty-seven

Esmé could hear Toby's tantrum before she opened the front door of number seven. It was the last thing she needed tonight.

The office had remained quiet all afternoon so Esmé had got through it by making plans for her date: quick dash home, bubble bath, hair, make-up and possibly, an outing for the straight legged black trousers, blouse and scarf combo purchased with help from Minnie.

Or would that seem a bit strange given that it would be connected to Greg's work?

Either way, Esmé had little else to wear that was suitable.

'Hi Russ, how are we?' asked Esmé, dropping by the lounge before heading upstairs. Toby was face down, spread-eagled, screaming into the carpet, his arms and legs flailing in all directions. Russ was staring at Cbeebies '*Charlie and Lola*' on the plasma screen.

'Great thanks, you?'

Esmé took in the scene and screwed her face up.

'Is he OK?'

'Oh fine, a fleeting visit given that we're away this weekend, so Rita's picking him up in a couple of hours.'

'*OK.*' Esmé stared down at Toby whose neck was deep red. 'He's gone a bit red.'

'Yeah, he does that – he'll stop in a minute.'

The child continued.

'Catch you later.' Esmé left the lounge and dashed up the staircase, eager to enjoy getting ready for her dinner date.

First things first, she laid out her outfit on the bed, ensuring she'd snipped the tags from each item. Then she selected a playlist from *iTunes* which was guaranteed to lift her mood and grabbed an armful of toiletries with which to pamper herself, before dashing to claim the bathroom before anyone else could.

*

At seven fifty-five, Esmé was preened, primed and peering through the stained glass section of the front door side panelling: waiting.

'You going out?' asked Asa, traipsing barefoot down the staircase in jeans and a tee-shirt.

Esmé nodded.

Now, is not the time to wind me up.

'You look nice. Have a good time,' he said, passing through the hallway into the lounge.

Esmé gave a polite nod.

As the door closed she heard him ask, 'Kane, is there any Friday night football on tv?'

Kane was here again! Did he ever go home?

Esmé returned to her peering.

She had money and credit cards, just in case. A spritz of perfume in her clutch bag. A packet of tissues.

'Earrings!' she'd forgotten to put on her jewellery.

Dashing up the two flights of stairs, she charged into her bedroom and scrambled round the bed to grab her earrings from the mantelpiece. Busily pushing them through each ear lobe as she scurried back down the stairs.

My heart's all of a panic, now.

She stopped mid-way.

Breathe. I'm ready to go. Just breathe.

Placing her hands on the banister she felt the gloopiness before the stickiness registered.

'Urgh!' Esmé stared at the smear of jam decorating her left hand. 'What the hell?'

Toby!

One ear listening for the doorbell, she turned and darted back to the bathroom, her offending hand outstretched.

She quickly washed her hands.

'If I'm late because…' she stopped muttering, having viewed her torso in the large vanity mirror. A blob of red jam sat on the front of her new blouse. 'Can anything else go wrong?'

Grabbing the nearest hand towel, she began dabbing at the jam blob. It smeared. She rubbed the blob some more, creating a large patch of transparent fabric.

Stepping back from the basin and mirror she straightened her blouse.

Could the patch be hidden by her left arm?

Esmé viewed her reflection, only if she held her arm at a strange angle – which would only be until it dried.

Esmé calmed herself enough to leave the bathroom, wiping the banister with a large section of toilet roll in passing, and made her way back to the front door.

It's not his fault. He's a little boy. Little boys have accidents with food, and toilets, and toys.

Patiently waiting beside the front door, Esmé felt back in control, her heart rate had slowed, her breathing was normal. She was going to enjoy tonight. Her first date since the break-up. It wouldn't be easy, but she would make sure she had fun.

The time on her mobile said five past eight.

'Is he late?' asked Russ, leaving the lounge and spying her in the hallway.

'I had an emergency with strawberry jam, so it's a good thing he's not on time.'

'*Really?* At your age?' laughed Russ, as he disappeared from sight.

'Yes *really*. No thanks to your son redecorating the house with his mucky paws each time he visits,' muttered Esmé, checking her mobile for a missed call or text message. Nothing.

Russ came from the kitchen carrying a beaker of milk and re-entered the lounge.

Asa instantly popped his head round the lounge door.

'How long's the time allowed for lateness before the female becomes irate?'

'What?'

'I said, what's the…'

'I heard what you said.'

'Why make me repeat it then?'

'Asa. Please go.'

'Hey, I paid you a compliment earlier… that was me being nice. You look nice, so I said… hey, what's happened to your blouse?'

Esmé changed her stance, hiding the wet blob with her arm.

'Nothing. It'll soon dry.'

'Do you want me to leave you alone?'

'Yes.'

'OK. Enjoy your night.'

Esmé checked her mobile for the time: 8:10 p.m.

He might be stuck in traffic.

8:14 p.m.

He might be lost, not everyone knows this area.

8:26 p.m.

He's not coming, is he?

Esmé remained standing at the front door, waiting.

Now what? Call him? That'll make me look even more desperate than I already am, having waited here for nearly thirty minutes. Call Roberto, see if he's free? No, that would be rude.

Esmé knew that the minute she went back upstairs to change her outfit then either a, Greg would show up full of apologies or b, the guys in the lounge would realise she'd been stood up and Asa would have a field day taking the mickey. She decided it was best to stay silent.

8:33 p.m.

8:36 p.m.

8:39 p.m.

Esmé slid her feet from her shoes, and slipped them onto her outstretched fingers. She opened the front door as wide as she could and paused. She knew she had to be silent and swift if this was going to work.

Esmé slammed the front door with an almighty bang and flew up the staircase as swiftly and silently as her stockinged feet could carry her. She didn't stop until she was safely behind her bedroom door, from where she threw her shoes onto the bed and let the tears fall.

What a fool! To be stood up on a first date by a loser who I'm so desperate to take me out to dinner. Idiot girl. Let that be a lesson to you!

She tiptoed away from the door and began to undress. Would they think she'd gone out with Greg for the evening?

Esmé quickly dashed to the light switch and doused the main light. She knew that the gap under the bedroom door emitted a strip of light onto the landing carpet. She'd use the bedside lamp for tonight, it would save face in the morning.

What time were the boys planning to set off on their weekend jolly?

*

Having changed into her pyjamas, Esmé lay on her bed reading. Her stomach was churning with hunger pains, her throat was so dry she could murder a cup of tea and yet, her pride was bruised to the extent that she couldn't leave her room.

Hours passed.

The creak of footsteps outside her room made her hold her breath for fear of the men knowing her dinner date embarrassment, but she could really do with something to eat.

She spied The Single Girl's Calendar on her mantelpiece, the packaging created long shadows on the wall.

She couldn't. It would ruin the experience each morning, having a task but no chocolate.

She stared at it some more, she couldn't focus on her book knowing the chocolate was calling to her.

Within seconds, Esmé ran her fingers along the length of the lip edge trying to yank the plastic tray inside out. But the flat box would not give up the chocolate.

Bloody manufacturers.

Esmé peered inside the open edge to see that the inner sleeve, moulded to contain the chocolate slabs behind each door, was glued to the front facia of the calendar.

Esmé stopped. It would be a shame to ruin the gift which had helped her so much these last two weeks, so she returned the calendar to the mantelpiece.

I'll leave it. Go without food tonight.

Who was she kidding?

Esmé took the calendar back to the bed and decided upon a plan.

She began to peel open each door, remove the chocolate slab and attempt to close each door without looking at the revealed task.

In ten minutes, the remaining sixteen doors were prised open, the chocolate slabs consumed and a guilt-ridden Esmé stared at her handiwork.

Esmé flicked open a couple of the unread doors to view their tasks. Some of them seemed much easier than others.

Plus, would it make sense if she chose her own order from now on?

She ripped the sixteen future doors from their cardboard hinges and lined them up along her duvet. This was much better, it would give her far more control and she now had some notice and preparation time for certain tasks.

Esmé felt a glow of positivity flow through her veins, she was in control despite what others may say. Greg may have stood her up, but tonight would end on a positive note. She pulled a plastic bag from beneath her bed: a child's rucksack and a tube of brand new tennis balls. She opened the packaging on both items and eagerly filled the rucksack with the yellow balls before she heaved the tiny straps over her shoulders and attempted to lie on her back to road test her bright idea.

Urgh, how uncomfortable was that?

Marvellous, thought Esmé, a suitable solution to my irritating snoring habit. Ha, Asa would never embarrass her again by complaining about her lying on her back!

Rap a tap tap.

'Esmé?'

'Yeah!' she called, before clasping both hands over her mouth.

Too late, I've blown it.

'I've brought you a cuppa,' said Asa, opening the door and bringing her mug into the darkened room. Esmé sat tall pretending she wasn't wearing a child's rucksack or been stood-up.

'Thanks.' Esmé scrutinised his expression, expecting to see a smirk, a grin or the slightest sign of smugness. Nothing, totally blank apart from his tattoo.

'No worries,' he said, heading straight out of her bedroom.

Chapter Twenty-eight

Day 17: Enjoy a relaxation and pampering session

This was bliss.

Esmé had the house to herself for an entire weekend. While the boys were away surfing in Newquay, this girl was planning to play, pamper, play. Esmé wrote her 'Weekend To-do List' as soon as she woke.

Luxury bubble bath – full works, candles and wine Saturday night take away – delivered Bottle of Prosecco – purchased already Luxury manicure and pedicure appointments at Skin 'n' Tonic – booked for 4:30 p.m. Sunday morning breakfast and papers at the corner café Reading book – Marian Keyes First flute lesson from Grace Set up the sewing machine Watch an entire comedy box set

Esmé had planned her perfect weekend. And now, she stood on the doorstep heartily waving goodbye to a camper van containing five males (housemates plus her brother) and enough beer to sink a battleship.

'Bye, enjoy,' she shouted as Russ turned over the engine of their hired vehicle. Jonah replied by signalling the VW hand gesture at the rear window, his tongue protruding down to his chin.

'Just hurry up and go, please,' muttered Esmé, eager to start her own weekend of pleasure. The vehicle shuddered, spluttered and then trundled off along Montague Road amidst a frenzy of waving hands and thumbs up.

Esmé watched the cream and orange paintwork turn the far corner, she stepped gingerly along the pathway wearing only socks on her feet and peered down the street to ensure they had really gone.

The road was empty. Esmé counted to ten in her head, then another ten just to be certain.

The boys had gone.

In utter delight, she ran back inside the house, dashed up the flights of stairs, grabbed her bottle of Prosecco from the carrier bag under her bed and flew back down to pop it inside the fridge door.

She placed the take away delivery menu by the landline phone ready for this evening: king prawn chow mien, prawn toast and a small portion of BBQ ribs had her name written all over them.

Esmé donned her rubber gloves and grabbed the cleaning products from under the sink to scrub her bathroom pristine so she could relax in peace in her bubble tub without the intrusion of male testosterone or floating chest hairs. On finishing the scrub, she placed her candle holders strategically along the window sill, the bath rollover top and the shelves – fetching the match box for use later.

She lined up her bottles of frangipani lotion, bath bombs and moisturiser on the closed toilet seat in order of use. Her face pack and hair bobbles lay by the sink, alongside soft face cloths and her tweezers. Within thirty minutes of the men leaving Esmé was out of breath with her synchronised activity to ready the house for her own indulgence.

And now, coffee.

Esmé shunned her jar of instant, took the cafeteria instead and spooned in her favourite ground coffee while the kettle boiled.

Nothing was going to ruin *this* weekend. Nothing.

She plunged the cafeteria. Within five minutes, she was curled on the couch in the morning room with her creamy coffee and her new Marian Keyes novel. The spring sun streamed through the window, warming her face as she turned to page one. She brought the crisp fresh pages to her nose and inhaled deeply.

Life didn't get much better than this.

Her manicure and pedicure were booked for four thirty but until then she could please herself. Esmé stretched out along the couch and spent an hour with her new book, while the dregs of her coffee cooled on the floor within reach of her right hand.

Esmé dropped her hand over the side of the couch, felt for her coffee mug but snatched it back on feeling something strange.

What the hell was that?

She sat up, put down her book and peered over the cushion edge: nothing. Her coffee mug stood alone.

Esmé returned to her reading, nothing was going to ruin her weekend.

*

Esmé wound her scarf around her lower chin and admired her beautiful nails crafted by Nina, whose healing hands had also worked wonders on Esmé's aching feet. With a renewed spring in her step, she waved goodbye and left the salon. So far, she'd had the nicest of days, all by herself. Asa was so wrong. She was independent, she could plan and could choose to do exactly as she wished.

Earlier she'd nipped next door to Grace for her first flute lesson. It was trickier than she'd expected; who'd have thought blowing across a flute head would be so difficult? But she'd created a squeak, eventually. After the lesson, she'd enjoyed a cosy cuppa with Grace and a giant piece of fruit cake.

Now with sparkling new fingernails and pert fresh feet Esmé felt like dancing along Corporation Street. She hadn't felt like this for such a long time…

Maybe she and Andrew hadn't been right for a while and she just hadn't noticed. Obviously, he had. He'd made alternative arrangements.

This is how life *should* feel, content and at peace with yourself.

*

Her bubble bath was sublime. Her wine chilled to perfection and the candle light allowed the worries of the past few weeks to melt away in a mellow glow. As her perfectly painted fingers and toes gently pickled beneath the bubbles Esmé lay back and enjoyed the silence of the house.

Rarely was the house silent. With Dam's constant coming and going, Jonah with his loud and proud ego, Russ with his daddy duties. And Asa with his crazy shift work that meant he came and went at all hours. It made for a house that revolved with bodies, voices and the front door constantly slamming… it really was a busy household… but…

What was that?

Something caught her eye by the skirting board.

Esmé sat up, leant over the bath's roll top edge and stared around the floor: nothing.

That's twice today.

She slid back beneath her bubbles, eyes fixed on the skirting board for several minutes.

Stop being so stupid, it's your imagination playing games.

Within thirty minutes, Esmé had wrapped the fluffiest of towels around her wet body and secured her hair into a towelling turban. A swirl of hot moist air swarmed around her as she opened the bathroom door, her face smeared with an apricot potion and her digits pickled.

Her flushed skin had calmed down, her wrinkled digits had regained their familiar smoothness and her messy eyebrows had been tamed.

Another hour of relaxation, then she'd order her take-away and pop the cork on the chilled Prosecco.

What a fabulous Saturday.

Esmé patted her reddened brows with aloe vera gel, lay on her bed and covered her eyes with a warm lavender scented towel. Breathing deeply and slowly she attempted to meditate.

The doorbell rang, disturbing her thoughts.

'Go away!' she muttered, from beneath her infused eye mask.

The doorbell sounded again in a continuous ring as if the person's finger was firmly attached to it.

The urgent tone launched Esmé from her meditation and down the flights of stairs in all her glory, but for her fluffy towel clutched to her breast.

'Yes!' she yanked open the front door to find Rita, tear-stained and crumpled, with Toby hanging from her wrist. 'Rita!'

'I need a favour, please, please have him for the night, he's already in his pyjamas, you know his routine and he'll eat whatever you give him – I need someone to babysit. I'll collect him tomorrow. Sorry. Bye.'

On cue, Toby ran inside and headed straight for the lounge as Esmé's mouth impersonated a goldfish.

'Rita! Toby, stop! Rita come back! No! I Can't! Please! Don't!'

Too late. Rita had dropped his overnight bag onto the doorstep and was backing along the pathway, mouthing 'sorry'. Within seconds, she was gone.

'Great! Bang goes my night on the Prosecco!' muttered Esmé, slowly closing the front door. 'Toby, do you want some orange squash?'

Having made the child's drink and settled him with a packet of custard creams, Esmé went back upstairs to comb her hair and get dressed.

She returned within minutes to find the discarded sections of custard cream mashed into the couch cushions and the volume on the plasma tv at maximum, though Toby was delighted with his roomy couch.

'Young man, you have one hour until your official bedtime, so what's it to be? Old fashioned *Bagpuss* or *Thunderbirds?*

'Bagpuss, fat furry cat-puss,' cried Toby, leaping from the sofa to the DVD collection.

'Excellent choice, though I'd have preferred a comedy box set but hey, that's how the cookie crumbles, given the state of our couch.'

*

It took hours to calm Toby after the glass of orange squash. He spent his time well. He raced around the lounge, trampled over the sofa cushions, gambolled around the kitchen, stripped from his pyjamas down to his socks twice and refused to wear his pyjama top on redressing, all before midnight. Eventually, Esmé carried the sleeping child upstairs, his head lolled softly with each step.

My room or his father's?

Esmé nudged open her bedroom door. It felt wiser to have him sleep in her room. Toby murmured as she lowered him onto the crisp white sheet and threw the duvet across his little bare chest.

Could she leave him to sleep alone while she read downstairs? Or did she now have to watch over him while he slept? This is why I'm not a parent, there are too many decisions to make about basic stuff.

Esmé made a quick dash downstairs to fetch her book and was part way up the second staircase when she saw it. Hanging from the corner of the ceiling as blatant as a beacon on the Yorkshire moors. Its eight hairy legs stretched, lifted and lowered alternately while maintaining its fixed position.

'The lying bastard!' screamed Esmé, staring between the tarantula and the safe haven of her bedroom door.

She couldn't stand there all night... but how could any sane person walk beneath that and survive?

Her heart began to palpitate. A hot sweaty gleam appeared on her brow. An itchy rash prickled at her neck and wrists, while her eyes remained fixed on the Chilean Rose.

Esmé began to recite all the names she was going to call Jonah when she next saw him.

Why hadn't she insisted that Russ search his room as proof that Rose had gone? She knew he'd complained about not finding a buyer for her giant tank but still, she'd trusted his word when he said Rose had found a new home.

She couldn't stand there all night. But what could she do? The guys weren't due back until four the next day – that would be sixteen hours frozen in terror while that critter stalked the landing.

Esmé considered waking Toby to ask if he was frightened of spiders? Would he mind dealing with it at the age of three? But she didn't have long to ponder. Suddenly Rose sprang from her corner location and landed on the carpet two feet away from Esmé's bare toes.

'Oh my life! She could go anywhere in sixteen hours and I wouldn't have a clue,' screamed Esmé, as she flew down the staircase.

Would it be wrong to call Andrew?

Esmé was instantly annoyed at her own thought process.

There was only one sure way to secure the house from an attack by Rose. Esmé dived under the staircase cupboard, grabbed the upright Dyson, its extra strong powerful suction guaranteed.

Within seconds she had clunked back upstairs, plugged in the life saving equipment and whipped out the extension hose – with a steady hand she aimed the long nozzle at Giant Rose.

'One flick of the switch and we'll be safe,' shouted Esmé, her killer instinct surfacing. 'I'll be given a bravery award for this.'

She flicked the switch and the powerful motor sprang to life, the spider was a blur of dusky pink lifted from the carpet which bumped along the corrugated tubing towards the powerful swirling jets.

The vacuum made a funny noise, then continued in its usual powerful whir.

Esmé calmly replaced the attachment, and the tubing and then cautiously peered inside the collection tub.

No Rose.

'Where is she?' asked Esmé, getting down on all fours to view the contents of fluff, dust and bent hair grips in the collection canister.

Suddenly Esmé's head filled with questions: what if she's climbed back out of the tubing? What happens if I switch off the vacuum and the drop in suction power frees Giant Rose?

Simple, leave it running.

Esmé lengthened the electric cord and repositioned the vacuum further along the landing, so there was no fear of it falling downstairs and spilling open to free the beast within.

She quickly stepped past the roaring vacuum and scurried into her room. She whipped back the covers to ensure that an army of miniature Roses hadn't infiltrated her room. Toby stirred as the cold air goose pimpled his skin.

She undressed sitting on the side of her bed, feet held high off the floor, her eyes scouring the carpet for any sign of Giant Rose's ghost.

She decided to leave the light on, too – it'd be best for Toby, though it might help her a little as well.

Esmé lay on top of the duvet beside a sleeping Toby and listened to the crazy roar of the vacuum. She wanted to cry and couldn't wait for the men to arrive home tomorrow.

How's that for a day of total pampering and relaxation?

Chapter Twenty-nine

'Esmé! You scared the life out of me. I thought you were upstairs when I heard the vacuum running. Have you had a good weekend?'

Esmé burst out crying at the sight of Asa, who casually strolled into the lounge just after half four on Sunday afternoon.

'Hey, what's wrong?'

'Bubble bath, Toby... pyjama top and Bagpuss,' she sobbed, her hands pointing in all directions as tears ran down her face.

'Slow down, I don't understand...' soothed Asa, his bare skin slightly tanned from the weekend outdoors.

'And Rita, she waved from the gate... and Toby, biscuits... crumbs everywhere... gambolling and tears and then... on the ceiling, she sat there looking at me – he lied, the bastard, he lied.'

'Who lied? Toby?'

'Jonah!' screamed Esmé, her face crumpled again beneath huge tears. 'Giant Rose at the top of the staircase and I... I... I...'

'The tarantula... he *kept* it?' asked Asa, his tone agitated and annoyed. 'So, why's the vacuum running?'

'I zapped her!'

'*No!*'

'Yes,' sobbed Esmé, nodding frantically. 'I daren't turn it off.'

'You seriously think it would survive the Dyson?' asked Asa. 'I'll take a look, shall I?'

'Please… before he comes in to find her, find me… find us.'

Asa calmly entered the hallway as if nothing was wrong; the other guys were carrying their baggage and belongings from the camper.

Esmé came from behind the lounge door, her tear-stained face greeting Russ, Dam and Kane.

'Who's left the vacuum running?' called Jonah, barging through the front door laden with his bags.

Esmé swallowed the urge to confess as Asa's eyes flashed a warning.

'Esmé's trying to run up the leccy bill again?' laughed Asa, as he ran up the staircase to sort out the vacuumed corpse.

'I was just tidying the house ready for your return, home sweet home and all that,' laughed Esmé, her arms waving around, vaguely suggesting polishing and dusting.

'I vote we hire a cleaner then… you're obviously not up to the job even with an entire weekend to complete the task,' laughed Jonah. 'The floor tiles are still dirty.'

'Kane?' Asa nodded towards Esmé, 'Would you?'

'Come on, Esmé, tell me what's happened… non-stop party time, hey?'

Asa darted up the second staircase and switched off the device. Silence descended for the first time since Saturday night.

'Esmé!' Asa leant over the banister, calling downstairs 'You've done an excellent job of eradicating dirt on the landing, full marks!'

*

Esmé held her breath as Jonah went about unpacking.

Any minute now he'd notice the empty tank.

It took two hours, several rounds of coffee and the first half of a film before Jonah poked his head around the lounge door to enquire if Dam was still around?

'He went to see his parents, why?' asked Russ, looking up from the action movie.

'*Nothing.*'

Three sets of eyes turned as Jonah's nonchalant tone died.

'Doesn't sound like nothing to me,' added Asa.

'I've mislaid something, that's all.'

'Anything of value?' asked Russ.

Esmé sank lower in her seat.

Jonah pulled a face.

'Kind of, though maybe not to everyone.'

'I think you have some explaining to do, son,' said Asa.

'I explain to no one, surely *you* know that.'

'The tarantula... you lied!'

'Oh shit!' muttered Jonah. 'Look I can explain... it wasn't fair for you lot to force me to hand her over...'

'Jonah, you git!' snapped Russ, glancing from Asa to Esmé. 'Seriously, all this time? You know she has a phobia.'

'Sod off, Russ, you're one to talk about coming clean.'

Esmé watched as Russ's face froze in terror.

'Fuck you, Jonah. If you'd sink that low, then do it.'

'Alright... thought not,' sniggered Jonah, seeing the fear in his mate's face.

'Enough!' shouted Asa, 'You boys need to calm it or take it outside... I think *she's* had enough this weekend.'

Esmé stared from one male to another trying to glean information.

Jonah left the lounge and slammed the door.

'Esmé, ignore him. It's emotional blackmail to make you suffer,' said Russ.

'I owe you an apology too, Russ. I was a little off with Rita when she collected Toby this morning…'

Asa stared at Russ.

'Well… yes… that may be, but she shouldn't have behaved as she did,' answered Russ, staring at the tv. 'I'll mention it when I see her.'

'But it must have been an emergency otherwise she'd…'

'Anything to add, Asa?' said Russ, his gaze fixed to the plasma screen.

'I think… that Jonah is right. We shouldn't comment on things we know little about.'

'Good dodge there,' laughed Russ.

Esmé sat looking from one to the other as they spoke.

Were they having a laugh at her expense? Or was there something else?

*

Esmé felt awful all Sunday afternoon. At six o'clock, having been reassured by the other guys that Jonah *really* was to blame, she selected today's task from the uncompleted ones lined up on her mantelpiece.

Day 18: Clear your conscience

Esmé eyed the task knowing she'd feel better afterwards. Something good had to come out of an entire weekend.

She found a piece of paper. Dated and addressed it.

7 Montague Road,
Edgbaston,
Birmingham.

Dear Jonah,

I am so sorry for killing your pet spider... I just wanted to say...

Esmé stopped, the words didn't flow. And so far, were also untrue. She wasn't sorry for killing it, she was glad it was liquidized by the powerful vacuum. He shouldn't have lied.

How can I clear my conscience – when I don't feel guilty?

She took a second look at the tasks lined up on the mantelpiece – 'Plan and host a dinner party' caught her eye. She'd need to organise, prepare and shop but that would be better than writing Jonah a fake apology letter. It would say 'sorry' to Jonah and 'thank you' to the others for being so supportive. And, given the recent vibe between the guys – a dinner might improve the house dynamics as the surfing weekend obviously hadn't managed to.

Either way, she could cook a wholesome meal tomorrow night, they hadn't sat down as an entire group since the house meeting.

Esmé pushed Jonah's letter aside. So, how could she clear her conscience? She gulped, as a tsunami of guilt was remembered. She had a niggling conscience about one thing, she could definitely write an apology letter and clear herself of that awful deed. She'd send it to the address she remembered, just a few streets from her parents'. If the family had moved, then so be it, she'd still written and sent the apology.

7 Montague Road,
Edgbaston
Birmingham.
March 2018

Dear Maxine,

You probably don't remember me but I used to sit next to you in year five during Mrs Salter's English class in primary school. It's OK, if you don't remember, I'm not offended. But I remember you. You were the girl that always had fresh plaits, tied with coloured ribbons, every school day. I noticed. I noticed how my plaits were messy and untidy with strands poking out and wispy bits sticking out but yours, yours were perfect.

I'm sorry if I was mean to you. I was jealous. Your plaits signified the time and attention spent each morning combing, dividing and plaiting your beautiful blonde locks. I imagined your mum to be very organised and mumsy doing your hair each morning. Whereas my mum was simply too busy keeping our heads above water to re-plait my hair every day. It was washed on a Sunday, plaited on a Monday, slept in for the Tuesday. Re-plaited on the Wednesday and maintained until Friday. Hence the wispy bits that stuck out. My mum simply wasn't a plaiting hair mum, I know that now.

You're probably wondering why you've received this letter, it isn't a crank one asking for money. But forgiveness. I'd like to ask for forgiveness for the last day of term in year five. You might not remember it, though something tells me you will. We'd been allowed to bring our favourite toy into school. So, amongst the Kerplunks and the Buckaroos was the electronic Simon game you played with your friends. Why did they make us do that? The class was always bored stiff by break time. Anyway, I watched you, stared at you, pretended to be you with your beautiful plaited hair and your Tommy Cooper golf game and… I snapped. I couldn't help myself. It's the closest thing I've come to an out of body experience, seriously. I felt as if I was floating on the ceiling, viewing myself playing Kerplunk by pulling plastic straws from the canister. I watched myself stand, walk to the plastic trays and retrieve a pair of scissors. Not the safety scissors.

I walked sensibly, I didn't run while holding the blade as Mrs Salter had taught us. I don't know what came over me but the touch of your hair was so tempting – that's one thing I do remember. Cutting through the chunk of your plait was like a Queen cutting through a twisted rope to open a shopping centre.

You screamed non-stop for forty minutes. I remember your mother collected you from the head teacher's office, where she'd given you a Spangle sweet to calm you down. I watched from the medical room, as you walked along the drive holding your mum's hand, your plait trailing from the other. I didn't receive a Spangle from the head teacher.

I know that nearly twenty years have passed, but I don't ever remember saying sorry... I'm not sure if you understand but now, as an adult I understand the pain and upset I caused you.

Truly sorry,

Esmé Peel x

'Are you for real?' laughed Russ, handing back the letter to Esmé.

'Yeah, why not?'

'Because she'll think you're a crackpot for sending it. All kids do stuff like that – it's expected.'

'That may be so, but that incident has haunted me and on occasions has kept me awake at night so I feel it is time to say sorry.'

'Is that the worst thing you've ever done?'

'Apart from the spider incident, yes.'

Russ laughed.

'Send it if you want but don't blame me if your name gets bandied around on Facebook with a load of nasty comments. You're asking for trouble sending that.'

'You're supposed to be supportive, helping me to gain independence and closure not laughing your tits off at my letter of apology.'

'Esmé... no one cares what happened when we were kids. You'd be better off not sending it and tell yourself that she forgave you a long time ago.'

'But did she?'

'Probably.'

Probably wasn't good enough at three in the morning when Esmé woke feeling that beautiful twisted plait with its pink satin ribbon between her hands and the scissors cutting through it in chunks.

'The guilt still niggles at me.'

'Fair play to you, are we talking about Maxine West?'

'Yeah, she used to live near our street.'

'While you're at it, could you mention that I'm sorry about the one night stand we had about six years ago after Jonah's birthday party. I really meant to stay all night but I couldn't sleep afterwards. I knew the whole morning routine would be as awkward as hell so thought it best to nip out with the dawn chorus. Cheers!'

Esmé stood open mouthed as Russ dashed along the landing to his own floor.

'Cheers, Esmé. I owe you one.'

Chapter Thirty

Day 19: Host a dinner party

Esmé ran around the dining room table lighting the candles, her heart pounding ten to the dozen. Five starters of warm goat's cheese tartlets were ready and awaiting her guests. She'd checked that each place setting had the necessary cutlery and glasses – she was aiming for a sophisticated evening, with wholesome food and good conversation.

She checked her appearance in the oval mirror above the mantelpiece. She'd grown used to her new hair style and colour, but the asymmetrical fringe still baffled her. Wearing the second of her new outfits suggested by Minnie, a dusky green dress with a chain belt detail, Esmé felt good, confident in fact.

The cooker timer sounded in the kitchen, announcing that the beef bourguignon would be cooked to perfection. Having prepped and set the slow cooker before work, she had arrived home to the delicious aroma. Her mustard mash and green beans would be tasty accompaniments.

Esmé donned the padded oven gloves, removed the heavy dish from the slow cooker and stared at the kitchen clock.

'Where are they?'

She'd given them all strict instructions to be home for seven o'clock and now, at ten minutes past, she had starters cooling on the table and a main course ready cooked but no dinner guests.

'That smells good,' said Russ, entering the kitchen and nosing over her shoulder at the offerings before he rummaged under the sink unit.

'I'm pleased, I did say I'd cook tonight.'

'Oh.' Russ stopped, looked up pretty sheepishly and winced. 'Sorry... didn't I mention I was heading out with a date?'

'No, you bloody well didn't... *Russ*! I did say last night.'

'Look, save me some and I'll warm it in the microwave when I get back.'

'Couldn't she join us for a bite to eat?'

'Nope!'

'*Russ*? This was my way of saying thank you for letting me move in,' adding. 'And for being so supportive about killing *his* pet.'

'Sorry,' he said grabbing a small tin of polish and brushing the front of his shoes. 'First date and all that... you know what it's like?'

'Ha ha, I was stood up on my return to dating so no, I don't know.'

'Until I know her a little better... we won't be doing friends and family introductions.'

'You've let me down big style,' said Esmé, stirring cornflour into the cooking dish to thicken the sauce.

'I'm sure Jonah will scoff the lot and as for your brother... *that* cooking pot wouldn't hold enough for his gut.'

Esmé collected the potatoes from the stove and began draining, ready to mash.

'Where's Dam?'

'His mum's.'

Esmé whipped around, her potato masher held high.

'*Tonight,* of all nights?'

'He always eats at his parents on a Monday.'

'I specifically asked him last night. What's the point of him even having a room – he only sleeps and showers here?'

Russ shrugged, finished polishing his shoes and put the tin away.

'Ask him, not me.'

'Ask me what?' called Jonah, entering the kitchen, dressed in faded jeans and a white shirt. 'How much would a replacement Chilean Rose cost?'

'Not you, *Dam.*' Esmé blushed, her guilt hadn't diminished during the day.

'He's always at his parents', so good luck with *that* task.'

'Exactly. Why pay rent when you can live at your parents and get fed each night?'

'He's pretty spoilt actually... though with six sisters he needs to be,' added Jonah, who pulled up a chair at the kitchen table and sniffed at the cooking pot which Esmé was guarding.

'Six?' queried Esmé, putting the strained green beans into a serving dish.

'I'm pretty sure it's seven,' corrected Russ.

'Either way, I'd move out,' muttered Jonah, adding. 'Are you serving or not?'

'I am when...' her sentence faded. Dam was out, Russ was going out, Kane was nowhere to be seen and Asa must be at work.

What a waste of time and a failed effort to be generous to her housemates.

Esmé stared at Jonah's eager eyes.

Dinner for two, it is then.

'Jonah, are you coming through or not?' she moaned, carrying two steaming dishes from the kitchen towards the dining room.

'Are we eating posh tonight?' asked Jonah, collecting the beef bourguignon pot en-route. 'I'd have dressed for dinner had I known.'

*

The candle light threw elongated shadows around the dining room.

'That was nice,' said Jonah, seated opposite her with his elbows on the table, dipping a hunk of bread into the ceramic cooking pot.

Esmé watched with disdain.

He chomped the dipped bread like a ravenous dog.

'*What?*'

'I was just thinking; my mother is desperate for me to settle down with one of your species. I honestly can't see it happening.'

'Why?'

'Now, there's a question.'

'Go on, shoot.'

'Men seem to be so alien and yet, I've spent a lifetime watching and chasing them only to realise I've learnt very little in the process... does it feel that way for you guys?'

'Nope. I know loads about women... more than they know about themselves.'

'Get lost!'

'Seriously... I do.'

Esmé eyed him. His stature oozed confidence simply by breathing. His golden hair flowed down his back, his clear blue eyes were steady in their gaze. His looks were dangerous when accompanied by candle light and dinner for two.

He's bluffing. This is ego talk.

'Tell me, then.'

'I learnt pretty early on that the majority of women have low self-esteem so I'm always onto a winner when I ladle out the flattery... some believe me straight away – which makes things very easy. Others take a little more convincing, but over a few dates they soon come round to my way of thinking. It might take a date or two but the results are the same.'

'The results?'

'Sex.'

'Jonah!' Esmé screeched.

Jonah dipped another hunk of bread in and chomped.

'It works every time. The older ladies are grateful for attention from any man, the young ones are flattered by *my* attention.'

She shook her head. She knew many intelligent, worldly wise and level headed women.

'You can shake your head as much as you like... I know what works.'

'No, you don't.'

Jonah's eyes widened.

'Oh boy, *I know.*'

'Such as?'

Jonah smiled.

'See, you're interested now.'

Esmé blushed. If he'd known how interested and for how many years he'd have bragged non-stop from the highest building.

'No. I'm not.'

'You want to know all my tricks with the ladies… sadly, I can't tell you.'

'Wow, that's my life ruined!' joked Esmé, hoping to cover her own embarrassment.

Jonah gave a wink.

'Uhhh!'

'If you play your cards right, you might get first-hand knowledge…'

'Er er! No thanks. I've had enough of men to last me an entire lifetime. Seven years ploughed into Andrew, a no-show dinner date and…'

She paused. Should she say? All evening her knowledge of the dining incident with Melissa had felt like a winning royal flush clutched in a sweaty palm. To come clean now and play her hand felt slightly deceitful.

'And what?' he asked, staring at her.

'I dined at the Italian Emporium the other week—'

'Did you?' he sat up and back, his hands stopped dunking bread in the sauce.

Esmé smiled.

'OK, don't judge me.'

'I'm not but do you seriously think that's the right way to live your life?'

Jonah shrugged.

'It was good while it lasted… yeah, we got busted but, hey!'

'Living amongst you lot is enough to put a girl off for life, do you know that?'

'On a date, were you?'

'No, but that's another conversation. Don't you feel bad for the husband?'

'Phuh! Melissa wanted fun. Melissa got her fun.'

'What if it's ended their marriage, don't you care?'

Jonah shook his head.

'I look out for me, and me only.'

'Oh Jonah!'

'I do.'

Esmé was irked by his attitude.

'Was that why you lied about the tarantula?'

'Of course, she was mine. I wanted to keep her.'

'But you lie and you cheat your way through life.'

'So?'

'One day that might happen to you… your wife might—' her words are interrupted by his bellowed laugh.

'Moi? Get married? Never!'

'Why not?'

'Because my life's good, too good to throw away on one chick.'

'But the single guy, shagging machine lifestyle can't last forever, can it?'

'*Why not?*

'*Because.*'

'Because what?'

'Jonah… one day you'll settle down.'

'No, I won't.'

Esmé smiled.

Such naïvety.

'Because that's what we all do. That's life. Even me, when I've got over Andrew and this whole disaster of a situation… I'll move on. I'll meet someone and in time will repeat the process and settle down.' She paused and picked at her finger nails. 'I can't imagine how I'll ever trust again given how I've been treated but in time, it *will* happen.'

'Why would I want that?'

'For love, family, security, children…'

'Children? You've got a high opinion of me, haven't you?'

'You want children, right?'

'Sod off… have you heard the noise that one kid makes when he comes for a visit? Why would anyone choose to have that twenty-four seven?'

'Jonah!'

'Seriously. I eat, drink, shag and sleep – what more do I need in life?'

Esmé watched as he continued to justify the ingredients of his life.

No responsibilities, no worries, no concerns.

'I'll never get ulcers, nor stress, nor cancer,' he laughed. 'Unlike the rest of you.'

'But you'll never find happiness either,' she added.

'Because after years of traipsing after one guy you're the picture of happiness, aren't you? And he's repaid you by knobbing someone behind your back!'

'I'd have you know that being loved by someone is the most beautiful thing in the world. Knowing that they care for you and you care for them, through the good times and the bad. I love being in love and being part of a couple and yes, you're right, right now, it hurts like crazy. I've felt sick nearly every day since we broke up. There are days I've felt very alone. But… but one day, when I least expect it, the man of my dreams will arrive and I'll take my time getting to know him, watch and learn what kind of character he has. And yeah, next time, I'll be cautious, hold back on giving too much of myself too soon and then, after we've discussed everything and know each other's hopes, dreams and opinions, inside and out, I *will* fall in love. Guaranteed. Because as much as Andrew has hurt me, and boy, he has definitely hurt me, Jonah. I *know* how to love and I know that love is the only thing that I am sure I want in my future,'

Esmé's voice cracked and her eyes welled with tears as she spoke so candidly.

Jonah stared, dumbstruck.

'*Really?*

'Yeah, really!'

'And he's going to feel exactly the same and will sweep you off your tiny little feet and you'll live happily ever after!'

'Yep.'

'*Wrong!*

'No!'

'Yeah! You'll fall in love and do all this...' he waved his hands in a large circle above his head, '... all this again and again and again. Esmé, you live in a dream world... wake up and smell the coffee. Human nature hasn't designed us to be faithful.'

'Mine has!'

Jonah burst out laughing.

'Faithful? Pull the other one, love. You name me the faithful one among us?'

Esmé stood up sharply, her body trembled with a passion for defending her future hopes and happy ever afters.

'Sit down.'

'No. How dare you claim that the likes of me and people like me should live like the likes of you!'

'When did I say that?'

'You're making out that we should all live like you... well, if that's your idea of a happy future, good luck, but I know what I want and one day, I *will* have it.'

'Along with a big white wedding, two point four children and tiny white picket fence...' laughed Jonah.

'Hey hey, what's with all the shouting?' asked Asa, as he entered the dining room and saw them sparring over the dirty plates. 'I thought a pleasant dinner party was booked for this evening.'

'Asa, a man after my own heart...' sang Jonah gleefully.

'Not quite. I think I've got standards compared to you!'

'Thank you, Asa,' cooed Esmé, as she collected the dirty plates to help calm herself down.

'Tell her, why would any man want to give up being single... tell her... we have the time of our bloody lives and yet these women, all they want to do is get us to settle down.'

Asa stared from Jonah to Esmé and back again.

'Are you pair always this passionate over dinner?'

'No!' snapped Esmé, as she covered the dish of left over vegetables for Russ's supper.

'Tell her man, she needs to hear it from someone she'll listen to – otherwise she'll waste her life chasing dreams.'

Asa pulled a face before speaking.

'What's it to you what *she* thinks… if you're doing what makes you happy, carry on. Maybe she wants something so different you can't even imagine it.'

'Bollocks!'

'Is it?'

'*Yes,* and you know it…'

'Do I now?'

Jonah paused, sat back and smirked. 'Asa, you do this every time. You talk the talk and yet when it comes to walking the walk you bail… every single time. You forget I know you of old before all this namby-pamby crap kicked in. Your job has gone to your head, mate… you were far better without all this touchy-feely business.'

'Jonah, you're talking out of your arse,' replied Asa, as he turned to Esmé. 'I came in to apologise for being late, I've just finished my shift but hey, it looks like dinner is over.'

'No problem. There's a trifle chilling in the fridge, if you want some.'

'Look at you playing house,' muttered Jonah.

'I have no idea where the conversation has gone or is going, so I'll clear the table and be done,' said Esmé, collecting the plates as the two men stared at each other above her head.

'Great dinner party, Esmé. We must do it again sometime, not!' called Jonah, as she carried a pile of dirty plates from the dining room. 'And it doesn't make up for you having killed my tarantula.'

⋆

'Are you OK?' asked Asa, as he spooned trifle from the chilled dish.

Esmé stood at the sink washing up by hand. The bubbles made her think of her teenage life at home, washing up after a Sunday roast.

'Me? Fine.'

'He doesn't get it… so don't take it to heart.'

'Point proven.'

Asa returned the trifle dish to the fridge and leant against the work surface to eat.

Silence descended.

'He doesn't get a lot of things. Doesn't get love, or commitment. Just shagging and drama and…'

'Life isn't just a tick list of things, you know?' said Asa.

'I do know.'

'I heard you rattle off a list like a grocery order… it shouldn't be like that either.'

'So now, I'm wrong?' Esmé stopped and turned, her soapy hands suspended. 'What's so wrong in wanting to be married by the age of thirty? Have children at an age young enough to keep up but mature enough to nurture?'

'No, but—'

'It sounded like I was being criticised then.'

'Hey, why snap at me? I'm trying to help you to understand what he's on about. You make out life is like picking cans off a supermarket shelf, once you've got the full collection you'll be happy. Tell me, how many people do you know who have everything you listed in life and yet, aren't happy? Happiness isn't guaranteed.'

'OK, not everyone's happy... but they're married and they have children, they're loved.'

'Are they? I wonder how many feel trapped, used or deceived. They bought into your tick list of life just as you have and now find they wish they hadn't been so narrow minded.'

'Is it *so* wrong to want what I want?'

'No, but don't expect everyone to want that, or be happy with it. Jonah won't have failed in life if he hasn't got a wife, two kids and a Volvo estate. But view it as you do, and you'd say he could never be happy without those things. We're all different.'

'Are we? Shucks, *that* never crossed my mind,' said Esmé, who huffed and puffed in frustration.

'I give in... see you.' Asa headed for the door, spooning his trifle as he walked. 'Cheers for this.'

'Asa?'

'What?' Asa turned back, holding the door open with his foot.

'What is it blokes want then?'

'To be happy with their lot… whatever *their* lot might be.'

Esmé stared at him as he ate his trifle. She took in his clean, strong and healthy, dark brooding features which were attractive from a certain angle. Together, that was the word for Asa. Whatever the rest of the world were searching for in life, Asa already had it sorted.

'And do you know what your lot is?'

'Yeah, and it's not a standard shopping list.'

He let the door close after his final word.

'Great! So, now my so-called 'shopping list' of life is being attacked,' muttered Esmé, cleaning the cutlery. 'Why do I have to be the one that starts again from scratch?'

Chapter Thirty-one

Day 20: Take time to listen to others

'Is that my Prosecco you're drinking?' asked Esmé, as Jonah sat on the garden wall drinking as dusk began to fall.

He pulled a face.

'It could be…' He finished his glass, and held it out to her.

'*Cheers*. I was saving that.'

'What, for another disastrous weekend home alone?'

'No, another dinner party actually.'

'Please don't invite me next time.'

'Oh, bugger you, Jonah. They're my bubbles, I'll fetch my own glass.'

Esmé darted inside the house and returned with another glass.

'Say when,' he asked, whilst pouring.

'When it gets to the bloody top, that's when,' laughed Esmé.

Esmé watched as the bubbles eased up the glass, and Jonah stopped pouring at exactly the right moment, without spilling a drop.

'So, what's new with you?' she asked, settling onto the wall beside him.

'Apart from not owning a pet spider anymore?'

'Yep, apart from that old news.'

'I'm waiting to hear about an industry award and possible interest in a photo shoot I did a week last Wednesday, the guy wants to fly me out to Milan for a specific shot... I'll be gutted if he doesn't phone.'

'That's not like you, you're usually more upbeat about work.'

'Not this one, I really want this one. This guy could make or break my career... a set of shots by him will help me no end.'

Esmé sipped her bubbles. He was being very polite and sociable given last night's heated conversation *and* his dead spider.

'When's the latest you'll hear by?'

'Yesterday.'

'Oh.'

'Exactly. Oh!'

'Never mind, you'll find something else. And the industry award?'

'Hmmm, not sure but it had better be mine this year.'

'Look at me, so much has changed in a few weeks.'

'Yeah, three weeks ago you were happy in a relationship, and now look.'

'You git!'

'Sorry, but it's true – don't kid yourself that happiness is around the next corner.'

'Maybe, but you don't have to rub my nose in it… anyway, at least I've made progress, I could have put up with his cheating and been walked all over for the rest of my days.'

Jonah looked at her square on, his brow furrowed.

'Is that how you see it?'

'I do… yes,' said Esmé. 'It sets a precedent in a relationship… I'd have opened myself up to a life of misery with a cheating partner.'

Jonah refilled his glass and pondered.

'And you've never cheated?'

'No!'

'Blimey!'

Esmé watched as he sipped his drink. His skin was flawless, his eyes a dazzling blue and his chiselled jawline was Hollywood perfect.

'You'd never trust the likes of me then?'

'No Jonah, as much as I'd love to… you aired your views last night.'

'I might have been pulling your leg.'

'I doubt it.'

His hand reached for hers. His thumb gently massaged the back of her hand in a circular motion.

Esmé watched as her skin gently rippled under his touch and a tingle ran along her spine.

So gentle, so soft and yet, she looked into his face, so very dangerous.

'What?'

'Things could have been so different for us, couldn't they?' he whispered.

'If you'd asked me out as a teenager, but you didn't.'

'You were my friend's kid sister.'

'I'm *still* your friend's kid sister…' Esmé retrieved her hand from his.

'You've grown, back then it would have been seen as me taking advantage of a puppy love crush.'

And that would have bothered you?

Esmé shook her head.

'Seriously… it was a no goer,' he whispered, moving closer.

'But now?'

'Now's different…'

Esmé stood, collected her glass from the wall and drank the remaining Prosecco.

'Now I'm older and wiser – which doesn't bode well for either of us, Jonah.'

'Are you going back inside? I thought we'd finish this together.' he said, indicating the nearly empty bottle.

She'd had enough of trying to listen to other folk for one day, whatever her calendar said. Penny hadn't appreciated the time she spent listening to her rant about her small children and their avoidance of bedtime routines. Esmé thought a problem shared might be halved, but sadly not. Likewise, Marianne only seemed narked by Esmé's effort to listen to others and eyed her suspiciously. So, Esmé had planned to return to her bedroom for a quiet night and a read.

'Enjoy!' Esmé began to move towards the house.

'Really? You'd bail out when we were finally having a pleasant chat?'

Esmé turned as he spoke.

'Jonah, Jonah, Jonah, you and I both know that we had the chance of a lovely chat last night and look where that ended. Asa called you an ungrateful git and I wanted to throttle you for your arrogance and lack of morals. Do you really wish to repeat the scenario?'

'We'll make a deal. I won't disrespect the 'M' word if you don't lecture me about the 'C' word – agreed?'

Esmé pulled a face. What the hell was he talking about?

'Marriage.'

'Yeah and…'

'Cheating!'

'Oh that! My guess is we'll have nothing to talk about then,' she laughed.

'Phuh! Ye of little faith!' Jonah patted the topping stone next to him. 'Please? Anyway, I have a favour to ask and if you go inside… you'll never hear what it is.'

She could do without this. An early night would be far wiser.

'Try me,' she said.

'Will you be my plus one to attend the industry awards a week on Thursday?'

'Wow! I am honoured!'

'Who else would I ask?'

'Jonah, don't flatter yourself…'

'Come on, say yes to being my plus one then we'll fetch a fresh bottle of vino and put the world to rights.'

*

'Emma, do you mind?' murmured Jonah, as he pulled the duvet from her side to cover his bare shoulder.

Esmé let go of the fabric, her warm section flowed sideways onto his body as a cold section slid across to cover her.

Great!

Esmé lay in the dark staring at his ceiling, outside the car headlights made abstract patterns as they came around the corner and parked.

How had she allowed this to happen? she thought.

One minute she was heading for an early night and a good read, the next he'd uncorked another bottle and they'd moved from the wall to make themselves comfortable on the wooden bench. 'Beautiful Esmé, come and have a drink with me,' he'd pleaded for the final time, as she'd stood deliberating and eventually threw caution to the wind, just as he knew she would. She'd fallen for his swagger. She was tonight's Melissa.

How had they ended up lying in the hammock? Squashed together like satsumas in a net? Hadn't she suggested that they top and tail – that would have been far safer. She wouldn't have ended up *here* if they'd topped and tailed!

They'd lain beneath the stars and rocked gently. The wine flowed, the conversation had followed and then, he'd kissed her. Not a boisterous, hard, intimidating kind of kiss that she'd imagined Jonah would give. But tender. Soft. Slow. Enticing. Which brought her guard tumbling down.

Esmé looked at the sleeping figure, his blond hair spread out on his pillow, the outline of his back and shoulders defined and muscular against the darkness. He was far stronger than Esmé had expected. Andrew would never have managed to carry her up the stairs in such a tangled embrace.

Had she fancied a nightcap or had she simply wanted his undivided attention? Just as Melissa had.

They were both consenting adults, they'd used protection. Everyone else did as they wished. Why shouldn't she have her fun, Andrew had? It wasn't as if she'd made a habit of such behaviour in her younger days but she was older, wiser and if she chose to spend the night with Jonah, it was her choice.

They'd felt good together. They'd enjoyed each other's sexual prowess and neither one had made false promises.

Meaningless sex. Wasn't that the excuse Andrew had used? Or had she made that up to feel better? Either way, Jonah clearly felt the same when he repeatedly called her Emma during his climax. Seriously, could the man not remember who he was bedding!

Esmé turned sideways and watched his bare back rising and falling as he slept. There was no denying he was incredibly attractive and sexually pleasing but… how awkward would this now be? She'd slept with a housemate, her brother's friend of twenty years.

She watched as another set of car headlights travelled across the ceiling and down the opposite wall. Should she try to sleep? Had he asked her to stay till morning or suggested she leave?

Jonah hadn't said anything much, apart from a general non-specific 'thanks'. As if she'd handed him a fresh coffee, a paper serviette, *or* sex on a plate.

Esmé lifted the duvet and climbed from his bed. Sleep wasn't an option, especially if she snored, as Asa claimed.

She felt around the floor searching for items of her clothing, which he'd eagerly removed and flung aside during their initial passion. Esmé counted the items: underwear, socks, tee-shirt, leggings. She made no effort to be quiet, she couldn't care less if he stirred or not.

Should she dress here or nip to the safety of her own room? Nipping upstairs would save an explanation if Jonah woke up. Though, he probably wouldn't care less either.

Esmé bundled her clothes into her arms and stared at the sleeping figure.

A beauty with a beast inside, she thought.

Esmé eased the door open and left.

The house was silent. The landing's frosted window permitted a small amount of light by which to see. Esmé swiftly nipped to the end of the landing and crept up the second flight of stairs, her bedroom door was slightly ajar, as she'd left it.

If Jonah could brush it under the carpet, then so could she. Two consenting adults, what's there to be ashamed of?

She reached the top stair, crossed the small area in front of the bathroom door and was a stride away from her own bedroom door when something moved further along the darkened landing. Esmé stopped in her tracks, her clothes clutched to her torso covering her nakedness.

From the shadows, Asa rose from the carpeted floor, straightened his back and stood squarely in the darkness. His face was hidden in shadow but his body was framed by a snippet of light from the landing window. Esmé's breath snagged in her throat.

'Goodnight,' he said, before slowly entering his bedroom and softly closing the door.

Esmé stood naked and frozen to the spot, horror etched upon her features.

Had Asa been waiting there all night? *Shit.*

She quickly entered her bedroom, closed the door, dumped her clothes into the laundry basket and flopped onto her bed.

Now what? Explain? Apologise?

She lay staring into the darkness, listening for any movement from Asa's room. There was nothing.

So, he knows we had sex, so what? Wasn't that what he'd taunted her about only the other day? If anything, he was probably congratulating himself on being *so* right. So accurate in predicting other people's behaviour.

Esmé sat up and stared at the dividing wall between their bedrooms. Was he lying the other side of the wall, annoyed with her? What was he trying to prove by waiting for her return?

Instantly, she felt dirty. She needed to shower. She wanted the hot water to scour and cleanse her skin. Sleep was the last thing she wanted.

Tomorrow, I might be able to ignore Jonah and pretend nothing happened, pretend our night was just a run of the mill thing, *but* Asa... Asa was a different story.

Chapter Thirty-two

Day 21: Take a risk

The next morning proved to be unsettling for Esmé. She hadn't slept well after her late night shower and so she left early and walked to work in a world of her own.

A bright blue sky was a beautiful back drop for the cherry blossom that was beginning to bud upon bare branches.

Her thoughts were a mish-mash dominated by Jonah and Asa. Two alpha males, who wouldn't admit it but were alike in many ways and yet, poles apart in other respects. Jonah with his Adonis body, his perfect complexion and sweet talking contrasted with the harsh exterior of Asa, his painted face, his abrupt manner and direct talk. One beauty, one beast. And yet, one beast and one beauty where their personality, morals and treatment of others was concerned. Had Jonah cared for her during her migraine? Had Asa belittled Crystal at the breakfast table? Images of the graveyard flowers, Dancing Queen and the Chilean Rose interpreted her internal monologue. Men – what complicated creatures?

How funny; two men sharing the same house and yet, reflections of each other: social, anti-social, arrogant, humble, accommodating, defiant, sexy, intimidating, Adonis, gargoyle…

Esmé blushed.

Now, that was unfair, how shallow am I?

Esmé corrected herself.

If viewed from his right profile Asa was as handsome as Jonah. He chose to destroy it with that ridiculous tattoo.

*

'Penny, have you ever thought of jacking it all in?' asked Esmé at lunchtime.

'Every day!' laughed her colleague, biting into a crisp bread cracker. 'Especially on days such as these when I need a broom up my arse to multitask and please the boss. Are you getting itchy feet then?'

'Well I have been here for nine years, six months and three weeks to be precise – I've worked it out,' said Esmé.

'I'd up and be off to pastures new, if I were your age,' said Marianne.

'But would you?'

'You never know what's out there till you go,' added Marianne.

'Spill the beans,' ordered Penny, as she scooted across the office on her chair.

'There's nothing to tell… just thoughts really.'

Esmé spent the next ten minutes explaining about her and Jonah's conversation from Monday night's dinner.

'Are you sure you just didn't take it as a rejection?' asked Marianne.

'No. It wasn't about me and him. I was offended that a guy should openly tell me that my dreams are farcical. As if I was in the wrong for saying what I want. Then Asa added his bit…'

'And?'

'He tried to smooth the waters but he reckoned that those that have what I want aren't really happy anyway, so why chase an impossible dream?'

Marianne and Penny nodded slowly.

'What?' Esmé stared at them.

'Well… he has a point,' said Penny, eventually, looking at Marianne.

'Slightly brutal but possibly correct…' she muttered.

'Are you pair stuck for words? Because I was relying on you both to put me back on track… and yet…' Esmé looked at each of them. They looked worried. 'What?'

'I don't know about you, Penny… but there are times when I wish I could go back and…'

Penny nodded.

'Yeah, oh yeah… I was too eager to rush into a relationship, then marriage and then the babies came along and then one morning you wake up and think…'

Both gave huge sighs.

'I don't believe I'm hearing this… are you saying Asa's right?'

Marianne shrugged.

'I didn't know that my Jimmy didn't want to be married… if I'd have known from the beginning,' muttered Marianne, as she gave another sigh. 'I'm happy. I love him. But his parents divorced, he saw a failed marriage and knew it wasn't for him.'

'But it's what you want?'

'It is, but I'd prefer to be with Jimmy as we are than married to someone else,' said Marianne. 'I have to accept his reasons.'

'I have everything on your list and still…'

Eyes turned towards Penny as she stalled and stopped.

'*Penny?*' whispered Marianne.

'I do wonder if it's all it's cracked up to be, that's all?' laughed Penny. 'Esmé… he might be right. Maybe there's more to life than doing everything by the book that everyone else lives by. Be your own person, be…'

Esmé sat speechless. Was she conforming to set ideas about life or had she made her own mind up about the future she wanted? Esmé had never heard either woman be so frank. And yet, three weeks ago they'd been encouraging her towards an engagement. Surely, life had to follow a plan?

'But I want to commit. I want a marriage. I want a family. I know what I want... I can't have it because it wasn't what Andrew wanted... and now, he's wrecked it.'

'So, make your own list based purely on you, leave others out of it, do as you wish... what is it they say? Go with the flow!'

Esmé blushed.

'It's funny you should mention that...' said Esmé, collecting the empty coffee mugs 'But first, I need to make a round of drinks because you're *never* going to believe what happened last night.'

*

The afternoon dragged as Esmé's mind reran her antics from last night and her colleagues' conversation from this morning in a never ending loop.

'You look deep in thought,' said Marianne, during afternoon break. 'I'll give you a penny for them.'

'You pair have unnerved me a little by agreeing with Asa… what is life about if really we're just supposed to please ourselves and only do stuff that makes us happy?'

'Exactly,' laughed Marianne. 'You can say that about everything.'

'You're just in a strange place at the minute, everything that anyone says is going to unsettle you given your circumstances. I remember when I felt like you,' said Penny.

'And what did you do?'

'I foolishly slept with a whole load of unsuitable men, then hated myself afterwards, but hey,' she laughed.

'Penny – be serious.'

'She *is* being serious,' laughed Marianne.

'And bloody honest… don't do that unless you want a stint of mind blowing sex.'

'Weren't you listening earlier, she's been there and done that last night!' laughed Marianne.

Esmé blushed, as a flash back of Jonah appeared in her head.

'I don't intend to make a habit of it,' muttered Esmé.

'Never say never,' added Marianne. 'Anyway, I travelled during my previous break-up. Went on safari, hiked across deserts and swam in tropical waters.'

'That was tame compared to my phase, ladies,' said Penny, scoffing bourbon biscuits.

'You need to do what makes you happy… take a risk,' said Marianne. 'You never know – it could be the making of you.'

*

Esmé sat back in her chair and looked around at her surroundings.

This three foot by four foot space, with its tea stained desk and the cardboard in-tray, which she always meant to replace, had been hers for nine years.

She watched the two females in front of her, their fingers dancing around keyboards as if their lives depended on it, their backs bent, Marianne's half eaten lunch propped on the side for later, and Penny's cardboard crispbread crumbs sprinkled down her front.

In five years' time, would she be sat here staring across the same office having filed a pile of invoices?

The answer rang loud and clear in her head. Asa was right, she had to start making plans for herself rather than tagging along in life.

Esmé tidied her desk, unpinned her Johnny Depp postcard from the side of her computer screen and collected her handbag from the bottom drawer of the filing cabinet. She knew the other two had stopped and were watching her every move.

'Esmé?' asked Penny, getting up from her chair. 'What's happening?'

'It's now or never, ladies,' said Esmé, her heart banging like a drum. 'And I have a funny feeling… it's now.'

Esmé gently kissed each colleague on the cheek, received a tight squeeze from Penny, and a bear hug from Marianne.

'It's not goodbye, because we'll catch up for coffee but I'm going to go and see Steely Stylo… and let's see what happens. I've got savings, I've got some qualifications and who knows what else.'

Esmé collected her coat and left their office. Within a minute, she was rapping on Steely Stylo's office door and ten minutes later she'd hailed a taxi.

Esmé gave a huge sigh.

This single girl's calendar was proving to be dangerous and yet, life changing, thought Esmé, as the taxi cut though the afternoon traffic towards home. What would her parents say?

Esmé was making plans and it felt good. She rummaged in her handbag for her mobile.

'Hello?'

'It's Esmé, you'll never guess what I've done.'

Chapter Thirty-three

Day 22: Donate to a worthy cause

'I walked straight in and told her, I quit!' explained Esmé, chomping cereal, while Russ buttered his morning toast. 'She didn't argue, or try to talk me out of it.'

'So, you haven't got to work notice... that's it, gone?'

'Pretty much. She was furious that I'd accepted a pay rise only last week and now wanted out.'

'And the plan is?' he asked, impressed by her gall.

Esmé shrugged.

'What, nothing?'

'Absolutely diddly squat,' laughed Esmé, as she sipped her breakfast tea.

'Are you serious?'

'I have no idea what I'll do, but I know I'll do something. I just have to find it.'

'Couldn't you have done that while working your notice?'

'Feel the fear and do it anyway!'

'You're a braver man than me,' laughed Russ.

'I'll think of something... by the end of today I'll have something.'

'Listen at you, confident or what?'

'You can mock.'

Within thirty minutes, Esmé sat alone at the breakfast table, the ticking wall clock the only sound in the house.

Esmé scribbled a list of her skills.

> Good listener
> Good organiser
> Good friend
> Decent cook
> Decent baker
> Decent at sewing
> Slightly decent house companion

Esmé scrubbed out the last line, knowing she probably wasn't a decent companion. She stared at her skills list – if they were to support her she'd have hardly enough to purchase her moisturiser let alone stretch to rent and food.

Esmé set about linking each skill to possible employment: counsellor, PA, Samaritans, kitchen work and homemade cupcakes.

Three coffees later, and without specific qualifications to support her employment ideas, Esmé's list looked very different.

> ~~Good listener~~

~~Good organiser~~
~~Good friend~~
~~Decent cook~~
~~Decent baker~~
Decent at sewing
~~Slightly decent house companion~~

She could purchase wool, colourful felt, some quality fabrics and lace trimmings and make a whole host of pretty craft things, maybe sell them at local fêtes or open her own eBay shop.

Esmé grabbed her coat, it seemed a morning at the local indoor market was necessary.

The day was looking brighter already. And, if I see a charity collection person on the street I may well give them all my change as a donation.

*

The freshness of spring filled the air, as Esmé stepped from the bus with her craft purchases wrapped in brown paper. The tree lined roads felt sleepy and bare branches overhead spread into a canopy with a smattering of tight buds upon every branch.

She hadn't seen Jonah since Tuesday night, so couldn't gauge how things would be. Had he chosen to avoid her or had her change of routine made it easier, less embarrassing, for both of them? Esmé hadn't seen Asa either but that still hadn't stopped her from calling him in the taxi after she resigned. She was so eager to share her decision, she'd forgotten about the night before. How ridiculous, that he would be the one she phoned first.

As she neared the parkland on the corner, she could see the stubby little bodies wrapped in duffel coats charging around by the roundabout or silhouetted at the summit of the climbing frame. A smattering of adults, mainly seated alone but a few in pairs, watched from a line of wooden benches.

I bet their hearts are in their mouths while they climb…

Esmé focussed her attention on the couple on the second bench, clearly holding hands. Russ and Rita.

Esmé smiled.

How lovely if they could get back together… and brave of them to give it another go. The upheaval of being apart with the joint responsibility of Toby couldn't be easy. No wonder he was coy about his date the other night, thought Esmé. He obviously didn't want to chance his luck and ruin what they had.

She nimbly left for fear of being spotted and arrived home with a warm fuzzy feeling deep in her stomach.

The first chance I get, I'll offer to baby sit Toby for an evening.

*

'Dam's just told me,' said Asa, bursting into the dining room as Esmé worked. He expression was alight, his persona energised and his tone excited.

'What?'

'That you went to blood donors in the city centre... well done!'

Esmé beamed.

'I hadn't planned on it. I'd never done it before but I nipped to the market area and walked past the billboard advertising for new donors and I thought why not?'

'I'm proud of you, good girl.'

Esmé blushed.

'Have you taken the white plaster off yet?'

'This?' Esmé proudly lifted her sleeve to show the adhesive dressing and tape, like a badge of honour, across her inner elbow.

'I suggest you remove it in the shower, unless you want some stinging and no hairs left on your forearm.'

It was the last thing she'd expected him to say. She wasn't about to admit that she'd felt faint and had eaten her body weight in biscuits afterwards whilst dunking them in strong cups of sweet tea.

'You did use condoms when you... spent the night with Jonah?'

Esmé frowned. What a question to ask!

'Excuse me.'

'If you didn't then you should have told them… you run the risk of…'

'Asa! Please!'

She was quite aware of Jonah's habits. The Crystal scenario on her first morning at Montague Road wasn't erased from her memory. She'd been honest, they'd used condoms and she'd filled out the appropriate forms with the truth and the best of intentions.

But yeah, she'd donated. Someone, somewhere, would be helped in the next two weeks thanks to a tacky cardboard calendar which sat battered and torn on her mantelpiece upstairs.

'What is that?' asked Asa, picking the remnant of navy knitting from the floor in the dining room.

'Don't start, I've just about had enough!' said Esmé, her temper frayed, looking up from her knitting machine. 'That is all I have to show for eight hours of work!'

'It's a beanie hat,' exclaimed Asa, forcing it onto his head.

'And it's crap! Look how badly I've sewn the edges?' Esmé was conscious of the last time they'd spoken.

'Maybe, but it's still a beanie… are you chucking it?'

'Yes, along with the other two I made over there.'

'Where?'

'Under the table and by the fire place… I threw them there when I got annoyed earlier.'

'*Nice.*' Asa scrambled on all fours and retrieved the items. 'Can I have them?'

'You can do as you like, I've had enough.'

'Self-employed work not suiting you then?'

'Ha bloody ha.'

'Seriously, I'm interested and asking…'

'First thing tomorrow, I might phone up Steely Stylo and beg for my job back,' Esmé held her hand to her ear like an imaginary phone. 'Hello Mrs Stylo, can I come and kiss your ass? We'll pretend that this never happened. Yes, of course I'll take yesterday as a day's holiday in lieu of wages… of course, I will admit I'm a total failure and yes, of course I shall never ask for another pay rise for as long as I live. Yes, I will work every holiday shift, fetch and carry like a skivvy if you agree to take me back. Good day!'

'That good, hey?'

'Unless you have serious advice for a delusional woman, I suggest you leave.'

'None, except for putting an advert in the newsagent's window to advertise your sewing skills.'

'Thanks…' said Esmé, unsure why he was now lingering. 'Please go!'

'As long as I can have these?'

'Yes, take, take, take… just go!'

Esmé watched the door close.

*

'Goodnight.' Asa peeled himself from the sofa and headed for the lounge door.

'Are you not going to talk about last night?' she asked meekly, looking up from her reading book.

He turned, having partly opened the door.

'I wasn't going to, except for the safe sex and blood donation issue mentioned earlier. I'd imagined it wasn't any of my business and that you and Jonah would do as you please… which I believe you did.'

'Asa?'

'What?'

'You sat on the landing… waiting for me to come back to my room.'

'Did I?' He stared at her.

'You know you did, don't play games, please.'

'Was I there for five minutes or two hours?'

'I don't know but either way you felt the need to do that… why?'

He shrugged.

'I arrived home from work and noticed your bedroom door was slightly ajar – I instantly knew where you were.' He paused. 'Maybe I was concerned for your welfare.'

Esmé shifted in her seat.

'I'm a big girl… who can look after herself.'

'Can you?'

'Yes.'

'Or are you trying your hardest to swing with the cool kids to destroy the meek and geek persona?' His manner was so different from earlier.

'You are such an arse!'

Asa's nostrils flared. He left the doorway, dropped to his haunches at the side of her armchair. His face level with hers, his flesh highlighted by the dimmed table lamp.

'So, tell me, has he spoken to you since?'

Esmé looked away, unnerved by his tone.

'Has he?'

Esmé shook her head.

'Precisely. In my book, he should have. Even it was a simply a bit of fun… for you both.'

'Maybe I don't want him to.'

Asa grimaced.

'Don't try that one on me, I know what I know.'

'Not always.'

'I know how it feels to have others not respond as you'd wish.' Esmé watched his eyes flicker about her features before he continued. 'But I'll be true to myself, don't ever lie to yourself, Esmé – there's really no point.'

Asa stood tall, looking down on her.

'So, make it happen,' she said. 'You can have what you want, if you're honest.'

'That easy, is it? I think not.'

'But Asa, you said…'

'Goodnight Esmé.'

In two strides, he was gone and the lounge door softly closed.

*

Esmé finished her day of beanie making just after ten o'clock. It felt like a wasted day. She'd have earned a day's wage at Stylos simply sat at a desk shuffling invoices.

An early night to bed, tomorrow's a new day.

As she drew the curtain, Esmé peered at the dusky shadows along the garden's back fence.

Someone was out there.

She doused the light and drew the curtain aside. It was difficult to make out but every now and then a movement of a hand or a head caught the glimmer of light.

Esmé counted the housemates. Dam was at his parent's, Asa was now at work – so, Jonah or Russ? Or Andrew, *again*. As her eyes grew accustomed to the darkness, she could see the outline of two people, facing each other.

I could stay here and spy or investigate.

Within seconds, Esmé was edging along the side of the house, sneaking around the corner to linger amongst the shadows by the shed. Above was a beautiful crescent moon in a clear night sky.

'I wouldn't know… it's not like we talk about you,' said a female voice.

'But surely you can guess,' said a male, adding. 'I don't want to ruin this.'

Russ? No. Jonah? Nothing like him. Dam? Yes, it was Dam!

'We won't but I can't keep pretending… it's not fair. I hate keeping secrets from her. She's had a hard time and earlier today she asked to meet up – I felt awful refusing her,' replied the female.

Carys!

Esmé thought back to the Ivy Bush – they'd talked all night. Carys had asked her questions when they went to the cinema with Jenny. How could she spoil their secret? But how could Carys not have told her before now?

Then the sound of kissing could be heard. Esmé looked around the side of the shed to glimpse Carys and Dam entwined.

She was pleased for them both, delighted that they'd found each other. Carys deserved some happiness after her recent dating disasters. Spying on them felt icky.

Esmé left and returned to the house.

*

Esmé couldn't wait any longer, she called Carys just after eleven o'clock.

'Hi Carys, thought I'd let you know how I was getting on.' Esmé kept talking, hoping that Carys wouldn't make an excuse to end the call.

'I was just thinking about you,' said Carys. 'So, how are tricks with The Single Girl's Calendar?'

It took Esmé ten minutes to summarise the past few days and the related tasks but she was too eager to hear of Carys's news, if she was willing to share.

'And you?'

'Nothing much happening at this end,' said Carys.

'Did you give Dam any more thought after we chatted?' Esmé held her breath. Would she spill the beans?

'Not really, he seemed really nice but it could be complicated with his family and his time… I'm not sure I'm ready for something so complicated.'

Why wouldn't she share?

'Esmé, are you still there?' asked Carys.

'Yes, of course, just tired, that's all. Are you free any time this coming weekend?'

'Hmmm not sure, I'll have to get back to you.'

Esmé mouth fell open. She had a good mind to blurt out the details and let Carys know she was fooling no one. But why spoil their fun if she and

Dam weren't ready to tell? Esmé couldn't focus on the conversation so within minutes had said her goodbyes and hung up.

'So far today, that's two secrets I've discovered purely by accident… let's hope they come in threes like bad luck,' she muttered.

Before she turned in for the night, Esmé straightened the line of daily tasks upon her mantelpiece purely to check there wasn't a 'keep a secret' task. Sadly, there wasn't but if there had been she'd have completed it with flying colours.

Chapter Thirty-four

Day 23: Embrace your inner spirit

'Can you sew anything?'

Esmé glanced up from her sewing to view Asa through the machine's archway. A swathe of mauve curtain material draped from the machine across the table onto the floor. Esmé's current project was to accessorise her bedroom with lined drapes, complete with pencil pleat gathers and a button detail, to hone her skills.

'Practically anything, why?'

'Just asking?' he said, pulling out the chair opposite and settling down with his coffee. 'Carry on, don't let me stop you.'

'If you're about to ask me to fix the hems of your jeans or a torn shirt – please don't... I have enough to do without being the house seamstress.'

Asa drank his coffee and carried on watching.

Esmé continued her work and the swathe of fabric glided beneath the machine's foot, her fingers swiftly feeding and securing the gathers into place.

'Would you be interested in making more beanies?'

Esmé took her foot off the pedal.

'What?'

'The beanie hats… would you consider making more?'

'They were on the knitting machine not this one…'

'I know… are you?'

'Who for?'

'*Friends.*'

Esmé stared as he sipped his coffee.

'How much?' she asked.

'Cheap… but as many as you can make.'

Esmé sat back. She'd bought the cones of wool already so it saved them from being wasted.

'When by?'

'No deadline, whenever you have the time.'

'Did you sell the other beanies then?'

'Nah, I gave them away… but the guys loved them. That's why I'm asking.'

'OK.'

Asa stood up, returned the chair beneath the table and snatched up his coffee mug.

'Cheers for that, I know you're busy.'

Esmé nodded as her foot brought the sewing machine back to life, Asa stood and stared.

'Anything else?' she asked, silencing the machine.

'Are you doing anything tonight?' he asked, passing the mug from hand to hand.

'I've just taken an order for beanie hats *sooooo.*'

'Ahhh, as I suspected, yet another thrilling Friday night in store for poor Cinders.'

'Shut up,' said Esmé, and repositioned her fabric.

'I've got a spare ticket for a concert, if you fancy going.'

'Tonight?'

'Yeah tonight, at The Symphony Hall.'

Was he for real?

'OK, if you're happy for me to tag along.'

'Quick then, go grab a coat… we need to leave.'

'But I need to change if I'm going out…' said Esmé, checking the time.

'No, you don't! You look fine, come on.'

Esmé unplugged the sewing machine as Asa grabbed her coat from the peg and threw it in her direction.

'Oy, you're so bossy! Why the race?'

'Because we're cutting it fine.'

*

A taxi dash into the city and a quick march across Broad Street found Esmé short of breath and suffering shin splints by the time they entered The Symphony Hall.

'Asa, slow down, will you?'

'Come on, keep up.'

Asa tugged at her coat sleeve to guide her through the warmth of the large foyer crammed with the hustle of bodies and noise.

'Who are we seeing?'

'Beth Hart.'

'Who?' Esmé pulled a face.

'Beth Hart… oh, you don't know who Beth Hart is?'

'Hey, I don't hang in your circles!'

'My circles? Bloody hell, Esmé… you need an education in life.'

'Oy, there's nothing wrong with my life, thank you.'

'And your plans for Friday night were… sewing. Yeah right, there's nothing wrong with your life!'

Esmé snatched her coat sleeve from his clutches.

Asa flipped a look in her direction, sensing her annoyance.

Esmé stood watching him from the foyer.

Asa was halfway up the first flight of stairs before he turned to see if she was following.

'If you want to go home, just say… I'll get you a taxi and you can head back to your sewing, otherwise change your face and come on, or we'll miss the support act.'

Esmé watched the crowd jostle past him as he beckoned to her over the chrome banister.

'Please?' His voice had softened. 'I think you'll love it.'

What the hell was wrong with this guy? He dashed from place to place, came up with crazy plans off the top of his head and thought it was normal behaviour. His energy was totally wrong, all up and down with nothing in between.

'Honestly, she's got a great voice…'

Esmé trotted up the staircase to Asa where his smile greeted her.

*

Esmé had never been inside the auditorium before, so allowed Asa to lead the way, directing her to their seats. He looked out of place in the refined interior of carved plaster and pillars.

'Wow, this is beautiful!' Esmé peered over the balcony at row upon row of identical seats filling the vast area below.

'Stunning design… have you never been here before?'

Esmé shook her head.

'See what I mean? Raised in Birmingham and yet…' he spread his hands wide indicating surprise, as he settled in his seat. She suppressed her irritation, the guy was right. So why did it irk her so much?

The stage set was in darkness, apart from a single strobe light which illuminated instruments and a microphone, Esmé couldn't sit back but looked around drinking in every detail like a child at the zoo.

Several times she caught Asa watching her.

'What?'

'You. You're looking around almost frantically – frightened of missing anything.'

'Look, I've only ever walked past here and nipped in once to use the ladies' toilets... sit back and be grateful that I didn't go home.'

Within minutes the support act of Colin James and his guitar partner entered and the stage came alive. The duo played their guitars like she'd never seen them played before. She couldn't help but tap her feet and bounced her hand against her thigh. Beside her, Asa sat with a smile on his face.

In no time the support act were finished and the audience clapped nosily before the lights came back up. Asa stood up from his seat.

'Drink?'

Trying to cover her surprise, Esmé agreed.

'I'll buy,' she said.

'Nope, tonight was my shout so I'll get these. What do you want? Wine?'

'A lager perhaps.'

'Which one?'

Esmé shrugged, she couldn't name a lager if her life depended upon it.

Asa laughed.

'Fair enough, I'll get you the same as me.'

Once he'd gone Esmé named all the lager adverts she knew: Kronenbourg, Budweiser, Heineken, Carlsberg, Fosters. The adverts filled her head until he returned.

'Here.' The plastic pint pot was thrust before her.

'What is it?'

'Heineken… that's all they had.'

'Cheers.'

Asa sat down, drink in hand and shook his head.

'What are you laughing at?'

'A minute ago you hadn't a clue, but suddenly you're an expert wanting to know what you're drinking… you make me laugh!'

'I can name lagers.'

'Go on then.'

Esmé listed all she could.

Asa sipped his lager nodding as she named each one.

'Very good, but it doesn't count if you had to sit here in the dark recalling every one yet couldn't answer my question when I asked what you wanted.'

'I… I… never.'

'It's OK not to know stuff you know.'

'So why do I always feel stupid when you ask me a question and I don't know the answer?'

'Who knows? I don't.'

Esmé turned away and sipped her lager.

'Does it taste like Heineken?' he asked, leaning over to her.

'Hmmm yeah, thanks.'

'No prob... but it shouldn't... it's Carlsberg!'

Esmé spluttered and stared at him.

'Argggh!' she retorted, as Asa settled back in his seat, his shoulders shuddering as he sniggered.

Suddenly, the auditorium lights faded to black as a powerful female voice cut through the darkness.

The hairs on the back of her neck stood up. Esmé and Asa simultaneously leant forward to view the stage but the direction of the voice played with their senses. A single spot light picked out the singer as she walked along the side aisles amongst the crowd, who jumped up, thrilled to be so close to her. Esmé watched as the barefoot singer, in a slinky tight fitting dress, slowly made her way through the crowd, hugging, dancing and receiving kisses as she sang. On reaching the front, she climbed up and took centre stage.

Esmé was mesmerised.

Throughout the performance, Esmé's emotions were snagged by previously unheard lyrics and jolted by the power of the one woman's voice that flew around the rafters and lighting frames of the auditorium.

'And now, my final song… I don't always play it because I try to let you think I'm strong but I'm not, so take it easy on me,' announced the singer, as her fingers drifted along the piano keys and a tsunami of tears spilt down Esmé's cheeks.

The song quickly finished, the audience rose to their feet to applaud and cheer. Esmé was making a mental note to download the back catalogue songs when the auditorium lights came on faster than she was expecting, revealing her tears.

'Here,' said Asa, handing her a tissue.

Esmé didn't try to cover up her reaction. She dabbed at her face as he watched.

'You OK?'

'Yep,' she said. 'Just being a soppy mare.'

'You're allowed,' he laughed.

'Her lyrics hit home, don't they?'

The audience flowed towards the exits quicker than kids at the school gates. Esmé and Asa sat in silence and watched them leave.

'Sorry, I'm such a sop to have cried but…'

Asa's eyes skittered about her face as she tried, but failed, to explain.

'Sorry, but I'm not really sure what I'm trying to say… one minute I was listening, enjoying the music and then the next minute a wave of emotion took over.'

'That happens sometimes… and usually when you least expect it.'

'Not to me, it doesn't.'

Esmé checked her mascara in her vanity mirror and took a deep breath.

'I feel such a fool.'

'Well don't.'

Esmé pulled a face.

'Seriously, something made a connection and you reacted emotionally – that's what happens in here,' he swept a hand casually towards the now empty seats of the auditorium. 'That's what music does, it evokes sensations and feelings that we're not conscious of having and delivers them to the surface to be aired… in public, but hey, what's it matter? The main thing is that you enjoyed it.' He fell silent.

'Do you do this often?'

'Sporadically really… I don't visit for months, then other times I'll come back to see the same performance, if I can get a ticket, on consecutive nights.'

Esmé laughed.

'Now, I know you're pulling my leg!' she laughed, clutching her sides. 'Why see the same thing over and over?'

Asa slowly shook his head.

'I'm not joking. If I enjoyed something, why not return to enjoy it again? There are days when I come here filled with resentment and hatred for the world outside and yet, within a few hours I'm OK... my emotions are calmed and something inside re-ignites... it might sound a bit wampy to you but it's true.'

Esmé stifled a laugh; his expression intensified, his eyes were lost to another world.

'Tonight, I was in a perfectly good mood, loving life, finding my feet after Andrew and getting on with life...'

'But are you, *really?*

'Yes!'

Asa gave a shrug.

'I'm not so sure. I think your 'finding your feet' seems more like a knee jerk reaction, almost manufactured... like your shopping list of life.' He stood and collected their empty plastic glasses. 'Come on, there's something I want to show you.'

Esmé picked up her handbag and followed.

When would others accept what she said? She'd taken control of her life in recent weeks and her actions were far from knee jerk reactions – they were her decisions following Andrew's confession. And, how many more times was Asa going to belittle her aspirations with the shopping list label?

Asa took her hand and dragged her down the spiral staircase in a hurried manner, Esmé stumbled in his wake, grateful that he was one step ahead in case she fell. The crowds had cleared, leaving just a few people milling around the foyer.

What was the rush?

On reaching the final step, Asa stopped abruptly and stared across the foyer.

'What?'

'Just look,' he said pointing towards a large painting in reds, oranges and yellows hanging on the far wall. 'I love this painting. Come and take a look.'

He tugged at her hand with an urgency. Esmé read the plaque beneath 'The Mahler Experience' by Norman Perryman, 23rd November 1993.

'Look at it, then,' whispered Asa, lifting her chin. 'What do you see?'

Esmé stood before the giant painting, her eyes flitting around the image of a tiny figure dressed in black, arms raised, emitting a swirl of white energy like a spirit or soul lifting towards the audience.

'That's where we've just been, isn't it?' Esmé pointed behind them towards the auditorium.

Asa nodded.

'Does it depict what happens when music…' Esmé's voice broke, she struggled to continue her sentence. '… conductor… and musicians… the spirit swirls around the audience?'

Esmé lowered her head wiping a tear on her sleeve.

'It's a specific Mahler concert actually but basically yes, touching the audience with a passion or energy to create a moment of pleasure... hey, don't cry.' His arm wrapped around her shoulders and pulled her close to his side.

'*That's* what's just happened to me. I couldn't help myself, it just came out and now *this* has made me cry too.'

'The painting has its own story... much like the music.'

'Did you know I'd react like this?'

Asa gave a nod.

'How?'

Asa released her shoulder and shuffled from side to side, his mouth opened several times to speak but then he thought the better of it.

'Can I be honest?'

Esmé nodded, her eyes flitting between the painting and Asa's features.

'You seem so erratic... the things you do, your behaviour... one minute hosting dinner parties, the next jacking your job in and then...' Asa paused. 'Your night with Jonah. I get it, it's a basic human instinct when there's a physical attraction but *seriously*, what are you doing?'

Esmé continued to stare.

'And your behaviour's normal?'

Asa shrugged.

'I embrace life and the experiences available to me... whereas you seem so pent up, chasing specific things which you hope will make you happy – it's back to that shopping list of life again...'

'Can you stop calling it that please?'

'OK, I'll stop. But I think you need to start being you, being more open to the world around you and definitely, more honest.'

'I am honest.'

'You're not. You pretend or cover up your flaws, uncertainties and insecurities all the time. Look at earlier with the lager – you hadn't a clue but instead of admitting that, you had to save face and pretend you're an expert. You're not, you're just someone who thinks you ought to know everything. And life's not like that, life's better when you are honest and embrace what's in front of you... I think tonight's outburst of tears is because you allowed yourself to be honest about the music – it struck a chord with you and you allowed it to – you let it.'

'I'm not dishonest.'

'Your life is a huge game of pretend... and it shouldn't be. Just be you.'

Esmé dried her eyes on her sleeve.

'Sorry, if it sounds brutal... but life's too short to pretend!'

Esmé stared at the painting, her gaze followed the swirl of yellow, and white haze twirled around the upper galleries of the auditorium.

'Do you think it touches us all in the same way?'

'I doubt it. Subconsciously we probably interpret what we see and hear into what we need and understand at the time.'

'Wow! You're deep.'

'At times,' laughed Asa. 'Come on, let's go and find a bar and get a drink.'

Esmé lingered in front of the painting for a moment longer, before she followed Asa out onto Broad Street.

*

It was just after one in the morning when Asa led Esmé from the bar, insisting that they go home after she'd downed several Jack D doubles and offered to sing to the entire bar whilst standing on the pool table.

'You just don't want me to have fun, do you?' she shouted as he led her along Broad Street towards Centenary Square.

'Believe me, I want everyone to have fun but you are heading for disaster come the morning because I don't think your head wants *this* much fun with alcohol!'

'Spoil sport,' chuntered Esmé, as she linked her arm into the crook of his. 'And you said I wasn't honest and now look at me, as honest as the day I was born…'

'*Really?* Such a change in one night,' muttered Asa, stabilising a drunken Esmé as she traipsed towards the Square. 'Let's hope it continues into tomorrow.'

'I bet you a tenner that it does!'

'I don't do bets.'

'I bet you you will with me. Live a little, Asa.'

'As I said, I don't bet.'

'Phhh, now who's being pent up? Closed in and the other stuff you said…' giggled Esmé, as she unhooked their arms and pointed wildly at him. 'Pent up emotion… that's the thing with you men.'

'Really?'

'Yes, really… whereas me… I'm free, easy and fluid just like the musical spirit spiralling in that painting.'

'Touching everyone's spirit and soul… wow, such an achievement and there was I thinking you'd organise your sewing tonight of all nights – how wrong I was.'

Esmé stopped walking, turned round and stared at the man walking towards her.

'You think I'm boring, don't you?'

'No.'

'You said my life was empty… but I'll show you, Asa Henson… I'll show you.'

With her final words Esmé dashed off towards the water feature in front of the city library.

'Esmé, come back, don't be stupid… you'll hurt…' She had climbed onto the edging wall and dropped into the icy water before he'd finished his warning. Asa approached steadily as she waded ankle deep in the shallow water. 'Esmé, will you please get out of the water?'

'See, I can be spontaneous. I can be fluid and open and honest… you're not the only one!'

'Esmé, you are going to slip and then we'll need an ambulance.'

'Join me!'

'No. Now *please* get out before you fall over.'

Esmé raced around in the water kicking and splashing, arcs of water swirled about her stomping feet. Asa stood patiently at the side and watched.

'Look at me, I'm the new Floozy in the Jacuzzi,' screamed Esmé, at the top of her lungs.

'Highly original… given that the original is only a stone's throw away and is now surrounded by plants,' shouted Asa, over the sound of dashing water.

Esmé stormed across the water feature towards him, stopped short and placed a hand on each of his shoulders.

'Asa, you might think you know all the answers to everything, you might think you know me inside and out but you have me wrong, really you do. After the other night, you think I'm being led astray by others, manipulated into doing things I don't really want to do… but guess what?' Esmé lowered her voice to a whisper. 'I did want to, honestly I did.'

Asa shook his head.

'See, I can do anything that comes into my head.'

'Go on then, do something amazing that will surprise me.'

'OK.' Esmé dropped her hands from his shoulders, took several steps backwards and then charged at him, grabbed his leather jacket and dragged him over the low wall into the water alongside her. Asa hastily grabbed for his phone and wallet to hold them up out of the water.

'What the hell, Esmé… I thought…'

'See, you didn't expect that, now did you? Be honest.'

Asa clambered to his feet, he was seething in temper.

'And neither are you expecting this…' Esmé took his face in both her hands and passionately kissed him.

Asa pulled away as if electrocuted and pushed her hands away.

'See, I'm not as boring as you think!' said Esmé, breathlessly.

'I never said you were boring. I said you weren't honest... and maybe that was a tad too honest of me.'

'Oh Asa, a girl can *never* be too honest, surely?'

'We'll see what you think about that in the morning.'

Chapter Thirty-five

Day 24: Make a promise

'Esmé, there's a woman at the front door who wants to speak to you,' said Dam, interrupting her knitting machine session in the dining room. 'She looks pretty frail.'

Esmé plodded past him to the hallway.

'Hello, how can I help you?' asked Esmé, viewing the elderly woman in a beige mac and sturdy boots.

'Esmé Peel?'

'Yes,' she confirmed.

'My husband opened this letter.' The woman retrieved a torn envelope from her handbag.

'I sent that to Maxine West a few days ago. I just wanted to say…'

'She's dead.'

Esmé's hands flew to her mouth as the words hit her like a thunder bolt.

'She died five years ago, an overdose.'

'I am so very sorry… I didn't know, Mrs West. I presumed—'

'Your generation all presume that you'll outlive my generation but sadly, not my girl… she was too sensitive for this world… so she's better in the next.' The woman's eyes became teary as she spoke.

'I'm so very sorry, really I am. I've thought about her so often over the years and always felt guilty for the way I'd cut her hair in school and…'

'I remember the incident, she was so upset that I was called to collect her.'

'I honestly regret it so much. And now she's not alive for me to say sorry well… I feel…'

'I wanted to drop by and tell you. It wouldn't be proper for us to ignore your apology and let you think she'd read it. Maxine never held a grudge, ever. So, don't feel bad about it.

Silence fell between them.

Esmé could see the grief etched upon the woman's face.

'Would you like a cup of tea?'

A soft smile appeared upon her powdered cheeks.

'I'd love one.'

'Here let me take your wet coat,' offered Esmé, unpeeling the lady from her dripping mac. 'We'll go into the kitchen, it's much warmer in there.'

Esmé made tea, ate biscuits and reminisced with Mrs West in the quiet confines of the kitchen.

'Did Maxine get married or settle down?'

'No, she was always a home bird. She never ventured far. We didn't hold her back but I always knew she wouldn't see old bones, if you get my drift. I just didn't expect her to give in like she did.'

'Have you any other children?'

'Just my Maxine.'

The words lingered as Esmé drank her tea. Of all the treasured children in her class, the smart ones, the naughty ones, Maxine West had always stood out as being cherished. A lump came to Esmé's throat.

How could I be jealous of a girl whose parents had to cram as much as they could into such a small window of time?

'I am truly sorry,' whispered Esmé, as she wiped her eyes on a kitchen towel.

'I always knew I wouldn't have her for long,' Mrs West continued. 'It was shorter than most mothers have and much greater than others ever know.'

Esmé watched as she sipped her tea.

'Is there anything I can do for you?'

'We want for nothing, lovey. Derek, my husband, he keeps busy in his shed, whereas I focus on my charity work. It does me good and has kept me active.'

'Where at?'

'I work in a St Giles' charity shop a few mornings a week. We take most household goods and quality clothing. If you were interested in donating.'

Esmé sat listening as Mrs West recalled the generosity of others, the gifts offered and the joy of a bargain for new owners.

Within the hour, they'd finished their tea and goodbyes were being said.

'I promise I'll drop by the charity shop… I have one or two bags of clothing that might be useful,' vowed Esmé, as she waved from the doorstep.

*

Long after Mrs West had left, Esmé still had a heavy heart so she joined Dam and Russ in the lounge as they watched an action film. It wasn't her ideal way to spend a Saturday afternoon but it was better than being alone with morbid thoughts about life.

Her days could be short lived, thought Esmé, as gun fire sounded from the plasma screen. Maybe she should make more effort to live a little.

Esmé cringed as Asa's phrase zipped through her mind.

'Russ, would you like me to baby sit one evening?' asked Esmé, as the commercials interrupted the film.

'Erm, no thanks,' he said, looking up from his sprawled position on the sofa.

'I'm serious, I just thought you could go on a proper date. It'd be nice.'

'You seeing someone?' asked Dam, glancing from one to the other.

'Nope,' said Russ, as his head shook vehemently from side to side.

Dam wound his finger around by the side of his head.

'Crazy wench alert.'

Russ nodded, his eyes big and wide.

Esmé stared at Dam, narked that he should be so cruel when he also had a secret that she hadn't spilt.

'Russ, I saw you.'

Russ sat up.

'Yes, I saw you the other day...' Now it was Esmé's turn to make big, wide eyes.

'You're seeing someone!' said Dam to his friend.

'No, I'm not. She's delusional.'

'I'm not, I saw you sitting on the bench.'

Dam watched the brief exchange, but given Russ's blank expression, soon settled back down as the film restarted after the commercials.

Esmé pulled a face at Russ, who lay back on the couch, though his steady gaze remained on Esmé and hers remained on him.

'What?' she snapped, after several minutes had passed. 'You keep staring at me... I want to know why?'

'I don't... and no reason.' Russ raised both hands in a questioning style.

'So, watch the film and stop staring,' demanded Esmé, slightly annoyed that her generous offer hadn't been snapped up.

You'd think he'd be grateful for the offer. In their position, I'd have jumped at the chance to go for a nice meal, have a dance and come home knowing someone sensible was looking after their boy. But no, instead he simply glared.

Russ's staring continued until the next commercial break. Dam jumped up.

'Time for the loo, don't pinch my seat,' he yelled, on leaving the lounge.

Russ jumped up too, surprising Esmé.

'When did you see me?'

'Thursday in the park.'

'With Rita?'

'Yes,' beamed Esmé, eager to repeat her offer.

Russ gave a huge sigh.

'We... sometimes we meet up... oh shit!'

'I get it, no one else knows?'

'Yeah, that's it. I haven't said... you know what it's like, early days and all that... so I'd prefer it if you don't...' He placed a finger to his lips.

'Absolutely, the pressure must be quite intense – I should think both families would be encouraging it for Toby's sake.'

'Yeah, yeah, something like that... but if you wouldn't mind, I... we would really appreciate it.'

The pounding of feet down the stairs indicated Dam's swift return.

'There and back with time to spare,' he laughed, slumping into his armchair.

Russ gave Esmé a fleeting glance, and she smiled in reply. His secret was safe, he'd probably needed time to mature and grow up. He must have missed out on a lot of Toby's young life simply by not being there. Esmé vowed she wouldn't ruin what they'd begun to rebuild. Hopefully they could start afresh as a family unit and prepare for their own happy ever after.

How funny that both men were keeping secrets.

Esmé smugly watched them return their focus to the film. A sense of pride ignited, Esmé could keep secrets better than anyone she knew.

*

Esmé heard Asa's boots pounding down the staircase on his way to work. She leapt up from cutting out a skirt pattern on the floor of the dining room and dashed to the doorway.

'Asa... I managed to make a few beanies. I only had two colours, sorry if you wanted others,' apologised Esmé, handing over a pile of carefully stacked beanies in navy blue and crimson.

'These are great... seriously, the guys will be chuffed,' beamed Asa. 'How much do I owe you?'

Esmé shook her head.

'Seriously, name your price?'

'I was experimenting really, with the new machine and the technique – so you've done *me* a favour.'

Asa looked surprised.

'Thank you, I really can't thank you enough for these,' he lifted the pile as he spoke. Esmé heard a softness in his voice and a glint appeared in his eye.

'And, I'm sorry about last night... the water and *everything*,' said Esmé, as she blushed, 'I really did enjoy the concert, I've downloaded some of her songs today... the drink... it made me a little too boisterous, that's not my usual style.'

'Apology accepted,' he said, adding, 'Stay clear of the lager next time – I don't think it's your drink.'

Esmé laughed at the memory.

Chapter Thirty-six

Day 25: Attend a sporting event

Esmé felt self-conscious walking arm in arm with Grace, amidst a crowd of racing punters all dressed in their sturdy jackets and jeans. She searched the masses but could spot very few women or children amongst the race track crowd.

'Not many ladies, are here,' said Grace, looking around too.

'Exactly what I was thinking, but we'll be fine, Grace.'

'I'm sure we will be once you've figured out where to place our bets. I'm feeling lucky today.'

Esmé smiled. The delight on Grace's face when she'd nipped round this morning to ask if she fancied a day out was a picture.

This morning, Esmé had kept her eyes firmly shut whilst she selected from the remaining eight tasks lined up on her mantelpiece. It wasn't purely her 'don't cheat, won't cheat' attitude, but her defiance on losing an hour's sleep due to changing the clocks to British Summer Time.

This particular task was one she was dreading, Esmé didn't particularly like sport. Yes, she'd won an egg and spoon race, aged five, and a drunken space hopper assault course challenge, aged twenty, but Esmé wasn't into participating in or spectating at, sporting events. So, she'd required numerous suggestions from her housemates during breakfast for a decision to be made.

'Get yourself up to Villa Park, you'll love it in the Holte End,' said Russ. 'Your brother will never forgive you but I wouldn't let that stop you.'

'I own a Villa hat, which could be useful,' laughed Esmé, not sure that being a stadium virgin attending alone was an ideal choice.

'Wrestling might be on at the Barclaycard arena,' offered Dam. 'Or you could go ice-skating.'

'Seriously?' jibed Russ.

'Stop laughing... it's a sport,' explained Dam. 'I'd like to hear you say it isn't to the guys that skate at Silver Blades.'

'Or skiing at the SnowDome at Tamworth?' added Russ, ignoring Dam's comment.

Perry Barr was only a few miles away, so the greyhounds won with the added bonus that it was an afternoon event which was ideal for Grace.

'I thought there'd be more families given the 1 p.m. opening time,' said Esmé, helping Grace into one of the few remaining seats at the track side. Esmé settled herself onto a hard plastic seat and flicked through the glossy programme.

'I'll be betting by numbers,' said Esmé 'I can afford to lose two pounds on each race and nothing more.'

'Fair play to you, but I'll be choosing names,' replied Grace, peering at her own programme, her biro in hand, marking her card like a professional gambler.

Within ten minutes, Esmé had chosen dog numbers four, four, five, three and two while Grace had circled dogs called Chicken Legs Galore, Blue Rinse, She's a Winner, Rolling, Rolling, Rolling and an unlikely winner in Last One Home.

'You'll be OK staying here, if I go and place the bets?' asked Esmé, clutching both lots of betting money.

'I'll be fine, you worry too much,' said Grace, waving her racing programme. 'On the way back bring a couple of drinks.'

'Hot beverage or alcoholic?'

'A nice G&T would hit the mark,' Grace said with a glint in her eye.

'Noted.' Esmé left the elderly lady seated contentedly, her handbag on her lap, staring at the huge track in front of her.

Esmé felt like a track pro thanks to the sweet gent at the betting counter. She'd simply blurted numbers at him and he'd produced two separate betting slips.

'Here you go, Grace. A double G&T with a nugget of ice,' said Esmé, side stepping along the row of plastic seats carrying two large plastic glasses.

'Doubles, ooh, I'll be singing 'Knees Up Mother Brown' in no time,' laughed Grace, taking her drink and adding. 'I'll pay for the taxi home.'

'Cheers!'

'Cheers, Esmé.'

Esmé explained that she'd passed the indoor seating area on the way to the betting office and it was crammed with noisy groups and young families.

'We're the bravehearts out here at the track side then,' laughed Grace before she added. 'Me and our Jack used to go to Hall Green all the time when we were first married. We *always* sat at the track side with a cup of Bovril.'

Esmé listened as Grace reminisced for just a short time about the laughs they had and the many years they were married.

'It must be lovely being settled,' said Esmé, more to herself than Grace.

'Oh, it is my lovely, but you'll see… your turn will come.'

'Doubt it… I've been foolish,' complained Esmé, before explaining about her disastrous few days.

'That's the difference between a boy, a man and…' Grace paused for effect, '… a gentleman!'

'There's my problem… I can't spot the boys from the men, plus I don't know any gentlemen,' laughed Esmé.

'Hmmm, I wouldn't say that,' muttered Grace, sipping her G&T just as the greyhounds and their handlers filed out for the first race.

*

The stuffed rabbit sped past on its rail as the clamour of six dogs lunged after it. A high-speed chase, over in minutes, with little reward. Esmé couldn't help but smile at the uncanny comparison to her late night antics with Jonah on Tuesday night.

'And have you spoken to him since?' asked Grace, marking her card with a winning dog thanks to Chicken Legs Galore.

'I can't face him just yet… no doubt he's chasing another woman by now.'

'No, not Jonah! Asa!'

'Briefly. He became stern and deep about it saying I was trying to hang out with the cool kid – as if he knows everything. After all, who in their right mind would sit waiting—'

Grace held up a commanding hand.

'Shush now, I won't have a bad word said about that one… he's worth ten of Jonah.'

'No Grace, you're wrong there... He's like Jekyll and Hyde. His mood swings are horrendous. One minute he's arrogant, moody and preaching at you... then on Friday night, he surprised me by taking me to a concert... though he still did a bit of preaching...'

Grace peered at her.

Esmé stopped talking.

'You are blind, young lady. Seriously you are. Wake up and smell the coffee, before it's too late.'

Esmé looked away. Couldn't anyone else see how Asa treated her?

'Look, the dogs are lining up for the second race,' said Esmé, faffing with her race programme, eager to change the subject.

'I bet they are...' chuckled Grace. 'And not just here at the race track!'

*

Two hours sped past. Grace collected another two wins on the second and fourth races with Blue Rinse and Rolling, Rolling, Rolling, while Esmé snatched a photo finish on the third race thanks to dog number five.

'I'll just nip to the little girls' room before the fifth race starts,' said Grace, hoisting her handbag on to her forearm.

'Do you want me to come along?' asked Esmé, standing to let her pass, not wishing to intrude but wary of her frailty.

'No, you stay here. I'll be fine, stretch my legs a bit...'

Esmé watched as her delicate frame slowly disappeared into the crowd of race goers. It must be lovely to be so spritely at her age and still have a sense of humour, not like her own grandparents who had definitely lost their place in the world as they grew older.

Esmé read the glossy race programme, trying to feign interest in the adverts.

'Hi.'

Esmé looked up to find Gregory standing in front of her, his expression sheepish and his eyes pleading.

'Oh, it's you! Well, better late than never,' said Esmé curtly, as her memory transported her back to Friday night at 8:33p.m. and the realisation that she'd been stood up.

'Look, I'm so sorry... please let me explain...'

'Gregory, give me two reasons why I should?' said Esmé adding, 'in fact... perhaps you could stand over there...' Her arm indicated a few feet away to her left. 'for about thirty minutes, and then I'll speak to you if I can be bothered.'

'Hey, hey, hey, look, it was rude of me. I should have called and I expected you to be annoyed but...'

'Sorry, there's no excuse. You had my contact details, you phoned me at work to make the arrangements so what stopped you phoning on the night or even afterwards?'

'My dad suffered a heart attack that afternoon, he got rushed to hospital and so... I was called from work and well... I didn't get a chance to call and so you thought...'

Esmé stared in horror. His face did look gaunt, his sparkling blue eyes not so alive.

'Honest, I went into autopilot and before I knew it I was driving my mum home at ten and I remembered I'd made arrangements.'

'Oh.' A wave of guilt flooded Esmé's throat. He hadn't stood her up. He hadn't changed his mind. He'd simply been a devoted son doing the right thing by his parents while all the time she'd bad mouthed him and vowed never to use the Personal Shopper service again.

'And now?'

'He's home and on the mend, it'll be a long road and the doctors warned us that he needs to take better care of himself.'

A silence grew between them, both shifted and shuffled in awkwardness.

'I called you every rotten name I could think of,' said Esmé, meekly.

'I thought you might, I felt the voodoo needles enter my spleen,' he half laughed. 'I am truly sorry. I just wanted to come over and explain.'

'Thank you… I'm sorry for jumping to conclusions when it was a family emergency but…'

'Excuse me, are you Esmé?' interrupted a young female steward in a yellow fluorescent vest.

'Yes.'

'Do you know a lady called Grace?'

'What's happened?' Esmé flew into a panic as the steward explained that Grace had had a fall.

Gregory and his explanation disappeared in an instant as she was hastily led from the plastic seats towards the race track toilets. The female steward explained how the wet tiles by the wash basin may have caused her to slip.

Within twenty minutes, the ambulance crew had arrived, assessed Grace and were carrying her out of the ladies' toilets on a stretcher wrapped in a NHS blanket. Esmé walked alongside the stretcher, holding Grace's hand.

*

The hospital corridor was busy, a stream of nurses traipsed back and forth, their squeaky shoes signalling their approach. It seemed rude to ignore them but she couldn't continue to look up and smile at each one.

Esmé sat flicking through the tatty magazines scattered on a table instead. Nothing could focus her mind, all she could think about was the frail old lady lying in a hospital bed a short distance away. She'd offered to stay during the examination but the nurses had asked her to wait outside for a few minutes while they assessed Grace and sorted out some nightwear for her.

That was thirty minutes ago. Nobody had spoken to her since.

Have they forgotten me? Or should I ask the next nurse where to go?

Esmé looked at her mobile phone for the umpteenth time: 18:15.

She closed her eyes and breathed deeply to ease her frayed nerves. This wasn't the day she'd hoped for. A pleasant day out had turned into a nightmare. What if Grace died? What if she never fully recovered from the fall and this was the beginning of her end?

'Any news?'

Her eyes snapped open on recognising his voice.

'Asa! Am I glad to see you!'

'There's a phrase I don't hear every day.'

'It's Grace, I took her for a day out and she fell over in the toilets.'

'I know, Dam called.'

'Are you still on duty?' asked Esmé, looking at his jeans and tee-shirt combo.

'Yes, but on a break so I have a few minutes to spare…'

Surely, he should wear a uniform of some description whether he was a porter, kitchen staff or a cleaner.

'Haven't you a uniform?'

'Not really, not for my role. Have they assessed her?'

'Yes, but they have forgotten to come back to me.'

'How long ago?'

'Ages.'

'Longer than twenty minutes?'

'Far longer!'

The bare side of Asa's face pales.

'Is that not good?'

'Time will tell. I'll go and enquire.'

Great, I'll wait for a little longer, shall I? Why was everyone wearing a uniform except for Asa?

*

Within no time, Asa re-appeared at the far end of the corridor and beckoned for Esmé to follow.

'Is she OK?'

Asa shook his head.

'Not quite, she's broken her leg in two places.'

Esmé's hands flew to her mouth.

'Is it bad?'

'Potentially, they think she needs surgery but she's suffering from shock mainly…'

'Shock?'

Asa gave her a quizzical look.

'Yes, shock, that's why it's taken so long to come back to you – they want to stabilise her first,' he said, leading her along a corridor. 'Would you like to see her?'

Esmé nodded as her tears began to flow.

'What are you crying for?'

'I can't help it, to think I took her for a day out and this happened… I caused this!'

'Stop it! Dry your eyes, she can do without seeing you upset.'

She wiped her eyes on her sleeve. She never had a tissue when she needed one.

Asa led the way through a warren of corridors, his head not moving to read the signage above each corridor. Esmé gave up trying to figure out the route.

'You know this place well,' she commented, trotting behind him.

'Like the back of my hand.'

'Doesn't it get to you working amongst all this sickness and ill health?'

'No, why, would it you?'

'Every day? Yes.'

'*Really?*' He whipped round and stared at her.

'Don't look at me like that. I'm being honest. I much prefer to be surrounded by fabric and wool or even go back to paper and pencils… than death.'

'Not everyone dies. Anyway, I see it as life. I'm surrounded by life here and the desperate attempt by some to hang onto that in whatever manner they can…'

Esmé stopped short.

'Funny, I've never thought of it like that.'

'Hmmm, maybe you should – here we are.'

Asa pushed open the double doors to reveal a small ward of neatly made beds, each with an occupant. Esmé instantly spotted Grace lying in the corner bed, with a nurse arranging her blankets.

'Grace, it's Esmé, can you hear me?'

'She's not deaf,' laughed Asa, standing at the end of the bed.

Grace gave a weak smile.

'Shall we sit you up a little, give you a better view,' said the kindly nurse, supporting the frail body and raising her a little. 'There, is that better?'

Esmé smiled appreciatively.

'Here's a chair, sit closer to her,' prompted Asa, placing Esmé nearer the head of the bed.

'Grace, how are you?'

The gentle blue eyes simply stared at the younger face. A tiny flicker of light danced on the watery surface.

'Just talk to her,' urged Asa, bringing a second chair into place.

'About what?'

'Anything.'

'Grace, I've phoned your son, David, he's on his way,' said Esmé, feeling conscious that everyone was listening to her. 'And I was reading a recipe for a banana loaf while I was waiting…. Don't tell the nurses but I've ripped it from the magazine and we'll make it once you get back home.'

Asa smiled.

"What?' mouthed Esmé, her brow furrowed.

'Carry on.'

Grace lay listening, her eyes fixed on Esmé.

'Anyway, I promise we'll keep an eye on the house while you're in here, so don't worry,' added Esmé, wishing that Asa would stop smirking at her. 'Russ has been to check that you locked the back door. Dam's not at home tonight – he's gone to his parents' for dinner. You always say, *what again?* whenever I say that line but it's true, he goes there a lot. He lives with them more then he lives with us, that's what we reckon over our cuppas.'

Asa laughed.

'Honestly, Grace says that every time I mention Dam.'

'What about me?'

'Oh you, you're a tortured soul,' gushed Esmé.

'Am I?'

'Oh yeah, Grace reckons there's another side to you that you hide from the rest of us… although I keep telling her there isn't, she won't have it. She reckons she's met you in a previous life.'

'*Really.*' Asa stared at the old lady, his eyes taking in her pale features.

'Yep, I swear.'

'And you?'

'Me?'

'Yep, you.'

'She thinks I'm naïve and don't know what's good for me in this world.'

'Touché, see someone else thinks the same,' laughed Asa, standing up to walk round the bed.

'I think she sees us as the entertainment next door, our comings and goings are more interesting than the tv,' laughed Esmé.

'Possibly, in the case of—' Asa stopped and coughed.

'What?'

'Nothing.' Asa busied himself reading Grace's bed charts.

'In the case of who?'

'Is that the time? I need to get back. The nurses may ask you to leave in a while but I'll see you back at the house, bye.'

Esmé watched as Asa hot footed it along the ward and exited, before she resumed her watch over Grace.

What was it he'd said? 'Possibly in the case of…' Dam? Russ? Jonah?

What's the big secret and why hadn't anyone included her?

Chapter Thirty-seven

Day 26: Show others you care

'Asa, thank you for coming with me, I'm sure Grace will appreciate another visitor given that her son David can't come during the day time,' said Esmé, standing in the hospital lift with Asa.

'Sure, though the other ladies might be unsettled given my appearance.' The lift doors opened and Asa walked out.

'Asa, this is the wrong floor,' said Esmé, as she snatched at his arm.

'No, it's not.'

'This isn't the floor for Grace's ward.'

'I know... this is where I work. I thought you'd like to see.'

Esmé stepped from the lift just as the doors slid closed. Once through a set of double doors her mouth fell wide open. She stared around at the youngsters perched on top of their beds watching tv or playing games on the floor.

'You work here?'

Asa beamed a cheesy grin.

'Great, isn't it?'

'Asa, they're children.'

'No shit, Sherlock!'

Esmé stared around the ward, the children were aged from about twelve to early adulthood, all in various fashions and all wearing navy or crimson beanies.

'Asa, I thought you were a porter.' She scurried alongside him.

'Did you now? Whatever gave you that idea?' said Asa, waving to various children along the ward as he walked.

'I assumed that with the...' Esmé pointed to his face.

'My tattoo?'

'Yes, your tattoo...'

'I can't have a proper job?'

'Sorry,' she whispered in embarrassment.

'*Soooo* small minded...'

Asa left her and began chatting to the nearest young man, who was seated on his bed with his blankets pulled across his legs and a woollen beanie covering his scalp. Esmé watched as they playfully fist bumped before Asa perched casually on the edge of his bed.

What was wrong with them all? They were just children and yet they all looked so poorly.

She stared around the ward at their physical weakness, sallow complexions and for some, their lack of hair. Then it hit her – many of them were wearing her beanie hats.

She nipped across to Asa, as if he hadn't noticed their head gear.

'Asa, these are my beanie hats!'

'You're quick today! Hey Stig, *this* one is on fire,' joked Asa to the young lad. Esmé watched as the teenager laughed politely. 'Stig, this is Esmé. Esmé, this is Stig… and yeah, she sewed your beanie hat.'

'Hello, Stig, nice to meet you,' blushed Esmé, trying hard not to stare at the young man's frailty.

'Sup!'

'Sorry?'

Asa laughed.

'She doesn't do cool talk, dude – try old lady chat,' joked Asa.

'Hello, nice to meet and greet you,' said Stig in a posh voice, thrusting a delicate hand in Esmé's direction. Her hand wrapped around his, and she could feel the delicate bone structure, just like that of a tiny bird she'd rescued as a child. 'Testicular cancer is my bitch and she's winning.'

Esmé was helpless, speechless and stared between the two males.

'I'm dying by the way, in case you were wondering.'

Her eyes bulged with tears, her stomach clenched with nerves and she lost the ability to speak.

'Ha ha, it works every time, doesn't it, Asa?'

'Sure does, kiddo, sure does. Come on, Esmé, spit it out,' said Asa, beckoning her nearer.

'When?' blurted Esmé.

'My sell by date was smudged during production so I'm not too sure, but it'll be a damn sight sooner than yours, I know that,' answered the young lad in a chirpy tone.

'It's not a game of Top Trumps, you know,' said Esmé, disconcerted by such flippant remarks.

'It is around here!' hissed Stig, as Asa belly laughed at the end of the bed.

'Asa!'

'He's right, the rules in this ward are different to those in any other ward… literally anything goes with these kids,' hissed Asa, through his laughter. 'Stop being so uptight, pull up a chair and chill out.'

Esmé wanted to rant, rage and rebuff everything Stig had just said. But looking around her everyone did seem relaxed, quiet and yet, busy. Busy with computer games, board games, chatting between beds – Esmé sensed that the only person looking uncomfortable was *her*.

'Anywhere?'

'Anywhere.' The two males stared at her as she self-consciously nipped to the nearest table, grabbed a hard back chair and carried it as if walking into assembly in primary school, before settling beside Stig's bed.

'OK?' asked Asa.

'Do you like the beanie?' she asked.

'You the gal that made them?'

Esmé beamed with pride. Never before had she made something so simple and yet, so fitting.

'I love it. Asa brought them in a few days ago,' he added.

'Have you taken it off yet?' jeered Asa, elbowing the lad's blanketed legs.

'Nah!' The teenager turned round and called along the ward. 'Oy Jonty! This here gal made the beanies… cool or what?'

Esmé blushed under the scrutiny of a second youth, lying in bed playing a computer game. She watched as Jonty paused his game, searched in his locker and brought out a crimson beanie, which he swiftly plopped on to his head, covering his baldness.

'Cheers, lady… Stig, my man, we're looking good!'

'See what a few hours spent creating 'stuff' can do?' whispered Asa to Esmé.

Esmé nodded, as the lump in her throat grew with pride.

'And the others?'

'I gave them out to others on various wards.'

'There are more wards… like this?'

Asa slowly nodded.

'Kids?'

He widened his eyes to answer.

'*Really?* And they're all… seriously ill?' Esmé whispered the final section of her remark.

Asa nodded.

'You don't have to whisper, lady, there's a big possibility you'll eat more birthday cake than I will,' said Stig, as casually as if they were chatting about the weather.

Esmé looked dolefully around at the handful of faces, all different and yet, all similar.

'Cancer, mainly,' said Asa, following her eyes. Esmé returned her saddened gaze back to him.

'She's going to cry, isn't she?' said Stig, turning to Asa.

'Probably, she's a wuss at home.'

'No, I'm not.'

'Did I mention what she did to the tarantula?'

'Is this the one?' asked Stig, his face beamed with life.

'This is *she.*'

'I'm not the wuss, I have a phobia,' she said.

Asa rolled himself from the bed and stretched.

'Come on, visit over. We need to head off to see your pal, Grace, before visiting hours finish… catch you later, Stig.'

Esmé watched as the two performed a complicated sequence of fist bumping, hand shaking bromance style farewell.

'See ya, spider-girl,' called Stig, as Esmé and Asa bade goodbye to the other patients.

'Bye,' waved Esmé to a sea of smiley faces.

As they exited the double doors Esmé couldn't hold back any longer, and let tears cascade down her cheeks.

'We'll take the lift up to ward seventeen and then… hey what's…?'

'Is this what you do? Look after children that are…'

'Dying? Why does that surprise you?'

Esmé stood in amazement and stared at his blurred features, her head slowly shaking from side to side.

'I thought you were a porter.'

Asa smiled.

'Seriously I did, every time they said 'he works at the hospital' – they made it sound like a services provider, that kind of stuff… not *this*.'

'Well, *this* is what I do… I'm a palliative care nurse. I thought you did quite well, back there, he's good at giving the verbal flack.'

'Lord no, I wanted to cry the whole time. I was trying so hard not to stare. How can they be so cheerful when… when…? Are they all going to die?'

Asa shrugged.

'Most… but it's amazing how they cope and live.'

'Live?' interrupted Esmé, wiping her face to clear the second flush of tears. 'Live?'

'Yeah, live, this is what they have… there's no second chances, they can hardly put life on hold while they focus on getting better for the glory days ahead… this…' he waved his hand around the clinical corridor, 'is their life, at the moment.' Asa pressed the lift call button.

'That's so sad. I can now see why you do what you do.'

'Exactly! There's no biding my time, no waiting for a better time to come along – I do it, I live as if tomorrow wasn't mine.'

Esmé watched as a spark of energy lit up his face.

'I imagine you're great at your job,' she said.

'I'm bloody fantastic at my job. I'm *me* and I do what it takes to make these kids smile.'

The lift doors slid wide open.

'Asa?'

'What?'

'Sorry for calling you an arse… you're far from it,' said Esmé, fighting the urge to giggle.

'Believe me, I can be an arse but a great one, with a *great* job.'

'You must have met some very special people?' They entered the lift, and Esmé pressed the button for the ground floor.

'For sure, and *they* don't waste their time unlike some I could mention.'

'Oy! Stop having a pop at me. I don't waste my life.'

'What's your plan for this weekend then?'

'Hmmm.' Esmé wished she could list a host of activities to fill the forty-eight hour window. Sadly, nothing came to mind.

'Point proven – you'll wait for others to invite you out or invite themselves around and then you'll have plans.'

'You've a bloody cheek.'

'That's because I'm an *arse.*'

Asa gave a wry smile and walked from the lift.

'You think you're so bloody funny… and you're not!' snapped Esmé following, irritated that yet again he'd hit the bull's eye.

'Those kids would switch places with you in a heartbeat… so stop wasting time and live a little.'

'I will.'

'So, what are you doing tomorrow?' asked Asa, striding towards Grace's corridor.

'Nothing. Why?'

*

Esmé struggled through the door of St Giles charity shop with two bin liners.

'Hi… I'd like to donate these please,' was all she could manage having carried the bulging bags from the bus stop to the High Street. She'd felt awful entering apartment number nine knowing that Andrew was on a day shift, but while she had a key and some belongings surely it was for the best that she cleared her wardrobe in the least painful manner.

She'd given a huge sigh of relief as she'd emptied those final shelves. It felt cathartic. Old life, old clothes and old dreams being stuffed into black bags ready for a new beginning.

'Oh, thank you, young lady… everyone loves a bargain in here,' said the chirpy lady who welcomed her donation with open arms.

'Could you tell Mrs West that Esmé dropped by?'

'Of course, she's in later, I'll mention it… a friend of Maxine's, were you?'

Esmé's breath caught in her throat.

'*Yes,*' she said, proudly. 'I was a school friend of Maxine's.'

'Lovely young woman, she was…'

Esmé smiled. Maybe one day I'll be remembered as fondly.

*

She hoped she was doing the right thing. Why wait around wasting time – do something, live a little as Asa would say, thought Esmé. Though would it be classed as interfering?

Esmé had asked herself that question repeatedly from the moment she'd left the house, throughout her twenty minute bus ride, a ten minute walk and now, on entering the concrete block of flats.

What if Rita thought she was being nosey? But shouldn't she offer help if it was needed?

She pressed the call button and waited for the lift to descend. On arrival, the metal door swept aside to reveal a mirrored box with a hand rail and a corner full of pooling urine.

'Stairs it is!' announced Esmé briskly to an empty lobby. 'Only fourteen floors – it'll do wonders for my thighs.'

She crossed the lobby and entered the stairwell: an endless spiral of concrete steps and a plastic rail greeted her.

How does anyone live comfortably in such horrid surroundings?

Finally, after much huffing and puffing, she reached the fourteenth floor. She stopped to shake her legs and ease the burning sensation which was spreading from her groin to her knee caps and catch her breath. Sweat trickled down the centre of her back and soaked into her cotton shirt.

Esmé peered at the slip of paper – flat number thirty-two. She quickly rapped on the solid wooden door, uncomfortable in the dimly lit communal landing.

'Hello,' she said meekly, not wanting to overwhelm Rita before she'd had her say. 'I wanted a quick chat.'

'Esmé! What a lovely surprise!'

Esmé sighed at her genuine reaction.

'Can I come in?'

'Sure, though ignore the mess…'

A sea of coloured plastic filled every inch of the carpet from the hallway into the lounge: cars, scooters, plastic wipe clean mats, wellingtons, a ride on and push along motorbike, stack and storage boxes. Everywhere Esmé looked her eyes viewed plastic.

'Eyo!' called Toby from the pile of Lego positioned in the middle of the lounge floor.

'Hello soldier, how are we?'

'Plane!' shouted Toby, holding aloft two long bricks joined in a cross shape.

'Good boy, aeroplane.'

'Tea or coffee?' asked Rita, as she collected empty mugs from the mantelpiece.

'Whatever you're making, with two sugars and milk for me.'

Rita disappeared through the nearest doorway. Esmé moved a pile of folded washing on the armchair and perched on the cushion edge. She'd have felt better sitting back but she didn't want to disturb Rita's system and there was no other empty surface on which to place the washing.

Esmé fixed a smile to her face as she stared around the lounge. Every surface was chock-a-block with stuff – they'd obviously outgrown this flat a long time ago. The mantelpiece was an array of everyday essentials, cotton buds, *Calpol*, electricity cards, keys, matches, mobile phone and not the usual decorative space for displaying things of beauty.

A thick layer of dust smeared the tv, and sticky paw prints were dotted across the plasma screen.

When was the last time she vacuumed in here?

'Here we are…' Rita broke her train of thought as she returned holding two steaming mugs. 'Drink, baby?'

'Bina!' called Toby, without looking up from his brick pile.

Esmé cradled her mug as Rita put hers down by the couch and returned to the kitchen for Toby's Ribena.

'Here.' She returned instantly, offering Toby a large bottle of purple squash.

'Ta!'

Esmé watched as the child slugged the bottle backwards and guzzled non-stop until bubbles appeared inside the bottle.

Rita settled on the couch and picked up her mug.

'So, what brings you over here?' she asked warmly.

'Rita… you can tell me to go to hell, but… I know about Russ.'

Rita stopped drinking and stared.

'OK.'

'And I wanted to say that if there is anything I can do to help the situation then I would be more than happy to babysit… to give you guys more chance to get back on track.'

Rita slowly nodded.

Toby suddenly began to splutter.

'Careful. Don't choke yourself,' said his mum, launching from the couch to pat his back. Toby jolted back and forth with her force, his eyes watering with the shock. 'He does that all the time, little gutsy, aren't you?'

Toby slung the nearly empty bottle aside and continued to play.

'As I was saying, if it's a night out at the pictures, a table for two… I really don't mind looking after him.'

'That's so lovely of you… though I don't know how Russ would feel about it.'

'Oh!'

'Don't get me wrong, I appreciate your offer. I was wrong to drop Toby on you the other weekend when the guys were away but I was desperate. My mum was suddenly rushed into hospital. So, thank you, Russ did say that I shouldn't have done it. The thing is, I'm just not sure Russ is ready for all the fuss that goes along with... us.' Rita looked at Toby who was busily bashing bricks together.

'I see...' said Esmé, slightly baffled. 'I just wanted to help, that's all. I can't imagine it's easy.'

Her suggestion had fallen flat, much like her conversation with Russ. What was wrong with these people? She felt foolish for having offered. If she'd been a single mum who was trying to get back with the father, Esmé imagined that she'd have jumped for joy at such an offer. Instead Rita sat sipping coffee and staring into space.

Within the drinking of a coffee, the visit was over. Esmé received a warm snotty kiss from Toby and a swift hug from Rita before the door of flat number thirty-two was rapidly closed.

Esmé called the lift to the fourteenth floor.

What a wasted journey. Esmé couldn't imagine being as laid back as Rita. And as for Russ, taking it easy... not certain... the man should be glad of a second chance to be a family.

Esmé entered the lift and pressed the ground floor button, the doors closed as her mind whizzed with thoughts, then she remembered the pool of urine in the corner. She stared in dismay as the trickle worked its way towards her new boots and wished the lift would descend at break neck speed.

She felt disheartened. She had followed her task of the day and the positive energy had failed to materialise. She hadn't meddled, forced the issue or interfered and yet, she'd clearly failed.

Chapter Thirty-eight

Day 27: Seek a thrill

The minibus arrived at the hospital steps at seven o'clock, as arranged. It was a typical hire vehicle plus driver affair, an aged fella with slicked back hair and nicotine stained fingers.

'Morning, minibus for eight people?' he asked, climbing from his seat.

'Morning mate, are you ready for us?' replied Asa, taking the lead role of organiser and driver's buddy.

'Ey, I am... quicker we're gone the sooner we're back,' said the driver, as he flung open the side door. The traffic was obviously more important than a teenager's dream day out.

Esmé had stood for fifteen minutes amidst a jumble of holdalls, blankets and first aid kits piled around her feet, acting as the official mini-bus look out. A deep-seated thrill rumbled in her stomach, a mixture of dread and excitement.

Was it morally right to tie a poorly... dying teenager to a high wire and hurtle him head first down a mountain side? Esmé cringed. Right or wrong, it was Stig's request.

'Oy Esmé, are you standing there all day or are you going to load some kit?' called Asa, as he beckoned her towards the rear doors to start loading their bags.

Within ten minutes, they had the group's belongings neatly stacked inside the confines of the storage area.

'Where's Stig?' she asked Asa, once the other medical helpers had drifted away.

'Don't you worry, he's in fine spirits... he'll be here any minute.'

Within five minutes, the cheery smile of Stig arrived by special delivery of a wheelchair and a brisk nurse.

'Park here, please,' ordered Stig, pointing beside Asa.

'Yes, your highness,' laughed the nurse, swivelling the chair around. 'Have a nice day and come back in one piece.'

'We'll try to,' laughed Asa, high fiving Stig.

'If not you can patch me together again,' shouted Stig to the retreating blue uniform, before speaking to Asa. 'Hey man, how's it hanging?'

'You up for this adventure?' asked Asa, as he scrutinised Stig's features.

The teenager pouted in a determined fashion.

Esmé watched the brief exchange.

She was thrilled to be asked to accompany them as a helper for the day but deep down was unsure what was required of her.

'So, what are you doing tomorrow?' Asa had asked when they'd visited Grace in hospital.

'Nothing. Why?'

'*Good*. Sounds like you're zip wiring then.'

'Doing what?'

Asa had explained the premise behind 'Make a wish days' and the zip wire was Stig's one wish.

It sounded amazing apart from the nagging uncertainty of such a thrill being safe enough for a young man whose delicate body was wracked with pain and suffering.

'OK folks, climb in, buckle up and we'll leave,' shouted the plump driver.

'Stig, say goodbye to your parents,' said Asa, smiling at a solemn middle aged couple standing a distance away from the minibus.

'See ya!' shouted Stig, waving from his wheelchair, before whispering. 'They're still mad at me for choosing this. My mum hoped I'd opt for an afternoon with dolphins.'

'Are they *still* mad at me for agreeing?' asked Asa, as he waved and smirked.

'Oh yeah, but then they get your motives, they just don't get mine,' said Stig as he propelled himself towards the minibus's side door.

'You lifting?'

'If you're asking!' joked Asa.

Asa's arms snaked beneath and around the teenager's frail body and hoisted him high above the wheelchair and onto the bench-like padded seat. After a quick argument about whose seat belt strap was whose, the lad was safely secured by the far window.

'Esmé, you next?'

'You can go in the middle,' she said, zipping her fleece. 'He'll be more comfortable having you cracking cool jokes and pulling his leg than my tedious efforts.'

Asa climbed in and untangled his seatbelt.

Esmé glanced towards the rear of the minibus, where three medical staff, accompanying them in case of an emergency, hurriedly loaded supplies whilst Stig was occupied and oblivious.

Esmé climbed in and immediately retrieved and opened her large bag of Skittles.

'You on a day trip, love,' called Stig, leaning round Asa's body to view her.

'Yes, thanks, I'll start the singing off in a few minutes so get your vocal chords warmed up,' she answered, matching his jovial spirit.

The minibus journey was as comfortable as could be expected given the age of the shock absorbers and rusty suspension. Within a few hours, Esmé's back ached and her thighs were numb from her swinging feet not touching the floor but her voice was in fine form. After seven renditions of 'Ten Green Bottles', endless rounds of 'Swing Low Sweet Chariot' and a dubious football chant, which Esmé was sure Stig's mother wouldn't approve of, but which Asa sang heartily, the mini-bus drew to a halt near Bethesda, North Wales.

The medical crew and helpers piled out, as Asa gently lifted Stig from the vehicle into his wheelchair.

The mist was low, the rolling hills high and Stig's excitement levels were entering the stratosphere.

Whoosh!

All eyes lifted skywards as two bodies suspended in nylon cradles came zipping overhead in bright orange jumpsuits.

'OMG!' shrieked one medical helper, introduced as Tara. 'Is that what you're going to do?'

'You got it!' cried Stig, his pinched face beaming with delight. 'Wow! Look how fast they go, Asa!'

'Faster than five miles an hour, hey?'

'You bet. I'll race you down, no problem.'

'Are you going down too?' asked Esmé.

'Of course, we'll go side by side, hey Stig – you and me?'

'Sure man… who is going with Esmé?'

'*Me?* Esmé screeched, looking amongst the group. 'Excuse me, I'm not doing that for no one. I'm here to watch.'

The group of faces turned and stared.

'I've news for you, you are!' whispered Asa, throwing a casual arm around her shoulder. 'Now buck your ideas up, don't be scared but the lad wants us all to do it.'

Esmé's worst fear had come true.

'I can't do that, I'm only here as a helper.'

'And this is your payment.'

'I don't *need* paying, thanks – I'm doing it purely to be useful.'

'Think of the thrill, woman,' laughed Asa, releasing his hooked arm.

'It'll be the fastest you *ever* move,' called Stig, his body doubled in laughter.

Esmé looked from Asa and back to another female helper, who seemed as shocked as she was.

'No one said,' muttered Esmé, knowing she'd have never agreed to help if this little plan had been mentioned. Was this her punishment for sleeping with Jonah?

Asa shrugged.

'Best foot forward, me thinks, live a little, Esmé.'

'I'll give you 'live a little', if you keep on with that bloody saying,' muttered Esmé, swallowing her pride.

They emptied the minibus, registered at the reception and were given a booking time before Esmé could catch up with the plans.

The Stig Six were ushered from one prefab shed to another to collect bright orange jumpsuits and endure the undignified ritual involving looped harness strapping being hoicked and tightened about their groins by an instructor, creating a puffy arrangement like an adult nappy.

'You've been Tangoed,' called Stig, as Asa knelt before him doing up his front zipper.

'Does my bum look big in this?' laughed Tara, as she pranced about.

The group stood and stared, no one dared answer her.

Great. Esmé was sure hers looked worse.

Esmé watched Asa and the instructor assist Stig with his strapping. Stig's tiny frame was overwhelmed by orange material and the strapping gave the impression of a desperate turkey trussed up in a fancy dress costume. The instructor tugged and tugged to get the child size strapping small enough, the force of his movements causing Stig's body to move violently.

'Grab a helmet and line up please,' called the instructor. 'We'll adjust and fit each one.'

Esmé joined the queue, butterflies dive bombing in her stomach.

What the hell was she doing here?

She stepped forward for the instructor to position and fit her safety helmet by twisting the appropriate dials.

'Don't look so frightened, love, you'll come to no harm,' he joked as Esmé walked off, the rigid plastic strapping biting the underneath of her throat.

'Asa, tell her to change her face…' called Stig, as he pointed at Esmé.

'Esmé, a request from Stig… change your face – you look like a bulldog chewing a thistle.'

'Ha, bloody ha, Stig! And you look like a Cadbury's chocolate orange gone very wrong in that jump suit, but hey, I'll forgive ya!' she called back, desperate to avoid the fear that was growing in her belly.

'Asa, she's history, isn't she?' said Stig.

'Sure thing, mate, sure thing!'

*

Esmé looked out at the thick steel cable which was slung between their platform and another platform a few hundred feet away. A drop of around fifty feet was below her.

'Could you lie down into a press up position please?' asked the young woman, her pierced eyebrows and lip distracting Esmé from her instructions.

'Press up?'

'Like we just demonstrated…'

Esmé stared around the group.

What demonstration? The Stig Six group had just arrived at this platform by foot… no one had performed a demo, not that Esmé was aware of.

'Wakey, wakey, Esmé,' shouted Asa, stepping forward from the group. 'Like this.'

Esmé watched as Asa went to the front of the platform, peered over the edge, crouched down, placed his hands flat to the steel grid-work and stretched his body backwards. His palms and boots supported his outstretched body.

How could orange jump suits look good on certain body types?

'Are you watching?' Asa's voice interrupted her thought.

'She's definitely looking, mate,' called Stig, as a titter of giggles ignited amongst the group.

'Stig!'

Esmé stared intently at Asa's hands to demonstrate her full concentration.

She watched as the instructor collected the rear sections of Asa's body harness strapping and clipped him to a suspended metal runner hanging from the wire cable.

Asa's body was lifted up, his fingertips hardly touching the metal ledge while his feet were lifted and positioned against a length of black strapping pulled from the rear of his harness.

He swung like a peg bag on a washing line.

'See? Now, Esmé, get down in a press up position on the other launch pad,' said Asa.

Esmé stared in horror as all eyes turned to look at her.

'*Me?*'

'Er yeah, we'll go down side by side,' said Asa.

'*Me?*'

'Esmé!'

Esmé followed the routine demonstrated so beautifully by Asa. The instructor performed the attachment routine at her rear and finally, her body was attached to the cable washing line.

Beneath and before her lay an expanse of scrub land, mature trees, rocky footpaths and groups of orange jumpsuits hiking up the hill towards the platforms.

'Now listen, as you near the metal strut in the distance, put your arms out by your sides like an aeroplane and it will help to slow you down, OK?'

A second instructor completed his safety check on both harnesses, clips and runner hooks. 'Perfect!'

'Excuse me...'

'Esmé, shhhh now!' called Asa, his arms held straight by his harnessed sides.

'But I can't...' Esmé glanced sideways towards her flying partner.

'You can. In thirty seconds, it will all be over,' laughed Asa.

'Ready, steady, go!'

Esmé felt her safety clip removed and whoosh! The rush of air took her breath away. Her body launched forwards and down, flying above the scrub land. Asa waved as he overtook her mid-flight.

On approaching the platform an instructor grabbed the cable with his giant hook and stopped her flying action in one move.

Within seconds, Esmé had followed the instructions given and was standing, knees knocking, back on terra firma.

She'd done it. She'd actually done it. Less than thirty seconds, as Asa had said. A wave of emotion lifted from her boots, up through her orange jump suit and snagged somewhere below her throat.

'Love, you OK?' said the instructor, looking concerned.

'She's fine, mate,' called Asa, as he offered her his arm. 'Esmé!'

Asa's fingers wrapped around hers and a spark of electricity flared.

'Ouch!'

'Exactly, but still give me your hand.'

'I'm fine.'

'You're actually green – you look far from fine.'

'But I did it.'

'You certainly did.'

'I nearly bailed out at the top.'

'But you didn't… full marks to you.'

*

They stood a distance away from the landing platform, and there was a whooshing sound overhead as two more of their small group zipped along the wire.

'Is it Stig?' asked Esmé, as she peeled herself from Asa's protective grasp.

'Yep, look at his face.'

Stig had the broadest smile, his face was alight and alive.

'Didn't he want to come down alongside you?' asked Esmé apologetically. 'I ruined the running order.'

'Oh well, he can do next time.'

'What we're doing *that* again?'

Asa stared at her.

'That was the practise wire… the real one is up there.' Asa pointed to a huge mountain away in the distance. 'You didn't think that little stunt was *his* wish come true, did you?'

'No, I... just... I thought that... you never said.'

'Bloody hell, Esmé. You don't think these instructors take someone up there without testing their nerve on a smaller set-up first?'

Esmé stared at the mountain.

'How high is it?'

'Just under five hundred metres *and* the zip wire is a mile long.'

'Are you serious? I've got to do that all over again? That...' she pointed to the practise platform. 'Was bad enough.'

'Live a little, Esmé. You only have to lie there and watch the view come towards you,' laughed Asa. 'Now hush, here comes Stig... you'd better grow a backbone double quick.'

'Asa!' called Stig. 'Wasn't that the best?'

'Certainly was... but now for the biggy,' shouted Asa, helping him down from the landing platform.

'Esmé, you were awesome,' said Stig.

'I was?'

'Yeah, you had fear written all over your face and yet, you launched... I thought you were just about to bail but no, off you went!' he laughed, holding his sides as Asa supported him. 'Asa, can I go down alongside her next time.'

A pause occurred before Asa spoke.

'Sure man. If that's what you really want.'

'No!' Esmé saw the surprise on Asa's face. 'I would prefer to go with one of the others, you should stick with the original plan and head down alongside Asa – you can have a race to the finish.'

'OK,' said Stig, turning to Asa. 'You and me then, mate.'

'You and me!' repeated Asa, his voice sounding hollow.

'Come on, we need to move on to the big one,' said Esmé, walking away from the pair. The look on Asa's face was etched upon her mind. Stig's suggestion had hit home. For a split second, she'd seen Asa's pain.

'Thank you... I really want to do this alongside him.'

Esmé turned to find Asa walking at her left shoulder, the helpers supporting Stig a short distance away.

Esmé stopped.

'You really care about these kids, don't you?'

Asa rolled his lips together and sighed. For an instant he looked vulnerable, his emotions bare.

'I get it, I really do,' she added.

'Good... because you'll stop talking emotional crap and get your ass up the hill so we can all move towards the big one and give this lad the thrill of his damned life,' said Asa, with a sudden glint in his eye.

The Stig Six didn't walk to the top of the mountain, they couldn't. Instead a refurbished cattle wagon trundled up the steady climb along the twisting quarry road to reach nearly five hundred metres up the mountain. Esmé hung onto the wagon's metal tubing rail, her knuckles whitening simultaneously with her face.

'Are you alright?' asked Tara.

Esmé nodded in a frantic manner.

'You can say… Stig will laugh it off.'

'Hmmm, but will I live it down?'

The helper inclined her head and smiled.

'From Stig maybe, but not where Asa is concerned.'

Esmé turned away to watch a set of daredevils launch from the quarry side and fly through the air towards the wagon, going straight over the top and away down the mountain side. She followed their progress across the quarry, above the blue lake and on towards the landing platforms, just tiny specks in the distance.

A wave of nausea swept over her.

Stig's voice rattled on about what he is going to do this time whilst flying: arms out, arms in, waving, singing or shouting as he raced Asa.

Esmé's gaze traced the outline beneath his orange jumpsuit – there was nothing of him, the fabric billowed around his stick thin limbs, his collar bone protruded and his sallow cheeks dipped inwards.

Why was life so cruel? She'd asked Asa questions earlier at home during breakfast.

'It's frigging unfair, that cancer is about to snatch the life of a young man who hadn't even learnt *how* to examine his own body properly to ensure that anomalies didn't go unnoticed. How sick is that? The bitch got him before he was old enough to know better.' Asa had said as he ate his morning toast. 'By the time his testicles were painful and swelling, it was too late. He was given the diagnosis in a matter of days.'

Esmé watched Asa and the others make Stig's planned adventure bigger, grander and more outlandish by suggesting song titles he could shout whilst flying.

'Come fly with me.'

'When I see an elephant fly.'

'Flying without wings.'

The group became rowdy and boisterous as the wagon continued the climb. Esmé's stomach churned as the wheels rolled.

Finally, the wagon drew to a halt on a large flat area of grey shale by a sturdy fence edging the quarry drop.

The billowing clouds were too close for Esmé's liking.

*

Within seconds they had unloaded Stig from the wagon and were lined up ready for the short walk to the platform and the waiting cable.

In her head, Esmé practised her announcement.

Asa, Stig, I'm so sorry but I really can't do this... the practice one was bad enough but this... up here, so high off the ground... I simply can't do...

'Come on, slow coach,' said Asa.

Esmé froze.

This was her moment to say it.

'Asa, look it's been a fun day so far but I really...'

'Want to do this and can't wait to get started.'

'No!'

'Yes.' Asa's hand grabbed hers and pulled her aside in an unceremonious fashion.

'Asa look... seriously, I can't go through with this.'

Asa's grip tightened. His head bent towards her ear.

'The lad's dying... and you're worried that you can't do this? Are you for real, Esmé?'

Esmé's eyes lifted to view Asa's stern expression.

'Take a look at that kid's face, think of all the wonderful things that face won't ever enjoy in life and then tell me that you going to deny him the enjoyment of watching you face a fear because he has asked you to. You are giving up just one moment of your selfish, timid, scared little life to him and his enjoyment because... and I mean this, Esmé, that lad hasn't got long left and this is the day he asked for. One day, where we all put aside our own worries and create a day to remember. And if you are really selfish enough to be able to face that young lad and tell him that you can't do this... you're not the woman I thought you were.' Asa's voice cracked on his final sentence. Esmé stared at him, a flush of tears threatening to cascade from her. 'Now, buck yourself up because you have got a damned sight more days to enjoy life and be the scared little girl that you are, than he has!' His final words were hurried, he dropped her hand and instantly turned away brushing a hand across his eyes and face.

'Asa?'

He ignored her call and strode towards Stig, as the helpers carried him towards the launch platform.

*

Esmé had no choice. She lay cradled in the harness and pinned to the zip wire cable. The wind gently swung her body from side to side as she watched them secure Tara. The rest of Stig Six stood behind her, huddled together, whispering and awaiting their turn.

Her stomach flipped, her limbs shook and she turned her head sideways as she couldn't face the view before her. Nearly five hundred metres' drop to a metal platform which she couldn't see and where she was to be caught by a giant hook.

Asa stepped forward and crouched beside her shoulder.

'Thank you, this means the world to him.'

Esmé's doleful expression was greeted by his warm smile.

'Sorry.'

Asa nodded before returning to the group.

'Ready, steady, and...'

Esmé didn't hear the word 'go' as the safety clip was released and the wind snatched her breath away for the second time. The cable whizzed and whooshed above her head and her body swung in the canopy as she flew over a bright orange wagon parked beneath her.

Silence descended as the quarry side fell away and there was nothing beneath her but distant land hundreds of feet below. Esmé looked around as if she had all the time in the world, the motion seemed to have slowed and yet, she knew she was still moving rapidly.

This is how a bird must feel.

The large lake beneath displayed a spectrum of blue hues as the water deepened and eased. In less than a minute Esmé had covered the mile long zip wire, and land was beneath her once more. She was greeted by the landing instructor's huge smile.

'How was that, love?'

'Awesome, I want to do it again,' shouted Esmé as she landed, the excitement bubbling in her voice.

She gingerly climbed down from the landing platform.

'That was the best thing I have ever done,' screamed Tara.

'Me too!'

She'd actually done it! She didn't let him down. Esmé was unsure if 'him' was Stig or Asa.

Chapter Thirty-nine

Day 28: Organise a girls' night out

It was supposed to be a girls' night out, that's what
The Single Girl's Calendar had proclaimed but it felt
good to have everyone together in one room. For
once, Kane hadn't joined the ensemble. Karaoke
wasn't Esmé's forte, nor a strong talent of anyone
who had graced the microphone with their chronic
warbling, so far. The Cube hired out karaoke booths
purely for private parties so shrouded everyone's
embarrassment in sound proof rooms alongside all
mod cons and alcohol on tap. Apart from a tuneful
singer, what more could a group of friends ask for?

The majority of the crowd had attempted to sing.
Penny and her husband, Keith, had annihilated a
Sonny and Cher cover, which everyone hoped
wouldn't lead them down the same marital pathway.
Marianne's long-term boyfriend, Jimmy, was too
busy parading and practising as Elvis Presley to
succumb to the star-studded line up that was Bucks
Fizz, despite the promise that he could attempt to rip
Marianne's skirt off in one sweeping move. Bucks
Fizz instantly became a trio as both Penny and
Marianne performed word perfectly behind Keith, a

single male but at least it gave Jimmy's top lip time to practise curling.

'Esmé, thank you for asking us. You've only been gone a few weeks but we've missed you so much already,' was Marianne's opening line that night. Esmé had to work hard to swallow the lump wedged in her throat on greeting her two colleagues and their partners.

'Old Steely Stylo keeps asking us when you're coming back?' added Penny, which made Esmé's heart feel heavier than ever. Nine years was a long time to work for one employer, but the freedom to find herself and develop her talents was far more important at this point in her life.

Esmé moved around the karaoke booth, going from table to table amidst the variously coloured strobe lights. She was trying her hardest to merge the two groups but the Stylo four seemed content not to associate with her housemates. Was it Jonah's model looks, Russ's morose expression or Asa's inked face that was creating the No Man's Land between the tables? Only Carys moved between the two camps as freely as Esmé did, laughing, joking and making sparkling conversation.

'Oy Esmé, come here a minute?' Jonah beckoned her towards his table, and pointed at the song selection book. 'Here, you pick a song any song and I'll sing it just for you,' he said, pulling her close into his body. Esmé felt his hand travel about her shoulder and linger before it travelled down towards the base of her spine where it stuck fast.

'Keep your paws to yourself, Jonah… Emma's not up for the likes of you tonight!' she warned.

'Ay, am I ever going to live that down?' he asked defensively.

'No, not really!' Esmé was unwilling to do anything that would put herself at the centre of his attention ever again. Naked or clothed.

*

The group cheered as Dam finally arrived an hour after the allotted arrival time.

'It's about time too… we thought you'd got lost!' called Asa, looking up from the song selection book. 'Or was it another dinner at your parents?'

'Dinner at my parents? Mmmm, touchy subject, man. I'm not in their good books at the moment, but hey, they'll come around. An extra few hours at work and every one thinks I'm up to something.'

'Dam, is there anything you'd like to announce?' called Esmé, across the karaoke booth.

Carys blushed, instantly busying herself on her mobile.

'Such as?' said Dam, shrugging and feigning confusion, as he settled beside Russ.

That was a cheap shot, that I shouldn't have said, thought Esmé. She's my best friend. I should be repaying her for the support she's shown me.

Esmé watched as Dam and Russ sat forlornly, both concealing love-interests and wishing they were elsewhere.

*

'Esmé, what are you singing?' asked Keith, Penny's husband.

Esmé protested frantically for the third time tonight, this really *wasn't* her scene, she'd only agreed to the venue and activity because Carys had made her vow to stick to the rules of The Single Girl's Calendar. Getting her various friendship groups together seemed like the logical thing to do.

'Not me, I sound like a mongoose playing a harmonica,' she joked, hoping that would finally stop the requests for the night.

Asa stared and pouted.

'I'll sing if you do,' he said, handing her the selection book.

'Honestly Asa, I can't sing... everyone is better than me.'

He pulled a face.

'Right I'll do it alone then,' he said, removing his jacket and making his way to the main microphone positioned on the mini stage. A succession of coloured strobe lights skimmed his features distorting his expression and body art.

Esmé leaned against the wall of their booth and watched as Asa composed himself before taking the microphone. He'd really been a tower of strength in recent weeks and she'd seen a whole new side of him with young Stig. A tenderness and strength that he'd previously hidden, though it was now perfectly clear why he'd been so attentive when he'd found her upon the bathroom floor with a migraine. Yes, she'd annoyed him with her initial refusal to go on the zip wire but he'd encouraged her and helped her to overcome her fear. And she'd ended the day as pleased as punch that she'd helped in giving Stig his dream day out. Be it two months, six months or a year he had left, Stig would never forget his magical day.

A sweet gentle intro drifted from the overhead speakers, Asa cleared his throat before his voice filled their booth. Everyone stopped talking and turned to watch. Esmé had expected him to choose a heavy metal track, a testosterone filled number full of power and anger but he hadn't. Instead, a delicate backing track of simple guitars was all that supported Asa's voice. Esmé watched as he openly sang to the gathered group, turning this way and that as the words filled their booth and on reaching her, his eyes stayed, lingered and remained fixed upon her.

Esmé's knees jittered. Her backbone prickled. His gaze bore into hers. It wasn't a song she knew, or recognised, but the repeating line of 'Let it be me' rang about the booth as the rest of the crowd faded and disappeared, leaving just the two of them standing a distance apart across the dimly lit room where strobe lights flashed and danced. Esmé held her breath. This was a moment she wanted to pause, rewind and review but within a minute or so, Asa's song had ended and the friends were on their feet clapping as he exited the mini stage. He retrieved his jacket and returned to being Asa, the housemate, the wind-up merchant, her brother's friend.

'Now your turn,' he said, when he reached her position.

Esmé shook her head.

'Chicken?'

'No, I just can't sing like you do – why force me to show myself up.'

'*Esmé...* it's a bit of fun, why be so serious?'

Why had he ruined it by calling her 'chicken'? He'd walked from that stage like a new man, as if the lights had depicted his true nature and worth. Yet, within seconds had ruined the illusion with a cheap jibe.

'I was half expecting you to sing 'Dancing Queen',' she said, narked that he'd called her chicken. 'You said *that* was your favourite.'

'No, I didn't, I said *that* was a favourite of *most* people... they love to hate it but secretly they love it. I just sang my favourite song... 'Let it be me', didn't you hear it?'

Esmé shrugged.

Asa glowered at her. His jaw clenched and released.

'Great, thanks a bunch.'

Esmé watched him walk off to collect another beer before making conversation with Dam.

'Are you alright?' said Jonah, as he snaked an unwelcome arm about her shoulder again, his right hand resting above her right breast.

'Oh me, yeah, of course,' lied Esmé, trying to switch moods.

'Forget him, he's got serious issues,' said Jonah, nodding towards Asa.

'It's nothing,' she said, at the exact moment that Asa looked up and saw Jonah draped about her shoulders.

'Anyway, tell me how Grace is... she's far more important than Asa.'

Esmé continued to explain that Grace was expected to stay in hospital for another week before being transferred to her son's home for some nursing by the family.

The karaoke continued in good spirit and as the alcohol flowed, everyone but Esmé attempted to sing during the evening. She couldn't bring herself to try, knowing that all eyes would be upon her.

Hadn't she made enough foolish errors in front of her housemates this month?

Asa's stare seemed fixated on her and each time their eyes met across the booth, she quickly looked away.

*

'Kiss me,' demanded Asa, as they leant against the brickwork of the house. He'd invited her outside for a chat while he enjoyed a cigarette.

'What?' said Esmé, scanning his features.

'I said… kiss me.'

'Asa?' Her tone lifted, unsure if he meant it.

'Go on then.'

'But Asa…'

'I'll kiss you then.'

'*Why?*'

'I thought you were after the thrill of a man… so, here you go.'

'Are you serious?'

'I'm as serious as you are.'

Silence. Esmé stared at him in the moonlight. She could see he was the worse for wear from drink but still, this wasn't Asa.

'Why?' she asked, unsure what game was being played.

'Why not?'

'But you said—'

'Ignore what I said… you want me, I want you… so, why not?' He took hold of her forearms and pulled her close.

'Asa?'

He paused, blinked and released his grip upon her upper arms.

'I get it.' He pulled away.

'Get what?'

'No. Sorry. I thought for just one minute that you *did* actually want what I wanted but no, I now get it, I see it, you hesitated. Sorry, my mistake. I can only apologise.'

'Asa.'

'What?'

'I don't get it?'

'Unfortunately, or rather fortunately for you, I do…' He rummaged inside his jacket pocket for his cigarettes and matches. 'Now run along, if you're quick, I'm sure you'll find Jonah upstairs preening himself… flash him your best smile and he'll be putty in your hands, *again.*'

'Asa!'

'Go on, Emma! Go and find Jonah. He'll do whatever you want, he's been chasing you all night,' he snarled, his voice was twisted in her ear as she scurried from the garden patio. 'Emma! Phuh! He can't even get your name right!'

Esmé dashed around the side of the house and leant against the wall to catch her breath. Her heart was booming, her lungs gasped, unable to function properly.

What had just happened? Why had he done that? One minute he was sweetness and light, a laugh a minute kind of guy yet in the next breath he was frightening. And why had he brought the Emma thing back up, even Jonah had finally got her name right.

Esmé stood panting in the moonlight.

'Go! Be used by that fecking slime ball...' his words were a husky whisper. 'Esmé, Esmé, Esmé... you have no idea what you do.'

She heard a match strike and smelt his cigarette smoke.

Silence descended.

Esmé peeled herself from the brick wall and tiptoed back inside the kitchen before Asa realised she'd heard him.

Chapter Forty

Day 29: Party with confidence

Esmé fingered the cerise dress fabric, it had cost more than she'd planned and had been difficult to sew due to the sheer and fine quality of the fabric, but it felt gorgeous. Now, with her hair jazzed and spiked with glitter, her make-up skilfully applied and sparkly jewellery she stared at her reflection and blushed. She looked as glamorous as any cat-walk model, and felt confident enough to accompany Jonah for the evening to his awards ceremony.

Rap a tap tap.

'Yes?'

'Jonah said if you're not downstairs in the next five minutes he's going without you,' called Dam from the landing.

'Tell him, I'm nearly ready… and I'm worth the wait!'

Esmé took one last satisfied glance and prayed that tonight she'd turn heads, despite her recent dalliance with Jonah, her underlying obsession remained. Things had been a tad awkward since, their polite conversations had been terse as they navigated about each other. Esmé knew it would pass, but still, she hadn't heard him mention another female since. She also knew that it wasn't about trying to impress the cool kids, like Asa had said. Instead, a month after her break-up with Andrew there was no denying she had a spring in her step, having transformed into a sassy, life loving, independent female! – *just* as The Single Girl's Calendar had promised!

Her entrance down the staircase was dreamlike. Esmé descended like royalty. Jonah was faffing with his bow tie and collar so had his back to her, but Dam's eyes lit up as he watched her glide downstairs: chin lifted, eyes smiling and a modest amount of flesh on show.

'You look beautiful,' said Dam, which made Jonah turn round.

'Boy! You scrub up well,' exclaimed Jonah, his eyes scanning her from head to toe and back up again.

'I hope it's suitable.' Esmé knew it was more than suitable, but it seemed polite to ask. She hadn't an alternative dress if it hadn't been. She re-arranged her hemline which started at mid-thigh and flowed into a long floaty train, emphasising her shapely legs.

'Wait till Mr J gets an eye full of you, boy, will he be narked.'

Esmé frowned.

Cheers, my aim wasn't to impress your friends.

'He's the big boss man,' added Jonah, as a car horn sounded outside. 'That'll be for us. Come on, see you, Dam.'

In seconds, Jonah was striding along the pathway, his blond mane sweeping rhythmically against his dinner jacket, Esmé tottered behind to catch up.

Where were his manners? He didn't even offer to help, thought Esmé.

'Bye, enjoy yourselves,' called Dam, from the doorstep.

A black limousine was parked at the kerb side, the uniformed driver climbed out to greet them and opened the rear door.

'Evening,' he smiled from beneath a peaked cap.

'Oh, hi,' said Jonah climbing into the rear seat without hesitation.

Lifting her skirts, Esmé settled beside him – the bemused driver closed the door.

By the time the limo pulled away from the kerb, Jonah had ransacked the mini-bar fridge and was uncorking the champagne.

'We have to make the most of it, Esmé. This may well be the only bonus I get, so let's enjoy ourselves – got it?'

'Got it,' chirped Esmé, taking the offered glass of bubbles, unsure that such extravagance was necessary, if not even a little wasteful, for such a short trip into the city.

'I've got no plans to hold back, let me tell you that!' added Jonah.

On hearing his spiel, Esmé was pleased she'd stretched to such expensive fabric, though she would need to eat porridge three times a day for a fortnight to pay it off her credit card bill.

'Hurry up, knock it back... we've only got a twenty minute journey to the venue,' ordered Jonah, hurriedly refilling his flute.

'Hold fire, I can't take my drink like you,' laughed Esmé, as he tried to refill her glass.

Esmé watched as Jonah gulped and glugged, his Adam's apple dancing in the process. Esmé would have preferred to savour each sip and every bubble – sadly, Jonah had other ideas.

*

As promised, the limo came to a halt after twenty short minutes. Jonah held the champagne bottle high and drained the final drips into his mouth as the uniformed driver opened the rear door. Esmé stared at Jonah and shook her head.

Was that really necessary?

'Madam.' The driver offered her his hand as she climbed from the vehicle.

'Thank you.'

'Sir.'

'Cheers man, will the fridge be refilled for the journey home?'

'Certainly, sir,'

'Excellent, throw in a few more snacks, if you wouldn't mind,' laughed Jonah, slapping the driver's shoulder. 'Or make it two bottles of champers!' Esmé cringed and gave the bemused driver an apologetic smile, as Jonah boldly walked ahead, once again forgetting his manners.

'Catch up, keep up,' he called over his shoulder as he climbed the steps of the hotel's grand entrance.

Esmé collected her floating hemline and scurried to follow Jonah's stride. He stopped before the main entrance.

'Esmé, listen. The industry awards are the place to be seen. There'll be some serious networking going on all night with the top brass – so, by all means speak to whoever, go where ever you like but make sure you ask their job title and that you mention my name if you're chatting to an agency boss or a photographer, OK?'

'Didn't that top guy call you about the job for Milan?'

'Cheers, thanks for reminding me. Would I be doing this if I had more work lined up?'

So, she was here to promote his career.

'I thought I was your plus one at an awards ceremony?'

'You are, but that's only a section of the entire night, Esmé… and I'm not going to waste the rest of the time. Now, here's a few of my contact cards, remember my portfolio can be viewed on-line and I'm prepared to travel for photo shoots if all expenses are paid… have you got that?'

'Jonah!' Esmé pushed away the wadge of business cards forced into her hand.

'Take them… it's important,' said Jonah. 'Why the face?'

'Because I thought I'd been asked out for a treat, an enjoyable night out alongside you where I could let my hair down… now I find that I'm on duty as your PR woman!'

'Opportunities in life, I can't afford to miss them,' said Jonah, accompanied by a shrug.

'Hmmm, I've noticed.' Esmé stuffed the cards into her handbag as Jonah opened the doors.

He stood back to allow her to pass and Esmé smiled, manners at last!

'Oh, Esmé, one other thing… make sure you're back here for two o'clock sharp – the limo won't wait for you, so if you miss it you'll need to get a taxi back.'

Esmé stared at him.

What a bloody joke! She must have been delusional to think this was a good idea, thought

Esmé, as Jonah walked ahead, waving to a crowd of beautiful people.

Esmé finally took Jonah's arm as they entered the hotel's assembly suite where the opulence was immediately apparent: the gleaming chandeliers, the oversized flower arrangements and the pristine waiting staff gloved, dicky-bowed and poised to serve.

'Cracking, isn't it?' said Jonah, unhooking Esmé's arm.

'Stunning, but as you said the awards ceremony is *fairly* prestigious, so it's to be expected.'

She looked around at the assembled crowd as drinks were served in the anteroom prior to taking their seats for the dinner. Some were blessed with good looks and an imposing physical appearance, others with personality and inner beauty.

'Here,' said Jonah, as he grabbed two champagne flutes from a passing waiter's tray. 'It's free.'

Esmé accepted the glass and gave him a terse glare, Jonah definitely belonged in the former category.

She could see a sea of white linen cloth on large round tables which filled the other two thirds of the assembly room, and at the far end the stage had been decorated in glittering banners and awards paraphernalia celebrating the industry.

Jonah was busy chatting to another beautiful male, who he hadn't introduced her to, but who she guessed was also a model.

Esmé busied herself as they spoke. She eyed the stage's podium. In less than ninety minutes Jonah expected to be squarely before it, proudly accepting an award and thanking those who had supported his career. He'd denied writing an acceptance speech when she'd asked earlier but within ten minutes, Esmé had heard him practising one to the bathroom mirror.

*

The celebration dinner was stunning, top quality food presented in an imaginative and intriguing manner by award winning master chefs. Esmé tucked into every course with gusto, despite the evident scorn of four svelte models on her table, who simply pushed their forks around their plates without lifting a morsel to their mouths. Esmé proudly scraped her plate clean.

Very few people had bothered to make conversation with her, so Esmé sat and watched the proceedings. Jonah was guffawing at every opportunity and knocking back drinks in between. The room seemed to be full of beautiful stick insects and wide shouldered hunks, all with shiny coats, clipped nails and good teeth. Esmé pondered on how much it resembled Crufts on the final weekend of showing. The air was filled with back slapping, air kisses and networking chatter.

Once the cutlery was silenced, and the coffee cups arranged, the industry awards began, category by category. Esmé could feel Jonah's nerves rising as his knee didn't stop pumping like a piston against her chair. The glamorous presenters, some highly respected duo, read out the category, opened the envelope and one by one the deserved winner stumbled up on stage to accept their gleaming token gesture of a prize and a cheque. Esmé clapped and smiled in all the right places, conscious that she hadn't a clue who these people were, but hey, she had manners and could feign interest.

Finally, the main award of the evening 'Model of the Year' was about to be presented. Jonah sat tall, straightened his bow tie, smoothed his jacket lapels and gave Esmé a cheeky wink.

This is it. His moment of glory.

The audience watched as Claudia Klauscroft, a supermodel from the Nineties, elegantly opened the gold envelope and withdrew the card.

'And the winner of 'Model of the Year' is…' A deafening drum roll was performed on the table cloths by the front tables, before Ms Klauscroft announced 'Leonardo Abbatai!'

Jonah's face autocorrected to cover his disappointment, as the audience applauded and stood for the dark haired guy in a glitzy emerald suit as he slowly made his way to the stage, with much back slapping and hand shaking occurring en route.

'Quick, let's get out of here, before the can-can girls come on stage,' jeered Jonah, tugging at Esmé's bare arm, as Mr Abbatai began his acceptance speech.

'I'd prefer to stay here and listen to him,' muttered Esmé, frowning at Jonah. His smile was fixed but he continued to pull at her wrist until she was on her feet. Jonah nodded to many beautiful people as they darted through the tables towards the foyer.

'Champagne?' asked Jonah, as a waiter neared their position.

'I could do with a glass of water, to be honest,' said Esmé, rubbing her wrist.

'Champagne or nothing, it's free.'

'Even so, I'd like a glass of water?' insisted Esmé.

'I don't see why I should fork out when it's being given away on tap.'

'So, if I said I was allergic to champagne, would you buy me a drink from the bar?'

'I'd tell you to get your purse out, lady.'

Esmé headed straight to the bar and purchased her own glass of sparkling water.

Jonah followed her, leant against the bar and began drinking from the first of the two champagne flutes he'd taken from the waiter's tray.

'Are you for real?'

'Sure thing, if this rich taste doesn't suit you then I apologise, but for me… it's champagne all the way.'

Bloody tight arse.

A gaggle of svelte beauties dressed like Jessica Rabbit walked past, and Esmé watched as Jonah's tongue hit the deck and his eyes shot out on stalks.

'Liking the view, Jonah?' muttered Esmé, sipping her sparkling water.

'Excuse me, but can you hold these,' said Jonah as he thrust his two glasses at her. 'I need to visit the gents.' He hurried after the gaggle of pert ass, and disappeared into a swirl of beautiful women.

*

Esmé entered number seven Montague Road just after three o'clock in the morning. The house was in darkness. Behind her Jonah struggled to put one foot in front of the other along the garden path, as he greedily clutched two bottles of champagne taken from the limo's mini fridge. She refused to assist him.

If he wanted to drink that much, then he was big enough and ugly enough to cope.

Kicking off her shoes in the hallway, she glanced in the mirror. Her hair remained attractive but her eye make-up had merged into a colour wash of shimmer. And, as for her dress, well. She fingered the rip in the train's hemline, if Jonah was any kind of gentleman he would have taken responsibility and apologised immediately for stepping on it and tearing it. But, he hadn't.

Esmé heard a noise in the kitchen.

Who's up and about at this hour?

Esmé forgot about her torn hemline and tiptoed towards and through the kitchen door.

The back door was wide open, the moonlight shone eerily upon the slate tiles.

She popped her head out and looked both ways: no one. She stepped barefoot onto the paving slabs and made her way round the corner to the garden. And paused.

Asa was crouched down, leaning against the house wall, apparently naked but for a pair of jeans, a cigarette in one hand, staring up at the moon. The moonlight shone on his torso and the various tattoos visible on his temple and neck, along his left shoulder and snaking down and around his lower back.

What was he up to?

Asa picked up a large bottle from by his side, took a deep swig and wiped his mouth roughly on the back of his hand. He drew heavily on the cigarette, before exhaling a plume of smoke into the dark night sky.

'Asa?' she whispered as she neared him.

He visibly jumped as she broke his reverie.

'How was your swish party?' The cigarette hung from the corner of his mouth.

'So, so… not much fun if I'm honest, look at my dress,' she said turning round to show the snagged and torn rear train. 'As I was walking, Jonah ripped it by standing on it.'

'Ha, ha, definitely showing a bit more thigh than you'd planned, just what the captain ordered,' laughed Asa.

'Hmmm.'

'Drunk?' His cigarette danced as he spoke.

'Out of his tree on all the free drinks. He's still crawling up the path.'

'That's Jonah, ponce as much as you can, pay the price later.'

His voice sounded thick, and slow.

Esmé could see the bottle was not full.

'What are you doing out here?'

'Having a smoke.'

'You're smoking a lot recently.'

Asa removed it from his mouth, looked at it and laughed.

'Am I?'

'Yes!'

'I got news for you…I've always…' he grinned and raised an eyebrow.

'Asa!'

He held up his free hand to silence her.

'Esmé… not tonight, please.'

'What's wrong?' she asked, as he settled onto the block paving and stretched his legs out in front of him. She could see the sheer size of his frame, he was far more muscular than his clothes suggested. His tattoos curved and swept about each taut line, a fascinating combination of colour and muscle. Esmé could make out a peacock's head on his shoulder, it's bright feathers lifting towards his neck and face. A tiger prowled over his left collar bone before slinking across his left shoulder and bicep. Several music staves and their notes drifted above his heart and pecs.

Asa watched as her eyes roved around his body.

'Did you live a little tonight, Esmé?'

She snatched her gaze away, embarrassed to be caught staring.

She pulled a face.

'Not really, I thought it was going to be more fun than it actually was, though you'll never guess who Jonah works for and who I've now met… our Mr Joshua… he owns the modelling agency, if you didn't know.'

'No, I didn't know,' he mumbled, snatching at the bottle and swigging from it. 'Did our shining knight live up to your expectations?'

'He dumped me to chase other women.'

Asa burst out laughing, a manic tone that filled the air.

'He's a bit of a git, *really*.'

'Just a bit? I'd say a first class git,' chuckled Asa. 'So?'

'So what?'

'You still interested in him?'

Esmé pulled in her chin and wrapped her arms around herself.

'I was never…'

'Sod off, you were gagging for him since the day you moved in… and you haven't taken your eyes off him since the night you and he… well… *and* he knows it.'

'He left me holding his drink… and was half an hour late returning to the limo's collection point. He said two o'clock but then failed to make it. I had to beg the driver to stay and wait for him.'

'Seriously?' Asa took a final drag on the cigarette and stubbed it out on the brickwork. 'What a man.'

Esmé watched as Asa pulled a pack of smokes from his jeans pocket and struck a match off the brickwork.

'Is that necessary?'

'It's all necessary tonight, Esmé,' he muttered, lighting the cigarette between words.

'Why? Give me one good reason.'

Asa leant his bare shoulders against the brickwork, withdrew the cigarette from his lips and pinched something away off his tongue. He stared up at her, his eyes tracing every inch of her face before speaking.

'Stig died today.' His eyes remain fixed on hers, drinking in the reaction.

'No!' Tears sprung to her eyes.

'Yep, this afternoon.'

'Oh Asa… I'm so sorry. I don't know what to say… you cared for him and were so close… and he admired you…' her words faded. 'Is there anything I can get you?'

Asa held up the cigarette and the bottle.

'I have everything I need, thanks.'

'Asa, that's not right.' Esmé began to wipe at her eyes.

'Why?'

Esmé dropped her head to the side and watched him. A sadness surrounded his every move.

'Don't give me that head tilt.'

'I'm not, this is *not* the answer.'

Asa pouted.

'Actually, it works every other time, Esmé.' Asa took a deep swig from the bottle, his Adam's apple dancing in his throat, then he held it out to Esmé.

Esmé simply stared at the offering.

'Either join me, or sod off... but don't lecture me on how to deal with this... *hurt*... that's sitting right there.' He prods hard at his chest with the bottle. 'Your choice.'

Seconds passed but it felt like an eternity.

Esmé had drunk enough tonight. Far more than she usually drank. She also hated whisky.

The bottle hung in the space between them.

'OK, I'll have a drink but not out of the bottle.'

'You wuss! Live a little... you might be dead tomorrow.'

In annoyance, Esmé snatched the bottle, wiped the neck clean, which made Asa smile, before placing it to her lips. She took a big swig. His dark eyes fixed on her features, drinking in every move. Esmé handed the bottle back, coughed, spluttered and pulled an expression of disgust.

'That's vile.'

'It's good!' groaned Asa, leaning against the wall. 'Do you want me to fetch you a diet coke?'

'Would you do that?'

'Yeah, you seem unsure of whisky.'

That's more than Jonah would do for a girl.

'Thanks, but I'll share your whisky.'

Esmé bent down, wiped the block paving with her hand before she eased herself down to settle beside him.

'You'll ruin your dress,' he murmured.

'Jonah's ruined it anyway, then claimed it wasn't him. Everyone kept staring at my legs for the rest of the night.'

'You've got decent legs, be proud of 'um.'

Esmé pulled a face.

'I saw them naked, remember.'

'Not quite, a bundle of clothes just covered my modesty.'

'Nearly naked then,' laughed Asa.

They sat in silence as a gentle breeze began to blow.

'Were you there?'

'Yep, with his parents and older brother.'

'Did he know it was happening?'

Asa turned towards her, his head resting on the brickwork.

'Was that a stupid question?' she asked, when he didn't answer.

'Pretty much. He battled and fought it the best he could but yeah, he knew,' he whispered, 'He wasn't frightened… if that's what you meant.'

Esmé nodded. It probably was what she'd meant.

'To you, young Stig, one in a million.' Asa held the bottle aloft towards the stars.

Silence descended.

'I couldn't do your job,' said Esmé, as a second wave of tears rolled down her cheeks.

'You could, it's all about being a human being and caring for people.'

'But the hurt and pain when... this happens – I'd get too close, and then they'd die.'

'But that's life, we all die. And yeah, it hurts, I feel sad that he lost his battle but I have a head full of memories. I know I helped him be a normal young man, we chatted about lads' stuff, we joked, we shared and... now, he's gone.'

Esmé began to sob uncontrollably.

'Sorry, I've upset you now... maybe it wasn't a good idea to join me.'

'No, I want to. Listening to you talk, you make it sound so beautiful, so... I don't know what the word is?'

'A privilege.'

'Yes, a privilege!'

'But that's what it is... to support someone at their end... my job is a privileged one. They've taught me so much over the years.' The bottle rocked up and down before he continued. 'And now, he's not suffering, he's up there skateboarding like he wished – we have to let him go.'

Esmé pulled a layer of cerise dress fabric to her face and wiped her eyes.

'That dress will be fit for nothing after tonight,' laughed Asa, watching her.

'I don't care…'

'That's the attitude… don't focus on the material stuff, focus on living.'

'They've shown you that?'

Asa smiled.

'You live the life you want, don't you?'

'Losing my mother taught me to do that.'

Esmé stared at his side profile, the tattoo glared back at her.

'I can see that… but still I just have to ask. Why did you have *that* done?'

'Nosey aren't yeah?' he laughed.

'Suppose, but you're a good looking bloke… then you have that and ruin…'

'Ruin?' he interrupted.

'Yeah, ruin your face.'

Asa turned to her; their faces a shoulders width apart.

'Would it make a difference to you if it wasn't there?' he asked, his voice as serious as she'd ever heard.

'I shouldn't say this but…'

'You don't have to explain.'

She playfully snatched the bottle from his hands.

'Yeah, but how shallow does that make me?'

'As shallow as a puddle but *that's* not entirely your fault.'

'*Thanks.*'

'Seriously, it isn't. Society has made it acceptable to tattoo the body but the face – argh! You're just the same as the majority of people I meet every day who shun me, or walk past and stare. But what do I care, it says more about them than me.'

Esmé grimaced, embarrassed that she and society were so superficial.

'It makes you look defiant.'

'Good, I am. I'll drop by and have another done tomorrow.'

'You don't need any more tattoos – you're covered.'

A wry smile spread across his whisky stained lips.

'It's what I do each time one leaves.'

'One what?'

'Buddy.'

'Do what?'

Asa leant forward peeling his back from the wall.

'Look,' he said softly.

Esmé looked at the expanse of back, his muscles as defined as his abs. From his lower left back drifting across his spine and upwards was a medley of tiny birds in a flight formation, in various colours, aiming for the billowing cloud positioned on his right shoulder.

'Tiny swallows flying high – one for each child,' he whispered, as Esmé stared at the large flock. 'Tomorrow, I'll have number fifty-eight added in blue.'

Esmé couldn't speak, his tattoos told his story.

Chapter Forty-one

Day 30: Be honest

Esmé woke to the shrill sound of Toby screaming outside her bedroom door.

'Go and find your daddy,' called Esmé from beneath her duvet. A new day registered, as her hangover was confirmed by the thunderous drum in her head. Stig's name instantly filled her heart and mind. He'd died. He'd lost his brave battle. They'd drunk whisky in his honour. She'd drunk far too much. Finally, they'd called it a night at four o'clock in the morning.

The child's screaming continued, with an additional hiccupping sound that developed within the cry.

Clad in her pyjamas, Esmé climbed from the warmth of her bed and opened the door. Toby was standing on the landing, tear-stained and ugly mouthed, one slipper on, the other in his hand, waving it in a tantrum.

'Hey, hey, hey. What's all this crying for? Come here, let's put your slipper back on then you'll be happy.'

Esmé knelt before him, took the offending slipper from his hand and raised his left foot. Toby placed his tiny hand on her shoulder to steady himself.

His skin was like velvet, soft, plump and…

Esmé's eyes nearly fell from her head on seeing his tiny foot. The high arch, the deep curve to the ball of his foot and the rounded rise of the big toe.

His slipper fell from her hand. Esmé sat back on the carpet, her legs outstretched, staring at a tiny bare foot and five wiggly pink toes.

Something was wrong, very wrong. Unless there was a really good explanation for the shape of this child's foot someone had a lot of explaining to do.

Esmé looked up into the hiccupping face of Toby, a fresh set of eyes scanning his features as a voice began to recall a series of events.

'Slipper on,' muttered Toby, pointing to his slipper lying idly on the carpet.

'Of course,' Esmé gently replaced his slipper and led him downstairs to find his daddy.

Esmé marched into the lounge, holding Toby's hand to find Dam lying on the couch watching cartoons.

'Oh no, daddy's not here, Toby,' she said in an overly bright and breezy manner, given her hangover.

Dam looked up, pulled a quizzical expression, then returned to his cartoons.

Esmé led Toby into the morning room, where Asa was scraping the inside of a marmite jar with a knife for his hot toast.

'No daddy here, either,' crooned Esmé, in an ultra-sweet voice, tugging Toby through to the kitchen area.

'Who are you looking for?' asked Asa.

'Now *there's* a question.'

Asa stopped, his knife suspended in mid-air. Esmé gave a wry smile.

'Something you'd like to tell me?'

Asa looked at the child, looked back at Esmé and slowly shook his head.

'Nope.'

'I *didn't* think so… thought I wouldn't find out, did we?'

'Esmé?'

'Don't Esmé me, Asa… I'm not stupid.'

'Seriously… you might not want…'

She held up a hand to silence him.

'You might want to eat your toast before it gets cold.'

'Fair warning, I'm out of this.'

Esmé turned to leave the morning room as Russ and Kane burst through the doorway, behind them stood Dam looking concerned.

'Oh, here we are, daddy's come to find you, Toby,' cooed Esmé, in a sickly-sweet voice, as she didn't want to upset Toby.

'I was just on my way, I heard him crying…' said Russ.

'Not you, Russ. I mean *daddy*… Kane!'

The atmosphere was electric.

Kane looked from Esmé to each of the males and then back at his younger sister.

'What?'

'Don't try that with me, I know.' She viewed his staring face. 'You all know what I'm talking about.'

'Esmé… don't talk crazy,' joked Kane. 'Little piggy's have big ears.'

'And feet!'

Esmé bent down and gently removed Toby's slipper, as if it were a game.

'Who has feet exactly like that, Kane?'

'Loads of people…' Kane stopped as all eyes watched the drama unfurl.

'Do you want me to ask them all to remove a sock just to show that no, not everyone has such a distinctive foot shape as that?' asked Esmé, her voice ice cold.

'Esmé… can I just explain?' interrupted Russ.

'No, you can't. This has nothing to do with you, you're not the father – you've only pretended to be the father or act like the father when I'm around as a cover-up job but *now...* I know too. Just like they do,' she pointed at Asa and Dam. 'And no doubt Jonah is in on it as well, just stupid little me left in the dark because guess what, I'm *your* sister, *his* aunt and *our* parents don't even know they have a grandson.'

'Esmé, let me explain,' begged Kane, snatching Toby up into his arms, the child nuzzling his head into his father's neck. His friends stood in silence.

'I'll give you plenty of time to do that before I nip round and explain to our parents, so please continue, I like to get my facts right.'

'Excuse me, but I'm off,' apologised Dam, who grabbed his car keys. 'I can spend the day at my parents' house.'

'Dam, can I jog along too?' asked Russ.

'Not really, Russ, he's probably going to Carys's instead,' said Esmé, nonchalantly.

'*What?* said Dam, his eyes wide.

'What?' chorused Russ and Kane.

'Kane's not the only one with secrets around here... hey Russ? Is there something you'd like to share about Rita?'

'Esmé!'

Asa began to belly laugh.

All eyes turned to view him, leaning against the counter top munching his toast.

'Don't mind me, I'll be over here enjoying my breakfast… I've heard all this before.'

'Dam, can you take Toby into the lounge to watch cartoons?' asked Kane, passing the boy over. 'I'll be through in a minute.'

Russ hastily followed suit. The remaining trio stayed silent until the kitchen door was closed.

'I'm not going to be part of your sordid little secret! I… we should be putting this right as quickly as we can but oh no, big shot Kaney-boy over there is too frightened to face up to his own responsibilities while his mates take the flack and cover for him. Like the weasel that he is…'

'If you breathe a word of *this* to *our* parents I will… I will seriously think about…'

'I don't give a flying frig what you want to do… you've done enough damage and I am going to put this right for *me*, *my* parents and *your* son!' shouted Esmé. 'And I simply don't understand why Rita was complicit!'

'You won't have a clue about anything until you've got a child of your own.'

'Kane, that is such a sorry ass excuse to throw at anyone without a child and even if I did have a child, I wouldn't deny him his family or his history, just to save face around the Sunday lunch table.'

'You're talking out of your ass.'

'You are the most selfish, arrogant bastard that I have ever met and if you continue I will have no choice but to drive across the city and deliver the news to our parents right now… you have no right to stop me!'

'Ah, happy families, is it?' interrupted Asa. 'I always wondered what that looked like being the only child of a single mother whose father didn't give a frig whether I had shoes on my feet or food in my belly or not… but thanks to the Peel family – I'm brought right up to date with what I missed.'

'Asa, save me from the demon that is called a younger sister, sort her out please?'

'Please continue… this is a whole new scenario for me,' said Asa, who flopped onto the small sofa and lay back, still chomping his breakfast.

'It's nothing to do with her so she should butt out!' droned Kane, pointing at Esmé, his arm pumping with each word.

Asa nodded.

'Screw you, this affects the entire family and our futures. How the hell do you date, marry and raise other children knowing you've kept this one a secret from our parents… it's impossible.'

'You're impossible… I said this would happen. I knew this would happen if they allowed you to move in. Asa, didn't I say that?'

'Yeah, but she had the deposit, which you didn't have and couldn't get, so we didn't have much choice.'

Both siblings turned and stared at Asa.

'Cheers,' grumbled Kane.

'Thanks a bunch,' spat Esmé.

'My pleasure.'

'Bingo, Asa, you pissed us both off with one comment – neat trick!' laughed Kane.

'Aren't you supposed to apologise when your family rift spills over into your housemates' world of peace and quiet?' jibed Asa, neatly folding his hands behind his head and settling down to watch the entertainment.

'Could I get you any popcorn?' hissed Kane.

'Maybe at half time.'

'Nice deflection, Kane,' shouted Esmé, her hands lifting to her hips. 'Relying on humour to avoid the real situation!'

Kane turned, his face raging with anger.

'You've wrecked it, that's what you've done. For three years, there's been no problem... but you moved in and bang the whole thing is blown wide open in a month.'

'It was always going to come out, whether it was now, then or when he's eighteen... your son can't be kept a secret for ever.'

Kane inched closer to his sister, his height advantage clearly in his favour.

'I promise you'll regret every word you utter.'

Esmé stepped backwards away from her brother's warm breath on her face.

'And I think you'll regret every minute that you've wasted not introducing him to our family… *his* family.'

Kane stormed from the kitchen, Esmé hot on his heels.

'And another thing, you lied to Rita when you said they wouldn't accept her… they'll welcome her with open arms… you wait and see.'

'Don't you dare!' spat Kane, his stare fixed and serious, his chin thrust forward. 'If you do… I swear… I'll… I'll…'

'What?' hissed Esmé, her hostile stance in close proximity to her brother's body. 'Tell Mum and Dad?'

'Esmé.'

'Kane.'

'I'm warning you.'

'Well, I'm warning you, too.'

Kane shook his head and lowered his gaze, he inhaled deeply and consciously. His chest and shoulders appeared to expand to twice their normal size before he slowly exhaled. Esmé had never seen Kane *this* angry before.

'Seriously, if you tell them... I will make sure you live to regret it.'

'Don't threaten me.'

Kane nodded slowly, his eyes fixed menacingly on his sister.

'Seriously Esmé, you'll no longer be a sister of mine.'

Esmé gasped. The pain of his words cut deep and straight.

'Are you saying...?'

'That you won't ever see him or me again if you breathe a word to either of them.'

'You bastard!'

'I'm not joking.'

'I didn't think that even *you* could stoop any lower but that is a whole new level, Kane.'

'Don't test me, Esmé.'

'Test you? Believe me when I say you're the last person I'll test on this topic. You deny your son the chance of a proper family, you deny his mother the correct support to help her successfully raise him as a single parent and you, Mr know-it-all Kane thinks that he's the one being tested. Get a grip man... how the hell do you figure that out?'

'I'm warning you, it'll be, bye, bye Auntie Esmé...'

Esmé's anger billowed from her boots, every cell in her body wanted to smack this arrogant, selfish bastard into the middle of next week.

Is *this* what brawling men felt like just before they threw the first punch?

'You're deluded!'

'May be, but *that's* my choice.'

Esmé span around to face the other way, she couldn't bear to see his gurning features any more. Never had she hated someone so much as she hated her own brother at that precise moment.

'He has rights.'

'I have rights, too.'

'*What?* Esmé spun round, unable to control her temper as a torrent of venom flared inside. 'You get a girl pregnant, secretly stand by her telling her a whole pack of lies about our family not existing, win her over with some sob story. And then tell more and more lies to anyone that'll listen to you... including your mates... who I'm sure have tried to talk some sense into you many times. But oh no, Kane knows best.'

The kitchen door swung open.

'Esmé, enough's enough – you've tried to talk sense into him,' muttered Asa, filling the doorway.

Esmé turned to Asa and lifted her hands in a helpless shrug.

'I know, I've tried too, but he'll do as he wishes,' said Asa calmly. 'You and the rest of us have to abide by his choices... none of us agree with him. Well, I never have anyway.'

'But how can he insist that...' Esmé turned to Kane, her eyes pleading. Kane stared angrily. 'If this is you, the real you... I don't want you as a brother but at least this way Toby and our parents will get to know one another despite your threats towards me. I'll cope without you!'

'Esmé, come here, please,' asked Asa, beckoning her back into the kitchen.

Esmé walked towards Asa's outstretched hand but then stopped and turned.

'In fact, I swear on my life that by this time tomorrow our parents will know they have a grandchild. They'll have seen pictures of him and if that means I no longer exist as far as you're concerned than fine, have it your way. But I am not going to keep *that* little boy a secret.'

Within a heartbeat Esmé was through the open doorway, Asa moved his foot, allowing it to close swiftly before wrapping his arms tightly around Esmé's sobbing shoulders.

Kane stood in the hallway, not knowing which way to turn.

Within seconds they heard Toby say goodbye to Dam and Russ, then the slam of the front door notified the entire house that Kane had chosen to leave.

Chapter Forty-two

The studio door buzzed as they entered. Asa was greeted warmly by two men covered with tattoos, setting up their work stations for the afternoon by wrapping cling film across every surface.

'Morning fellas, anyone available to squeeze me in?' asked Asa, looking between them.

'One of your birds?' asked the older male, his ear lobes stretched to golf ball size.

'Yeah Tony, he died yesterday.'

'Oh man, I'm sorry...' continued the tattoo guy, 'We don't need you to tell us how much they struggle to stay alive.'

'Exactly, but yeah, he asked for it in blue ink.'

'Who did?' asked Esmé.

'Stig.'

'He asked for a blue bird?'

'I ask them what colour they want... they know what I do once they've gone.'

'Free hand?' asked Tony.

Esmé stood in awe as both guys offered to squeeze Asa in before their booked clients arrived. It seemed surreal to watch the two burly men speak so softly and respectfully.

'Do you always come here?' asked Esmé, interrupting their flow.

'Always, these two are responsible for everything I've got inked,' explained Asa, waving a hand at the duo. 'You might want to take issue with them for ruining my skin.'

'Not to your taste, hey, lady?' asked the younger one in the corner, displaying a pair of tattooed sleeves that stopped at his knuckles.

'He's one of our regulars,' laughed Tony, pulling on a pair of latex gloves.

'Asa!'

'You said it, not me!' retorted Asa, unbuttoning and removing his shirt and indicating a position to the top of his right shoulder.

Esmé wanted to look away but couldn't. The sight of his naked torso in full daylight as he settled face down on their black couch was hypnotic.

'Pull up a chair if you want?' said the older guy, as he grabbed wipes and began cleaning the area.

'No, I'll stay here…' answered Esmé, touching the counter top a short distance away.

Asa's head lifted, then he turned and smiled at her.

'Stop being a chicken, come and watch… you never know, you might fancy one yourself after this,' he said, his eyes twinkling.

Esmé tried to think of a smart retort, but she had nothing. He'd won.

Let's live a little.

'I doubt it, but I'll pull up a seat and watch you squirm in agony.'

Asa pulled a face.

'It doesn't hurt, you wuss.'

'Hmmm, it might,' she said, as she dragged a wooden stool across and sat near his head.

'Wooooo, more like she's *hoping* it hurts you!' laughed Tony, using a purple pen to draw a tiny bird freehand. 'Now, who am I to please, him or her?'

'Me! I'm paying,' laughed Asa.

'You ready?'

'Yep.'

Asa's gaze lifted to meet Esmé's.

'I'm glad you came along. I thought you'd bail out.'

'Yeah, me too,' smiled Esmé. 'I like proving you wrong.'

'Mmmm, do you now?' he whispered, as the artist stretched the skin on Asa's back and the whir of the needle began.

*

'What do you think?' asked Asa, minutes later as he stood in front of the large mirror, clutching a smaller mirror to help view his shoulder.

Esmé couldn't speak. Her tears had flowed from the minute the navy ink started to seep into his skin.

'Hey, you big softy. I'm asking for your opinion and all you can do is snivel; does it look OK?'

'It… looks… beautiful…' she hiccuped, into the tissue hastily offered by the younger guy. 'Stig… would… have… loved… it.'

Asa handed back the small mirror and wrapped his arms around her quivering shoulders as the booked client arrived looking bewildered.

'Come here, you daft one, there's no need to get so upset.'

Esmé inhaled his warmth, deep and musky with a hint of freshly applied deodorant.

'It's… just… that I've never seen something as beautiful as that before… you've actually given up your own skin to remember them… all of them.'

Asa pulled back to view her tear-stained face.

'Exactly, but shhhh, that really isn't rock and roll, is it?'

'Nope, quite the opposite.'

Asa squeezed her tightly before releasing her.

'It certainly is. Now, dry your eyes or this customer will think you've sobbed like a baby having your own tattoo.'

Esmé frantically wiped at her face as Asa sat down for protective wrapping to be taped to his shoulder and back.

'You know the rules, look after it, care for it and it'll last you a lifetime,' laughed Tony.

'Thanks,'

'Always a pleasure, you know that.'

*

'Does it hurt?' asked Esmé, as they walked back home.

'Sometimes, but I can hardly complain, can I?'

'Suppose not, given the endless pain they endured.'

'That's life, petal. Endure the pain to receive the peace.'

Esmé stared up at him, as they strode along.

'You talk in riddles a lot of the time, don't you?'

'Not really, if Stig was here right now he'd know exactly what that meant... but you, you've not known the pain, so why should you get it?'

'I've known pain.'

'When?'

'I broke my arm at nine, I've had wisdom teeth come through all at the same time, I've had...'

'That's *shite* pain... I'm talking real pain, loss, death, injury, serious illness – *that* pain.'

Esmé shook her head.

'Exactly, and until you do… you haven't a clue about life.'

'Asa!'

'I'm not trying to patronise you, but honestly, if you had you'd know I don't talk in riddles, I speak the truth, known by those who know.'

Esmé thrust her hands deep into her side pockets.

'Don't get arsey.'

'I'm not.'

'You are. I can tell.'

'You think you know everything…'

'I know about life.'

'Go on then, let's hear it… let's hear about the pain you've suffered to know everything there is to know, when I know nothing.'

'Drink?'

'Yeah, if it helps.'

'Are you sure you've got the time, I thought you were planning to visit your parents' to discuss Toby?'

'I've plenty of time. I'll phone them later today and make arrangements to visit on Sunday, it'll give Kane a chance to talk to them before I do.'

'Esmé, drink doesn't help but it'll give you something to cry into when I tell you, that's all.'

'Ha bloody ha.'

Within minutes Asa had cut down one street, crossed a main road and was hauling her through the doors of a distinctly grubby looking pub.

'You seem to have a taste for dives,' said Esmé, staring around the darkened room where a handful of customers cradled pint glasses.

'Quite the opposite actually, I just don't judge on face value as much as you do,' whispered Asa, as they neared the lengthy bar.

A sense of déjà vu overwhelmed her as she struggled to climb onto the bar stool.

'We're not sitting at the bar,' said Asa. 'Go grab that corner table, I'll bring your JD over.'

Esmé did as she was told.

He's got a bloody big chip on his shoulder, he thinks he knows everything about everybody – well he doesn't.

Within minutes, Asa was carrying a full tray of glasses towards her.

'How many?'

'JD and coke. I cancelled the ice and two whisky chasers each.' Asa settled the tray before settling himself.

'Can you hear my liver screaming 'no'?' laughed Esmé.

'Nah, but if I do I suggest we ignore it, it'll cope.'

'I've drunk more since moving in with you guys then I ever have before.'

'Cheers!' Asa gulped at his JD. Esmé followed. 'How good is that?'

'Great!' mocked Esmé.

'You see there's one huge difference between us. I savour the little things, the taste of a drink, the smell of the place – you simply gulp it down and don't recognise or acknowledge the enjoyment of it. That…' pointing to his glass. 'Tastes great.'

'So, I don't sample life like you, that doesn't mean to say I don't feel what you do.'

'But you don't.'

'I do.'

'Nah, you don't.'

'Asa!'

'Esmé!'

'I do.'

'You don't and here's why… and I don't mean this nastily but you've been brought up in a lovely little life where every pain and danger has been removed or eased.'

'No.'

'You have. You've never gone hungry, you've never known loneliness, hurt, pain, fear…'

'Here we go again,' mocked Esmé, busying her hands by sipping her drink. 'I'll remind you that we came in here to hear your story, so why focus on mine? Are you avoiding the topic?'

Asa shook his head.

'Not at all.'

'Let's hear it then...'

'OK. It'd been just me and mum, my father skipped out and moved on at the teenage pregnancy stage. Anyway, we lived in a small flat in a terraced build the other side of town. Mum worked... I went to school. *That* was the routine.'

Esmé hung on his every word. Her eyes flicking about his face as he seemed to return to the two bedroomed flat of yesteryear.

'Anyway, it was getting near to Christmas, Mum took on an extra job to earn some pennies, so I used to go to my Gramp's house after school until Mum collected me. One night I had to stay there even longer than usual, she mentioned something to do with more overtime – that kind of thing. Turned out she'd been busy decorating the lounge with Christmas decorations ready to surprise me when I returned.'

'Like a reward?'

'Exactly.' He swigged his JD drink.

Esmé got it. A working mum making the most of things, adding in the treats as and when she could and trying her best to make ends meet.

'Anyway, Gramps walked me home, Mum opened the door with a big grin, she covered my eyes with her hands and we walked into the centre of the lounge. I remember counting to three, then she whipped her hands away.'

Asa's face softened. The hard edges had gone and a mellowness hung around his eyes as he stared into the distance some way beyond Esmé's right shoulder.

'It was fab, she'd decorated the entire room in tinsel, coloured streamers, a real Christmas tree stood in the corner – the full works. She really had spent ages on it. I was thrilled, we'd never had anything like that in previous years but this year was going be different. She'd said so, so many times.'

Asa took another swig of his JD and coke, before he returned to his story.

'She was happy – I know that now… to be able to thrill a child and hear his delight after you've spent hard earned money on a few bits and bobs stapled around a room – that gave her pleasure.' A lengthy pause occurred, Esmé waited, ready for him to resume his story.

'Anyway, bedtime came and she always went to bed at the same time as me, there was no point her staying up on her own… it made sense to close the flat down for the night. So, while I warmed my pyjamas by the fire she went round blowing out the candles that she'd lit around the room: on the mantelpiece, the bookcase, the window ledge. I can see her now, moving quietly to each one, blowing them out and wafting the whisper of smoke away with her hand.'

Asa ignored his JD and coke, grabbed a whisky shot and downed it in one gulp.

'We were asleep when the noise from outside woke me in the middle of the night. My room was thick with smoke. I got out of bed and looked out of the window, I could see the neighbours outside pointing up at our flat. I started to call for Mum, she should have been in the room next to mine, but when I ran in she wasn't there. The bed had the clothes pulled back but nothing. I started along the corridor towards the lounge door and that's when I saw the fire. A total blaze, everything in it was on fire, including the couch on which my mum was lying.

I couldn't leave her there, by this time people were banging on the front door, trying to smash it down, I was trying to wake my mum. I shook her. I yelled at her... but nothing. I understand now that she was overcome by the smoke because her face had black soot marks on it. She knew nothing about it.'

Esmé exhaled in a gasp, having held her breath for much of the story. Asa's focus returned to the room and he blinked, as if he'd forgotten where he was. He sipped his JD and continued.

'That's it really, the neighbours came charging in once the door had given way, the fire brigade arrived soon afterwards and Gramps was called.'

'Your mum?'

'Dead… it was too much to fight once the door was open, the fire used the additional oxygen and the intensity was just too much, even the fire brigade had a job on their hands, let alone the neighbours trying to save her.'

Orphaned at nine, thought Esmé.

She snatched up a whisky shot and downed it in one. No face pulling, no twisted expression, nothing. Asa watched her intensely, his eyes deepening into glistening pools as he stared.

'That's how I got this,' he pointed to the left side of his face.

'The tattoo?' mouthed Esmé, her brow furrowing deeply as she peered at his face.

'No, you fool. I was nine! You broke your leg, I received a burnt face.'

Esmé stared, speechless. Her eyes peeled away the colour of feathers and fine lines to imagine the scarred tissue beneath. The uneven skin, the bumps and stretched web effect now apparent and clear to see despite the peacock's colouring.

'I had the tattoo to cover up the scar tissue.'

'But a tattoo of all things? It must draw more attention than any scar?'

'Are you joking? People used to stare more at my burns with revulsion as if I was a freak of nature… with this,' he pointed to his tattoo. 'They glance once or twice, some stare but the disgust and revulsion has disappeared. They simply stare.'

'I assumed you were thuggish... and uneducated.'

'That's better than being labelled as Quasimodo, or socially unacceptable, purely through no fault of my own.'

Esmé grabbed her second whisky shot and necked it in one. She gave a satisfied gasp on returning the shot glass to the tray.

'Easy, tiger,' laughed Asa, 'you're getting quite a habit.'

'*That...* is possibly the saddest story I've ever heard.' Esmé's voice cracked as tears flowed.

'And me,' added Asa, as his eyes glistened.

'Why peacock feathers?'

'They symbolise immortality and resurrection.'

'They may look beautiful but have you ever heard one calling?' asked Esmé, her face screwed up in disgust, as she wiped her eyes. 'They sound bloody awful... beauty and the beast wrapped in one.'

'Doesn't that apply to most things in life?'

Esmé thought about Jonah – yep. Andrew – possibly. Asa? Yes, but in reverse with a beastly scar but a beautiful heart.

'I think that last whisky is yours,' said Esmé, pointing at the tray of glasses.

'Cheers.' Asa necked the final whisky and sat back. 'So, there you are… the reason I live my life as I do, it's precious – don't waste it.'

'I am so sorry, Asa – it never occurred to me that *that,*' she pointed to his face, 'covered anything.'

'You assumed I was a thug who wanted to be different and shout it loud and proud?'

'Something like that, sorry.'

'No worries… now, *you* know different.'

Chapter Forty-three

Day 31: Make plans for the future

The studio door's buzzer sounded as Esmé entered to escape the thundering downpour. Shaking her sodden jacket, she tried and failed to make her hair look decent in the large gilt mirror.

'Can I help you, lady?' called the older guy, looking up from his current client's naked back.

'I just wanted a look…' stammered Esmé, pointing to the design charts plastered around the foyer wall.

'Help yourself, take a load off your feet and browse… there's more designs in the photo albums on the table and a hot drinks machine, if you want one.'

Esmé smiled politely, the awkwardness she knew she'd experience hadn't subsided.

As directed, Esmé flicked through the photo albums and sipped her hot chocolate while a smatter of chatter and laughter punctuated the hypnotic drone of the artist's needle whirring and whizzing.

Esmé flipped the pages revealing a Madame Tussaud's of body parts decorated in various colours, patterns and inscriptions. Her fingers quickly flipped past the pages of tribal art, spider's webs and skulls but lingered on the butterflies, unicorns and music staves traced upon taut white, yellow, brown, olive skin tones – each body headless and nameless.

Music staves? Esmé quickly turned back the page. Was that Asa's chest?

She stared at the positioning of the flowing stave – right hand side of his chest, olive skin, toned muscular build... her index finger stroked the headless image. If this was him, where were his other tattoos? Or was this an early version of his tattoos before the collection grew. Her eyes drank in the detail, the curve of the ribcage, the dusting of body hair from navel to denim waistband...

'Find anything that takes your fancy?'

Esmé jumped and immediately blushed, having been caught in a fantasy world of her own.

Her furtive eyes met the kindly face of the older guy, the one that had added Stig's bird to Asa's flock.

Esmé shook her head, reluctantly closing the album.

'What were you thinking? Dainty and pretty? Or symbolic?'

'I want something with meaning to signify this point in my life but...' she waved at the closed album. 'Nothing.'

'I thought you were going to ask for the music staves when I came over, not so pretty on a female's chest but on a thigh or hip bone it would look stunning.'

'Is it an actual tune?'

His face burst into a smile.

'Do you seriously think people have just random notes tattooed on… of course it's an actual tune. If I remember correctly it's his favourite tune – a song his mother used to sing.'

She wanted it. She wanted the same. She thought he was an arse for the majority of the time but now she wanted a matching tattoo, which he hadn't agreed to. Why?

'Look, you've been in three times today, looked through the albums, had various conversations with me and the other guys and yet…' he grimaced. 'You're either serious about this or I suggest you go and get a henna design from the local beauty salon and it'll wear off in a matter of weeks.'

Esmé blushed.

'Sorry.'

'Don't apologise… we have young women like you come in here all the time… literally torn about doing it, but my advice would be to wait until you are sure.'

Esmé stood up, handed back the album and made for the door. She wanted to cry. The buzzer sounded as she left the studio, and she vowed she'd never return.

Today was the last day of her Single Girl's Calendar and yet, she'd just proven to herself that nothing had changed. She'd wasted her entire month. She wasn't a sassy, independent woman with a spring in her step. She was simply too chicken to live a little.

*

'Hellooooo!' called Esmé, entering the warmth of number seven. 'Anybody home?'

'In here,' shouted Russ from the morning room.

Esmé peeled off her coat, not waiting for a moment to show off her bravery.

She found Russ seated at the table eating beans on toast.

'Look what I've got!' She lifted the edge of her jumper to reveal a large square of cling film and white medical tape.

'Not you, too?' choked Russ, as beans spluttered into his lap.

Esmé gently peeled back the large protective square, on which some plasma had seeped.

'It'll look better when it's healed, but look…'

Russ stared, his expression dropped.

Did he like it? Or not?

'Russ?'

'What do you want me to say?'

'I don't know… but you haven't said anything.'

'Esmé, is that henna or a *proper* tattoo?'

Esmé shook her head and swallowed. His expression and tone had changed.

'Wait till your parents hear about this… I'm dead meat. They think that I look out for you, correct the other guys if they mistreat you and all the bloody time you're going behind our backs and doing shit like…' He pointed to her bare stomach.

'Hi,' Asa entered the kitchen and glanced briefly between the two. 'Sorry, have I just walked in on something?'

'Nothing,' muttered Esmé, quickly correcting her jumper.

'Nothing? Esmé, are you for real?' asked Russ, his annoyance showing. 'Asa… have a word with *her.*'

Asa disappeared beneath the kitchen archway, he grabbed the kettle and filled it from the tap.

'What about?'

Esmé frantically shook her head at Russ to shut him up.

'About the shit she's had tattooed on her stomach, that's what!'

Asa's face appeared around the archway wall.

'The what?'

'It's nothing,' said Esmé, quickly.

'Show me.'

'No.'

'Show me!' he demanded.

'Excuse me, I don't have to show anyone my body if I don't want to and I choose not to show you.'

'You showed me,' interrupted Russ.

'You're different,' said Esmé.

'Bollocks is he, now show me!'

'No!'

Asa walked across and stood before her, his eyes flashing with annoyance.

'What's it of, Russ?'

'That frigging stupid phrase you keep sniping at her.'

Asa stared down at Esmé's covered torso, as if he could read the tattoo through her folded arms and jumper.

'He…' he jerked his thumb over at Russ, '*had* better be joking.'

'I'm not, you wait and see… her parents are going to go ape-shit,' said Russ, standing up and taking his plate to the dishwasher. 'I've got nothing to do with this… I've never said that phrase to her and I think those that have need to step up and take—'

'Shut the fuck up, Russ! If this is a wind up – I'm not laughing… so now's the moment to quit yanking my chain!' said Asa, as his gaze flashed between Esmé's crestfallen face and Russ's shaking head.

'Asa, it's no joke. She's just shown me what she's had done and I'm not impressed.'

Esmé squirmed as Asa's focus returned solely to her.

'I'm out of here, see you later,' said Russ, exiting the morning room.

Silence descended. Esmé sat herself on the couch, curled her knees to her chest and rested her chin on top of them, with her arms wrapped round her shins. Her tattooed torso protected and hidden.

Asa walked backwards, his eyes never leaving her frame and sat down at the kitchen table.

'You have a serious problem, you know that, don't you?'

Esmé shrugged nonchalantly.

'Well, you have... it seems to me you'll do anything to please others, to make them like you... even force them to like you because you copy the things they like.'

'No, I don't.'

'You do. You have.'

'I haven't.'

'You have never mentioned wanting a tattoo. Your reaction towards me suggests you dislike tattoos and yet today, some crazy idea has swept through that brain about a tattoo. Why?'

Esmé shrugged.

'Stop it. Stop hiding, stop running, stop playing games. Why, Esmé?'

'Don't speak to me like that, my parents wouldn't dream of speaking to me like that so don't you dare!'

'Maybe they should… then you wouldn't go through life copying others and doing stupid things purely to be noticed… you'd please yourself and not the rest of the world.'

'What's it to do with you anyway? It's my body!'

'How old are you, fifteen?'

'Phuh!'

'Yeah, phuh! Show me.'

'No.'

'Otherwise I'll phone your mother and she can sort *this* out.'

Esmé outstared Asa, her defiance grew like a fifteen year old grounded for the weekend.

'Fine, I'll phone her,' Asa retrieved his mobile from his pocket and began to search his contacts list.

Esmé jumped up.

'Here. Look all you bloody want!' She lifted her jumper, wrenched off the white tape to reveal the black italic lettering '*Live a little*' neatly inked across her hip bone and the soft contour of her stomach.

Asa's mouth fell open. He eased himself from the kitchen chair, dropped to his knees and stared at the offending script.

'You went to Tony's?'

'Yep.'

'Tony did this?'

'Yep.'

Esmé caught her breath as Asa's finger gently stroked the embossed welt. Her stomach fluttered beneath his warm touch.

'Why?' he sat back on his haunches, almost on bended knee, his doleful gaze meeting hers.

'I wanted it.'

'No, you didn't.'

Asa dropped his head forward. His neck extended and Esmé stared at his nape contoured and decorated in artful colours.

'This is my fault... I kept needling you to try stuff, getting under your skin and now... *this.*'

'I can think for myself, you know!'

'Really? Jonah said he liked red hair so you dyed yours. Grace plays the flute and now you're having lessons. Carys had a stupid calendar and you've lived by it all month. Tomorrow's the first day of a new month... so who's plan are you following then? Because it certainly won't be your own!'

Asa stared at her intently, his eyes scanning every inch of her face.

'What?'

'Nothing.' Asa stood up, straightened the legs of his jeans, and walked through the kitchen archway.

'What?' called Esmé, watching his retreat. She heard the kettle switch flick.

'Oh Esmé,' came the sigh from Asa.

'Don't *oh Esmé* me, you know nothing… so stop kidding yourself.'

His head appeared around the archway wall.

'*Me?*'

'Yeah, don't kid yourself, Asa.'

'Me kidding myself?' he prodded his index finger into the middle of his chest. 'Never!'

'Yeah, you!' she scowled, standing to her full height, her temper ignited by his arrogance.

Asa walked under the archway, his eyes fixed on hers. His chest rapidly inflated and fell beneath his tee-shirt. In a flash, he stood before her, too close to talk. His hands cradled each side of her jaw and his mouth landed hard on hers. The energy from his mouth forced her head backwards and his warm lips worked at her mouth. Her breath snagged in her throat as his hands pulled her face closer and deeper into his kiss, before one hand glided around her earlobe and slid into her hairline. Minutes passed as Esmé responded and her hands roved around his waist and wide back.

It was over as quickly as it started. Asa pulled his face back from hers, his eyes alive and on fire, his breathing deep and troubled.

'That! That's what you just told me.' His hands released her jaw and the base of her hairline as he stepped away into his own space and watched her quivering expression. Esmé watched as he rolled his lips inwards as if re-tasting their kiss. He turned and slowly walked back towards the boiling kettle. 'And you've stupidly had *that* tattoo, to impress me… so, let's stop the pretending. I can read you like a book.'

Oh my life, he knows everything.

*

'Hey Asa, my man,' called Tony, from behind the counter top.

'Tony, I'm not impressed!'

Esmé stood a foot behind staring at the floor like a pupil awaiting the headmaster's wrath.

'Can't she speak for herself?'

'No, she damns herself every time.'

'No, I don't,' muttered Esmé.

'That tattoo sounds like a discount store slogan, I want you to add to it – same style and script but it'll make it a little more acceptable.'

'Who to?' Esmé asked.

'Me!' Asa glared over his shoulder. 'And don't give me the 'it's my body crap'.'

'As you were earlier,' muttered Tony, waving Esmé towards the nearest couch station. Esmé pulled a face, slid off her coat, positioned herself and lifted her jumper to reveal the fresh script.

'Uncovered?' said Tony, cleaning the area.

'For now, yes… as you need to add extras,' said Asa, as he pulled up the nearest chair and plonked himself down without an invitation. He pointed to the offending script on her hip bone. 'Here, you need to add 'dream' and then a few tiny flowers and possibly a star or a glitter swirl… but that, urgh!'

'Are you criticising my work?' asked Tony, writing free hand on her stomach.

'No, just your judgement… on this one.' Asa pointed to Esmé, whose brow creased.

The needle began to whir, Tony's head lowered and his hand altered the phrase as requested. Asa's expression softened as he watched the needle glide across Esmé's torso. His eyes intense, as if they were burning the image into her skin, a solid look, absorbing every inch of her naked stomach and yet, not leching as other men would.

'Stop staring at me,' grunted Asa, his eyes fixed on her stomach.

'I'm not.'

'Don't lie.'

Esmé's mouth fell open.

'This is the thing with you – you always think you are right… well, this time you're not… you seem to think I got this,' she jabbed towards her flesh. 'For you… and I *didn't*.'

Tony glanced up from his handiwork and looked between them.

'Exactly Tony, who is she trying to kid?' muttered Asa. 'Shhhhh woman, you doth protest too much.'

'You're such as arse!' growled Esmé, her jaw clenched as the needle snagged her pain barrier.

'You keep saying,' mocked Asa.

'You pair argue like a married couple,' joked Tony.

'Mmmm,' grunted Asa, as he stared at her stomach.

Esmé remained silent as her phone began to vibrate in her pocket.

'Is that your mobile?' asked Asa.

'Yeah, I'll let it go to answer machine, it won't be anything important.'

Within minutes the stark black script is transformed into a pretty, feminine version with the addition of '*dream*' and a delicate floral decoration.

Chapter Forty-four

'Mum, what's wrong?' asked Esmé, as she bustled into the foyer of the MacDonald Burlington hotel in a state of panic having received a brief text message from Kane. 'I was going to call you later.'

Sue rose as Esmé entered the double doors, smoothed down the front of her peach and cream dress coat, and supressed the nervous giggle that rose to her throat.

'You look nice. Why are you dressed like that?' asked Esmé, oblivious to the fact that her first question hadn't yet been answered.

'Calm down, nothing is wrong... quite the opposite.'

'Mum?' Esmé stared about the foyer. 'Kane said it was urgent, that I must make haste and now... where's Dad? Is there an emergency?' She'd dashed through town at break neck speed having left Asa at the tattoo studio paying for her additional ink. How rude was that? She'd quickly had dressing applied and thanked Asa, even she had to admit that the additional word 'dream' and the decoration now made a worthy enhancement to her skin.

Sue patted her arm and gently led her away from the double doors to sit on the elaborate couch upon which she'd been waiting for twenty minutes since speaking to Kane, her eldest.

'Mum, what's going on? Is this about my argument with Kane?'

'Kane? No. Now, I know you've had the most unpleasant month and no one more than me understands just how much that has affected your relationship with Andrew…'

'*Mum?*'

'Esmé, let me finish, please. Anyway, I wanted to show you something,' said Sue, standing to collect her belongings.

She led Esmé past reception, where Esmé had signed for a room just four weeks ago, down a long corridor to stand before a set of elaborate double doors.

Esmé was still not comprehending how Kane's urgent message equated to this calm situation but still, all seemed well.

'Please just think about it,' said Sue, opening both doors to reveal an exquisite dining room of white linen cloth, decorated with crystal chandeliers and an array of cream and apricot flower arrangements at the centre of each table. 'Go on.'

Sue led her inside to stand amongst the most perfect wedding reception breakfast that any bridal magazine could have photographed. A five tiered wedding cake stood in the corner complete with a silver cake knife and two empty champagne glasses ready for a toast.

'Who's this for?' asked Esmé, looking around, her eyes wide and taking in every minute detail.

'Well, it's prepared for a wedding at four o'clock this afternoon, but I asked if I could show you exactly what this hotel's wedding package looks like.'

Esmé turned round on the spot, every surface displayed a detail that she'd dreamt of *had* Andrew proposed just four short weeks ago.

'Stunning, isn't it?'

'Beautiful, everything is just as I'd dreamed… but I don't understand.'

'Apparently the bride's having a horse and carriage, eight bridesmaids, three page boys, though I think one is plenty for carrying the rings… top hat and tails, champagne and a honeymoon in Rome…' Sue's voice faded to silence, as she watched Esmé turn around, taking in the spectacular room.

'Mum?'

'Esmé?'

'*What's* going on?'

'Now, please give him a chance to explain… hear him out… he's been very busy and I have to say, I'm very proud of what he's achieved in such a short time.'

'Esmé.' Standing in the doorway, dressed in a top hat and tails, complete with a carnation button hole was Andrew. His hair had been cut, his shave was impeccable and his eyes were locked on her. 'Esmé.'

Esmé's heart rate sounded like a drum beat locked within her chest. Andrew looked impressive, so smart, so fetching and *so* over dressed for a Saturday afternoon.

'Do you like it?' he asked, as he approached and stood before her.

'Yes, it's lovely. I'm sure the bride and groom will be delighted but what's this got to do with me, and my mum?'

'Esmé, I have something to ask you.'

Esmé watched in silence as he gently took her hand and slowly, but very deliberately, lowered himself onto his bended knee.

*

'A bloody house meeting on a Saturday evening, are you having a laugh?' moaned Asa, plodding barefoot down the stairs having been summoned from the shower with barely enough time to pull on a pair of jeans.

'It's not my idea, Kane said it was important,' answered Dam, leading the way to the morning room.

As the door swung open Asa could see they had guests.

At the table sat Jonah, Russ, Kane and another chap, who looked familiar but Asa couldn't place him.

Dam sat down, and Russ kicked out a chair for Asa.

'I'll cut straight to the chase,' said the guest. 'Esmé has decided to move out of this property and to return to our apartment at Symphony Court.'

Kane lowered his head and stared at his hands.

'Where is she?' asked Asa, looking around the kitchen for the missing housemate.

'She's decided that she will move out immediately and so I've come round to discuss the finances as I understand that it could potentially leave you guys in—'

'Hang on a minute, who are you?' asked Asa, his lip curled in distaste.

'I am her fiancé, Andrew.'

'Fiancé?' chorused several males.

'I don't think so!' spat Asa.

'This is Andrew,' introduced Kane, his eyes firmly focussed on his hands.

'The ex-boyfriend, as far as I know!' said Asa, adding 'You arrived one night and harassed her – I asked you to leave.'

'Not quite, but yes, that's probably how you'd remember it. *Anyway*, today Esmé accepted my marriage proposal and so, she'll be—'

'No way!' Asa stood up, his chair scraped against the tiles. 'Where is she?'

'Asa, sit down… it's her decision,' said Kane, not raising his head.

'And you agree with *this,* do you? He cheated on her… she's done pretty well the last few weeks and now, she is expected to revert back to what she *had?*

'Look mate, I really don't understand what your problem is, but my fiancée and I will be getting married in sixteen days' time, it's the quickest I can organise things, given the special license, and I'm trying to be proactive to ensure you guys have a replacement housemate.'

Kane shifted in his seat.

'So you've organised this in secret and then sprung it on her?' asked Asa.

'Hey, now I really don't think it's your place to tell me what I'm allowed to organise for my fiancée. In fact, my soon to be mother-in-law also organised—'

'Cut the crap! I don't want to hear it. Dam, what have you got to say about this?' asked Asa, standing at the edge of the table.

'Isn't it her decision?' said Dam, with an embarrassed shrug.

'He's got a point,' added Jonah.

'Russ?'

'Asa man… it's her choice, at the end of the day.'

'Seriously?' Asa looked around the group of forlorn faces. 'Nah! I'm out of here. You guys discuss whatever you want. Kane, welcome to the house, because it looks like your sister's made way for you after all.'

Asa stormed from the kitchen, knocking his chair over as he went.

Chapter Forty-five

Tuesday, 10th April

The church was heaving with mourners. She'd expected a sea of black filling every pew, instead every colour imaginable was in front of her. Bright Hawaiian shirts worn by teenage boys, a rainbow of sparkles and sequins twinkled upon young ladies in prom dresses. Claret and blue football shirts dominated three rows on the far side. The navy blue berets of sea cadets, dark green and yellow of scout leaders and even a row of black leather biker jackets filled the rear corner of the church. The sea of colour was sporadically punctuated with formal black. Esmé sighed with relief, she hadn't made a complete mistake by sticking with tradition.

Clutching the order of service, Esmé squeezed through the crowd to find a seat by an archway.

Flowers covered every surface: stone windowsills, pew ends, the altar table and decorative garlands hung between the large stone pillars alongside looped football scarves.

'Amazing,' sniffed the lady seated beside her, on viewing the floral decorations. 'It looks more like a flower festival than a funeral.'

'Simply beautiful,' answered Esmé, unsure if such words were appropriate at a funeral.

'He planned it all, poor lamb,' added the lady. 'They've done him proud.'

'They have.' Esmé swallowed the wave of emotion billowing inside her chest.

It'll be OK to cry when everyone else does – surely, before wasn't the done deal.

The dulcet tones of Sinatra began to croon 'Come fly with me' as the gathered congregation automatically stood in honour of the passing coffin carried high upon the pallbearers' shoulders.

*

The service was beautiful, not a dry eye in the church. As the funeral procession glided towards the church doorway she stared at the intricate carvings on Stig's wooden coffin. She replayed his cheesy grin and complex fist bump farewell in her mind. And, she smiled through the tears.

'See you, Stig – farewell,' she whispered.

The family followed the coffin, their eyes red raw and hearts heavy with pain, in a slow shuffle into the April sunlight.

Esmé walked amidst the crowd towards the exit and stood watching as the pallbearers organised themselves to cover the short grassy distance to the prepared plot.

And, this is it. This is what it *all* comes to in the end for each of us. Ashes to ashes, dust to dust.

'Esmé!' cried a voice above the crowd.

She hesitated as Asa, dressed in a black top hat and tails, cut a path through the crowd and chased her morbid thoughts sky high. Esmé hadn't seen or spoken to any of the housemates since the Saturday afternoon she'd dashed out on Asa at the tattoo studio.

'Beautiful service, don't you think?' he said, his voice was full of life, not sombre or muted.

Shhhhh, mouthed Esmé, staring at his attire complete with pink carnation button hole.

'Why? This is what Stig wanted… a glorious day, bright flowers and a crowd of wailing mourners as large as a football crowd – he's got his final wish.'

'How can you be so upbeat? And dressed like that at a funeral!'

'How come you're not?'

'I'm at a funeral.'

Asa leant in closer to whisper.

'I'm not, I'm at his stag-do come wedding day.'

Esmé winced.

'You wouldn't deny Stig his last laugh, would you?'

Esmé moved her head away from Asa's whispering mouth.

'No? Well then… we do what we must and give the lad his last wish and let his funeral be a combination of the biggest parties he would ever throw… so here's his year eleven prom, eighteenth and twenty-first birthdays, a graduation, his boys' boozing holiday in Zante, a wedding, even his fortieth, fiftieth…' listed Asa, adding, 'Otherwise you deny him all the good times… like cancer did.'

Esmé's eyes welled, the other mourners shuffled along leaving her and Asa suspended by his last words.

'Come here,' he grabbed her hand and wrapped it around the crook of his arm. 'I hear congratulations are in order.'

Esmé blushed. She had hoped he wouldn't mention it.

In silence, they walked arm in arm across the grass, behind the pallbearers' procession.

*

'Are you coming back for a glass of sherry and bite to eat at the hotel?' asked Asa, as they walked away from the graveside.

Esmé looked sheepishly at him.

'I wasn't planning to... there's things I need to prepare for...' she said, hesitantly.

'So, you're still going ahead with Saturday?'

Esmé gave a nod.

Silence lingered until Esmé couldn't stand it any longer.

'Look, I know you're angry with me, I can feel it, but seriously, this is what I want. This is what I've *always* wanted.'

'But he—'

'Please don't!' interrupted Esmé. 'That's all forgotten.'

Asa walked her to the car park and without another word, just a peck on her cheek, they said goodbye.

Chapter Forty-six

Saturday, 14th April

'If any persons present know of just cause why they may not lawfully be married, speak now: or else for ever hold your peace.'

Esmé stared at the wooden crucifix as the vicar's words rang about the church of St Paul's on a clear and beautiful spring day.

She felt Andrew's shoulders tense as the silence lengthened and the vicar looked intently around the wedding guests seated in wooden pews.

The vicar gave a little cough before he continued.

'I require…'

Esmé sighed and Andrew relaxed.

'Stop!' a breathless voice rang out from the back of the church. 'Esmé! Listen to me.'

Everyone turned in unison to stare at the interruption – a man who was bent double like a marathon runner was positioned in the middle of the aisle, panting and holding aloft a small piece of paper in his right hand. His face was tattooed along one side.

Esmé stared. Her hands fell to her tulle skirts and hastily fingered the delicate fabric.

This was real. This was *actually* happening to her, it wasn't one of the nervous dreams she'd been having for the last two weeks. The nightmares that her mother had said were stress related. This wasn't a Friday night chick flick. This was *her* wedding day… and she was standing at the altar, in her dream dress, about to make her vows and now, everyone was staring at a guy who'd called out her name at the most inappropriate moment of her life. Feck!

'Carry on,' said Andrew, turning back to the vicar on seeing who had interrupted.

The vicar raised his hand to dismiss the instruction.

'I'm sorry, is there something you wish to say, young man?'

'Yes, I need a minute… to speak to Esmé. Sorry, please… Esmé?' said Asa, as he stumbled the length of the aisle. All eyes in the church watched his every move as he stood waving his piece of paper.

'Esmé, ignore him, turn round,' said Andrew, his brow furrowed in anger, as he reached for her shaking hand.

She snatched her hand away and turned to face Asa. This wedding was everything she'd ever wanted and yet… her breath snagged in her throat, eager to hear his reasons.

'Young man, what is it you wish to say?' asked the vicar, stepping forward between the couple to address the newcomer.

'Esmé... I found this.' Asa held aloft the paper which the guests could see had a small amount of writing on it. 'You left in such a hurry, you didn't say goodbye to any of us and I found this in your room... alongside the torn calendar... but it's important Esmé, so please, hear me out and then... then if you still want to marry him... then go ahead and do it.'

Esmé was frozen to the spot, her painted eyes wide and staring at the emerald and navy ink swirled about the strong features of another man.

Asa began to read aloud.

'One, to fall in love again. Two, to get married. Three, to plan a family. You wrote this, Esmé, and dated it March of this year. Esmé, you titled it "my dreams" and... I've figured out that these were written to complete a task from the calendar your friend bought for you. The Single Girl's Calendar that was supposed to help you overcome a broken heart. The broken heart that *he* caused! Remember?'

Esmé nodded, her lips had gone dry and her fingers twitched uncontrollably upon her tulle skirt.

'I found all your tasks lined up on your mantelpiece... the haircut, the make, bake or create, your donation, the clear your conscience task... it suddenly made sense to me, Esmé. Why you did all those random and erratic things… you were simply following the instructions in the calendar and trying to find the real you. And this piece of paper, Esmé, I truly believe is the real you!'

Esmé looked towards the front pew where both her parents stood in shock alongside Kane and his son Toby. Carys's mouth was wide open, her eyes stared.

Asa continued. 'Esmé… these dreams are what you *truly* want in life. But Andrew is never going to be able to deliver them to you, *ever*. He'll say his vows, he'll declare he loves you and yeah, in the future he might even father your children but Esmé, he ruined it. Ruined it before he even started by breaking the foundation on which your dreams are built. Will you be happy hearing his vows knowing that he can cheat behind your back? Can you place a ring on his finger knowing that he can take it off whenever he chooses for a night with another Sadie? And can you honestly say that he'll never disrespect his children in the same deceitful way he disrespected you?'

The guests were on the edge of their pews now, silent and listening.

Esmé glanced at Andrew, who was shaking his head.

'Esmé, listen to me when I tell you… you marry him and you'll never know peace, there will always be a doubt in your heart, a deep-seated niggle in your mind because he's done it once before. He hurt you, Esmé. He knew it would but he still did it.'

Esmé moved a step away from Andrew.

Asa stepped forward and offered her the piece of paper, her eyes glanced at her own handwriting and she gently took it from his grasp.

'You didn't write *his* name beside any of your dreams, Esmé. So, I'm begging you, please don't do this… leave now, with me and I'll make all three dreams come true! Me and you, Esmé… could live a little dream – *together*. So please, I'm begging you… let it be me.'

A hushed murmur ran through the church pews.

Esmé scanned Asa's upturned face, his deep dark eyes and the surrounding ink of peacock feathers.

'Esmé?' said the vicar, 'have you anything you'd like to say?'

'I'm sorry,' came her hushed voice.

*

Asa drove the one hundred and eighty-five miles on the A74 as fast as he could. One thought raced and repeated through his head for every moment of every mile.

She chose me!

Beside him, Esmé sat quietly watching the miles glide by. In the passenger seat, her tulle skirts billowed about her knees. She wasn't quite sure how she'd left St Paul's church without signing the register as Mrs Nixon, but she had. Was Carys still holding her fresh bouquet of orange blossom and lily of the valley? Had smelling salts brought her fainting mother round?

It took over three hours to drive from England to Gretna Green on that bright April day, but drive they did in order to book a wedding, a much smaller wedding but one where the marriage certificate would be successfully signed by both bride and groom.

Epilogue

'Congratulations!' chorused the welcoming party, and an explosion of confetti and party poppers filled the air as the new Mr and Mrs Henson entered the morning room.

'Thank you, guys,' gushed Esmé, overcome with gratitude. 'You shouldn't have.'

'Yeah, seriously, you *shouldn't* have,' added Asa sarcastically to the small gathered group, as he carried his new bride over the Montague Road threshold and gently placed her feet on the tiled floor of the morning room.

'Tell us all about it!' demanded Marianne, slapping a glass of champagne into Esmé's hand. Penny squeezed in close to hear the details.

'It was simply beautiful, just the two of us, with a couple of hired witnesses… just what we wanted.'

'No party, no cake, no flowers?' asked Carys, leaving Dam's side for an instant to re-bond with the females.

'Of course, I had flowers, what girl gets married without flowers, but yeah… ten pounds each we paid the witnesses, total strangers but so thrilled to be part of our day,' explained Esmé, her left hand being lifted and lowered by her friends as she spoke. 'It was lovely.'

'And private,' added Asa, above the simultaneous 'ohs' and 'ahhs' of the women at the sight of Esmé's gold band. 'Any of you fellas want to see my wedding band?'

A tsunami of head shakes occurred, as Asa grabbed a champagne flute from Russ.

Esmé spent an age reliving every detail of the ceremony, from the Scottish piper that walked them down the aisle, her dream dress which, courtesy of Andrew and her mother's planning, was perfect for their elopement, and the hand tied lily-of-the-valley bouquet quickly arranged by the local florist.

'No horse and carriage?' asked Carys.

'No bridesmaids?' asked Penny.

'No guests?' asked Marianne.

Esmé shook her head, a profuse apology sat upon her lips.

'No, and yet… everything was perfect, just as we'd dreamed,' sighed Esmé.

Esmé felt strange asking if anyone had heard from Andrew, but it felt necessary to ask. Carys quietly told her that he'd taken it badly, had spent several days at home on the sick but was beginning to piece his routine together again. She reinforced that in time he'd be fine. Carys had dropped in on her parents while Esmé had been away too, just to make sure they'd survived the shock departure of their daughter alongside a tattooed stranger.

'Any news on Grace?' Esmé asked, eager to catch up on the details.

'She's recovering nicely, her son David phoned only yesterday to say Grace wants to arrange for you to go and visit her, very soon,' explained Dam. 'I think she's hoping for a slice of wedding cake.'

'Hmmm, and to gloat about her choice of man,' said Esmé, giving Asa a cheeky grin.

'We've got news too,' announced Russ, his arm draped about Rita's shoulder. 'Rita and Toby are joining me here, so the house sharing has increased.'

'Fabulous news, and Kane, you get to spend more time with Toby living under the same roof,' added Esmé.

'True, very true. Now, I can be a full time dad. Did you bring us any presents?' interrupted Kane, slouched upon the couch, having not bothered to stand to greet the happy couple.

'Same old Kane, putting your needs first,' mocked Asa. 'Esmé has brought presents actually, we stopped off to buy them in the city centre prior to driving home.'

'Great! A souvenir from Brum city centre,' moaned Kane, shaking his head and downing his beer.

Esmé dashed to retrieve a series of bulging plastic bags from the hallway, Asa stood proudly awaiting her return.

'It isn't much but we wanted to show our gratitude to our friends with a small gesture so… I'm sorry they aren't wrapped but here goes,' said Esmé, bringing out a slim box from the first bag. 'Kane… here's your very own Single Guy's Calendar… please complete each day and do every task.'

Asa handed the boxed treat to his new brother-in-law. His gratitude was a mumbled 'thanks'.

'Russ, here is your New Step-dad's Calendar… I hope it contains lots of fun activities to share with little Toby… and Rita,' said Esmé.

One by one the guests each received their calendar: The Modern Man's Calendar for Jonah and Dam, a Fabulous at Forty for both Penny and Marianne, a Thrilling at Thirty for both Rita and Carys. Everyone began searching for their daily task behind day one's door, except for Marianne.

'Marianne?'

'Is there any chance of a return and refund?' said Marianne, holding her calendar aloft. 'I *actually* need The New Mum-to-be Calendar!'

The morning room erupted into more celebratory cheers.

'I don't need to be married to know my Jimmy loves me, that shopping list of life only works for some girls, the rest of us find our own way.'

'Too right!' said Esmé, as she flung her arms around Marianne in a warm embrace.

After a few nibbles, the ceremonial cutting of a small shop bought cake and a few more drinks, Esmé was happy to be amongst friends. She scanned the morning room as everyone mingled and chatted happily.

How could life change so much in such a short time? How had a heartbreaking situation led her to such a beautiful relationship? Esmé viewed her husband from across the crowded room. His mouth wide open, belly laughing at his friend Dam's re-enactment of a family gathering to introduce Carys to their fold, one side of his face fresh and pink, the other inked in blue and emerald but neither side as beautiful as the heart within.

'I can't believe you've done it,' said Russ, slapping Asa on the back. 'Seriously man, I never thought you would.'

'We had to wait the twenty-nine days after booking so all the legit stuff could go through but yep, she's made an honest man of me,' laughed Asa.

'I can't believe that back in March I was planning on a June wedding and actually it ended up being a

May wedding… far sooner than I'd anticipated,' said Esmé.

'Yeah, and to a different bloke!' shouted Kane.

'Well, if it goes tits up for us, Esmé, and you change your mind about being married to me…' said Asa, above the noise of the rabble, 'Don't you worry, I found Roberto's mobile number while cleaning out your room so you can always give him a ring.'

Esmé swiped him for being cheeky. Poor Roberto, she'd never phoned him or given him a second thought, but hey, what will be, will be. Here was her chance to live a little… *dream.*

The End

We hope you enjoyed this book.

More addictive fiction from Aria:

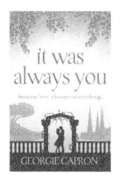

Find out more
http://headofzeus
.com/books/isbn/
9781786693358

Find out more
http://headofzeus.
com/books/isbn/9
781786698070

Find out more
http://headofzeus
.com/books/isbn/
9781788541862

Acknowledgements

Unreserved thanks to my editor, Sarah Ritherdon and the team at Aria Fiction – it has been a joy working alongside you all and together we have produced two beautiful books.

A belated 'thank you' to Debbie Clement for designing such eye-catching book covers for both 'The Single Girl's Calendar' and my debut, 'A Christmas Wish'.

David Headley and his dedicated team at DHH Literary Agency – the backbone for any author are the support team who work tirelessly behind the scenes. I couldn't ask for a more experienced and professional team.

My dear writing friends within The Romantic Novelists' Association – we definitely know how to support each other! We're not bad at glamming up, chatting and drinking bubbles either, especially the noisy girls Bella, Christie and Philippa on the 22:00 from Euston London. Eternal thanks to Katie Fforde and Jo Thomas for continuing to be my fairy godmothers having granted my greatest wish in 2017. I will always 'give back' to our writing world.

Helen Phifer and Donna Ashcroft, my partners in crime and romance – thank you for all the positive vibes.

Tamworth and Atherstone libraries for entertaining an author and providing me with time and space to chat to readers. Special thanks to Charlotte Horton, Debbie Smith and Fiona Morton – the best local support an author could wish for.

Thank you to the National Novel Writing Month: November, where each year I attempt to write 50,000 words in 30 days. I've completed the challenge for the last seven years, 'The Single Girl's Calendar' was my project for November 2016. My debut novel 'A Christmas Wish' was my 2014 project – yay, for www.NaNoWriMo.org!

NHS Blood Donors for enabling me to give 63 blood donations to help others, and a mighty big 'thanks' for feeding me biscuits and hot tea over many years! I hope there will be many more occasions, with love from donor H0086120H x www.blood.co.uk

The Macdonald Burlington Hotel, Birmingham – my first day and last day of 2017 were spent with you and what a fabulous year it has proven to be!

ZipWorld, Penrhyn Quarry, Bethesda - my birthday, spent conquering both your zip wires, was truly an amazing day. I felt as free as a bird. It's probably the fastest this body will ever move.

Sincere thanks to Norman Perryman, a kinetic painter, whose talents created 'The Mahler Experience' dated 23rd November 1993 which hangs inside The Symphony Hall, Birmingham. You made my day when you answered my email request and we met to discuss my idea. It was slightly nerve wrecking explaining my interpretation of your masterpiece but your praise was appreciated.

Ben Johnson – tattoo genius at Original Sin Tattoo Studio, Atherstone, Warwickshire for his advice and talents at turning bare flesh into works of art. Sorry for asking *so* many questions regarding scar tissue and tattooing ethics. And thank you, for my reverse script – I love them.

Darren Carter – tattoo artist and school friend, for his advice and views about tattooing and associated ethics.

To my Mum, thank you for always being there. Birmingham was the city in which both you and Dad were raised – creating a fitting backdrop for my imagination.

Everlasting thanks to my husband, Leo, – in Gretna Green, Scotland, on 31st December at midday, just the two of us, and yet it was simply the best day of my life!

Heartfelt thank you to my readers, you make my day when you contact me and share reviews about my novels. Without you guys my happy-ever-afters would simply be daydreams wasted on a bookshelf.

And finally, to a stranger waiting at a bus stop on Tuttle Hill, Nuneaton, Warwickshire – I took one look at your face and my imagination was on fire!

About Erin Green

Erin was born and raised in Warwickshire, where she resides with her husband. She writes contemporary novels focusing on love, life and laughter. An ideal day for Erin involves writing, people watching and copious amounts of tea. Erin was delighted to be awarded The Katie Fforde Bursary in 2017 and previously, Love Stories 'New Talent Award' in 2015. For more about Erin, visit her website or follow on Twitter.

Find me on Twitter
https://twitter.com/ErinGreenAuthor

Visit my website
http://www.ErinGreenAuthor.co.uk

A Letter from the Author

Dear Reader

Thank you for reading my novel – I hope that you've enjoyed the time spent with my book.

Books have played a vital role in my life. My ideal reading books are those where I race through and gobble up the story with passion but as the ending draws near I slow my pace in an attempt to delay the end of my enjoyment. Then afterwards, wish I could forget the story and reread, as if it were the first time.

My reading habit was step one to be becoming an author. And now, I have the delight of spending my time daydreaming and crafting stories for you. I love that my stories revolve about love, life and laughter – much like our daily lives. If you've enjoyed my novel – could you let me know by writing a review. I love to hear from my readers, so tell me which character did you like? Who did you fall in love with? Did you laugh or cry, or both? Reading your reactions to my work is one of the nicest parts of my day – so please, feed my curiosity.

If you'd like to ask me a question about my writing or wish to connect via social media, please follow the buttons below.

If you'd like regular updates on my writing, inspirations and events please visit my webpage where you can sign-up for my newsletter. You'll also find a competitions page where I regularly offer goodies and signed copies of books to lucky readers.

I truly believe that being an author is the best job in the world – but without my readers my books would sit unloved on a shelf.

Love Erin x

Also by Erin Green

Find out more
http://headofzeus.com/
books/isbn/9781786697
950

Find out more
http://headofzeus.com/
books/isbn/9781786697
967

Visit Aria now
http://www.ariafiction.com

Become an Aria Addict

Aria is the new digital-first fiction imprint from
Head of Zeus.

It's Aria's ambition to discover and publish
tomorrow's superstars, targeting fiction addicts and
readers keen to discover new and exciting authors.

Aria will publish a variety of genres under the
commercial fiction umbrella such as women's
fiction, crime, thrillers, historical fiction, saga and
erotica.

So, whether you're a budding writer looking for a
publisher or an avid reader looking for something to
escape with – Aria will have something for you.

Get in touch: aria@headofzeus.com

Become an Aria Addict
http://ariafiction.com/newsletter/subscribe

Find us on Twitter
https://twitter.com/Aria_Fiction

Find us on Facebook
http://www.facebook.com/ariafiction

Find us on BookGrail
http://www.bookgrail.com/store/aria/

Addictive Fiction

First published in the United Kingdom in 2018by
Aria, an imprint of Head of Zeus Ltd

9 7 5 3 1 2 4 6 8

A CIP catalogue record for this book is available
from the British Library.

ISBN (E) 9781786697967

Aria
c/o Head of Zeus
First Floor East
5–8 Hardwick Street
London EC1R 4RG

www.ariafiction.com

Printed in Great Britain
by Amazon

79567991R00332